NEW YORK REVIEW BOOKS
CLASSICS

T0000250

RED PYRAMID

VLADIMIR SOROKIN was born in a small town outside of Moscow in 1955. He trained as an engineer at the Moscow Institute of Oil and Gas but turned to art and writing, becoming a major presence in the Moscow underground of the 1980s. His work was banned in the Soviet Union, and his first novel, *The Queue*, was published by the famed émigré dissident Andrei Sinyavsky in France in 1985. In 1992, Sorokin's *Their Four Hearts* was short-listed for the Russian Booker Prize; in 1999, the publication of the controversial novel *Blue Lard*, which included a sex scene between clones of Stalin and Khrushchev, led to public demonstrations against the book and demands that Sorokin be prosecuted as a pornographer; in 2001, he received the Andrei Bely Award for outstanding contributions to Russian literature. His work has been translated into more than thirty languages. Sorokin is also the author of the screenplays for *Moscow*, *The Kopeck*, and *4*, and of the libretto for Leonid Desyatnikov's *The Children of Rosenthal*, the first new opera to be commissioned by the Bolshoi Theater since the 1970s. His most recent novel is *Inheritance*. He lives in Berlin.

MAX LAWTON is a novelist, musician, and translator. His translations of Sorokin's stories have appeared in *The New Yorker*, *Harper's Magazine*, and *n+1*. In addition to more than ten of Sorokin's books, forthcoming from NYRB Classics and Dalkey Archive Press, he is currently working on translations of works by Michael Lentz, Antonio Moresco, and Louis-Ferdinand Céline. He lives in Los Angeles.

WILL SELF is a writer. He lives in London.

OTHER BOOKS BY VLADIMIR SOROKIN

The Blizzard
Translated by Jamey Gambrell

Blue Lard
Translated by Max Lawton

Day of the Oprichnik
Translated by Jamey Gambrell

Dispatches from the District Committee: Selected Soviet Stories
Translated by Max Lawton

Doctor Garin (forthcoming)
Translated by Max Lawton

Ice Trilogy
Translated by Jamey Gambrell

Marina's Thirtieth Love (forthcoming)
Translated by Max Lawton

The Norm (forthcoming)
Translated by Max Lawton

The Queue
Translated by Sally Laird

Roman (forthcoming)
Translated by Max Lawton

The Sugar Kremlin (forthcoming)
Translated by Max Lawton

Telluria
Translated by Max Lawton

Their Four Hearts
Translated by Max Lawton

RED PYRAMID

Selected Stories

VLADIMIR SOROKIN

Translated from the Russian by

MAX LAWTON

Introduction by

WILL SELF

NEW YORK REVIEW BOOKS

New York

THIS IS A NEW YORK REVIEW BOOK
PUBLISHED BY THE NEW YORK REVIEW OF BOOKS
207 East 32nd Street, New York, NY 10016
www.nyrb.com

Library of Congress Cataloging-in-Publication Data
Names: Sorokin, Vladimir, 1955– author. | Lawton, Max, translator. | Self, Will,
    writer of introduction.
Title: Red pyramid / selected stories by Vladimir Sorokin; translated by Max
    Lawton; introduction by Will Self.
Other titles: Red pyramid (Compilation)
Description: New York: New York Review Books, 2024. | Identifiers: LCCN
    2023029933 (print) | LCCN 2023029934 (ebook) | ISBN 9781681378206
    (paperback) | ISBN 9781681378213 (ebook)
Subjects: LCSH: Sorokin, Vladimir, 1955– —Translations into English. |
    LCGFT: Short stories.
Classification: LCC PG3488.O66 R43 2024 (print) | LCC PG3488.O66 (ebook)
    | DDC 891.73/5—dc23/eng/20230703
LC record available at https://lccn.loc.gov/2023029933
LC ebook record available at https://lccn.loc.gov/2023029934

ISBN 978-1-68137-820-6
Available as an electronic book; ISBN 978-1-68137-821-3

Printed in the United States of America on acid-free paper.
10 9 8 7 6 5 4 3 2 1

CONTENTS

INTRODUCTION

FUNDAMENTAL to the fiction of Vladimir Sorokin is not the pornography his detractors accuse him of producing but the paradoxical topologies his carefully spun tales evoke. Each of his stories is a sort of mutant Möbius strip, in which to follow the narrative is to experience the real and the fantastic as simultaneously opposed and coextensive. There comes a point—it may be early on; it may be comparatively late—when the strictures of orthodox plotting seem to overwhelm its author, such that idiom and plain speech converge even as events spiral ineluctably out of human control.

What Sorokin losing the plot looks like can be highly disconcerting because, mark this: He is a fictional artificer of a high order, and we believe in the worlds he has caused to be—both as reflections of our own and in their own right. To convert James Joyce's criticism of Oscar Wilde to praise: Sorokin really does have the courage of his own perversions. When his characters begin to indulge in wanton or obtuse sexual behavior, baroque violence, coprophilia, or cannibalism, we're obliged to unbuckle and chow down beside them.

Moreover, while in all of Sorokin's stories there is arguably more than a little signposting—and certainly, once you've read any one by him, you cannot claim to be shocked by any other—but that very particular moment still arrives unexpectedly when the reader realizes once again (and yet, for the Eliotic first time) that Sorokin's imagination has taken flight. It's a giddy sensation when, at precisely the point where the effort of suspending disbelief is becoming unbearable, it's relieved, quite suddenly, by the helium lift of the writer's unbridled fantasizing.

Born in 1955, in the Moscow region, Sorokin trained as an engineer before beginning to publish experimental fictions in the semiunderground Russian magazines of the 1970s and '80s. The transition from technician to literary incendiary is marked in this selection of stories by the odd elision of Soviet bureaucratese with his trademark depictions of those transgressive behaviors that take us *a vagina ad anus*, then *et iterum*. These stories also convey their readers from the suffocating atmosphere of the late Soviet era, with its embalmed-alive politburo and its sophisticatedly psychotic system of government—every state institution shadowed by a party one, every free utterance gagged—to the delirious current one, wherein history, having failed to end with the fall of the Berlin Wall, continues to body forth the moral antinomies that have bedeviled relations between Russia and the West for time out of mind, but in new and frightening forms.

East and West are themselves an instance of these antinomies—as are Red and White, right and left, good and evil, Slavophile and Europhile, theist and atheist. Supposedly generated by the violent collision between such opposites, the regime that gave shape to the young writer's carnal imaginings, then itself became radically disembodied. In the modern Russia, all such binaries—in a truly Sorokinian manner—are now so hopelessly, topologically confused that even the simplest line between right and left has been all tangled up in black. As I write this Russians are fighting Ukrainians under a relentless barrage of mutual bemerding, each side accusing the other of being... fascists.

Sorokin's status as perhaps the most pertinent of contemporary Russian writers was underscored in the wake of the escalation of the conflict, in February 2022, when his text figuring Vladimir Putin as a demonic figure, nourished by the "black milk" of corrupting power and intent on resurrecting the imperial ambitions of Ivan the Terrible, was widely published in the Western media. Pertinent? That seems, perhaps, a little lame—a step down from relevant; not even within shouting distance of... significance.

But then this has been the enduring fate of Russian writers in the West since 1989: Both deprived of the historic cachet associated with those epochal, pre-Revolutionary "Russians"—Tolstoy, Dostoyevsky et al.—and also robbed of the sickly allure bestowed by Western liberals, as a matter of course, on all of those whose suffering they approve, they have necessarily struggled to find translators, publishers, and readers. Meanwhile, in their domestic market, returns on the literary product have been just as scarce—so scarce that despite all literary production being privatized, Russian works of fiction and, by extension, their creators have avoided being commoditized.

From the Russian perspective, lauding this state of affairs may seem at best patronizing and at worst idiotic. Who but a fool, as Dr. Johnson tartly observed, would write for anything but money? This noted, the extravagantly idiosyncratic development of Sorokin's oeuvre, throughout a writing life, the vast majority of which coincides exactly with the post-Soviet era, cannot be accounted for by literary influences alone, any more than by biographical facts. Rather, just as the Sakoku period of isolation in Japan fostered and strengthened the singularity of its culture, so contemporary Russian literature's abstraction from the commoditized realm of contemporary globalization (for which, read "Western+," given China's own effective and willed isolationism) produced conditions uniquely propitious for the development of a Sorokin-alike writer, if not necessarily this very one.

A trope that chimes with the science-fictional interest in historical counterfactuals that has typified his longer-form fiction: The cataclysmic internal collapse of the Soviet regime was both the culmination and the commencement of a mass exercise in what-ifery, and Sorokin—as befits his status as Russia's prose laureate—has been one of its principal exponents. In this collection, we find "A Month in Dachau," published a year after the fall of the Berlin Wall: a polymorphously perverse exploration of a counter-reality in which, presumably, the Molotov-Ribbentrop pact was kept.

There are too many transgressions—of taste, or propriety, or morality, of the very temporal order itself—on display here for these to be, in any meaningful sense, what the story is *about*; indeed, for Sorokin, what-ifery is, in and of itself, sufficient to fully supplant what-aboutery. The presence of two nonidentical twin lovers, whose sexual contortions are congruent, once again, with the queered topology of Sorokin's fictional universe, and whose attentions are devoted to the unnamed narrator—a Sorokin-alike Russian writer—might give pause to the psychoanalytically minded, if, that is, they're aware that the writer has, himself, two nonidentical twin daughters.

But really, the solecism of such criticism is sideswiped by overdetermination: nonidentical twins equals alternative outcomes beginning from the same point of origin. The British filmmaker Adam Curtis titled his series of films charting the collapse of the Soviet Union and the shivering into being of its successor regimes *TraumaZone*. Comprising reams of found footage from the BBC's archives, this doomy evocation of a complex society coarsening into quasi-barbarism speaks to those of us who lived through this era—but emphatically not these events—in disconcerting ways. Who knew there *was* this much footage, and of such a granular kind: Russians experiencing everything from food shortages, to arbitrary justice, to weird new TV shows of their own, to the very attempted coup against Boris Yeltsin that, in retrospect, marked the point at which the kleptocracy of Vladimir Putin and the oligarchs became inevitable.

If Russia, before the Berlin Wall fell, was for the West a mirror world, seen through a glass darkly, then afterwards, that glass was either completely occluded—history not being written by the losers—or even more powerfully distorted than heretofore. Sorokin's stories show us what we need to know in order to understand this, certainly, but by resisting all the obvious dichotomies, including those between tale and teller, diegesis and mimesis, and, naturally, signifier and signified. Commonly typed as a postmodernist, precisely because of his disdain for the predictable narrative parabolas of premodernism, Sorokin's resistance is in fact rooted in the archaic: the deep time from which great modernist works such as Joyce's *Ulysses* and Marcel Duchamp's *The Bride Stripped Bare by Her Bachelors* emerged. It's here, in an everynow before historiography—if not history—that their creators have done battle with the Enlightenment order.

A story such as Sorokin's "Nastya," which subjects that Chekhovian sense of *douceur de la vie* specific to a feudal society vermiculated from within (a perception of the plays and stories which, perhaps, owes its salience almost entirely to the retrospective glow cast on them by the fiery revolution ahead), to the stress test of familial and socially enjoined cannibalism as a rite of passage, is nonetheless not, fundamentally, a literary matter. A revolution may not be a dinner party, but a dinner party at the Sablins' manor house in the last summer before the twentieth century can be, in Sorokin's universe, a revolution. One that should return his readers to the elemental, the Real: the material-organic substratum, the ever-inchoate, ever-evolving stuff of life that, in this view—an article of faith for many contemporary Westerners—is *all* life is. To confuse Sorokin's apophatic theology, which bodies through his prose fiction in innumerable ways, with the clickety-clack *Glasperlenspiel* reasoning typical of, say, contemporary academic discourse in the arts and humanities, is to do a grave injustice to reason as much as faith.

A convert to Orthodoxy in his mid-twenties, at the very apogee of Soviet godlessness, what does this say of the writer? Apodictically, this was a young man serious about the assertion in the Gospel of John that "the world is passing away, along with its desires. But he who does the will of God will abide forever." If converts to Western Christianity seem often to be driven—psychologically, at least—by a need for forgiveness from a largely absent deity, then what can be said about those who find God down the back of an old record player?

In "Tiny Tim," the eponymous hamster, having partaken of prosphora himself, is able to direct the protagonist's son as to where to relocate the fragment of holy bread lost by his mother decades ago. Sorokin describes the hamster—as seen by the narrator, in extremis—as "entirely new and transformed. Unbelievable grace flowed forth from him. But an even greater grace trembled and wavered with unearthly light behind his back. A graceful sea of light trembled behind Tiny Tim's back." He isn't being facetious at all—let alone fanciful.

For the Orthodox confession, God's totalizing presence cancels out all the shilly-shallying between the Deity's immanence and/or imminence that typifies the Western churches and engenders their obsession with catechism. For Sorokin—as for all Orthodox believers—when the prosphora is eaten the communicant gets it all: the blood, body, soul, and divinity of Jesus Christ. Meanwhile, the necessary devotion is not to interrogate the nature of God so He can somehow be worshipped *better* (a very Weberian idea) but to have no fear of saying all those things that God most emphatically is not and, more important, *does not enjoin*; since given He is all, and all is He, every single thing we say and do can be construed as a form of worship.

Looked at this way, Sorokin's propensity for pitilessly describing violent delights and their violent ends may well be an enormous tease, a sort of peek-a-boo, where no matter that the reader tries to look away, he can't help being returned to the central problem of faith—and its conspicuous lack in himself—again and again. I'm reminded of Schopenhauer's dismissal of Kant as a man who attends a masked ball and dances all evening with a fascinating woman, only to discover when she removes her disguise at the stroke of midnight that she is his wife.

Except that Sorokin never pretends to Kantian uxoriousness: he is Ivan Karamazov, declaring in Father Zosima's cell that since God is dead, *everything* is now permissible. The starets who ends the penultimate story of this collection—which, sensitive readers will be pleased to learn, has a conclusion not exactly happy but indubitably uplifting—ensures his hermetic state by walling himself up in a cave, with bricks made from his own excrement. We are, it would appear, to be delivered from the earth that defiles us by the very thing we believe, um, defiles us. By extension, it's noncoincidental that Tiny Tim is a hamster: Sorokin's faith is not in the afterlife conceived of as a celestial retirement community but in an unknowable, ineffable, and ineluctable panpsychism: this thing really is bigger than all of us.

Which is why in story after story in this collection, such a reality is not merely alluded to but directly described. The black pearl given to Nastya by Father Andrei, the pervert priest, for her birthday, is then swallowed by her, tempered, and eaten again—passing through two members of a female line, and fire, before ending up as the smoking, curvilinear mirror within which Sorokin scries a whole world:

"black sky, black clouds, black lake, black boats, black pines, black juniper, black shallows, black footbridges, black willows, black hillock, black church, black path, black meadow, black alley of trees, black manor, and black woman, opening the black window of a black bedroom."

In his fabulists' vade mecum, "Tlön, Uqbar, Orbis Tertius," Jorge Luis Borges tells us that the heresiarchs of Tlön abhorred mirrors because, in common with copulation, "they increase the number of men." But the objects that transact the business of Sorokin's fictions couldn't possibly lead us back in the direction of those tedious, long since abandoned, dichotomies—they urge us on, into a realm at once monist and transcendental: this single black pearl, swallowed by a sixteen-year-old girl, reflects *everything*; while in "Horse Soup," what becomes of paramount importance—the active principle, rippling through an entire reality—is the act of consuming, rather than what is consumed, as Sorokin shows how a very human folie à deux can build a world entire.

In "The Black Horse with the White Eye," the universalizing monad is the title itself—in "Monoclone," it's a deformity—while the title signals the synecdochal character of the tale; in "Tiny Tim," as discussed, it's the bit of holy bread the pet hamster didn't eat, and which the little girl hid down the back of a record player. And in "White Square," it's a TV pilot of a televised debate—whither Russia—that provides the Sorokinian lift-off point, such that a re-creation of *The Flaying of Marsyas* becomes this curious object, one that simultaneously enacts the fate or the world, is the world, and yet is also a mere part of it. In Sorokin's postlapsarian fictions, all actions can be communion, all objects prosphora.

Throughout the stories of *Red Pyramid* we find stray bits and fugitive pieces of *zaum*, which is the term coined for this sort of indeterminately poetic language by the futurist poet and theorist Aleksei Kruchenykh. Just as their creator succumbs, time and again, to the sheer buoyancy of his own inspiration, so do his characters succumb, again and again, to the mere incommensurability of what can be understood with what may be expressed, causing them to break down into inarticulate bleating and blurting. "Nao!" Burmistrov, the eater of horse soup cries, as he reaches his perverse climax: "And this is na-a-o. And this is na-a-a-o!" A meaningful echo of the verbal tic displayed by his accomplice, Olya's violin teacher.

Instruments and instrumentality. For Sorokin, this is what incarnate humans are and the mode in which they view one another, which means all interactions necessarily become transactional: there's no love lost in his fictive world because, for the most part, there's no love. When language itself breaks down, and Sorokin's perfectly evoked characters begin to moan and garble, the reader may think of that revolutionary ferment, out of which came the radical experimentalism of Vladimir Mayakovsky and the proto–flash fiction of Daniil Kharms; just as when, in the title story of the collection, we're introduced, on a sleepy station platform, to this anachronistic oddity, Mikhail Bulgakov's *Master and Margarita* is summoned: "His summer clothing was old-fashioned: a white panama hat, a beige summer suit, and a white *kosovorotka* with an embroidered collar. White calico shoes peeked out from underneath his loose beige trousers."

Bulgakov was another believer, who took the defunct materials of Soviet realism, then twisted and shaped them in such a way as to confound those engineers of the human soul. When Sorokin asks us to follow the flayed skin of a television presenter, which has been rolled up into a scroll, as it's transported hundreds of miles by gravity, avian power, and then haulage into the hands of a near-destitute ne'er-do-well who survives by selling honey at a roadside stall, he's also reminding us that every intelligible human utterance rests on this: the invisible structure of universal grammar itself—which projects into the vacuum of the immediate future, so guaranteeing our meanings are always belated and traumatic. In the Godless West, this leads us to the *zaum* of Derrida, but in the Holy East things are different: there is no specter haunting Russia—it became embodied then took up residence more than a century ago, and everyone remains absolutely fucking terrified.

The skin scroll of "White Square," which, after being chucked out the window of the studios, is first picked up by a crow, then dropped onto the roof of a truck that drives for six hours and eighteen minutes away from Moscow, recalls the copper cylinder secreted in the walls of the Bastille and abandoned there by the Marquis de Sade when he left the prison eleven days before it was stormed on July 14, 1789. Inside the cylinder was a paper scroll twelve meters long and eleven centimeters wide: the manuscript of *The 120 Days of Sodom*. Sade never recovered it—and in a way, the travels of this scroll, with its painstaking inscription of depravities, mirror those of Sorokin's skin scroll: both objects becoming vectors for the transmission of absolutes through eras of increasing relativism.

Pornography, insofar as it is the propaganda of perversion, rather than merely a little extracurricular titillation, is a technical language. What typifies *The 120 Days of Sodom* is just this: its repletion with numerical data—the sizes of genitalia, the ages of the corrupted, the amounts of penetration, the tabulations of ecstasies, and their degrading divisors. A single page of Sade bears comparison, no doubt, with the technical engineering journals Sorokin had to write and edit at the outset of his career.

With the five last stories of this selection of Sorokin's shorter fiction, we come up to the pre-present and encounter a Russia still dominated by the subsonic "red roar," which the writer's acute senses allow him to hear emanating from the titular edifice—a numinous structure, implanted beneath Moscow's Red Square. For Heidegger, the questionable nature of technologies is the way they frame our perception of the world, and in so doing encourage us to take it for granted; in his words, we treat it as "standing reserve." It is the genius of Sorokin's fiction—both overall and particularly in these stories— to use the lexicon of pornography to show how, in our benighted era, East and West, Red and White, right and left, good and evil, Slavophile and Europhile, theist and atheist alike have all been complicit, not just in treating the earth and its resources as standing reserve but each other's bodies, souls, and divine natures as well.

—WILL SELF

RED PYRAMID

PASSING THROUGH
1981

"WELL, comrades, on the whole, your district is working well this year." Georgy Ivanovich smiled and leaned back slightly. "That's what I've been assigned to communicate to you." The people sitting at the long table smiled back at him and began to exchange glances.

Shaking his head, Georgy Ivanovich spread out his hands. "When it's good, comrades, it's certainly very good, and when it's bad, what's there to argue about? Last year, you were late with the sowing, your factory couldn't stick to plan, and there were a great many blunders with the sports complex, remember? Hm? Remember?"

Sitting to the left of him, Stepanov nodded. "Yes, Georgy Ivanovich, it was a sin, of course, we were to blame for all that."

"Yes, you were, you're the governing body, and you somehow thought the builders would get by without you and that the deadlines would hold fast. But, really, they're just the implementers of the plan—why should they hurry? Your factory is notorious through the entire Soviet Union, and, oh ho ho, how badly we need plastic, but you were only at 78 percent last year...Well, that's no way to do business. Panteleyev came to me and said, 'We're at 78 percent.' What am I gonna say? Definitely not 'Thank you, Comrade Panteleyev, for the proper organization of your district industry,' hm?"

The assembled company smiled. Georgy Ivanovich sipped from his cup of cool tea and licked his lips.

"And there's something deeply pleasant in this. Your new secretary, too bad he's not here now, he came to me back in the spring, Panteleyev, he would've waited till the autumn—at least—but Gorokhov, he came in the spring. And he laid it out in a businesslike way, y'understand, all of the reasons why, and everything was really businesslike, he explained everything. The builders were bringing in cement from another district. Well, where's the sense in that? Panteleyev couldn't make it to the Kirov district for six years. It's a stone's throw away, 160 kilometers or so, a dry plaster factory, and next to it's a cement factory. I mean, what can I say about that?"

"The thing is we used to work with them, Georgy Ivanovich." Vorobyov leaned forwards. "But, that one time, they immediately refused us. They were connected with the Burkovsky factory and with the construction site, but now they've split up and they're free, so it worked out—"

"If there hadn't been pressure from the top, they wouldn't be giving us anything now either," Devyatov interrupted him. "Everyone needs cement."

"Of course, Georgy Ivanovich, Panteleyev was to blame, we ought to've put pressure on back then, maybe they had some reserves."

"Of course they did, it can't be that they didn't, they did, they certainly did." Georgy Ivanovich finished his tea. "Generally speaking, comrades, let's not make guesses at random and, in the future, we have to be more professional. You couldn't come up with it yourselves—shake the deputies, consult with the managers and the workers. And, in the future, let's continue to hold fast, like we did this year; as you began, so shall you finish. Agreed?"

"Agreed."

"Agreed, of course."

"Agreed, Georgy Ivanovich."

"We'll do our best."

"We'll try hard."

"Well, that's very good." Georgy Ivanovich stood up. "And I'll see your secretary next time. Hopefully he won't be upset that I didn't warn him I'd be here. I'm just passing through, after all. Let's hope he gets better. What is this lunacy? Tonsillitis in August? It can't be."

The assembled company also began to stand up.

"He's strong though, Georgy Ivanovich, he'll get better. It's just a matter of chance, he rarely gets sick. It's too bad that it had to be when you were passing through."

Smiling, Georgy Ivanovich looked them over.

"It's no big deal, no big deal. Now I'm always going to come visit without warning. And you know what, whenever Panteleyev used to come into my office, it was immediately clear: he'd come to repent."

Everyone laughed. Georgy Ivanovich continued: "But here I am now glancing in as I'm passing through and—all's good. That means there's a new secretary. Well then, comrades..." He looked at his watch. "Past two, we've had our fill of sitting...Tell you what, why don't you all please go to your places, and I'll walk around for a half hour and have a look at how you do things."

"Maybe we could get lunch instead, Georgy Ivanovich?" Yakushev walked over to him. "It's right nearby, we'd already agreed—"

"No, no, I don't want to, you have lunch, do your work—generally speaking, just *do your thing*. And, please, don't follow me around. I'll go from floor to floor on my own. On the whole, just occupy your places, comrades."

Smiling, he walked out through the reception room and into the hallway. The workers of the district committee followed him out, then, looking around, began to disperse. Yakushev was about to follow after him, but Georgy Ivanovich threatened him with his finger and, smiling, Yakushev fell back.

Georgy Ivanovich moved down the hallway. It was cool and booming. The floor was molded from light-colored stone slabs and the walls were of a calm pale-blue tone. Square lighting fixtures shone down from the ceiling. Georgy Ivanovich walked to the end of the hallway, then walked up a broad staircase to the third floor. Two colleagues passing by greeted him loudly and welcomingly. He returned their greetings.

On the third floor, the walls were pale green. Georgy Ivanovich stood next to the information board for a moment. Picked up a tack that had fallen from its notice and fastened the notice back into place. A woman came through a neighboring door.

"Hello, Georgy Ivanovich."

"Good day."

The woman set off down the hallway. Georgy Ivanovich looked at the neighboring door. A metal plate was fastened to the light-brown upholstery:

V. I. FOMIN, HEAD OF THE
PROPAGANDA DEPARTMENT.

Georgy Ivanovich cracked the door open. "May I?"

Sitting at his desk, Fomin lifted his head, then leapt up. "Please, please, Georgy Ivanovich, come in!"

Georgy Ivanovich walked in and looked around. There was a portrait of Lenin hanging over the desk and two massive safes in the corner.

"I've just been sitting here doing my work, Georgy Ivanovich." Fomin walked over to him with a smile. "So much work always piles up in the summer."

"That's because everyone hibernates in the winter." Georgy Ivanovich smiled. "You have a nice office, real cozy."

"You like it?"

"Yes, not too big, but cozy. What's your name?"

"Vladimir Ivanovich."

"Well there, we're both Ivanovich."

"Yes," Fomin laughed, tugging at his jacket. "And both heads of our departments."

Georgy Ivanovich grinned and walked over to the desk.

"So then, Vladimir Ivanovich, you say you've got a lot of work?"

"More than enough." Fomin became more serious. "The print workers' conference is coming soon. And the newspaper people are kinda sluggish, we're having problems with the factory's anniversary album. We can't seem to solve them . . . Various difficulties . . . And our secretary's sick."

"I'm not sure I'm following. What kind of album?"

"Our anniversary album. Our factory is turning fifty this year."

"That's quite a number, of course. I didn't know."

"That's why we're planning this anniversary album. I mean, it's already done. I'll show you." Fomin drew forth one of the drawers in his desk, pulled out the mock-up for the album, and handed it over. "Here's the mock-up. Two guys from Kaluga made it for us. Good designers. Our factory's on the cover and our lake and pine grove are on the back."

Georgy Ivanovich flipped through the mock-up. "Mhmm...yeah... it's a beaut...What's the problem?"

"Well, the main deputy doesn't like it. He says it's boring."

"What did he find boring in this beauty? It's a wonderful view."

"That's what I say, but he doesn't see any beauty in it."

"Is it Stepanov?"

"Yeah, and the secretary's sick. We haven't been able to get it approved for two weeks. And we're delaying the designers and the printing house."

"Well, I have a thought. Let me sign for it."

"I'd be very grateful to you for that, Georgy Ivanovich. You'd be taking a great weight from my shoulders."

Georgy Ivanovich took out a pen and wrote on the inside of the cover, "I approve this view onto the lake," then signed quickly.

"Thank you, really—thank you." Fomin took the mock-up from his hands, looked at it, then put it away in his desk. "Now, I've really got 'em with this mock-up. I'll say that the head of the regional committee approved the lake. No more dragging our heels."

"You tell 'em that." Georgy Ivanovich smiled, then, squinting, examined various papers surrounding a paperweight. "And what's this that's so neatly arranged?"

"It's the June directive from the regional committee."

"A-a-a-a-h, about how the harvest is to be carried out?"

"Yes. You probably know more about it than we do."

Georgy Ivanovich smiled.

"Ye-e-e-e-a-h, I really had to tinker with that. The secretary came twice and we sat around puzzling it over ."

Fomin nodded seriously. "I understand."

"Yes," Georgy Ivanovich sighed, "there's no rest for the weary, Vladimir Ivanovich. We'll calm down when we get carried away."

Fomin nodded sympathetically and smiled. Georgy Ivanovich took the directive and looked at the neat typewritten sheets, flipping through them and shaking them slightly, which set the pages to trembling.

"Well, what do you think of it, Vladimir Ivanovich?"

"The directive?"

"Yes."

"Very businesslike, in my opinion. Everything's concise and clear. I read it with great interest."

"So, we weren't tinkering around in vain."

"A necessary document, there's nothing more to say about it. It's not just administrative red tape on paper, but an honest document worthy of the party."

"I'm glad you liked it. Usually, directives like this just gather dust in safes. I'll tell you what, Vladimir Ivanovich—take this directive and put it on top of one of the safes."

"On top of it?"

"Yes."

Fomin took the sheaves of papers from him and carefully laid them on top of a safe. At the same time, Georgy Ivanovich walked over to the desk, pulled out a drawer, and took out the mock-up of the album.

"It's good I remembered." He began to leaf through the mock-up again. "You know what we'll do, Vladimir Ivanovich . . . I'll tell you what . . . here . . . I'll tell you what . . . so there won't be any . . . I'll tell you what . . ."

He placed the open mock-up on the desk, quickly threw off his jacket, tossed it over on the chair. Then slowly clambered up onto the desk, stood, and straightened up. Smiling in surprise, Fomin watched him. Georgy Ivanovich undid his pants, pulled them down, lowered his underwear, and, looking back at the mock-up, got into a squat. Clasped his thin hands out in front of his body. Mouth gaping, Fomin continued to watch. Georgy Ivanovich glanced back again, took an awkward step with his bent legs, then froze, grunted, and stared past

Fomin intently. Pale now, Fomin began to back toward the door, but Georgy Ivanovich spoke to him in a strangled tone: "Here...yourself..." Fomin walked over to the desk cautiously and raised his hands in bewilderment.

"Well, Georgy Ivanovich, how on earth...why...I don't understand—"

Georgy Ivanovich grunted loudly, his bloodless lips pulled apart, his eyes only slightly open. Avoiding Georgy Ivanovich's knees, Fomin circumnavigated the desk. Georgy Ivanovich's flat buttocks hung over the open mock-up. Fomin reached out for the neat little book, but Georgy Ivanovich turned his furious face toward him: "Don't touch, don't touch...oof...buzz off, dickhead."

Fomin walked back over to the wall-shelf. Georgy Ivanovich passed gas. His hairless buttocks swayed. Something brown appeared between his cachectic cheeks, then began to grow and lengthen rapidly. Fomin swallowed convulsively, twisted away from the wall, and put his hands over the mock-up of the album, shielding it from this brown sausage. The sausage broke off and fell into his hands. Another one came out right after it—a thinner, lighter sausage. Fomin took that one into his hands as well. Georgy Ivanovich's short, white penis swayed, then a broad yellow stream burst from it and set off fitfully across the surface of the desk. Georgy Ivanovich passed gas again. Grunting, he squeezed out a third portion of sausage. Fomin caught it. Urine dripped down from the desk and onto the floor. Georgy Ivanovich reached out, pulled several sheets of satiny scratch paper out of a little box on the desk, wiped his butt with them, threw them on the ground, then straightened up, grabbing his lowered pants as he did. Fomin was standing behind him, holding the warm excrement in his palms. Georgy Ivanovich pulled up his trousers and looked absent-mindedly at Fomin.

"Well, there...and why is it you—"

He straightened his shirt, jumped down from the desk awkwardly, picked up his jacket, and, holding the jacket under his armpit, picked up the phone, which was slightly spattered with urine.

"Yes, listen, how can I call that fellow of yours...erm, the head...I mean, what's his—"

"Yakushev?" Fomin muttered, barely able to part his lips.

"Yes."

"327."

Georgy Ivanovich dialed. "It's me. Well, yes, Comrade Yakushev, time for me to go. Probably. Yes, yes. No, no, I'm with one of your comrades. With Vladimir Ivanovich. Yes, in his office. Yes, in two minutes would be best, yes, you can do that right away, right now, I'm on my way. Good, yes, yes."

He put down the phone, put on his jacket, glanced at Fomin again, then took his leave, closing the door behind him. A plentiful scatter of drops was still dripping from the edge of the desk down onto the floor and a puddle of urine glittered motionlessly atop the polished wood. In this puddle were glasses, a notebook, a cigarette holder, and the edge of the mock-up. The door cracked open and Konkova's head appeared. "Volod, was he just with you? Why didn't you call me, you idiot?"

Fomin quickly turned his back to her, hiding his excrement-filled hands. "I'm busy, not now, not now—"

"Hold on. Tell me what you were talking about? It's really stuffy in here..."

"Not now, you can't be in here now, I'm busy!" Fomin shouted, going crimson and drawing his head down into his shoulders.

"Okay, enough, enough, I'm leaving, just don't yell."

Konkova disappeared. Fomin watched the door close, then quickly bent over and was about to stick his excrement-filled hands underneath the desk when a protracted honk blared outside the window. Fomin straightened up and ran over to the window. There were two black Volgas and a black Chaika next to the entrance to the district committee. Surrounded by district committee workers, Georgy Ivanovich descended the granite steps toward the cars. Yakushev was saying something, gesticulating joyfully. Georgy Ivanovich was nodding and smiling. The Chaika turned and, rolling over to them, stopped across from the stairs. Fomin observed with his forehead pressed against the chill glass. The excrement he was holding in his palms had begun to break apart; one of the little brown sausages fell from his hand and plopped down onto the toe of his shoe.

A HARD-NOSED PROPOSITION
1981

"YOU UNDERSTAND, guys, we don't print those *to-be-continued* novels." Avotin shoved his cigarette butt into a jar of water and waved his hand, dispersing the smoke that had gathered around his face. "This isn't a monthly journal but an institutional factory newspaper."

Savushkin grinned. "Yes, that's clear, of course. But this isn't just any novel; it's the belletristic account of a geological expedition. Those are two separate things."

"It's still monstrously long, Vitya!" Avotin stood up and, sticking his hands into his armpits, began to pace around the narrow editorial room. "It's almost two whole printer's sheets! Our limit is ten type-written pages. What is it you're planning—to stretch this diary over five issues?"

"I mean, why not?" Kershenbaum interjected. "This certainly isn't Agatha Christie—it's necessary, relevant material. The work of ge-ologists."

"And, in my opinion, it's pretty well written." Kolomiyets shrugged.

"It's so, so long-winded," Avotin muttered, pacing around. "Long-winded and verbose."

"Why long-winded? Is it really long-winded?"

"Yeah, I'd say it's written in a *businesslike way*. Concisely!"

"And the descriptions of nature are so good! Sasha really worked hard."

Avotin walked over to the table and leaned heavily on it with his palms. "Well, I'll tell you what. If you want us to print it, edit it down fifty percent. Then we can try to fit it into two issues, I think. Nothing will come of it otherwise."

The students sitting across from him exchanged surprised glances:

"By fifty percent? What are you saying?"

"What! By! Fifty percent? What would even be left?"

"Like . . . what's there to cut out?"

Avotin sat down at the table, yawned, then looked at his watch. "It's past eight—we've oversat again."

Kershenbaum walked over to the table. "That's really not possible, Seryozh. How will we cut that much? There are so many facts and discoveries. What about the local folklore? And the description of the Urals? What do you want—for us to toss all that out?"

"Not to toss it out but to cut it down. I'm not telling you to toss anything out. Cut it down. Your profession is literature. Therefore, you can cut it down in such a way that the folklore and the Urals and everything else stays in."

"But you gotta understand that we're dealing with extremely dense material. There are almost no extraneous bits. Only facts."

"Facts can also be laid out briefly and clearly."

"But Seryozh, you're contradicting yourself now. Last time, you said you wouldn't spare any columns for the sake of good, relevant material. And now? You want us to cut it all, right off the bat? That's the easy way out."

"No. It's the hard way out, my dear. To write briefly and clearly is the hardest thing of all. And, at the end of the day, what is it you're suggesting? To print it over nine issues?"

"I mean, why not?" Savushkin stood up. "We shouldn't be ashamed to make full use of such material."

"Of course not. And everyone will read it with great pleasure."

Avotin sighed impatiently. "Listen! Do you understand what an institutional factory newspaper is? It's two columns! Two! If I had four, I wouldn't mind stretching out your material over five issues, of course not. But that's not possible now. Not possible. And, more generally, let's round off this meeting—how long can a body sit?"

"What do you mean 'round off'? What about the material?"

"Cut it down. There's no other option."

"That's not possible, Sergei."

"It's possible. When you cut it down, it'll be even better."

"Well, this is foolish . . ."

"Okay, my eagles, time to go home. Cut it down, bring it back, then we'll talk."

The students were silent.

Avotin stood up and began to stuff the papers lying on the table into his briefcase. Savushkin also raised himself up, then began to speak firmly: "You know, Seryozh, if this is how it all turns out, we'll have to consult with the Komsomol Committee."

"Which would be proper," Kershenbaum nodded. "We'll show Losev. Let him decide."

"That's your right," Avotin spoke up drily. "I've said my piece. I'll say the same to Losev. At the end of the day, the question of the length of such materials was decided at the party committee . . . And now I bid you good evening. I have more work to do at home . . ."

The students began to leave in silence.

"Stay for a minute, Gena," Avotin spoke up as he fastened his briefcase. "Something came from the Voluntary People's Druzhina about your article, I totally forgot to mention it."

Kolomiyets walked over to the sofa and sat down again.

After fastening his briefcase, Avotin rubbed his chin and glanced out through the open door. "I was thinking about that mess with the construction team yesterday. You know what . . . I have a hard-nosed proposition for you."

Kolomiyets nodded with a smile.

"Shut the door," Avotin spoke up quietly.

Kolomiyets stood up, walked over to the door, then, having shut it, rotated the lock's round handle twice.

Then he turned to Avotin and smiled even wider, baring his regular, white teeth.

Avotin slowly got up from behind the table, approached him, then, holding out his hand, ran his trembling fingers across the boy's smoothly shaven cheek. Kolomiyets laughed quietly and laid his palms on

Avotin's broad shoulders. For a moment, they were looking into each other's eyes, then their faces slowly came together.

They kissed for a long time, leaning against the door as they did. Avotin stroked Kolomiyets's curly head of hair, then began to unzip his fly. Kolomiyets pushed his hand away.

"Not now…"

"Whaddaya mean—let's do it here!" Avotin whispered in his ear.

"What are you saying…"

"No one'll see. You can't see anything through the window…"

"No."

Avotin shrugged. "What're you afraid of?"

Kolomiyets smiled. "Nothing."

"Then what is this? C'mon, Gen."

"I'm not gonna," Kolomiyets muttered capriciously and, leaning against the door, looked up at the ceiling.

Avotin stroked his cheek. "I mean, shall we go to my place?"

"To your place?" Kolomiyets repeated gloomily.

"To mine."

"That's a long walk."

"We'll get a taxi, then. Fifteen minutes on the road. Let's go."

Kolomiyets stretched out. "I don't want to."

"Why, Gen?"

"I don't want to. And, anyways, erm…" He walked over to the window. "I didn't say the main thing on my mind."

"What?" Avotin asked warily.

Kolomiyets sighed, then began to speak after a long pause. "I sniffed at Ma's thing again yesterday."

Avotin went pale.

Kolomiyets turned to him, then repeated himself, grinning strangely. "I sniffed."

Avotin was silent. Kolomiyets sat down on the windowsill and was also silent.

"Gena," Avotin pronounced in a strangled voice, "you promised, you…"

Kolomiyets looked out the window.

"Gena! Gena!" Avotin got down on his knees, crawled over to Kolomiyets, and, shoving his face onto his lap, began to weep.

"Come on, stop, come on, what is this—" Kolomiyets pushed him away gloomily.

"I ... I ... this ... you promised," Avotin sobbed. "You ... you promised ... Bastard! Bastard!"

"Come on, enough ... really ..."

"Bastard! Bastard!" Avotin wept, shaking his head. "You want to torture me, huh? To torture me? What am I to ... am I to ... kill her? Or hang ... myself ...? Bastard!"

"Come on, what are you jabbering on about ... get up ... get up right the hell now."

"Bastard! I'll kill her! The ragged bitch! The whore! I'll kill her!"

"Be quiet! Get up, you're like some kinda ... get up ..."

"Such an asshole! And you! You yourself! You promised! You swore back in ... Yalta! You swore!"

"Come on ... enough ..."

"No! What am I ... am I a doll to you? Yeah? A pawn? Like Perfiliev? You ... you really don't consider me to be a human being? What am I to you? Say it, say it! And to her? To her? Some kinda asshole! Some kinda monster!"

Kolomiyets held Avotin's head in his hands and covered his mouth with one palm. They were silent for a little while. The only sound was Avotin's muffled sobbing. Finally, Avotin got up from his knees, took out a handkerchief, wiped at his face, and spoke up drily. "Yes ... well, in general, this is, of course, your business. You're the selfish one here. You only think about yourself. And I was thinking about you ..."

He walked over to his desk, pulled out the middle drawer, and removed a package bound with pink ribbon. "Here. A present for you."

He walked over to Kolomiyets and tossed the package onto the windowsill. "For all the good times."

Kolomiyets took the package, placed it on his lap, and undid the ribbon. Then he unwrapped the paper and dropped it on the floor. All that remained in his hands was an elongated plastic box.

Kolomiyets opened it.

A sloppily severed segment of a man's face had been squeezed into the box. The edges of the cleaved, shriveled skin were caked in gore, and a single unshaven cheek was visible between glossy blue cheekbone and twisted jaw; tobacco-stained teeth, two of which were crowned in gold, stuck out from between split lips; a whitish eye, squeezed forth from blackened socket, reposed in the corner of the box.

Staring at the contents of the box in stupefaction, Kolomiyets rose up from the windowsill.

Avotin smiled restrainedly.

Kolomiyets suddenly tossed the box to the ground and threw himself around Avotin's neck. "Seryozhka!"

Avotin hugged him back. Kolomiyets kissed Avotin's face rapturously. "Seryozhka ... Seryozhka ..."

Calming down, he shook his head. "Seryozha!" His face shone with admiration.

"And you say 'jelly'!" Avotin grinned.

"Seryozhka!" Kolomiyets kissed him once more.

"You bring me other kinds of gifts, you little shit." Avotin smiled contentedly. "Well then, shall we?"

Kolomiyets nodded joyfully.

"To my place?" Avotin shook him by the shoulders.

Kolomiyets nodded.

"Shall we take Petechka?"

Kolomiyets nodded.

"And we'll use wadding? Later?"

Kolomiyets nodded, winked mischievously at Avotin, then whispered, "But, I gotta say ... it's still so sweet to sniff at Ma's thing in secret, ohh, how sweet it is, Seryozhenka!"

Avotin clenched his fist and brought it up to Kolomiyets's beautiful face. Kolomiyets kissed his hairy fist and laughed.

OBELISK
1986

THE PASSENGER bus on the Lyudinovo–Bryansk route turned off the highway, which was wet with rain, and toward the Mozhaevo bus station, then, after taxiing for a little while, stopped.

The driver opened the wide door of the bus, reminiscent of an airplane hatch, then, covering his head with a regional newspaper folded in four, trotted over to the unsightly one-story bus station building, managing to let forth a mischievous shout to the passengers as he walked. "I invite you to stretch your legs! We'll be stopping for five minutes!"

He was young, filled with energy, and hadn't yet grown tired of joking with his passengers.

They appreciated his joke and, smiling, watched through the rain-spattered glass at how he leapt over puddles, merrily mumbling as he did, ran over to a brown door, then disappeared behind it.

It was cool in the bus's cabin; the people had only spent two hours on the road and still weren't tired; obviously, none of them even thought of stretching their legs—some of them were munching on something and some of them were quietly conversing with their neighbors; two flaxen-haired five-year-old twins cheerfully fooled around on the wide back seat.

Suddenly, two women on the left side of the bus got up from their seats; one was plump and elderly and the other was forty-seven. They were mother and daughter and they were going from Zhizdra to Bryansk.

The daughter was tall, firmly built, and had a pale, unremarkable face.

The mother was the total opposite of her daughter.

Among Russian women, there is that well-known type: the elderly rural mother whose whole life has been spent in a brutal struggle for her children, a struggle against nature and the cunning of time. Having been born in an enormous peasant country during a cruel period of revolution and civil strife, these women have already taken the heavy burden of peasant motherhood upon their shoulders by the age of twenty and been harnessed to that harsh life for all time, a life full of privations and incessant hard work, a life that only *born peasant women* are capable of bearing. Having passed through the fierce times of collectivization, having lost their near and dear ones in Stalin's war against the people, they then imbibed the bitter cup of the years of World War II and those years directly following the war, never—not even for a moment—ceasing in their righteous struggle for life and for their children. And now, coming to the periphery of their lives, having aged in the course of their eternal labor, they carried an eternal memory of that struggle on their work-mutilated hands and in their wrinkled, weathered faces.

But even so, it was not their hands or wrinkles that were so stunning: it was their characters.

How had they held on to their kindness and tenderness, their gaiety of temper, and their breadth of spirit? Wherefore was there such energy and indefatigability in these broken bodies that had been wheeled over by their century? What was it that had helped them to withstand and to survive, their souls never becoming stale nor their human goodness impoverished? Many passengers were probably asking these very questions as they looked upon the elderly gray-haired woman, the mother of the other provincial woman. In any case, this woman couldn't be called "old"—her young, life-loving character wouldn't allow for it. On the contrary, next to her, her daughter looked older and more indifferent to life than she did. Galina Timofeyevna (this was precisely the woman's name) hadn't closed her eyes for a single moment of the two-hour journey: she japed with her neighbors, told her daughter the latest village news, treated the twins to her vatrushki, and presented the driver with a big red apple, speaking to him as she did. "Eat, my son, eat for yer health, and don't ye rush to get us where we're goin'!"

To which the cheerful driver replied, "Thank you, Mama. I'll get you where you're goin'!"

A good half of the passengers already knew that Galina Timofeyevna had lived in her village of Kolchino for nearly seventy years and that she'd brought nine children into God's world, two of whom she'd lost in the terrible famines of '46, when they were all laboring on the collective farm for workaday check marks in the filthy ledgers and baking bread from potato skins and crushed linden leaves. They knew that she was going to see her son Sergei (Seryozhka as she called him), that Seryozhka lived in Bryansk, that he was the head of a workshop in a Bryansk machine factory, and that "his family's sound, but his kids're real spoiled 'cause there's no one to lay down the law."

Having said this, she straightened her white kerchief, covered in little blue polka dots, with a quick, practiced motion, then smiled, making it clear that she wasn't going to Seryozhka to *lay down the law* for her grandkiddies, not at all.

"I knitted 'em lil' socks, I bet they'll last for the next three years, I baked a big ole' gingerbread, I boiled up some jam, the grandkids'll eat their fill all right!" She spoke to the woman sitting in front of her with the sort of sincerity and openness of which—alas!—old women in cities weren't capable.

And it seemed there would be no end to her lively stories, recollections, and advice, but suddenly, as soon as they'd crossed the bridge and the neat little Mozhaevo houses had begun to flash by, it was as if someone else had taken Galina Timofeyevna's place; her smile slid off her tanned face, she fell silent, and it was as if she'd instantaneously begun to act her age.

At first, the neighbors exchanged looks—was it possible someone had inadvertently offended the old woman? But, having understood that the issue lay in something else, they calmed down, not wanting to meddle in anyone else's affairs without permission . . .

And, meanwhile, it was as if Galina Timofeyevna were getting ready for a trip: she put on her old plush jacket, straightened her kerchief, and, putting her voluminous, world-weary bag on her lap, began to hastily search for something amongst her bundles. At that moment, her untalkative, pale-faced daughter began attempting to convince her mother not to get off the bus.

"Why get off now, Mom? You were here real recently." She spoke in an even, slightly annoyed voice, which was as colorless as she herself was. "It's raining and you're still trying to get off. We're only stopped for five minutes—the bus won't wait for you."

"If it doesn't wait for me, then God be with it," the old woman muttered, taking two small bundles out of her bag.

"Aw, what's the point of this, Mom? What's the point of upsetting yourself so much each and every time? C'mon, let's stay."

"I'll tell ye what, daughter, don't ye lecture me," Galina Timofeyevna pronounced firmly, as she picked up the bag with one hand, pressed the bundles to her plush bosom with the other, then walked down the narrow aisle toward the door.

Sighing, the daughter fastened her old-fashioned blue slicker, picked up her own bag, and followed after her mother.

They made it down to the wet asphalt at the very moment the bus driver, having filled out a route report in the unsightly bus station building, leapt over a puddle and ran over to the bus.

"Uh-oh! Were you gettin' ready to stretch your legs?" he cheerfully called out to the women. But when he noticed their serious faces, he asked, "Did something happen?"

"It's nothin', my son," Galina Timofeyevna replied. "Our old man was laid to rest over there. We're goin' to pay him a visit. And should we be late, don't ye wait for us—just get goin'. We're not far from where we're goin', we'll make it on our own."

The driver looked over toward a small linden grove by the highway.

His face became understanding and serious "Is it over there . . . where the star is?"

The old woman nodded, loosening her grip on her bag.

The driver shifted his gaze from the grove and over to his bus, then asked, "Will fifteen minutes be enough?"

Galina Timofeyevna exchanged an uncertain look with her daughter.

"That'll be enough, of course," her daughter replied.

"That's fine, then. Take your time and don't rush. And I'll wait for you, as you've such important business. I'm on schedule, I'll make up for the lost time on the road."

"Thankee, my son, may God give ye health," Galina Timofeyevna bowed her head to one side.

"It's no big deal." He turned and got on the bus.

The women walked quickly toward the grove.

Light rain drizzled down, everything around them was wet, and the occasional car drove by on the highway.

The old woman walked ahead of her daughter, her boots cheerfully slapping through the roadside puddles.

"At least give me your bag, Mom!" her daughter called out, but Galina Timofeyevna kept on walking right to the grove, not turning and not responding.

The grove consisted of eight young linden trees planted around a small square, fenced in on one side by a little white wall that was three bricks tall. The square was covered in gravel. In the middle of the square, in a small flower bed, stood a voluminous five-pointed star in the shape of an obelisk, slightly shorter than human height. It was welded from steel plates and painted silver. At the center of the star, these words had been beaten onto a nickel-plated metal square:

HERE, ON THE 7TH OF AUGUST, 1943,
A GROUP OF RECONNAISSANCE FIGHTERS
OF THE 141ST INFANTRY REGIMENT

DIED A BRAVE DEATH DURING
A BATTLE FOR THE VILLAGE OF MOZHAEVO

I. N. GOVORUKHIN

V. I. NOSOV

N. N. BYTKO

I. I. KOLOMIYETS

E. B. SAMSONOV

Galina Timofeyevna walked over to the flower bed, put her bag down on the gravel, placed the bundles down on it, crossed herself, then, bowing her head, pronounced: "Hello, Kolyushka."

Her daughter approached from behind and stopped next to her mother. She didn't put her bag down on the gravel but held it in her hand.

"Here … right here …" The old woman sighed, adjusted her kerchief, and crossed her arms across her stomach. "Here's where our dear one lies …"

She fell silent.

The finest of rains fell almost inaudibly around them, round, sonorous drops dripping from the linden trees and into the puddles. The grass and flowers in the flower bed glistened with water.

"Here's where ye just lie and lie, Kolenka," the old woman pronounced, then began a chantlike wailing: "Ye lie here, Kolyushka, ye lie here, our goldenun. And what's to be done, what're we to do, nothin' to be done … And now yer wife Galina's come to visit ye and yer daughter Marusya too, yes, they've come here to visit ye and yer just lyin' there. And how is it we're still livin' without ye and we're still havin' such a hard time without ye. And we've thought ye straight through with our whole heads and we're still grievin' and grievin'. And, Kolyushka, how is it yer just lyin' there without us, all alone, look at how yer lyin' there. And we still remember, Kolyushka, and we still're keepin' ye, our goldenun. And we still remember everythin', Kolyushka, and I remember, I remember how ye taught us the Testament, and I remember how ye taught us yer own Testament. And we remember how we used to do everythin' accordin' to that Testament and how ye did everythin' to us as ye had to, and we remember everythin'. And we remember how ye had to do everythin' accordin' to the Testament and how we did everythin' accordin' to yer Testament and how we still do everythin' accordin' to yer Testament and how ye told us. And here's yer little daughter Marusya and she and I do everythin' accordin' to yer Testament, we do everythin' as we must, and now I'm layin' a holy cross onto ye and we do everythin' as ye told. And here's ye daughter Marusya, she'll tell ye everythin', how she does everythin' accordin' to yer Testament, so that ye can sleep all soundly forevermore..."

Galina Timofeyevna wiped away her tears with trembling hands and looked at her daughter. After pausing for a moment, her daughter put her bag down on the gravel, clasped her hands over her stomach, quickly bowed her red face, and began to speak in an uncertain, stammering voice:

"I... every month, I make a juice from shits' squeeze. Oh my daddy, my darling, every month I take the pail, the pail you ordained. And on the second day of each month, I wipe it over with your mitten. Then we, then every time, then my mommy wants to go potty... I... I wash her ass over the basin, then I suck it out from the ass all honestly, I suck it out and spit it into the pail..."

"Oh and how she sucks, Kolyushka, so honestly, she sucks it out of my ass all honestly and spits it into the pail, just as ye taught her to do when she was six!" Galina Timofeyevna interrupted her, trembling and weeping. "She sucks me and sucked me, Kolyushka and, oh my darling, she sucked and shall suck for ever and ever!"

"Then... then, every day, I when my darling mommy wants to go potty, I suck from her ass eternally," the daughter continued, lowering her head even more and beginning to tremble. "I then when the pail is filled up, I put it on your roof bench, I put it there, in the sun, so the flies land on it and the worms set in to it..."

"And so that the worms, that the white worms set in! So that the worms set in as they must, as ye insisted, Kolyushka!" the old woman wailed.

"Then I'll wait for the worms to set in, then I'll tie off the pail with your undershirt, then in the corner it'll wait with the worms..."

"And it'll sit there with the worms, with the white worms, so that everything'll be good, as ye ordained, Kolyushka!"

"It'll sit there, Daddy, it'll sit so the worms procreate all proper..."

"And so that they procreate all proper, so that they procreate, and so that they stew, oh my Kolyushka!"

"Afterwards, Daddy my dear, the pail'll sit for seven days and start to smell." The daughter's shoulders shuddered and she sobbed, gazing down at the ground. "And when my darling mommy and I open the pail, and everything in there's all full 'cause of how they ate their fill..."

"And they ate their fill, ate their fill, the worms ate their fill of my shits, Kolyushka! And they ate their fill like ye ordained, we did it all as we had to!"

"Then my dear, darling mommy assigns me gauze, I wrap this gauze around the pail, then I upend it and put it over your other pail. And that there's how I make a juice from shits' squeeze with my dear, darling mommy..."

"And she makes a juice from *my* shits' squeeze, Kolyushka, she does it all as she must, oh my darlin'!"

"Afterwards, my dear daddy, when the shits' juice gives way to the evenin', I undress, get down on my knees in front of your photograph, and from the preached mug, I drink the juice from my dear, darlin' mommy's shits, and Mommy hits me on the back with your cane..."

"And I hit her on the back with yer cane, Kolyushka, I hit her with all my might, and she drinks the juice of my shits in yer name, Kolyushka, oh my goldenun!"

"And that's how I drink juice from my dear, darling mommy's shits every three days, I drink it in your name, oh my darlin' daddy..."

"And every third day she drinks it all as she must, she drinks it all the honest way, oh my Kolyushka!"

"Oh darlin' Daddy, I drank, drink, and shall drink, as you ordained, as you ordained, my darlin'..."

"And she drank, Kolyushka, drank, and shall drink the honest way, oh my darlin'! In yer holy name shall she drink the juice of my shits, may I lay the holy cross upon ye!"

The old woman crossed herself and bowed. Her daughter crossed herself too.

For a little while, they silently shuddered and sobbed, wiping away their tears with their rain-spattered hands. Then, bowing her head, the daughter began to mutter: "Thank you, Daddy, for instructing me in your Testament."

"And thankee, Kolyushka, for instructin' her in your Testament!" the old woman affirmed.

"Thank you, Daddy, for starting to feed me with your shits every third day when I was six."

"And thankee, Kolyushka, for feedin' her with yer shits, for feedin' her!"

"Thank you, Daddy, for starting to have me drink of the juice of your shits when I was six."

"And thankee, thankee, Kolyushka, for havin' her drink of the juice of yer shits, for havin' her drink of it!"

"Thank you, Daddy, for hitting me with the cane you ordained!"

"And thankee, Kolyushka, for beatin' her with yer cane, ohh, for beatin' her with yer cane!"

"Thank you, darlin' Daddy, for teaching me to suck from mommy's ass the honest way."

"And thankee, thankee, Kolyushka, for teachin' her to suck from my ass the honest way!"

"Thank you, darlin' Daddy, for sewin' me up forevermore."

"And thankee, Kolyushka, for sewin' her up forevermore!"

The daughter went silent and, covering her face with her hands, stood still and wept.

Galina Timofeyevna sighed, then began to quickly mutter: "And here, Kolyushka, now yer darlin' daughter, yeah, she'll say everythin', how she all is, she'll say and tell everything 'bout who she is, what she is, and how she is right now."

The daughter wiped her mouth and nose with her hands and began to speak: "I know, Daddy, that I'm a pissing piggy."

"And she knows that she's a pissin' piggy!" the mother affirmed.

"I know, Daddy, that I'm a manured reptile!"

"And she knows, Kolyushka, that she's a manured reptile!"

"I know, Daddy, that I'm a whorish rent."

"And she knows, Kolyushka, that she's a whorish rent!"

"I know, oh my darlin' daddy, that I'm a beastly pubic louse!"

"And she knows, she knows that she's a beastly pubic louse!"

"I know, Daddy, that I'm purulent guts."

"And she knows, Kolyushka, that she's purulent guts!"

"I know, Daddy, that I'm a shat-over bitch."

"And she knows that she's a shat-over bitch!"

"I know, Daddy, oh my darlin', that I'm a torn ass!"

"And she knows, she knows that she's a torn ass!"

"I know, Daddy, that I'm shameful and whored-through."

"And she knows that she's shameful and whored-through!"

"I know, Daddy, oh my darlin', that I'm a shit-ass bastardess!"

"And she knows, Kolyushka, that she's a shit-ass bastardess!"

"I know, Daddy, that I'm a rottin' lil' pussy."

"And she knows, o-h-h how she knows, that she's a rottin' lil' pussy!"

"I know, Daddy, that I'm an unfucked fallen woman!"

"And she knows, Kolyshenka, that's she an unfucked fallen woman too!"

"I know, Daddy, that I'm a fuckin' sick lil' bitch."

"And she knows, oh she knows, that she's a fuckin' sick lil' bitch!"

"I know, Daddy, that I'm an un-shat-out cocksucker."

"And she knows, Kolyushka, that she's an un-shat-out cocksucker!"

"I know, Daddy, that I'm snotty and un-fucking-needed."

"And she knows, oh my Kolyushka, that she's snotty and un-fuckin'-needed!"

"I know, oh my daddy, that I'm a horsey cunt-fucked-through."

"And she knows, oh how she knows, that she's a horsey cunt-fucked-through!"

"I know, Daddy, that I'm green upchuck!"

"And she knows, oh how she knows, that she's green upchuck!"

"I know, Daddy, that I'm a wretched eye of the cunt."

"And she knows that she's a wretched eye of the cunt!"

"I know, Daddy, that I'm an oaken dick-jerker."

"And she knows, Kolyushka, that she's an oaken dick-jerker!"

"I know, Daddy, that I'm a piggish dickface!"

"And she knows, oh how she knows, that she's a piggish dickface!"

"I know, Daddy, that I'm a big galoot."

"And she knows that she's a big galoot!"

The daughter fell silent. Her face was pale and wet with tears and rain. She stood there motionless, her head bowed and her hands clasped over her stomach.

"Ooh..." Galina Timofeyevna sighed, took the two bundles, then walked over to the star.

At that moment, the bus honked.

Galina Timofeyevna turned around, looked at the bus by the bus station, and, muttering "just a sec, just a sec," began to quickly unwrap the bundles. In one of them was a piece of yellowed lard about the size of a fist and in the other were some brown crumbs.

Having quickly scattered the crumbs across the flower bed, Galina Timofeyevna began to wipe the star over with the lard, speaking as she did:

"And as it all was, and as it all is, and as it all shall be ... and as it all was, and as it all is, and as it all shall be ... and as it all was, and as it all is, and as it all shall be ..."

The bus honked again.

The old woman turned to her daughter. "Why're ye just standin' there, ye bedeviled mare! Run on now, I think they're leavin'!"

The motionless daughter shuddered, grabbed both of their bags, and ran back toward the bus.

Having wiped over the whole star, Galina Timofeyevna laid the lard down in the flower bed, cleaned her hands on her skirt, and ran back to the bus with a limp.

A MONTH IN DACHAU

1990

5/1/1990. SATURN in opposition to Jupiter. On my trigram, the I Ching indicates "Successful Completion" and "Owl's Cry." The Slavic calendar promises a "Birch Path." Aquarius fatally dependent on Venus. Everything, absolutely everything depends on everything else—total mediation and unfreedom. We exist in this dependency like flies in honey and our slightest movement gives way to waves, waves, waves. Which whelm others. Frightening, but one must make peace with it. I went to see THEM for the third time today. It all came to pass with terrible agony, tension . . . and humiliation. Megatons of humiliation. That pig in uniform stamped down his stamp. But, oh Lord, at what price! Again with the slaps, the hoarse promises to "gut you upon your return." Again with the monstrous, inhuman conversation. I can't speak to them. How they love to humiliate and how ably they do so! That Nikolai Petrovich clearly thinks of himself as *the boss*. How much, how much more, oh Lord? But I again practiced the doctrine of noninterference. And the faces, the faces. Like slabs of raw meat. But I endured. When there's a goal in sight, one can endure anything. The main thing:

AUTHORIZATION

Vladimir Georgeyevich Sorokin, unaffiliated Russian citizen, is hereby granted unhindered departure from the USSR to the

German Empire, where he is to spend his summer vacation (28 days) in the Dachau concentration camp.

Signed,
Deputy Head of the Moscow Department
of Visas and Authorizations
Colonel N. P. Sokolov, MGB*

5/2/1990. Belorussky train station. Train to Munich: 20:07. The I Ching indicates "Contemplation" and "the Army." Dangerous, perhaps. The Arabs promise "Three Fourths." The Slavic calendar promises precisely the same "Birch Path." Hope. Everything is alive with hope. I hope it'll turn out well. Oh Lord, help me on this, my difficult path. A monstrous train station. Reeking peasants in bast shoes, Gypsies, and American pilgrims with their idiotic wave-shaped embroidered sleeve patches. Everything filthy and covered in spit. And the apotheosis of poor taste: an eight-meter-tall Stalin of black granite next to a six-meter-tall Akhmatova of white marble. And Pioneers with their dull faces in an honor guard. Little boys in the Hitlerjugend, two nondescript (apparently Mongolian) officers laying down wreaths. Faces, children's faces. So heavy to see a generation of such indifferent youths, infected with apathy as children. And it's unquestionably *our* fault and not the fault of the people with the meaty mugs. We're even guilty for the fact that they first lay the wreaths at Stalin's feet, then at Anna Andreyevna's. And everything's built on blood and tears, everything covered in dirt. Our whole life is essentially a train station, as Tsvetaeva said. Eternally waiting for a train, our Russian train, for which our grandpas bought tickets way back when. And we're still saving them, these yellowed bits of cardboard, in the hopes of leaving. Oh Lord, I don't mind being late, staying behind, crawling along rusty rails... But wither? A whole crowd of invalids and beggars. Dear, darling Russian people with no legs. Your song is "Our Enemies

*Ministry of State Security

Have Burnt Down Our Hearth" and my song "A Long Road with Troubles of Diamonds." A red-faced porter who's seen it all shoves 'em aside with two of my suitcases and they tumble onto the spat-over platform, then immediately pop back up like bottom-weighted dolls. An obvious analogy, the tears spill themselves. Nerves, nerves god-damn them. We've already been without legs for half a century—they knock us down and we spring back up, they piss in our faces, just like Nikolai Petrovich pissed in my face during the first interrogation, and we wipe ourselves off. It's nice the conductor's a woman and not a man. But what a beastly physiognomy: Nehmen Sie, bitte, Platz! She's gazing at me quite evilly. A gaze of total incomprehension, aggressive rejection, a gaze of mental intolerance. The chasm between us is, alas, ontological. The porter brought in my suitcases and there was immediately a pleasant surprise: I was alone in the compartment. Was this the beginning of a l u c k y streak? God willing. The most boring thing in the world is a compartment on an international train. What could be more melancholy than these beech panels, nickel-plated handrails, silk curtains, and plush sofas? But how much torment there is in this melancholy, how much expectation ... Six months ago, on a black December evening, I was imagining just how I'd stride into this dull compartment. How I'd sit down. The train would push off, they'd bring me tea, and a boiled egg would roll across the little table. Thanks be to God! I still have yet to endure this gloomy ritual, the Eucharist of the Ministry of Transport so to speak. I always have a hard time with it. The conductress enters, silently shoving the door open. I stand up. She silently proffers me a Box. I take it, open it, and sniff at it. She hands me a spoon. I scoop into the Box, I eat. I return it to her. That's all. But my heart pounds every time. What is this? Fear? But of what? I must fight it and fight it. The Germans eat the same thing when they set off for Russia. The Vienna Treaty of 1987. Well, that's that. The door locked, I change into my robe and begin to smoke my pipe. The endless Moscow suburbs crawl past and crawl past and crawl past. Back in 1958, as a joke (nice joke!), the glossy von Ribbentrop called Moscow an overgrown tumor whose benignness was highly problematic. Khrushchev smiled uncomprehendingly. My

God, my God, what's happened to my native city? And why has it been given precisely *to me* to witness its terrible rebirth? Oh Lord, how beastly and heavy this all is—how shameful. Though Berlin, I must admit, also exists in a state far from harmony: Kuppelsberg's gigantism, Arno Breker's tasteless titans, the unbearably vulgar Fountain of Victory, Turkish shit on the Kreuzberg pavement . . . Broadly speaking, the twentieth century is—alas!—antiaesthetic. I can understand that—but precisely *why that is*, I cannot, will not, and do not wish to! She brought tea. We entered a forest. Immediately easier on the soul, easier to breathe and think. Better to live with the trees. Only Nature is truly capable of calming us. I'm exhausted. A monstrous year. Life is not given to us for happiness, as Leskov wrote when he was dying. But not for suffering either, as Kaltenbrunner convincingly demonstrated. Sleep.

5/3/1990. An unexpected awakening in Brest. A vile and disgusting tradition. Dragged into Customs from the warm tangle of sleep. While I was lying naked on the urine-spattered floor (everyone here pisses themselves from fear), the blue-nosed Belarusian lieutenant droned that my authorization didn't exempt me from inspection. He looked me over thoroughly. A stupid cow with the mentality of a pig. Judging by the nose and the acne: a lover of moonshine, lard, and mashed potatoes. Oh, ye unhappy creature. In Russia, everyone's unhappy, victims and executioners alike. Forgive us all, oh Lord. And have mercy. When I returned to my compartment, I found another traveler had joined me—a gray-haired, intelligent-looking SS-Obersturmbannführer with a briefcase, cross, and the ribbon of the Leibstandarte Omega on his sleeve. I must confess that I don't love military men—there's nothing to be done about that—but my compartment-mate turned out to be a pleasant exception to the rule, surprising and delighting me with far from superficial refinement. After half an hour, we were already speaking intimately, like old friends. It turned out he had been in Minsk on the occasion of their May Day parade and was now returning to Warsaw, to his illustrious division. When he found out I was a Russian writer, he perked up and said that he used to write poetry at the institute, had had four articles printed in *Militärischer Beobachter*, had thought of becoming a war correspondent but that had been before his service had taken its toll. He seemed to be about fifty-five, a kind and clever man—otherwise he wouldn't be a lieutenant colonel, I suppose. The conductress brought us coffee and biscuits. We began to speak about German literature of the current century. "Each generation of German culture has its own Scylla and Charybdis," he says, brushing biscuit crumbs from his sleeves with a napkin. "For my generation, it was Thomas and Heinrich Mann. The neoromanticism of the first and the neoclassicism of the second was a unique, two-poled magnet through which my generation passed. And, believe me, those who managed not to be attracted to either of them were few and far between. I couldn't resist either." The Obersturmbannführer grins and strokes the swastika on his sleeve with a slight sadness. "I must admit, even now I'm ready to drink the moisture from behind Madame Chauchat's kneecap as if it were the Holy Grail. And my friend Walter, the doctor of our division, can't fall asleep without *Buddenbrooks*. We German intellectuals have two extremities: either the divine Friedrich's Turin euphoria or the great Immanuel's categorical imperative. But forgive me for just rambling on about Germans. Tell me, is it true that Soviet literature is currently going through a fairly dramatic period?" And he looks at me as only a German can: trustingly and with deliberate attention. How, how am I to respond to this adorable individual? That the cultural situation in the country is terrible and the literary situation monstrous? That arrogance, nihilism, and ignorance have been elevated not only to the rank of virtues but to that of qualities necessary for successful scaling of the bloody literary staircase? That crowlike flocks of murderous scoundrels—critics, they say—greedily peck at the body of a Russian literature that's fallen on its ass? That my literary generation is squeezed behind two deadly millstones—lead-headed Stalinist veterans and young literary Herostratuses who consider Russian culture in the ominous light of their own pyromania? That I'd lost my three best friends in the last month? That I'd chopped my typewriter up with an axe? That I'd spat in the face of my own mother? That I often dreamt of people with rotting heads? That I couldn't see my own hands in the evening? That I was afraid of chests of drawers? Holy God, Holy Mighty, Holy Immortal, have mercy on us.

5/4/1990. I'm quite hopeless: I always sleep through that which is most important. Fatum. Having barely peeled my eyes open, I raised my head and understood that we'd already gone through the Forehead a long time ago and were riding along the Nosebridge. Yesterday's interlocutor had disappeared together with his briefcase. For the third time in my life, I'm crossing into Germany and for the third time in my life, I've slept through the Forehead. What is this? Russian anarchism? Or am I just another Oblomov? Or perhaps it's premature aging? Stupid, stupid. Yesterday evening, sitting in the restaurant car, the Obersturmbannführer and I were washing down Magyar pálinka with Czech beer when several gigantic fells of proper form appeared on the western horizon, to which my counterpart immediately suggested we drink. I agreed after a brief spell of hesitation. All paths from Russia to Germany pass through Braunau. Entirely in the spirit of the times, entirely… Here, over the last eleven years, enormous excavation projects have been carried out on an area of more than 10,000 km². Under Speer's leadership, thousands of people and machines have created HIS face—penetrating the sky—out of the local landscape. Both photography and aerial shots are categorically forbidden. But I know that Armstrong and Stafford shot HIM from space. And our people probably also shot, shoot, and shall shoot. Funny. Now, the train is riding along the Nosebridge, moving to the very tip of the Nose. Where shall be: our stop, customs, the painful rite of Crossing the Border, telescopes for the observation of space ice, an altar made from the bones of conquered peoples, bio-greenhouses, a columbarium… In all of this there's too much of an encroachment into the realm of unhealthy gigantism. A sense of proportion, a sense of proportion. How lacking it is in the twentieth century! Such pagan temples create not genuine artists but art apparatchiks. Corbusier would have done things differently. There will be a long stop, six hours, then the train will be lowered down into the Nasolabial Fold on special elevators. That's where the town of Braunau lies, serving as the Mustache. They had to broaden it a bit to take on the desired shape. Farther on are the Lips and Chin. But why, why am I always so unsettled about what's to come next? Why and whence comes this inability and unwillingness to live in the present moment? For how long shall the Russian consciousness have to balance between the past and the future, never noticing the present? Is there a limit to our epistemological thirst or our metaphysical ambitions? For how long shall we have to continue this Manichean dance around Geist, opposing it to the Being we humiliate? Where is our relativistic sanity? Where is the relevancy? My God, when shall we learn to simply LIVE? Berdyaev is right: "All Russians are inclined to interpret everything in a totalitarian way." Wherefore, oh Lord?

5/5/1990. 4:18. I didn't oversleep, thank God. Already getting light, forty minutes until sunrise. Saturn still in opposition to Jupiter but has shifted toward Mars. The I Ching promises the unintelligible "Deep Well" and "Squirrel's Screech." The Slavs are also unintelligible. The train crawls along like a snail on a straight razor. Remember, remember everything. Live in the moment. There are the rails, the concrete ties, there's the fog, there's the bulk of the Munich train station coming out of it, there's the switchman, there's the guard patrol with two German shepherds, there's the platform, the platform, how lengthily, lengthily, lengthily it stretches forth. How lengthily, oh Lord! We'll have to wait for our whole lives, hoping, believing, and trusting that the MAIN THING won't pass us by. And if it passes us by, will we whirl around in place like distraught Nebuchadnezzars, eating the grass we've set fire to? Can it all be in vain, oh Lord? The final centimeters of the torturous road. Oh Lord! Stop. Out. I immediately saw those who'd come to meet me: three men in uniform two cars ahead. They came over. Unterscharführer Willy and two soldiers from the camp's internal guard. Willy smiles. "Wie geht's, Herr Schriftsteller?"

"Danke, Willy! Nicht schlecht."

I shake his thick Bavarian hand and the soldiers pick up my suitcases. We move through the station crowd and set off on our way on two motorcycles with voluminous sidecars. The road from Munich to Dachau lasts thirty minutes, only thirty, a half hour, but this road, no, ROAD, road, or, oh God, road, this nervous trembling, this taut accumulation of the heart's pulsations, this languor of expectation, this, this predawn Bavarian breeze, calm and order, blossoming chestnuts swimming past, peasant greetings—Grüss Gott!—this morning erection, these (finally!) two gusty bends of the highway, these bushes, this grass, those camp watchtowers, this Stacheldraht, this hair, those camp gates ... My papers being checked, excruciatingly sweet, clouding the mind, the abrupt questions of pretty boys, young eyes looking out from under their helmets with adorable gazes, the enchanting growls of German shepherds, the rustle of a red-leather Soviet passport in trusty German hands, the intoxicating clang of a latch, a creak, no, no, a rustle, a whisper, the sound of opening gates, heart spasms, the cold of hands, the hot of cheeks, a foggy pince-nez, the gravel, the odor, no, the o d o r of the CAMP, that holy, familiar, enchanting smell, depriving you of speech, tearing into your heart, the slow, slow, slow movement across the gravel, oh, that I not lose consciousness, a heartfelt prayer and hope and love and BELIEF in the might of the PLEASURE growing in my chest like a mad baobab tree, oh how embarrassingly wonderful are its roots, growing ruthlessly through the lungs, stomach, and intestines, branching out in veins of peristalsis and filling the cavernous bodies of the penis with seething joy, oh, how longed for is its crown, as it expands into the brain in billions of divine, sparkling leaves, how longed for is its trunk, as it ruthlessly bursts my throat! We stop. Appellplatz. Oh Lord! Heart, heart, halt. Learn to drink the wine of pleasure drop by drop, don't choke it down. Get out of the sidecar, step along the fragile morning gravel, look into the ocean of fog, fatty as a Bavarian widow's milk, distinguish the familiar outlines: a single barrack, an administrative building, a prison, a memorial to the fallen, and there, in the distance, in the milky nirvana—like a beacon of rotten Doves—the crematorium's chimney, the chimney, the chimney of Your Hellish Jericho, oh Lord, the chimney of Paradisiacal Suckage, the First Trumpet of the Orchestra of the Correctors of the Human Genus, the OMEGA TRUMPET, the trumpet of the Eternal Orgasm of Those Flying Away, and the Brown Tornado of Rebirth. A Manmade Elevator into the Halls of the Jade Emperor, the Catapult of the Main Leap, the Terrible Evaporator of Souls, no, no, not Everything at once, everything in time, oh d e s i r e d one, slowly, gradually revive the Divine Mechanism of Realization, unwind the sparkling flywheels of that which is DEAR-EST, with sperm, with sperm shall I lubricate your golden bearings, blood, my own blood shall I pour into your silver carburetor, the meat of my own body shall I hurl into your roaring furnace, sparkle, sparkle, oh you Platinum Spokes of the Wheel of Pleasure, crunch, crunch, oh Gravel of Anticipation, prepare me for my Main Meeting with You, DIVINE, INHUMAN, TORTUROUS, WORSHIPPED, TERRIBLE, DEAREST: she always appears unpredictably and on time, in the space of expectation, like crystal in a supersaturated solution, just as it is now, with a segment of sun and bird from behind the wire, and the odor, the odors and crunching, SHE comes to me obliquely out of the fog across the Appellplatz, passing between gallows and guillotine, SHE's a two-headed woman in a black Gestapo uniform. My Infernal Darling, Margarethe on the left and Gretchen on the right. Margarethe: my darling, white-gold, soft, silent, Lorelei's hair, Lilith's eyes, Sappho's lips, the tenderness of Zhivago's Lara and of Lotte in Weimar (in terms of enchantment). Gretchen: blackish-blue, a raven's wing, Brunhilde's eyes, Brunhilde's face, Brunhilde's voice, Salomé's lips, Lady Macbeth of the Mtsensk District's decisiveness, the intransigence of Sacher-Masoch's Wanda, the licentiousness of Sade's Justine. YOU'RE 23, YOU'RE BOTH 23 ("Ruin" according to the I-Ching and the Slavs say "Deer's Rib"). You appeared in the world at the moment of the atomic bombing of London, Glasgow, Liverpool, and Manchester under, oh be still my heart, the Lord of Power and Glory, under the rumbling growth of Plutonium Champignons, your parents died a valiant death five years later, no, no, My Dichotomous Darling, during the New York landing, YOU were raised by our Motherland, Margarethe is an SS-Hauptsturmführer and Gretchen is a Sturmbannführer, we first met a year ago in Moscow at the Exhibition of the Achievements of the People's Economy, I was just strolling around thinking about my new book, walked unwittingly into the Pig Breeding pavilion, never mind its odor, walked down the aisle between the corrals, enormous pigs that couldn't even stand were lying around, and I stopped in front of the final corral. You were standing nearby in a leather SS slicker with white lapels, fiddling with a riding crop through your gloves, looking at a hog that weighed 1,500 kilos, watching in silence, and I said that that was probably nirvana—to live in such a body, a body that can only sleep and eat, Margarethe smiled, and Gretchen grinned coldly, I offered to show You the other pavilions, especially the Virtual World, and you agreed, and a few hours later, my Siamese Delight, you gave yourself to me atop a narrow bed in the Intourist pavilion, Margarethe and I were kissing and Gretchen was looking on from the side, chewing gummy bears, feigning indifference, and I was crying, kissing the mediastinum of your necks.

DO

N'T

PLEASE

PLEASEDON'T

PLEASEDON'TPLEASE

PLEASEDON'TPLEASEDON'T

PLEASEDON'TPLEASEDON'TPLEASE

PLEASEDON'TPLEASEDON'TPLEASEDON'T

PLEASEDON'TPLEASEDON'TPLEASEDON'TPLEASE

PLEASEDON'TPLEASEDON'TPLEASEDON'TPLEASEDON'

TPLEASEDON'TPLEASEDON'TPLEASEDON'TPLEASEDON'T

PLEASEPLEASEDON'TPLEASEDON'TPLEASEDON'TPLEASE

DON'TPLEASEDON'TPLEASEDON'TPLEASEDON'TPLEASED

ON'TPLEASEDON'TPLEASEDON'TPLEASEPLEASEDON'TPLE

ASEDON'TPLEASEDON'TPLEASEDON'TPLEASEDON'TPLEA

SEPLEASEDON'TPLEASEDON'TRESISTTHEPRURULENT-
LUNATICDECOMPOSINGOOZINGBLOODYSPERMYRAPING-
DICKOFTOTALITARIANISMPLEASEDO
KNOWHOWTOGIVEYOURSELFTOITWITHGREATPLEA-
SUREANDMAKINGYOURSELFUSEFULFOR
THECOMMONCAUSE. V. I. LENIN

CHAMBER 1 immediately adorable when in the chair as if it were a dentist's and the pliers and you my darling with the riding crop and down below totally naked and they tie me up tile lots of light and at first you hit me across the legs with a swish until blood begins to flow and I'm crying then the pliers and the nail from my little finger and you my love are saying take that Russian swine and I scream and piss all over my beaten legs and feet and I cry and you laugh and show me the torn-out fingernail between the pliers an hour later look it looks like a geranium petal eat it and I swallow it.

CHAMBER 2 cold very warm rats arm and legs hurt behind the wall they're raping an American oh Lord how much suffering there is in this world you and Georg come in and when they hung me up I screamed as if it were my childhood Mommy electrodes one attached to the scrotum another to my earlobe Mommy Gretchen kisses George Margarethe screams at me to admit everything Mommy everything everything I'll sign and they still they still I'll sign my darlings I'll admit to everything they kiss I cry out and the American moans I signed that I took active part in the testing of the first gas chamber they wrote fascist on my forehead.

CHAMBER 3 soft furniture television Georg you Kurt show how they tortured me you're all supping they don't let me I watch myself on the television Kurt asks tell me about Dostoevsky I tell them you eat and drink beer watch me and listen to me then thank you for the lecture Mr. Writer take turns pissing in my face just like Nikolai Petrovich.

CHAMBER 4 concrete and boards you repeat my lecture over a loudspeaker Gretchen one sentence Margarethe the next I want to eat so weak why did I come here you're simply merciless, it really isn't becoming for a woman to be so.

CHAMBER 5 flogging in the morning and oh Lord please don't do it till I bleed and you cry out for me to tell you about Dostoevsky about Raskolnikov's repentance again and I please leave my balls out of it only I was crying and three riding crops and oh Lord and you don't feel for me Gretchen and Margarethe screams into my ear and I tell them then I'm on the ground and it's painful and your heels are on my chest and I tell you about his repentance and about Sonechka Marmeladova and you look down from above and Kurt and Stefan touch you down below and I can't breathe and the heels are sharp and they touch me and you're crimson Gretchen and Margarethe screams at me louder louder louder swine then again flogging me across the ankles and you ask about Sonechka and you hit me again and Kurt and Stefan stroke you and drink their beer.

CHAMBER 6 you came in throwing runes this morning rest and expectation I beg you for something to eat or drink I really kiss your boots I beg terrible thirst and hunger left laughing a hatch in the ceiling and you lowered down a rope I'm begging lowered down a piece lowered down a piece of lamb a grilled leg of it pours I present my mouth fresh lamb's blood I catch it with my mouth I'm choking I catch it I drink until I can't anymore then bite the meat I yank you yank Margarethe laughs and Gretchen says have pity I gnaw lower then higher indescribably delicious I eat darling I eat and your faces in the hatch my beloved adored one I eat as if it were the first time in my life as if I'd just been born we're reborn like phoenixes by way of food like Osirises like Dionysuses like Christs and you were laughing Margarethe Gretchen wouldn't allow wouldn't allow gnawed round white bone on the rope then you announced over the loudspeaker that I'd eaten a Russian girl's ham her name was Lena Sergeyeva that I'd drunk her blood you threw me a photo an adorable adorable Russian face oh Lord I wept and prayed until night fell the bone on the rope fell asleep dreamt of my mother taking me to the church on Obydensky I'm a little boy and pieces are falling from her back I catch them in a string bag and weep and all around they're singing Christ has risen from the dead and Mommy smiles.

CHAMBER 7 they didn't appear for a long time everything is made of rough lacquered wood then you came in Kurt four soldiers with a German shepherd you threw runes Gretchen said wonderful entirely fortuitous the soldiers held me down the male dog carried out a sexual attack on my anus then they hammered a cork into my anus put me in a straitjacket threw me down Gretchen said look a Russian writer with a German shepherd's sperm in his ass how long will you hold out?

CHAMBER 8 fantastical luxury marble walls an enormous bath they put me into it all tied up then left music music up above from the ceiling Wagner Lohengrin blue light a big gilded tap and a viscous stream thick as my leg brown slime and worms a monstrous odor it flowed out flowed out quietly and Wagner and I'm chained to the bottom and it flowed out and flowed out oh Lord and it slowly slowly fills up with warm manure and languorous worms up to my stomach up to my chest up to my throat I crane my neck chin to my mouth trembling I'm afraid to budge the door opens a long blue hallway you're at the very end in white Wagner Wagner and Gretchen's singing Lohengrin's part and Margarethe's singing Elsa's a duet it's all over silence there's only the quiet rustling of worms Kurt came in with a ladle Georg with a plate eat this soup made from the best body parts of your young female compatriot I tremble eat this or we'll feed you worms I open my mouth and swallow I pray ladle ladle one two three Holy God Holy Mighty Holy Immortal eighteen ladles I weep they laugh I'm afraid to barf I'll choke on the worms they were laughing smoking then Kurt you dumbass this is veal broth we were joking they left I wept but calmed myself Wagner again Twilight of the Gods and you came in wearing a charming white dress and Margarethe was watching sadly and Gretchen was watching distractedly then they both said those bumpkins were joking that was Lena Sergeyeva soup.

CHAMBER 9 stomach bloated intestines hurt I'm bound up swaddled in straitjacket straw not much light they took me out of the bathtub in the morning washed me carried out a force feeding of pea mash with knödel I begged painfully all day lying there cork all the way inside me she leads excursions local population pointer Russian writer with a cork up his ass children and the elderly didn't believe they show them the cork please I weep my rectum's gonna blow Gretchen the Russian intelligentsia can take an awful lot Margarethe looks on with a sad smile there will be another feeding at three I cried out I thrashed about they whipped me across my legs beat me with boots fed me vegetable ragout made with Lenochka's lard poured me dark beer then oh no dessert strawberries with cream ice cream with fruit they shoved me I lowed and oh Lord oh Lord they shove apple pie pour coffee mocha mocha ground by a gilded electric grinder our poor people oh Lord sufferings oh Lord how much suffering Mommy bursting I'm bursting exposition excursions at night in the evening dinner Lenochka's liver in sour cream no potatoes no shoved over kicked through Mommy beer beer beer blood and beer pineapple no and I'm afraid God have mercy on us in your greatness rupture play with a stomach rupture with a German head cork in the ass oh Lord interrogation at night sign we'll let you shit don't sign it you won't shit and I Mommy I oh Lord I signed.

CHAMBER 10 at night unconsciousness woke up on the square a crowd of locals a women's battalion a rostrum chair with a hole in its bottom microphones underneath the hole Mom your photo in the coffin Mommy forgive me and they're saying Russian mommy Russian writer Mom and by the decree of the SS-Gruppenführer points over there Mom he's been allowed to shit they pulled the rope and oh Lord this cork it's there and I I forgive about Mom I this loudly loumommy Mommy I they pulled Mom I Mom to youoffin to native Mo I loudly and laughter and I Mom forgomommy I'm innocent to all of Germany I loudly to Mom dead forgive then signed in the chamber that I'm an agent of the CIA I signed Mom that you cut up Dad.

CHAMBER 11 a cozy modest space quiet table bed bookshelf enormous portrait of Lena Sergeyeva on the wall I'm reading spring torrents by Turgenev it calms me in those days they still knew how to love sincerely ideals were alive belief was strong love for one's country for one's parents everything the cynical twentieth century covered in blood and trampled in the mud at supper Lenochka fillet with mushrooms Beaujolais nut ice cream liqueur I refused the mushrooms risky after Chernobyl then work stuffing pillows for invalids with women's hair significantly less blond hair I was thinking about Margarethe how much softer and more feminine she is than Gretchen flogging at six masturbation in front of the third company of the women's battalion at eight.

CHAMBER 12 I'll sign everything please don't I'll sign everything please don't not there forgive me I'll sign I'll sign please don't I won't anymore I'll sign not only there please don't I'll sign everything I'll sign everything I'll sign I'll everything please don't I'll sign everything please don't I'll sign everything please don't I'll sign my good women please don't I'll sign my good women please don't I'll sign still please don't please don't any deeper I'll sign deeper please don't I'll sign deeper please don't I'll sign deeper please don't deeper.

CHAMBER 13 solitary confinement concrete sack then to work in the quarry then could at least give me gloves before supper heavy broth made from Lena's offal pea knödel made with Lenochka's lard ersatz bread but the water is clean better than in Moscow work work work macht frei rocks rocks time collect them and refrain from hugs with autism and introversion work clears the head it's no wonder Tolstoy used to plow yes the plow is ready your excellency rocks rocks rocks like Khlebnikov's boards of fate how much has our intelligentsia taken upon themselves without bothering to read the cuneiform of its destiny of our alphas and omegas PRIDE ANARCHY OB-LOMOVISM those are the three whales the three stone turtles supporting the fate of our woes and sufferings always always a deficit of modesty and internal culture not in the sense of spirituality and genius but in the sense of the culture of behavior oh Lord how many slaps my face has suffered how much spit has dangled from my beard and not even from the proletariat or the bourgeoisie that's what's worrisome spitting on ourselves we deprive ourselves of a future we put the gene pool at risk and meanwhile the situation mirrors the end of last century with alarming precision the idols of the past are de-crowned without fear the coming dark likc a sea before the threat and the human race stands between a coffin full of ashes and an empty cradle six hang the American on the Appellplatz concise commands drumroll farts before the unlucky man's death scary scary as a rule every hanged man gets an erection an ocean of suffering washes away your throne oh Lord until evening flogging then a lecture about contemporary Soviet prose if only I could remember their last names Babaevsky Bondarev Bitov Bananov.

CHAMBER 14 there you liquid swine there you swine there there liquid swine there swine liquid swine there swine liquid swine there there swine there swine there liquid swine there swine swine liquid swine swine you there liquid swine there swine there liquid you bastard there swine there liquid swine there you there liquid swine there swine liquid swine there liquid swine there liquid swine liquid bastard there liquid swine liquid you swine liquid swine there swine there.

CHAMBER 15 perforatorio and puncturio needle needlework of Christ Christ-skinned godmeat corpsobeatio offalothrottlo clank clanko clank this rotten rottenified corpse-skinned virgomaro corpse-skinned virginmaiden foroxomplo clank clank clank.

CHAMBER 16 a salon type room shower wc round mirror over the sink every time I have to leave Russia it's like a strange metamorphosis comes over my face my facial features somehow indiscernibly move out of place creating a new face vaguely reminiscent of the previous one such an aberration of the physiognomic topography eyes nose mustache beard everything else even my pince-nez shines differently movements how much automatism toothbrush mustache trimmer nail clippers comb here are our eternal slavemasters Derrida is right every automatic movement is textual every text is totalitarian we're in a text and consequently in totalitarianism like flies in honey and the exit exit can it be only in death no prayer prayer and repentance today I prayed for travelers and infants slaughtered in innocence before supper I was reading a hunter's album then slept glued boxes at nine they didn't bring me dinner I lay down with nest of the gentry ten eleven at midnight a soldier with a bundle change clothes they're waiting for you on the Appellplatz oh Lord unrolled white smoking jacket top hat gloves shoes cane went up in the elevator nervous trembling nighttime stars in place of the gallows a wonderful table set for two candles four servants in white and you in a marvelous evening dress two cigarettes in white and black mouthpieces lovely dinner Vivaldi string quartet seasons and champagne and dessert and you my darling and the cool and the chinchilla across your shoulders and a nightingale in the grove next to the crematorium and Gretchen's eyes and Margarethe's smile and the machine gun behind the trees at the shooting range and our stroll and the wind in the barbed wire and eyes burning in the darkness soldiers in their watchtowers and your hands and the gravel beneath your heels and the darkness and Margarethe's kiss and Gretchen's embarrassment and all three of our hot whispering and a manteau cast off into the darkness and your adorable desirable shoulders and Margarethe's trembling and Gretchen's choked nein and my lips and Margarethe's and Dunkelheit and kisses and Gretchen's desire to go and steps steps and again embraces and liebling and nein and an unexpected tumble into a ditch of rotting corpses and Margarethe's awe and Gretchen's awe and the Nachtigall and the Maschinengewehr and the crackling of velvet and lacy linen and the sweet moisture of your delightful Möse why why only one for both of you and Margarethe's moans moans moans and Gretchen's nein nein nein and meine meine bezaubernde schatz mein liebling meine meine meine liebe meine zarte deutsche blüme meine ma meine ich ich ich möchte dich bis auf grund ausschlürfen.

CHAMBER 17 whip with whalebone handle buffalo leather woven into four strips lead wire plaited into tail bamboo stick with split end riding crop of elm rod covered in kid skin rubber hose with olive oil three cellophane bags an enema disposable syringes two steel wedges a glove made from Jewish skin four hatchets a hook a selection of saws and files artificial respiration apparatus vice jars with Englishmen's lymph nodes crucifixion dental drill handcuffs silk noose brass knuckles Macintosh computer.

CHAMBER 18: all of the hairs have been pulled off her ass and everything's been powdered and I'm swaddled in wet so's it all tightens slowly and her sphincter's shaped like a cross and over her face and a cross of excrement on her face and a cross of excrement on my face.

CHAMBER 19 blue jelly-like after tension after strainings and tremblings after sucking it in and gradual intermittent nein nein nein nein nein nein nein nein nein nein nein nein nein nein nein nein nein nein nein nein nein nein nein nein nein nein nein nein nein nein nein nein nein nein nein along the guiding along the cerebrospinal along the nein nein nein nein nein nein nein nein.

CHAMBER 20 hounded by German shepherds before lunch forced to run over beams catch sticky stones humiliated a sumptuous meal three hours eight courses she said congratulations this isn't Lenochka anymore but a Jewish boy Osya Blumenfeld that's how gluttonous Russian writers are they hung his picture next to Lenochka's they gave me his biography I wept they looked down from the wall two adorable childish faces Lenochka grew up in the Smolensk region in a very simple peasant hut ran along the river for raspberries kissed a calf on its silky forehead learned to weave bast shoes nursed her suckling brother Fedka Osya was born in Zhitomir in the large family of a Jewish shoemaker he studied difficult letters aleph beth waw helped his father to wax laces climbed his way through an old cemetery with his boys went to the synagogue with his grandpa to watch old people sway so adorable so adorable seriously they could have met in ten years or so somewhere on the Arbat or on Khreschatyk Street to fall in love with each other and combine the quickness of the Jewish mind with the breadth of the Russian soul to give the world a new Afanasy Fet but they didn't have the chance to meet on the Arbat instead they met in the stomach of an unfortunate man so's to be bound together in decaying cells and to pass in soft zigzags of peristalsis, passing into the light of God as a reeking monument to our inhuman era oh Lord and why must it all pass through me why oh Lord did you choose my flesh as the testing ground for your whimsies why do torments and sufferings fall upon me like great rotten bears why is everything trampled wasted and sold why are we doomed to take the pauses between tortures as happiness when the torturer goes out to have a smoke and change out his tool where lies the purity in perceiving the world where is the immediacy where is the innocence?

CHAMBER 21: eat for me and I'll come back eat eat with all your might eat when dreary greasy rains tell you nothing's right eat when snow is falling fast eat when summer's hot when no one else is eating and all the past's been eaten yesterday eat when it seems from fatty places no fat will ever come eat even when those that also eat are bored and tired and glum those that did not eat they will never understand how amidst the strife by your eating for me dear you had saved my life how I made it we shall know only you and I you alone knew how to eat we alone know why you don't like to don't want to hump oh you are so beautiful and cursèd to fly—alas—I am too plump though as a child wings from me bursted you with the fattest of nuts they resemble rippling sails slurping juice from the depths of my cunt-guts voices in gales in one unbelievable screwing you've lived your rotten, puss-filled time and the stems of your genitals bluing up the snow does climb.

CHAMBER 22: schmerz schmerz schmerz proposed to Margarethe and schmerz schmerz and Gretchen turning palschmerz schmerz schmerz endure and hide our feeschmerz schmerz schmerz we're not children enouschmerz schmerz schmerz I'm thirty-four schmerz schmerz schmerz I loschmerz schmerz and she also loschmerz schmerz and I came here onschmerz schmerz we entirely gave ourschmerz schmerz it would be proper to underschmerz schmerz schmerz schmerz schmerz Gretchen should underschmerz schmerz the main thing is not to be led around by an egoischmerz schmerz that we can't get along without schmerz schmerz our love is written in the schmerz schmerz I'm prepared to demonstrate it nowschmerz schmerz schmerz.

CHAMBER 23: yesyesyesssssssss looks cheesy but worse more beastly softer I'm sure that having a solid supply of last year's partially processed substance 88 we can hope for a well-timed eucharistic fascistic intimately applied divinely human child-hating technologi-cal positivistically permissible alloyed psychosomatic government-related justification for gum decay and the arthropodal parasite set forth in the child.

CHAMBER 24: crucified crucified crucified like like Peter head upside down light Jupiters Saturns masked ball Strauss champagne laughter laughed laughing gentlemen officers und Soldaten und und GretchenMargarethe und un tour de valse with all with all of the gentlemen Offizieren of the division and from the ritual licking of the soles I do them laughed undressed GretchenMargarethe and bootlicking for me and her undressing and all 112 officers of her division masturbieren and the sperm-washing of GretchenMargarethe and gave out vibrators and 112 vibrobodyings across the sperm-washed Gretchenmargo amplification of the voice vibromoano voluptostrobo and the lowering of the cross and my my oral beneath her anal and vibrators and two lines of fifty-six Offizieren to the oral Gretchen and to the oral Margarethe suctions suctions suctions suctions dick-officero and Wagner Wagner to me to me into my oral your darling excremental Valkyries leberwurstcremento flights of Valkyrecremen-tofly into moutho into moutho into moutho excrement you you jak jak jakcremento warm Wagner removal from the cross placing into white of coffin on the dining room I'm naked gentlemen Offizierohehe and into myobodocoffino defecascheissen onto me by ten by ten und Soldaten and scheisse scheisse scheisse schmekt das besser und I forced myself to pull my hand out of the excrement and pressed the abdrucken of the pistol roulette and pressed pressed when they defecascheisse and to the gray-haired Russian mother's temple pressed five times and she's alive alive alive from the Soldaten's excrement and GretchenMargarethe hat gesagt award award für russische Schriftsteller and I'm into the excrement the excrement face next to Osya Blumenfeld's rotten head and Lenochka's Lenochka's too and into the excrement the German excrement and the Russojewish bones and GretchenMargarethe to me in the cocaine tubo to the nostriline over the excrement the Rheingold Wagnexcremental and musicaine musicaine of the body in the excremental coffin musicaine of the body in the excremental coffowhite I love you aroundo alles Offizieren urinoxcremental duft duftsterbergescheiss of my soul and you and you I must above my coffoxcrement copulated the Obergruppenführer Walter Dietrich and I love you you you.

CHAMBER 25: stretched out stretched out stretched out across across the pressed laichenorot slid acr across the corpsorot recenoschwerkraftobodily and washed the spill of pussostream when I spill the oberstozaubermachen wash the guest from off in the distagnant and Gutnachrichten Reichsführer authorized our our wedding authorized the wedding did the Reichsführer the Reichsführer authorized our wedding.

CHAMBER 25:

durch das lamm das wir erhalten wird hier
der genuß des alten osterflammes abgetan und
der wahrheit mousse das zeichen und die nacht
dem lichte weichen und das neue
fängt nun an dieses brot
sollst du erheben welches
lebt und gibt das
l
e
b
e
n

the wedding proceeded according to Catholic-Russian-Orthodox rite, which certainly suited Margarethe, me, and all other interested persons, a group in which I cannot, however, include Gretchen whose behavior has been strange, to say the very least. On the eve of the wedding, while dressing the bride, she suffered an overpowering hysterical fit, she was screaming at Margarethe, calling her "a lascivious swine sold out to the Bolsheviks," weeping, swearing that she would get an audience with the Reichsführer and tell him about Margarethe and Dietrich's crimes and betrayals, she tore the clothing, and threatened to defecate in the church at the very moment of "wedding." Naturally, I was forced to call the regimental doctor, who immediately gave her an injection in the head; she fell into a drowsy state, in which she remained until the wedding night. The wedding rites were lengthy and they apparently calmed her down even more, she took in the solemn voices of the gray-bearded Father Pimen and the close-shaved Pater Wiese and a nervous convulsion passed across her face only twice: when they sang hallelujah and when Margarethe and I kissed. But how miraculous, how marvelously charming was the visage of my beloved! The divine light of love emanated from her, Margarethe's blue eyes shone, and her golden strands curled up next to tender cheeks. With an almost painful shudder, I looked at her lips, pronounced *ja!*, and this sound concussed my heart with the music of the unpredictable, the voluptuous, and the beloved. A dream, an acerbic, waking dream was carrying us on steel German wings: Munich, the palace of newlyweds, passing between swastikas of ice and fire, paying our respects to the Heroes' Ashes, kissing the relics, laying down wreaths, visiting the Soviet consulate, returning to the camp, a triumphal procession past the heads into the main hall of the basement, a cross-shaped table, white roses, black ice, candles and torches, SS officers and champagne, division banners and standards, leopards in bloody cages and guillotines, blue marble and pink offal. The motion, the motion of a surgeon's skillful hands, the entry, the entry of the scalpel into a Florentine youth's carotid artery, blood, blood, igniting the crystal facets of the glass: sip, sip it, my blue-eyed angel, wine aged for millennia in the cellars of World History, the wine of life, the wine of Humanity. The music of the spheres, the elixir of immortality, confusion of the feelings. You drink, I see your fantastic face, I love you, my Lorelei, we kiss with bloodied lips: music music music of the chamber orchestra, sweet Vienna in a lacy froth of women's underwear, hands, your hands, the silver oval of a dish of stuffed ears, a spiced convulsion of white sauce, a salted spasm of the heart muscle: English, African, Russian, Jewish, German, and Chinese ears, which had, until recently, been listening to the fearsome chorale of our era and have now been baked with the brains of their former owners, oh pierce, pierce the ruddy golden auricle with a silver fork, reach out, my darling, and, yes, in this sweet crunch we shall feel the Music of the Eternal Return, and, yes, we shall wash it down

with the Steaming Wine of Life, and, yes, we shall rejoice at Our
Black-and-White Union, and, yes, we shall taste of the Food of the
Gods: lead, lead me to the Silver-Crystalline Paradise of the Table of
Our New Life, feed, feed me Jellied Breast of Dutch Girl, most ten-
der Ham of French Girl, bring, bring me Magenta Blood Sausage of
Greek Girls, slide, slide over to me a dish of Jewish Tongue, dish up,
dish up to me a dish of Polish Pâté, eat, eat together with me the
finest Roast Beef of English Girls framed by a wreath of Irish Flow-
ers and Sausages, lay, lay a bit of Arab Kidney soaked in Montenegrin
Blood into my mouth, and finally, finally bring, bring me to the
Highest and Final Dish of Our Accordance, stretch out, stretch out
Your Proper Hands, raise up, raise up the Golden Plates over the
Heads of Your Friends and Colleagues, bring me, bring me, bring me
the Last and Consummate Refection of Our New Life: the Heart of
the Novgorod Artilleryman Larded with the Fat of the Bavarian
Nurse, His Burgundy Flesh breathes hot, hot steam, you slice, slice
in half In Half the Meaty Pomegranate of Our Love with the finest
Solingen knife, Your Knife flashes, flashes blue and white, they steam,
they steam with the Steam of Flesh, the Hot Halves, the Gold of Our
Union flashes, flashes, flashes, the Crystal of Our Ringing Souls Sings,
it demands, demands the Icy Blood of a Conquered Europe, churned
by the Nocturnal Oxygen of Our Repast, drink, drink, drink, drink
with Lips and Collarbones, drink, drink with Eyes and Elbows, drink,
drink with Lungs and Cheeks, drink with Tracheas and Genitals,
drink, drink, drink the Wine of Hellish Revelations, the Wine of
Paradisiacal Communion, the Wine of Our Touchings, Wine from
the Snowy Basement of Fields and Mountains, the Wine of the New
Testament of Hatchets and Flowers, drink it to the dregs, drink it to
the dregs, and drop the Glass of Transparent Derivations onto the
marble floor of Autumnal Riches, cry out, cry out with the Cry of
the Dark Blade, tear, tear, tear the Dress of Foremost Merits, outstretch
the Hands of Sturm und Drang, pull, pull, pull the Trigger of Red
Wishes, shoot, shoot, shoot, shoot your friends and companions with
the Machine Gun of the Blond Beast's Joy, shoot, oh Crowned One,
shoot, oh Inhuman One, shoot, oh Swordlike One, aim, aim, aim

the Searing Barrel of the Will of Representations at Heads and Bodies, at Fates and Relationships, at Ancestral Lines, at Business Patterns, eliminate, eliminate everyone with the Stream of Leaden Love, everyone except for me, everyone except for me, command, command me to tear at and drink, tear at and drink, command, command me to topple, command me to topple You over, oh Visage of Mars, onto the Warm Corpses of Friends, onto the Chill Corpses of Enemies, let me, let me choke on the Bitter Foam of the Lacy Underwear of Your Convictions that has splashed, splashed onto my face, onto my Salivary Glands, onto the violet Contour Philosophizing Concrete-Reinforced Power and Glory that has forced Me to understand Your Anti-Generic and Anti-Buddhist Principle of Selected Dependencies, Your Principle of the Pseudo-Magical Packaging of Sensual Antinomies, Your Principle of Arrows and Lilies, force, force me to penetrate into the Westerwald Foliage of Your Veins and Arteries, into the Thickets of Sincere Pseudo-Presence, into the Clefts of Sacrificial Weaknesses, into the Phosphorescent Lacunae of Inseparability, order Me to authorize Charming Excesses in relation to Your Hot, Continuous, Incompletely Original, to Your Secretive:

ME: blue hammers and wild boars of a love tree I catch blows I know how to direct but I don't know how to wait in the name of study.

MARGARETHE: how I loved in the name of the icy fire in the name of the childish tendons I knew the possible intersections of violet.

GRETCHEN: to not do and not speak about the tassels and canopies to be silent to depend on the heavy dawns on the brick on the refusal.

MARGARETHE: oaks and lindens celestial milk and the promise of bloodletting lilies crushed by the bricks of wardrobe Lilliputians harpoons and dragnets of vestments.

ME: the past divisions of cotton hopes the door having opened after the bilious communion the pink demands of noblemen.

MARGARETHE: the lilies of the left-handed hyacinth of desires for the leaden gift the song of the petrified bird-catcher the strawberry of bloody heroes

ME: kiss the steel and eavesdrop know the pseudo-paths of early gods

listen to the music of the morning press believe in the astral sod-
omite

MARGARETHE: on the islands of communist dreams we shall search
for the raw bits of the lost loaned-out defeat of not entirely honor-
able heroes and their wooden doctors.

ME: basically if we want to speak of the bluish end of the extremity
and the jellied then I'd prefer the following sequence:

1. fillo my stomacho wormos dovooring gretchen's hd
2. sew garethe's head to my lef should
3. ampute my limb worked-ov in glued glue wallpaper in
4. full me recto eyes with germanorusso chillun
5. amputo my dck worked-ov in shoe-police gif t o cent committ
6. larde my bod in gold of jewis teeth
7. shoto my bodo into the sk big bertha germy is gret

NASTYA

2000

A GRAYISH-blue lull before dawn, a slow boat upon the heavy mirror of Denezh Lake, emerald caverns in the juniper bushes creeping menacingly toward the white wash of the river reach.

Nastya turned the brass knob of the door to the balcony and pushed it open. The thick, reeded glass swam to the right, splintering the landscape with its parallel flutes and mercilessly dividing the little boat into twelve pieces. A damp avalanche of morning air flowed through the open door, embraced her, and shamelessly flew up into her nightgown.

Nastya inhaled greedily into her nostrils and walked out onto the balcony.

Her warm feet recognized the chill wood and its boards creaked gratefully. Nastya lay her hands on the railing's peeling paint and her eyes sucked in the surrounding world to the point of tears: the left and right wings of the manor, the garden's milky green, the severity of the linden grove, the sugar-cube church on the hill, the willow branches that reached to the ground, the stacks of mown grass.

Nastya rolled her wide, thin shoulders, let down her hair, and stretched out with a moan, listening to her vertebrae crack as her body woke up.

"A-a-w-a-w-h . . ."

Over the lake, the spark of morning began to slowly catch and the damp world turned, offering itself to the sun's inevitability.

"I love you!" Nastya whispered to these first rays, turned, then walked back into her bedroom.

Her red chest of drawers looked out gloomily through its keyholes, her pillow smiled broadly, like a peasant woman, her candlestick screamed mutely with its melted mouth, and the highwayman Cartouche grinned triumphantly at her from the cover of a French book.

Nastya sat down at her little desk, opened her diary, took out a glass pen with a purple nib, dipped it in her inkwell, and began to watch her hand carry itself across the yellow paper:

August 6

I am now sixteen years old! Me, Nastassia Sablina! It is truly strange that this does not surprise me in the slightest. Why is this? Is it good or beastly? I am probably still sleeping, though the sun has risen and has illuminated everything around me. Today is the most important day of my life. How shall I spend it? Shall I remember it? I must try to remember it down to the smallest detail: each drop, each leaf, each one of my thoughts. I must think positively. Papa says that kind thoughts light up our souls just like the sun. Then, let my sun light up my soul today! The Sun of This Most Important Day. And I shall be joyful and attentive. Lev Ilyich arrived yesterday evening and, after dinner, I sat with him and Papa in the big gazebo. They were arguing about Nietzsche again and about what it is necessary to overcome in one's own soul. Today, I must overcome. Even though I have never read Nietzsche. I still know very little about the world, but I love it very much. And I love people, though many of them call forth boredom in me. Must I love boring people as well? I am happy that Papa and Maman are not boring people. And I am happy that the Day we have so long been awaiting has finally come!

A ray of sunlight hit the end of her glass pen, which flared forth into a tense rainbow.

Nastya closed her diary and stretched out once more—sweetly

and achingly placing her hands behind her head. The door creaked open and her mother's soft hands closed around her wrists.

"Ah, my little early bird . . ."

"Maman . . ." Nastya threw her head back, saw her mother's inverted face, and hugged her.

An unrecognizably toothy face hovered there, hiding the stucco cupids on the ceiling from view. "Ma petite fillette. Tu as bien dormi?"

"Certainement, Maman."

They froze in their embrace.

"I saw you in my dream," her mother pronounced, stepping back from her daughter and sitting down on the bed.

"And what was I doing?"

"You were laughing a great deal." She looked at her daughter's hair streaming down in the thin beam with intense pleasure.

"Was I being stupid?" Nastya stood up and walked over to her—lean and delicate in her semitransparent nightgown.

"How would laughter be stupid? Laughter is joy. Sit down, my little angel. I have something for you."

Nastya sat down beside her mother. They were the same height, with similar builds, wearing nightgowns of an identical blue. Only their shoulders and faces were different.

A jewelry box of crimson velvet opened up in mother's delicate fingers, a diamond heart glittered, and a delicate golden chain was pressed against daughter's collarbone.

"C'est pour toi."

"Maman!"

Nastya bent down, took the heart. Her hair gushed round her face, and the diamond menacingly flashed blue and white.

Daughter kissed mother upon still-youthful cheek.

"Maman."

Sunlight lit up mother's green eyes. She carefully parted the chestnut curtain of her daughter's hair; Nastya was holding the diamond before her lips.

"I'd like for you to comprehend what today is."

"I already do, Maman."

Mother stroked her head.

"Does it suit me?" Nastya straightened up, puffing out her taut, youthful bosom.

"Parfaitement!"

Daughter walked over to the tripartite mirror growing sharply out of the colorful tinsel on the table, upon which it sat. Four Nastyas gazed out at one another.

"Ah, how glorious..."

"Yours forevermore. From Papa and me."

"Wondrous... And where is Papa? Still sleeping?'

"He woke up early today."

"Like me! Ah, how glorious..."

Mother picked up the bell next to the candlestick and rang it. A growing shuffling behind the door slowly made itself heard, and Nastya's big, full-figured nanny walked in.

"Nurse!" Nastya ran over and threw herself into her plump arms. The chill dough of Nurse's arms closed around Nastya.

"My goldenun! My silverun!" Nurse swayed and trembled as if she were about to weep, and laid the quickest of kisses upon the girl's head with big, cold lips.

"Nurse! I'm sixteen! Already sixteen!"

"Goodness me, my goldenun! Goodness me, my silverun!"

Mother looked at them with intense pleasure.

"Was just yesterday ye were in yer swaddlin' clothes!"

The nanny's bosom shook—she was breathing heavily.

"Only just yesterday, Lord Jesus! Just yesterday, Mother Mary!"

Nastya turned away fiercely, ripping herself away from the kneading trough of Nurse's belly.

"Take a look! Is this not the most beautiful of things?"

Still not able to see the diamond through the tears that had filled her eyes, Nurse solemnly shook her heavy hands. "Oh Lord!"

Barely able to restrain her joy, Nastya's mother whirled over to the door. "We'll breakfast on the veranda, Nastenka!"

*

Having washed Nastya's body with a sponge soaked in lavender water, Nurse rubbed her over with damp and then dry towels, dressed her, then began to plait her hair.

"Do you remember your sixteenth birthday, Nurse?" Bowing her head defiantly, Nastya looked down at a red ant crawling across the floor.

"At yer age, goodness me, I was already with child!"

"So early? Oh, but I remember—you were betrothed at fifteen!"

"Just so, my darlin'. And my precious Grisha was born by the Nativity Feast. The darlin' littlun passed on from an ear infection, oh Lord. Then came sweet Vasya, then lil' Khimush. By the time I was twenty, I had one runnin' around, another cryin' in the cradle, and a third waitin' in my tummy. God's truth!"

Nurse's swollen white fingers flashed through Nastya's gilded-chestnut waterfall of hair; the heavy braid grew implacably.

"But I've never had a baby." Nastya stepped on the ant with the tip of her canvas shoe.

"Oh Lord, what a thing to bellyache about, my goldenun!" Nurse cried out. "Ye want to give up yer beauteousness for a fam'ly? *Ye've* been shaped to another purpose."

The braid stretched forth like a dead python between her shoulder blades.

On the white veranda, the garish samovar wheezed chokingly, the cunning ivy climbed through the open windows, and Pavlushka, their new lackey, was thundering down dishes. Her mother, father, and Lev Ilyich were sitting around the table.

Nastya ran up to them. "Bonjour!"

"A-a-h! The name-day girl!" As ungainly and angular as a broken chaise longue, Lev Ilyich began to stand up.

"My little sauteuse!" Her chewing father winked.

Nastya kissed him on the clearing between his black beard and his firm nose. "Thank you, Papa!"

"Let's have a look at our Russian beauty!"

She backed away instantaneously, rose into first position, and spread her arms apart: an embroidered olive-colored summer dress, a beaded ribbon around her head, naked shoulders, the gleaming diamond at the mediastinum of her long clavicle.

"Voilà!"

"Our *Lady Macbeth of Mtsensk*!" her father laughed white-toothedly.

"None of that, Seryozha!" Her mother waved her napkin.

"She could be a bride!" Lev Ilyich was standing up and holding his terribly long arms out in front of him.

"Bite your tongue, brother!" Her father picked up a crimson piece of salmon with his fork and slapped it down on his plate.

"Last night, Nastenka, I could barely restrain myself from giving it to you when we were talking about Mr. Mustache." Lev Ilyich reached into the inside pocket of his tight-fitting blazer. "But thank God I didn't rush!"

"Haste makes waste!" Her father began to shred the salmon rakishly.

Lev Ilyich held his bony fist out to Nastya and opened it. In his palm, as dry, flat, and swarthy as a piece of wood, lay a golden brooch made up of Roman letters. "Transcendere!" Nastya read. "What's that?"

"The transgression of limits," Lev Ilyich translated.

"Hold on, brother." Her father froze with his fork by his mouth and shook his steep-browed head. "You're accusing me of literal-mindedness with that definition."

"If you'll allow me, Nastenka, I'll clip it on you." Lev Ilyich held his arms out to her ominously, like a praying mantis.

Nastya took several steps toward him and gazed out the window at the cook's flaxen-haired twins who were carrying five buckets on a single yoke along the edge of the water. *Why are they only using one yoke?* she wondered to herself. Tobacco-stained fingers with long, uncut nails fiddled their way across her bosom.

"Of course, it's your birthday, not your name day . . . but should Sergei Arkadeyevich truly be the champion of progress he says he is—"

"You'll ruin my appetite with all this talk!" Her father chewed lustily.

"How is it possible to hang five buckets from one yoke? Strange..."

"There we are..." Lev Ilyich dropped his hands and, squinting, moved back abruptly, as if he were getting ready to butt Nastya as hard as he could with his little head. "It suits you."

"Merci." Nastya curtsied quickly.

"They complement each other well." Her mother looked at both the diamond and the brooch.

"And Father Andrei, what he will do-o-o is that is he will gi-i-ive Nastassia Sergeyevna another bijou and that is ho-o-ow our Nastassia Sergeyevna will become—a Christmas tree!" Father winked to daughter as he cut into a warm roll.

"Then, you'll stand me in the corner, Papa?"

Everyone laughed.

"Let's have some coffee." Nastya's father wiped his full lips.

"The cream's cooled, master. Shall I warm it up?" asked the freckled lackey.

"Don't call me 'master.' This is the third time I'm telling you." Her father rolled his strong shoulders irritably. "My grandfather was a plowman!"

"Forgive me, Sergei A-ryka-dievich ... and the cream ... suppo—"

"You don't need to warm it up."

The taste of coffee reminded Nastya that she had to go to the riverine backwater.

"I won't make it! It's already struck eight!" She leapt up from her chair.

"What do you mean?" Mother raised her beautiful brows.

"The washbasin!"

"Ah—it's so sunny today..."

Nastya ran off the veranda.

"What's the matter?" Lev Ilyich asked, buttering his bread.

"Amore more ore re!" Father replied, sipping his coffee.

Having jumped down from the porch, Nastya set off for the backwater at a run. She saw the flaxen-haired twins walking toward her from the hill, carrying the inverted yoke with five full buckets hanging from it.

"Just look at that!" Nastya smiled at them.

The barefoot twins gazed at her, having forgotten the weight of their load. Milky snot was trembling in the first one's nostril. Water dripped from all five buckets.

The granite semicircle of the backwater struck by a rash of white moss, the heavy silhouette of an oak tree, velvety hazel leaves, and a ripple of light across the stern ranks of sedge.

Nastya walked down the mossy steps to the dark-green water and stopped dead: the sundial on the cracked column showed a quarter past eight. A pocket of damp cold hung over the water in a barely discernible fog. At the center of the backwater stood a marble Atlas up to his knees in water and bearing a crystal orb upon the yellowish-white musculature of his back. Bird droppings covered the statue's head and shoulders, but the orb shined with transparent purity—the birds could not land on polished glass.

Nastya squinted her left eye: enormous leaves blurred together in the orb, the stalks of imaginary plants, darting rainbows.

"Oh Sun! Gift it to me!" She squeezed her eyes tightly shut.

A quarter of an hour passed by in what felt like a moment. Nastya opened her eyes. A broad stream of sunlight forced its way to the crystal orb through the canopy of oaks, which pulled forth a refracted needle of golden light from the orb that then pierced the thickness of the water.

Holding her breath, Nastya watched.

The needle of light slowly crawled along the surface of the water, leaving a tender vapor in its wake.

"I thank you . . . oh, I thank you," whispered Nastya's lips.

The Moment of the Mystery of Light passed.

The ray was extinguished as unexpectedly as it had come into being.

Having torn a young branch off of the pecan tree and brushed its tender leaves against her lips, Nastya started off home through the

Old Orchard. She opened the rotten gate, walked through rows of cherry trees, even standing by the blue beehives for a moment, waving off the bees with her branch. She then passed by the New Orchard with the glass cone of the orangerie, then ran along the dusty boards past the barn, the hayshed, and the animal yard.

From the stables came the sound of heated voices. Three girls carrying empty baskets ran through the gate laughing, then turned toward the New Orchard, but, seeing Nastya, stopped and bowed.

"What's going on in there?" Nastya approached them.

"Pavlushka's bein' flogged, Nastassia Sya-a-argevna."

"What for?"

"For callin' his master 'master,' they say."

Nastya strode toward the gate of the stables. The girls ran for the orchard.

"Uncle Mityai! Uncle Mityai!" Pavlushka's shrill voice rang out.

"Don't be afeard, don't be afeard…" the stableman said in his basso tone.

Nastya started to walk into the stables but stopped short. Turned around, traced a path along the building's log walls, peered in through a murky little window. Made out that the two stablemen Mityai and Lash were binding Pavlushka to a bench in the half-light. They pulled down Pavlushka's dark-blue pantaloons and his drawers fell to his ankles. The stablemen were quick to strap him down, then Lash sat down by his head and grabbed hold of his arms. The stocky, red-bearded Mityai pulled a bundle of long birch rods from a bucket of salty water, shook them off over his head, crossed himself, then began to whip Pavlushka with great force, directing his blows at the boy's small, pale behind.

Pavlushka squealed.

"Understand! Understand! Understand!" Mityai declaimed.

Lash looked on indifferently from beneath his fur cap as he held the lackey's arms.

Nastya watched his buttocks shuddering in the half-light, his thin legs twisting and turning. Pavlushka's young body was jerking as he tried to bend away from the blows, but the bench wouldn't allow him to. He whimpered in time with the blows.

Nastya's heart pounded in her chest.

"Un-dar-stand! Un-dar-stand! Un-dar-stand!"

"Agh! Agh! Agh!"

Behind her, someone laughed quietly.

Nastya turned around. Beside her was Porfishka, the village idiot. His tattered white shirt had come untucked from his striped trousers, bast protruded from his ruined sandals, and his pockmarked face glowed with quiet insanity.

"I done locked the lady frog in the banya! So that it might have a lil' frog from me!" he said, his blue eyes shining, then laughed without opening his mouth.

Nastya gave him the pecan tree branch, then set off home.

Father Andrei arrived around midday in his new droshky. Slim, tall, and with a beautiful Russian face, he squeezed Nastya's head between his strong hands and kissed her firmly on the brow.

"Well, my wingless seraphim, the very picture of beauty! I'd been hoping to celebrate your name day, but a birthday's better than nothing: siiix-teeeeen years old! That's quite a mouthful!"

He rustled around inside his slightly blue, mostly lilac-colored cassock and, suddenly, a small red box of morocco leather rose before Nastya's face. The priest's strong hands opened it: in a tiny depression in the pink silk was a black pearl.

It's as if Papa could see the future! Nastya thought, then smiled.

"This precious pearl is from the bottom of the ocean." Father Andrei bored into her with his strong, honest eyes. "It is not an ordinary pearl but a black pearl. Ordinary pearls are created when the shell opens underneath the water and lets in the sunlight, then it begins to shine with that same light. But this is a different kind of pearl. A black pearl. This pearl is carried through the depths in the mouths of wise fish who listen to the voice of God with their gills. They carry them for a thousand years, then become dragons who guard rivers. An enigma!"

"I thank you, Father!" Nastya took the little box from his hand. "And how do I...wear it?"

"This isn't to be worn; it's to be kept."

"As a fish would?"

"Yes, like a fish, perhaps," Father Andrei chuckled. Then, stroking at his beard with a quick motion, he looked into the cold light of the sitting room. "Well, are they going to ask me in for a drink?"

"Hold on, Father." Sablin stepped into the sitting room. "We'll have plenty of time to make merry later!"

They embraced, both strong-bodied and tall, with similar beards and faces, then exchanged three loud kisses.

"Oh how jealous I was of you three days ago, brother!" Sergei Arkadeyevich shook Father Andrei by his lilac shoulders. "The blackest envy! The *black*est envy!"

"Why was that?" The priest arched his thick eyebrows.

"Sashenka!" Her father's voice boomed through the entire house. "Just listen to this! I'm driving past his farmstead, I look, and he's got a whole company of maidens tidying up his hay! Such maidens too— the very picture of health! Nothing like my delicate ladies here."

"Yes, well, my mother got them from Mokroye," Father Andrei laughed. "They'd been baling in Mostki, when suddenly—"

"Oh, but I didn't see your mother there! Only those maidens! Such maidens!" Nastya's father laughed.

"That's enough!" Father Andrei waved his hand.

"Is Sablin japing vulgarly once again?" Nastya's mother came in and exchanged kisses with Father Andrei. "It's time, Nastenka!"

"Already?" Nastya showed her the pearl.

"How charming!"

"A black pearl, Maman!"

"O-o-h!" Her father embraced her mother from behind and looked over her shoulder. "From deep underneath the sea, all the way from Buyan Island! Beautiful."

The clock struck midday.

"It's time, Nastyusha!" Her father nodded severely.

"Well if it's time, it's time." Nastya sighed tremulously. "Then I'll...just..."

Walking into her bedroom, she opened her diary and wrote in enormous letters: IT'S TIME! She removed the diamond on the chain from her neck and looked at it. She put it under the mirror next to the brooch. She opened the little box with the pearl, looked straight at it, then looked in the mirror.

"Inside me?"

She thought for a second, opened her mouth, then swallowed the pearl with ease.

The dark-blue silk of her father's study: a star chart affixed to the ceiling, a bust of Nietzsche, stacks and stacks of books, a huge ancient battle-axe taking up a whole wall, hands holding Nastya firmly by the shoulders.

"Are you strong?"

"I'm strong, Papa."

"Do you want it?"

"Yes, I want it."

"Will you be able to?"

"I'll be able to."

"Will you overcome?"

"I'll overcome."

Her father approached her slowly and kissed her on the temple.

The red stone fence of the inner courtyard, fresh whitewash on the newly built Russian oven, their cook, Savely, naked to the waist, sticking a long poker into the oven's mouth, her father, her mother, Father Andrei, Lev Ilyich.

Nurse undressed Nastya, neatly laying her clothes down on the edge of a rough oak table: dress, undershirt, underpants. Nastya was left standing naked in the middle of the courtyard.

"And her hair?" her father asked.

"Let it . . . be, Seryozha." Her mother narrowed her eyes.

Nastya touched her braid with her left hand. She was shielding her thin pubis from view with her right.

"A righteous heat." Savely straightened up and wiped the sweat from his brow.

"In the name of the Eternal." Father nodded to the cook.

Savely put an enormous iron shovel with chains dangling from it onto the table.

"Lie down, Nastassia Sergeyevna."

Nastassia walked over to the shovel uncertainly. Nastya's father and Savely lifted her up and laid her back down on the shovel.

"Let me move yer lil' legs . . ." The cook's white, wrinkled hands bent her legs at the knee.

"Hold onto your knees with your hands." Father bent down.

Gazing at the tufts of cloud drifting through the sky, she took her knees into her hands and pulled them to her chest. The cook began to chain her to the shovel.

"Be easy on her.." Nurse raised her hands anxiously.

"Don't be afeard." Savely tightened the chains.

"Undo your braid, Nastenka!" her mother advised.

"It's fine how it is, Maman!"

"Tuck it under your back or it shall burn." Father Andrei looked on with a scowl, spreading his legs apart and trifling with the cross on his chest.

"Hold onto the chain with your hands, Nastenka." Lev Ilyich looked on fussily.

"No need . . ." Her father waved his hand impatiently. "They're better like this . . ."

He shoved Nastya's wrists underneath the chain, tightening them to her hips.

"He's right," the cook nodded. "Otherwise she goan git loose just as soon as she starts wigglin'."

"Are you comfortable, ma petite?" Nastya's mother took her daughter by her smooth, quickly reddening cheeks.

"Yes, of course ..."

"Don't be afraid, my little angel, the main thing is don't be afraid ..."

"Yes, Maman."

"The chains aren't too tight?" Her father tugged at them.

"No."

"May the Eternal be an aid to you." He kissed his daughter's forehead, which was dotted with cold sweat.

"As we've always said—be strong, Nastenka." Nastya's mother rested her forehead on her daughter's shoulder.

"God be with you." Father Andrei crossed himself.

"We'll be right here beside you." Lev Ilyich smiled tensely.

"My goldenun ..." Nurse kissed her slender legs.

Savely crossed himself, spat in his palms, took hold of the shovel's iron handle, grunted, picked it up, staggered over to the oven, then, almost at a run, pitched Nastya into the oven in a single movement.

Her body erupted into orange light. *There we are! It's begun!* Nastya managed to think, looking at the slightly sooty ceiling of the new oven. Then she felt the heat. It overwhelmed her like a frightening red bear and called forth a wild, inhuman scream from her bosom. She thrashed around on the shovel.

"Hold on tight!" Nastya's father shouted at Savely.

"Stands to reason ..." He locked his short legs and gripped the handle forcefully.

The scream became a roar coming from deep inside her.

Everyone gathered around the oven; only Nurse moving off to the side, wiping her tears off on the hem of her apron, and blowing her nose.

The skin on Nastya's legs and shoulders tightened and soon blisters began to ripple over her body like drops of water. Nastya wriggled around and, though the chains had less and less of her to hold onto, they held fast. Her head shivered very slightly and her face turned into one gigantic red mouth. A scream tore itself loose from her in an invisible crimson stream.

"You need to poke the coals, Sergei Arkadeyevich . . . so that her rind catches . . ." Savely licked the sweat from his upper lip.

Nastya's father took the poker and stuck it into the oven, but was unable to rake the coals.

"Goodness me, not like that!" Nurse ripped the poker from his hand and began to rake the coals toward Nastya.

Another wave of heat gushed over Nastya. She lost her voice and, opening her mouth like a big fish, wheezed weakly. Her eyes rolled in her head, their whites now red.

"Over to the right, to the right." Nastya's mother glanced into the oven and directed Nurse's poker.

"I can see wither." The nanny raked the coals more forcefully.

Nastya's blisters began to burst, spattering her body with lymph, and the coals hissed, their blue tongues flashing. Urine flowed from her and immediately began to steam and boil. Her jerking began to subside and; she could wheeze no longer, now merely opening and closing her mouth.

"How hastily the face changes," Lev Ilyich muttered. "It's no longer even a face . . ."

"The coals have caught!" Her father bustled about. "Make sure not to burn the skin."

"We'll close her up to let the insides bake. No chance she'll get loose now." Savely straightened up.

"Don't overcook my daughter!"

"Clear as clear can be . . ."

The cook let go out of the shovel, picked up the thick, new flap, and put it in place over the oven pipe. The hustle and bustle instantaneously ceased. All had grown bored almost immediately.

"Then you . . . .that . . ." Nastya's father scratched at his beard and looked at the handle of the shovel sticking out of the oven.

"She'll bake up in three hours." Savely wiped the sweat from his brow.

Nastya's father looked around, searching for someone, but he waved his hand. "Very well . . ."

"I'll leave you gentlemen to it," Nastya's mother muttered and walked away.

Nurse followed her with a heavy tread.

Lev Ilyich stared numbly at the crack in the oven pipe.

"Well then, Sergei Arkadeyevich . . ." Father Andrei placed a reassuring hand on Sablin's shoulder. "Shall we test our diamond-covered spades against our clubs? A little round of cards?"

"While we've got the time, we might as well, no?" Sablin squinted at the sun perplexedly. "Come on, brother, let's play."

The shovel's iron handle suddenly jerked and the tin flap chattered. They heard something like a hoot come from inside of the oven. Nastya's father darted over and grabbed the hot handle, but everything was already gone quiet.

"Her soul leavin' her body." The cook smiled exhaustedly.

The oblong, semicircular windows of the dining room, evening sun on the weathered silk of the drapes, layers of cigar and cigarette smoke, scraps of unrelated conversations, the slovenly clinking of eight thin glasses: while waiting for the arrival of the roast, the guests were finishing a second bottle of champagne.

Nastya was brought to the table toward seven o'clock.

She was met with the delight native to mild intoxication.

Gilded-brown, she was presented on an oval serving dish, clutching at her legs with now blackened fingernails. White rosebuds surrounded her; slices of lemon covered her chest, knees, and shoulders; white river lilies bloomed innocently from her nipples, pubis, and forehead.

"That's my daughter!" Sablin stood up, glass in hand. "This evening's special, ladies and gentlemen!"

Everyone applauded.

Sitting at the beautifully decorated table with the Sablin couple, Father Andrei, and Lev Ilyich were Mr. and Mrs. Rumyantsev and Dmitri Andreyevich Mamut with his daughter Arina, who had been

Nastya's friend. Savely stood at the ready in his white apron and chef's hat, a large knife and a two-pronged fork in hand.

"Excellent!" Rumyantseva said in French as she looked hungrily at the roast through her lorgnette. "How wonderfully she was laid out! Even this suggestive pose can't spoil Nastenka."

"I can't bear it." Sablina pressed her hands to her temples and closed her eyes. "It's beyond my strength."

"Don't spoil this special day for us, Sashenka." Sablin gestured over to Pavlushka, who had begun to bustle about with the bottles. "We don't eat our daughters every day, so this is a difficult time for all of us. But also joyful. So, let us rejoice!"

"Yes!" Rumyantseva affirmed. "I didn't rattle around in that train for seven hours just to pine away!"

"Alexandra Vladimirovna is simply tired." Father Andrei laid his smoking cigar down in the giant marble ashtray.

"I can certainly understand your maternal instincts." Mamut turned to her. He was fat, bald, and resembled a june bug.

"My dove, Alexandra Vladimirovna, don't think bad thoughts. I'm begging you!" Rumyantsev looked at her with his fish eyes and his coarse face, pressing his hands to his chest. "It's a sin to be melancholy on a day like today!"

"Think good thoughts, Sashenka!" Rumyantseva smiled.

"We're all begging you!" Lev Ilyich winked.

"We're all ordering you!" the fiery-haired, freckled little Arina spoke up.

Everyone laughed. Pavlushka filled the glasses, his face downcast and puffy from crying.

Sablina laughed, sighed, and shook her head with a sense of relief.

"Je ne sais pas ce qui m'a pris . . ."

"It shall pass, my angel." Sablin kissed her hand and raised his glass. "Ladies and gentlemen, I hate toasts. Therefore—I drink to the overcoming of limits! I will be glad if you join me!"

"Avec plaisir!" Rumyantseva exclaimed.

"A toast!" Rumyantsev raised his glass.

"A real toast!" Mamut's fat lips flapped.

The glasses came together and rang out.

"No, no, no . . ." Sablina shook her head. "Seryozha . . . I don't feel well . . . no, no, no . . ."

"Well then, Sashenka, my dove, then . . ." Rumyantseva pouted. But Sablin raised his hand authoritatively: "Silence!" he said in French.

Everyone was quiet. He put his unfinished glass back onto the table and looked at his wife attentively.

"What do you mean 'not well'?"

"No, no, no, no . . ." She shook her head faster.

"What do you mean 'no'?"

"I don't feel well, Seryozha . . ."

"What do you mean 'not well'?"

"Not well . . . not well, not well, not well . . ."

Sablin suddenly slapped her face with great force. "What's wrong?" She put her hands over her face.

"What's wrong?!"

Silence reigned over the table. Pavlushka was hunched over with bottle in hand, completely frozen. Savely stood there with a doomedly uncomprehending visage.

"Look at us!"

Sablina had turned to stone. Sablin bent down to her and, as if he were carving every word into being with a heavy knife, pronounced, "Look. At. Us."

She took her hands away from her face and looked at the guests gathered round the table, her eyes suddenly narrowing.

"What do you see?"

"Peo . . . ple . . ."

"What else do you see?"

"Nas . . . tya . . ."

"And why don't you feel well?"

Sablina said nothing and stared at Nastya's knee.

"It's strange that you would be so open in your dislike of us, Alexandra Vladimirovna," Mamut spoke up weightily.

"You should at least learn to dissimulate your hatred, Sashenka." Rumyantseva grinned nervously.

"It's far too late"—Arina looked at her sullenly—"at forty years old."

"Hatred is damaging to the soul." Father Andrei cracked his knuckles. "He who hates suffers more than he who is hated."

"How stupid all of this is ..." Rumyantsev shook his head sadly.

"Evil is not stupid. Evil is vulgar," Lev Ilyich sighed.

Sablina shuddered. "No ... ladies and gentlemen ... I'm not ..."

"What are you not?"

Sablin stared at her firmly.

"I ..."

"Savely! Give her the knife and fork!"

The cook walked over to Sablina cautiously and held the handles of the carving utensils out to her. "Please."

Sablina took them and looked at them, as if she were seeing such instruments for the first time.

"You're going to serve us." Sablin sank back down in his chair. "You're going to cut the pieces that we ask for. You're free to go, Savely."

The cook left.

"Ladies and gentlemen, let's eat before Nastya gets cold." Sablin tucked the corner of his napkin into his collar. "As the father of the newly baked, I'll order the first piece: give me the left breast! Pavlushka! Bring us the Bordeaux!"

Sablina stood up, walked over to the serving dish, stuck the two-pronged fork into Nastya's left breast, and began to cut into her flesh. Everyone listened intently. Beneath a brown, crispy crust flashed forth white meat and a yellow strip of fat. Her juice flowed freely. Sablina put a slice of breast onto a plate and handed it to her husband.

"Please, everyone! Don't be shy!"

Rumyantseva was the first to come to her senses:

"Cut me some itsy little bits from the ribs, Sashenka, the tiniest bits!"

"I'll have some rump!" Mamut sipped his wine.

"Shoulder and forearm for me, Alexandra Vladimirovna." Rumyantsev rubbed his hands together, as if he were counting invisible money. "Make sure it's nowhere near the hand...on the forearm itself...the very forearm..."

"I could have some of the hand." Lev Ilyich coughed modestly.

"I'd like a bit of head!" Father Andrei cheerfully rested his fists upon the table. "So as to take a stand against the testimonium paupertatis."

Arina waited until Sablina had fulfilled everyone else's orders. "Alexandra Vladimirovna, can I have..." She fell silent and glanced over at her father.

"What?" Mamut leaned down to his daughter.

Arina whispered something in his ear.

"You have to ask like a grown-up if you want that part," he advised.

"But how?"

Her father whispered something in her ear.

"What would you like, Arinushka?" Sablina asked quietly.

"I would like...the mons veneris."

"Bravo, Arina!" Sablin exclaimed and the other guests applauded her.

Sablina looked her daughter's body up and down searchingly: her groin was impossible to get at between her legs.

"It's not always so easy to get to that mysterious corner!" Rumyantsev winked and a burst of laughter filled the dining room.

"Hold on, Sasha..." Sablin stood up, took hold of Nastya's knees resolutely, and pushed hard, attempting to spread her legs apart. Her pelvic joints cracked, but her legs would not move.

"What a thing!" Sablin pushed harder. His neck turned purple and the hedgehog of hair on his head quivered.

"Slow down, Sergei Arkadeych!" The priest stood up. "It would be a sin to overstrain yourself today, brother."

"Am I not...a Cossack? I've still got...some! some! some! powder left to shoot with...yes! yes! yes!" Sablin grunted.

Father Andrei grabbed hold of one knee and Sablin grabbed the other. They pulled, grunting and baring their beautiful teeth. The joints cracked juicily, the roasted legs fell open and were parted, and juice sprayed out of the meat as it was torn apart. Protected by the thighs from the heat of the oven, her pubis still shined a tender shade of white and seemed to be made of porcelain. Two dark pubic gashes filled with twisted bones and steaming meat enshadowed its sides. A stream of brown juice flowed onto the serving dish.

"Sashenka, s'il vous plaît." Sablin wiped at his hands with a napkin.

The cold knife cut into Nastya's pubis, as if it were white butter: the trembling of sticky little public hairs, the submissiveness of the semitranslucent skin, the innocent smile of her childish labia only slightly parted and occasionally dripping.

"Here you are, my angel."

The pubis lay on the plate in front of Arina. Everyone was staring at it.

"It's a shame to eat such beauty." Mamut was the first to speak.

"Like ... a wax angel," Arina whispered.

"Every moment is precious, ladies and gentlemen!" Sablin raised his glass of Bordeaux. "We shall not let the meat cool. To your health!"

They clinked the crystal glasses together. They drank quickly. Their knives and forks entered the meat.

"M-m-m ... m-m-m ... m-m-m ..." Rumyantsev shook his head while he chewed, as if he had a toothache. "There's something ... h-m-m-mit's ... something ..."

"Magnifique!" Rumyantseva tore off a chunk of meat with her teeth.

"Good," said Father Andrei, chewing a piece of Nastya's cheek.

"Your cook, brother ... he's really ..." The meat's crust crunched between Lev Ilyich's teeth.

"A perfect roast." Mamut carefully examined the piece of meat speared on his fork, then put it in his mouth.

"A quarter of an hour ... m-m-m ... on the coals and three hours in the oven ..." Sablin chewed cheerfully.

"Just so," Mamut nodded.

"No ... this is something ... this is something ..." Rumyantsev screwed up his eyes.

"How I adore the chest ..." Rumyantseva smacked.

Arina carefully cut off a piece of the pubis, put it in her mouth, and, chewing carefully, stared at the ceiling.

"How is it?" Mamut asked her, sipping his wine.

She shrugged her plump shoulders. Mamut delicately cut a strip of meat off of the pubis and tried it. "M-m-m . . . like celestial sour cream . . . Eat while it's still warm. Stop making faces . . ."

"And what about you, Sashenka?" Sablin's moist eyes turned to his wife.

"Don't undo our harmony, Alexandra Vladimirovna." Rumyantsev wagged his finger.

"Yes, yes . . . I . . . without fail . . ." Sablina gazed numbly at the headless body, swimming in its own juice.

"If you'll allow me, madame, your plate . . ." Father Andrei reached over for it. "What you need is the most delicate meat."

Sablina handed him her plate. He stuck the knife in beneath Nastya's jaw, made a semicircular incision, jammed his fork into it, then slapped her steaming tongue down onto Sablina's empty plate. "The most tender bit!"

Her tongue lay there, a question mark made of meat.

"Thank you, Father." Sablina accepted the plate with an exhausted smile.

"Ah, how delightful your Nastenka has remained," Rumyantseva mumbled through the meat in her mouth. "Just imagine . . . m-m-m . . . whenever I saw her, I thought . . . that this . . . that we would . . . m-m-m . . . that . . . no, it's simply stunning! What delicate, exquisite ribs she has!"

"Nastassia Sergeyevna was a remarkable infant." Lev Ilyich crunched into the fire-polished skin of the pinkie finger. "Once, I arrived directly from the Assembly as tired as a rickshaw, a terribly hot day, and naturally, in the simplest way . . . m-m-m . . . I decided to, you know, go directly to the—"

"Wine! Pavlushka! More wine!" cried Sablin. "Where is the Falero?"

"You had asked for a Bordeaux, sir." Pavlushka spun his head on his white, tight-skinned neck.

"You idiot! Bordeaux is just a prelude! Hurry now!"

The lackey ran off.

"Devil take it, it's so delicious!" Mamut sighed corpulently. "And it's completely, entirely correct that you've gotten by without any spices whatsoever."

"Good meat needs no spices, Dmitri Andreyevich," Sablin said, chewing and leaning back in his chair. "As is so with any Ding an sich!"

"That is certainly true." Father Andrei looked around. "And where, if you'll forgive me, is the ..."

"What, brother?"

"The teaspoon ..."

"Here you are!" Sablin reached out.

The priest stuck the teaspoon into one of the roasted head's eyes and twisted decisively: Nastya's eye was now on the teaspoon. The pupil was white, but the iris was still the same shade of greenish-gray. After salting and peppering the eye hungrily, the priest squeezed lemon juice on it and put it in his mouth.

"I can't eat fish eyes," the slowly chewing Arina said drowsily. "They're bitter."

"Nastenka's are not bitter." The priest took a gulp of wine. "I would even say they're quite sweet."

"She loved to wink. Especially when she spoke Latin. She got written up for that three times at school."

"Nastya knew how to look at things in a surprising way," Sablina spoke up, thoughtfully moving Nastya's half-eaten tongue around her plate with her knife. "When I gave birth to her, we were living in St. Petersburg. Every day, the wet nurse would come to suckle Nastenka. And I would just sit there. Once, Nastya looked at me in a very strange, a very unusual way. She was sucking the wet nurse's breast and looking at me. But this was, above all, not a childish gaze. To be honest, her gaze made me feel uneasy. I turned away, walked over to the window, and began to look outside. It was a winter evening. The whole window was covered over in frost. Only in the middle was one melted patch. In that little dark spot, I could see my Nastenka's face. Her face was ... I don't know how to describe it ... her face looked like it belonged to an adult. An adult who was significantly older than I was. I got scared. And then, for some reason, I said 'Batu.'"

"Batu?" Father Andrei wrinkled his brow. "As in ... Batu Khan?"

"I don't know," sighed Sablina. "Maybe not him. But what I said was 'Batu.'"

"Have some wine." Sablin moved a glass over to her.

She drank obediently.

"Sometimes, the devil can seem to appear even in those closest to us." Rumyantsev held out his empty plate. "I'd like some thigh, please, just that bit there."

"Where?" Sablina got up.

"The well-done part there."

She began to cut off a piece.

"Sergei Arkadych"—Mamut wiped at his greasy lips—"enough torturing your wife. Call the cook back."

"What on earth do you mean?" Sablina smiled. "I find serving you to be extraordinarily pleasant."

"I look after my cook's health." Sablin took a gulp of his wine. "Give me some of the neck, Sashenka, and don't forget the vertebrae ... Yes. I look after his health. And I respect him."

"He's a good cook"—Father Andrei took a crunchy bite of Nastya's nose—"if also a little rustic."

"Rustic, brother? His jack snipe in lingonberries is even better than at Testov's. There's not a sauce he can't make. Do you remember his suckling pigs on Easter?"

"But of course!"

"I brought him eight cookbooks. Yes yes yes! To the cook! How could I ..." Finishing his bite, Sablin stood up, grabbed Nastya's foot, and twisted it.

Bones cracked.

"Cut a strip there, Sashenka ..."

Sablina made the cut. Sablin tore off the foot, picked up the half-empty bottle of Falero, and walked from the dining room into the kitchen. In the stuffy, vanilla-scented air of the kitchen, the cook was laboring over a lemon-pink pyramid-shaped cake, covering it with buttercream roses from a paper tube. The scullery maid was whipping cream and blueberries next to him.

"Savely!" Sablin was looking for a glass but found a copper mug instead. "Here—take this."

Having wiped the cream from his hands onto his apron, the cook humbly accepted the mug.

"You tried hard today." Sablin filled the mug to the brim. "Drink in memory of Nastya."

"Thankee very much." The cook crossed himself carefully, so as not to spill the wine, brought the mug to his lips, then slowly drank it down to its dregs.

"Eat." Sablin handed him the foot.

Savely took the foot, gave it a once-over, then bit down hard. Sablin stared at him very directly. The cook chewed weightily and thoughtfully, as if he were working. His carefully trimmed beard moved up and down.

"How does my daughter taste?" Sergei Arkadeyevich asked.

"Real fine." The cook swallowed. "She roasted up somethin' glorious. That oven works magic."

Sablin slapped him on the back, turned away, and walked into the dining room.

Everyone was arguing.

"First, my father would sow lentils, then, once they came up, he would immediately plow and plant wheat," Father Andrei explained weightily. "By the Feast of the Transfiguration, the wheat was so tall that my sister and I would play hide-and-seek in it. You didn't have to drag it into the threshing barn either. If you gave the sheafs a shove, they would simply fall over. We had straw for the stove all through the winter. And you talk to me about steam-powered threshing machines!"

"In that case, Father, why don't we just return to the Stone Age?" Rumyantsev laughed cruelly. "It'll be like a song: they plow with bast shoes and reap with their nails."

"We can return to the Stone Age"—Mamut relit his cigar—"as long as there's something to plow."

"How can it be you're talking about bread again?" Sablin tucked a new napkin under his collar. "Devil take this conversation! I'm sick of it. Can it truly be there are no other subjects, friends?"

"They're men, Sergei Arkadych." Rumyantseva swirled around the wine in her glass. "You can't just feed them bread, they also have to argue about all the mechan—"

"What?!" Sablin banged his fist on the table, interrupting her in a contrivedly menacing tone. "Where do you see any bre-ad?! Where, my fair lady, do you see any bre-ad?! I didn't invite you here to break bread! What bre-ad? Let me ask you this—with what kind of bread do I feed men?! Hmm? With this bread here?" He picked up Arina's plate with the half-eaten pubis on it. "Does this look like French *buns* to you?"

Rumyantseva stared at him with her mouth hanging open.

Silence reigned.

Mamut took an unlit cigar from his mouth, moved his massive head forward as if he were about to collapse onto the table, then began to laugh heartily, his plump belly convulsing. Rumyantsev seemed to draw his head down into his standing collar, then waved his hands, as if he were being attacked by invisible bees, squealed, and let forth a shrill giggle. Lev Ilyich covered his face with his hands as if he were preparing to tear it from his skull, then began to laugh nervously, his bony shoulders twitching. Father Andrei banged his palms against the table and laughed a vigorous Russian laugh. Arina sprayed laughter into the palm of her hand and shook silently, as if from a fit of vomiting. Rumyantseva shrieked like a girl in a meadow. Sablina shook her head and laughed wearily. Sablin leaned back in his chair and roared with delight.

Laughter shook the dining room for two minutes.

"I can't ... ha-ha-ha ... I'm dying ... dying ... oh ..." Father Andrei wiped the tears from his eyes. "You deserve to be sentenced to hard labor, Seryozha ..."

"What for ... ha-ha ... for buns ... ha-ha-ha ... puns, I mean?" Mamut calmed down with some difficulty.

"For torturing us with this laughter ... oh ... he-he-he ..." Rumyantsev wriggled around in his chair.

"Sergei Arkadeyevich would be a wonderful ... oh my ... Grand Inquisitor." Rumyantseva sighed, now very red.

"An executioner! An executioner!" Lev Ilyich shook his head.

"Forgive me, Arinushka." Sablin put the plate back down in front of her.

"How am I supposed to eat that now?" she asked sincerely.

The guests were once more overwhelmed by a wave of laughter. They laughed until they cried, until they had stomach cramps. Mamut pressed his crimson forehead against the table and roared into his shirtfront. Rumyantsev slid to the floor. His wife squealed, shoving her fist into her mouth. Lev Ilyich wept uncontrollably. The priest laughed simply and vigorously, like a peasant. Sablin grunted, snorted, wheezed, and kicked his feet against the floor. Arina giggled delicately, as if she were beading a necklace.

"That's enough! Enough! Enough!" Sablin wiped at his wet face. "Finita!"

They began to come back to their senses.

"It's good to laugh, of course, it clears the mind . . ." Mamut sighed heavily.

"You could get your intestines in a twist laughing like that." Rumyantsev took a drink of wine.

"No one's ever died of good ol laughter." The priest stroked his short beard.

"Ladies and gentlemen, let us continue." Sablin rubbed his hands together. "While Nastya is still warm. Sashenka, oh light of mine, could you give me"—he squinted thoughtfully—"some tripe!"

"I'd like some of the neck!"

"I'd like some shoulder, Sashenka, my dove . . ."

"Some hip for me! Hip and only hip!"

"Can I have some . . . from the crusty bit there . . ."

"Some hand, Alexandra Vladimirovna, if you please."

Soon, everyone was chewing in silence, washing the meat down with wine.

"Even so . . . human meat has quite an uncommon taste . . . wouldn't you say?" muttered Rumyantsev. "What do you think, Dmitri Andreyevich?"

"Meat as such is strange fare, that's for sure." Mamut chewed weightily.

"Why is that?" asked Sablin.

"Because it's made from a living thing. Is it worth killing a living thing only so as to eat it?"

"You find that to be sad?"

"Of course it's sad. Last week in Putyatino, we were on our way to the Adamovichs. But right when we left the station, a hub broke. We managed to drag ourselves to a saddlemaker nearby. While he was making us a new one, I sat by a willow, in the shade. And a pig wandered over. An ordinary sow. It stood there looking at me. Looked at me in such an expressive way. A living being. A whole universe. But for the saddler it was a mere seven or so poods of meat. And I thought, What ridiculous game this is—to devour living beings! To end a life and destroy its harmony only to further the process of digesting food. Which ends we all know how."

"You're reasoning like Tolstoy." Rumyantseva grinned.

"I have no divergences with Count Tolstoy regarding the issue of vegetarianism. If eating meat means accepting evil, it must cease!"

"What does it mean to end a life?" Sablin peppered Nastya's liver. "Is it not possible to end an apple's life? Or to kill a stalk of rye?"

"The stalk feels no pain. But the pig squeals. Which means that it suffers. And suffering is the destruction of worldly harmony."

"Maybe the apple also hurts when it crunches," Lev Ilyich said quietly. "Perhaps it cries out in pain, writhes, and moans. Perhaps we just don't hear it."

"Yes!" Arina suddenly spoke up, pulling one of Nastya's pubic hairs out of her mouth. "Last summer, we had a grove of trees cut down and poor, dead Mommy shut the windows in every which place. 'What's wrong, Mommy?' I ask. And she just says: 'The trees are crying!'"

They ate in silence for a little while.

"The hips really turned out well." Rumyantsev shook his head. "As juicy as . . . I don't know what . . . the juice just sprays out . . ."

"A Russian oven is a remarkable thing." Sablin sliced into the kidney. "Would it turn out so well in a normal oven? Or on open coals?"

"Only pork can be cooked on open coals," Mamut suggested weightily. "Lean meat dries out."

"Precisely so."

"But how do Circassians cook their shashliks?" Rumyantseva raised his empty glass.

"Shashlik is raven feed, my darling. Right here, we have three poods of meat." He nodded at the serving dish with Nastya in it.

"Well, I love shashliks," Lev Ilyich exhaled.

"Can someone pour me some wine?" Rumyantseva touched her glass to her nose.

"Hey half-wit, wake up!" Sablin shouted at Pavlushka.

The lackey rushed over to pour the wine.

"Well, milady Alexandra Vladimirovna has eaten almost nothing at all," Arina reported.

"Is it not delicious?" Rumyantsev spread out his greasy hands.

"No, no. It's very delicious," Sablina sighed. "It's just that I'm … I'm just exhausted."

"You've barely had anything to drink," Mamut concluded. "That's why the meat's getting stuck in your throat."

"Drink as is ordained, Sashenka!" Sablin brought a full glass up to her exhaustedly beautiful lips.

"Drink, drink with us!" Rumyantsev blinked excitedly.

"Don't neglect your duties—drink!" Rumyantseva smiled, her face now pink.

Sablin grabbed his wife's neck with his left hand and slowly, but resolutely, poured the wine into her mouth.

"Oy—Seryozha—" she sputtered.

Everyone applauded.

"And now the most capital of chasers for the wine!" Mamut commanded.

"Have some fatty meat from the rump, Alexandra Vladimirovna." Lev Ilyich winked.

"I know what you need!" Sablin leapt up, grabbed hold of the knife, and plunged it into Nastya's belly with all his might. "Nothing goes with *wine* like intes-*tine*!"

Cutting off a piece of intestine with his knife, he then stabbed it with his fork and hurled it onto his wife's plate. "Tripe is the most superfluous meat and, thus, the most vital! Eat, my angel! You'll feel better right away!"

"Correct! Entirely correct!" Mamut shook his fork. "Though I always eat offal with partridge."

"I'm not sure . . . perhaps some white meat would be better?" Sablina stared at the grayish-white guts, which were dripping with greenish-brown juice.

"Eat quickly, I'm begging you!" Sablin grabbed her by the nape of her neck. "Then you'll thank each and every one of us!"

"Listen to him, Sashenka!"

"Eat it now, Alexandra Vladimirovna! Without fail! This is an order from on high!"

"You mustn't shirk your duty to eat food!"

Sablin speared a piece of offal with his fork and brought it up to his wife's mouth.

"You don't have to feed me, Seryozhenka." She grinned, taking the fork from him and tasting the meat.

"Well, how is it?" Sablin stared at her intently.

"Delicious." She continued to chew.

"My darling wife." He took her left hand and kissed it. "It's not simply delicious. It's divine!"

"I agree," Father Andrei chimed in. "To eat one's daughter is divine. It's a shame that I have no daughter."

"Don't feel bad, brother." Sablin cut himself a piece of hip. "You have a great many spiritual offspring."

"And I've not the right to roast them, Seryozha."

"Yes, but *I* have the right!" Mamut pinched his daughter's cheek as she chewed. "You won't have to wait much longer, my little fidget."

"When will it be?" Father Andrei asked.

"October. The sixteenth."

"Not for a while then."

"These two months shall fly by."

"Are you getting yourself ready, Arisha?" Rumyantseva asked, gazing at one of Nastya's severed fingers.

"I'm tired of waiting." Arina pushed away her empty plate. "All of my friends have already been roasted and I'm still waiting. Tanya Boksheyeva, Adèle Nashyekina, and now Nastenka too."

"Be patient, my little peach. We'll eat you soon enough. Children must be eaten without fail. Why do we birth them, hmm? To eat them, eat them, eat them!"

"I'm sure that you'll be very sumptuous, Arina Dmitriyevna!" Lev Ilyich winked.

"Of course, she'll need some fattening up!" Mamut laughed, tugging at her ear.

"We'll bake her like a teacup pig." Sablin smiled. "In October with a spot of vodka, a spot of rowanberry vodka—oh, how crispy our Arinushka shall be . . . ooh-ooh-ooh!"

"Won't you be nervous?" Rumyantsev was gnawing at a knuckle.

"Well . . ." she rolled her eyes thoughtfully and shrugged with plump shoulders. "A little. It shall be very uncommon!"

"No doubt about that!"

"On the other hand, many people are roasted. I just . . . can't imagine what it will be like to lie in the oven."

"Hard to picture, huh?"

"Mm-hmm!" Arina grinned. "It must be so painful!"

"Very painful." Father Andrei nodded his head seriously.

"Horribly painful." Mamut stroked her crimson cheek. "So painful that you go insane just before you die."

"I don't know." She shrugged again. "Sometimes, I light a candle and put my finger in the flame to test myself. I screw up my eyes and make a decision: I shall hold it there to the count of ten. But then I begin to count—one, two, three—and I can't stand it anymore! It's so painful! And in the oven? How shall I stand it in there?"

"In the oven"—Mamut grinned, peppering another piece—"it

won't just be your finger in the flame, but your whole naked little body. And not over a two-kopeck candle, either, but atop red-hot coals. The heat shall be fierce, hellish."

Arina lost herself in thought for a moment, raking her nails across the tablecloth.

"Alexandra Vladimirovna, did Nastya scream very loudly?"

"Very." Sablina was eating slowly and beautifully.

"She struggled until the end." Sablin lit a cigarette.

Arina wrapped her arms around her shoulders as if she were cold. "Tanechka Boksheyeva fainted when they tied her to the shovel. She came to in the oven and cried out, 'Wake me up, Mommy!'"

"She thought she was dreaming?" Rumyantsev stared at her with a smile.

"Mm-hmm!"

"Well, it wasn't a dream." Sablin began to fuss around the serving dish in businesslike fashion. "Ladies and gentlemen, your final orders! Hurry! One cannot eat a cold roast!"

"It would be my pleasure." Father Andrei held out his plate. "One must eat good food and a lot of it."

"At the right time and in the right place." Mamut also held out his plate.

"And in good company!" Rumyantseva followed their example.

Sablin shredded Nastya's still-warm body. "Durch Leiden Freude."

"Are you being serious?" Mamut lit his extinguished cigar once again.

"Absolutely."

"How fascinating! Explain yourself, please."

"Pain tempers and enlightens. It heightens the senses. Clears the brains."

"One's own pain or the pain of others?"

"In my case—the pain of others."

"Ah, there we have it!" Mamut grinned. "So, you're still an incorrigible Nietzschean then?"

"And I've no shame in admitting it."

Mamut exhaled smoke disappointedly.

"Well well! And I had hoped I was coming to dinner with a

hedonist like myself! Does this mean you cooked Nastya not out of love for life but for ideological reasons?"

"I cooked my daughter out of love for her, Dmitri Andreyevich. You can consider me a hedonist in that sense."

"What kind of hedonism is that?" Mamut grinned biliously. "It's Tolstoyism pure and simple!"

"Lev Nikolayevich hasn't cooked his daughters yet," Lev Ilyich objected delicately.

"Yes and it's unlikely that he shall." Sablin cut off a piece of Nastya's leg. "Tolstoy is a liberal Russian nobleman. Therefore, he is also an egotist. Nietzsche, on the other hand, is our new John the Baptist."

"Total demagoguery." Mamut sipped his wine. "Nietzsche has pulled the wool over all of your eyes. The eyes of all radical thinkers in the intelligentsia. They can no longer simply and clearly see that which is. No, this is total delirium, a general state of lunacy, the second dimming of our minds! First, there was Hegel, to whom my grandfather literally prayed, and now this mustached fool!"

"What is it about Nietzsche that bothers you so much?" Sablin was serving everyone pieces of sliced meat.

"It's not Nietzsche who bothers me but his Russian followers. Their blindness bothers me. Nietzsche did not create anything fundamentally new in the world of philosophy."

"Is that so?" Sablin handed him his plate with a piece of Nastya's right breast.

"A dubious statement," Lev Ilyich remarked.

"Nothing, *no*-thing, fundamentally new! All Greek literature is Nietzschean! From Homer to Aristophanes! Amoralism, incest, the cult of strength, contempt for the common man, hymns to elitism! Think of Horace! 'I hate the vulgar crowd!' And the Greek philosophers? Plato, Pythagoras, Antisthenes, Cinesias? Who among them did not call for man to overcome that which is human, all too human? Who among them loved the demos? Who among them called for mercy? Perhaps only Socrates."

"But Nietzsche was the first philosopher to write about the Übermensch," Sablin retorted.

"Nonsense! Schiller used that very word. Many others wrote about the idea of the Übermensch—Goethe, Byron, Chateaubriand, Schlegel! But never mind Schlegel—devil take him! In his little article, Raskolnikov sums up all of Nietzsche! Body and soul! What about Stavrogin and Versilov? Are they not Übermenschen? I say 'Let the world go to hell, but I should always have my tea!'"

"All great philosophers find a common feature or, better yet, a common denominator for that which has intuitively accumulated before them," Father Andrei spoke up. "Nietzsche is no exception. He did not philosophize in a vacuum."

"Nietzsche wasn't looking for a common denominator! He puts forth no common feature!" Sablin shook his head violently. "He made a great leap forward! He was the first in the history of human thought to truly liberate man and show him the way!"

"What is this way, then?" Mamut asked.

"'Man is something that shall be overcome!' That is the way."

"Every religion in the world says the same thing."

"If we keep turning the other cheek, we won't change anything."

"So we'll change it by giving the falling another shove?" Mamut drummed his fingers on the table.

"How else would we change it?" Sablin looked around for the gravy boat and picked it up; thick red sauce flowed over the meat. "By freeing the world from the weak, from those not capable of living, we are helping a healthy youth to grow!"

"The world cannot be exclusively made up of strong, red-blooded people." Having cautiously rested his cigar on the edge of the ashtray, Mamut cut off a bit of meat, put it into his mouth, and crunched through well-done skin. "There have already been attempts to create just this sort of 'healthy' society. Think of Sparta. And how did that end? Every society that kicks the fallen when they're down ends up falling itself."

Sablin ate with enormous appetite, as if he'd just sat down for the first time. "Sparta is no argument . . . mmm . . . Heraclitus and Aristocles didn't have the experience of fighting against Christianity toward the creation of a new morality. Because of that, their ideas for state were entirely utopian ... The situation in the world is different now ... mmm ... The world is waiting for a new messiah. And he is coming."

"And who, might I ask, shall he be?"

"A man. Who has overcome himself."

"Total demagoguery ..." Mamut waved his fork.

"The men are stuck on serious subjects again ..." Rumyantseva loudly sucked on Nastya's collarbone.

Father Andrei served himself some horseradish. "I've read two books by Nietzsche. He's talented, but on the whole, his philosophy is alien to me."

"What do you need philosophy for, brother? You have faith," Sablin mumbled with a mouth full of food.

"Don't play the fool." Father Andrei gave him a serious look. "Every human being has a philosophy of living. Their own. Even an idiot has a philosophy by which he lives."

"Which would be ... *idiotism*?" Arina asked cautiously.

Sablin and Mamut started to laugh, but Father Andrei turned his stern gaze onto Arina.

"Yes. Idiotism. And my doctrine for living is this: live and let live."

"That's a very proper doctrine," Sablina pronounced quietly.

Everyone suddenly fell silent and ate for a long time without speaking.

"An angel of silence has passed over us," Rumyantsev sighed.

"Not just one. A whole herd of 'em." Arina held out her empty glass.

"Don't give her any more," Mamut said to Pavlushka, who was bending over to do just that.

"But Daddy!"

"At your age, a person should be happy without wine."

"Live and let live," Sablin spoke up thoughtfully. "Well, Andrei Ivanych, that's a commonsense philosophy. But—"

"But! Always but!" the priest grinned.

"Please don't get offended. But your philosophy is badly moth-eaten. Just like the whole of old morality. At the beginning of the nineteenth century, I would certainly have lived by this doctrine. But today, ladies and gentlemen, we stand on the threshold of a new age. Only six months remain until the beginning of the twentieth century. Six months! Until the beginning of a new era in the history of humanity! Which is why I drink to the new morality of the coming century—a morality of overcoming!"

He stood up and drained his glass.

"And what kind of morality shall it be?" Father Andrei looked at him. "One without God, I'd imagine?"

"Certainly not!" The knife squeaked as Sablin cut the meat. "God has always been and shall always be with us."

"But doesn't Nietzsche discourse about the death of God?"

"Don't take that so literally. Every era fits its own Christ. The old Hegelian Christ has died. In the coming century, we'll need a young, strong, and resolute Savior, one who shall be able to overcome! One who shall be able to laugh as he walks over the abyss on a tightrope! Yes—he must laugh, not simply whine and pull faces!"

"So, in the coming century, Jesus must be a tightrope walker?"

"Yes! Yes! A tightrope walker! We shall pray to him with all our hearts, we shall overcome ourselves with him, and we shall set off with him to a new life!"

"Follow him across the tightrope?"

"Yes, my dear Dmitri Andreyevich, across the tightrope! Across the tightrope over the abyss!"

"That's insanity." Father Andrei shook his head.

"It's common sense!" Sablin banged his hand against the table. The dishes rang out.

Sablina shrugged her shoulders shiversomely. "I've grown so tired of these arguments, gentlemen. Might we get by without philosophy, Seryozha, at least for today?"

"Russian men fly to philosophy like flies to honey!" Rumyantseva declaimed.

Everyone laughed.

"Sing for us, Alexandra Vladimirovna!" Rumyantsev demanded loudly.

"Yes! Yes! Yes!" agreed Mamut. "Sing! You must sing!"

"Sing, Sashenka!"

Sablina clasped her thin hands and rubbed them together. "It's true, I ... today's ... such a day ..."

"Sing, my joy," Sablin wiped at his lips. "Pavlushka! Bring in the guitar!"

The lackey ran out.

"I've also learned to play the guitar!" said Arina. "When Mommy was alive, she used to say that some romances were only good on the guitar. Because the piano is a severe instrument."

"God's truth!" Rumyantsev smiled.

"Two guitars ring out, begin their plaintive howl ..." Mamut stared gloomily at the table. "Excuse me, but where's the mustard?"

"Je vous en prie!" Rumyantseva handed it to him.

Pavlushka brought in a seven-string guitar. Sablin moved a chair over to the carpet. Alexandra Vladimirovna sat down, crossed her legs, picked up the guitar, and, without seeing if it was in tune, began to play and sing in a quiet, soulful voice:

> "Do you remember the eloquent look you gave
> that revealed the depths of your love for me?
> In the future, it would be a happy guarantee,
> Every day, it would set my soul to rant and rave.
>
> In that shining moment, I smiled back
> and dared to sow the seeds of hope in you ...
> How much power I had over you, 'tis true,
> I remember everything, do you remember too?
>
> Do you remember the moments of elation,
> When the days flew by so fast for us?
> When you hoped I would reveal my infatuation
> And your lips swore our love would never rust?

You listened to me, happy and admiring,
The fire of love was burning in your eyes.
You would do anything for me without tiring.
I remember everything, do you remember too?

Do you remember, when we were apart,
I waited for you, mute with memory and care?
The thought of you was always in my heart;
The thought of you in the distance when 'twas only air.

Do you remember how timid I became,
When I gave you the ring from my finger?
How thrilled I was with your joy and acclaim?
I remember everything, do you remember too?

Do you remember that when night fell,
Your passion was transmuted into song?
Do you remember the stars as well?
Do you remember how I could do no wrong?

I'm weeping now, my breast is pining for the past,
But you are cold and your heart is far away!
For you, the feeling of those days has passed,
I remember everything, do you remember too?"

"Bravo!" Rumyantsev cried out and everyone applauded.

"I have one joy in my life, one sun that never sets..." Sablin kissed his wife's hand.

"Ladies and gentlemen, let us drink to Anna Vladimirovna's health!" Rumyantsev stood up.

"Without fail!" Mamut turned to her as he stood up.

"To you, our darling Sashenka!" Rumyantseva held out her glass.

"Thank you, friends." Sablina walked back to the table.

Her husband handed her a glass.

Lev Ilyich stood up with a glass in his hand.

"Ladies and gentlemen, allow me to say," he began, "that Alexandra Vladimirovna is a remarkable individual. Even an inveterate misogynist, egotist, and hopeless skeptic like me could not resist the charms of Sablina as a hostess. Six—no—almost seven years ago, I found myself here for the first time and"—he lowered his eyes—"fell in love instantly. I have loved Alexandra Vladimirovna for these seven years. I love her like no other. And ... I'm not ashamed to talk about this today. I love you, Alexandra Vladimirovna."

He stood there, drawing his head down to his bony shoulders and rotating the narrow glass in his large, thin hands.

Sablina walked over to him, stood up on tiptoes, and kissed him on the cheek.

"Kiss him properly, Sashenka," Sablin pronounced.

"You'll allow it?" She stared fixedly into Lev Ilyich's embarrassed visage.

"Of course."

"Then, hold this." She handed her glass to her husband, put her arms around Lev Ilyich's neck, and kissed him hard on the mouth, pressing her delicate, pliable body against his.

Lev Ilyich's fingers unclenched, his glass slipped, fell to the rug, but didn't shatter. Lev Ilyich squeezed Sablina's waist with his inordinately long arms and pressed his lips back against hers. They kissed for a long time, rocking back and forth, their clothes rustling.

"Don't hold back, my joy." Sablin stared at them with bloodshot eyes.

Sablina moaned. Her legs trembled. Lev Ilyich's wiry fingers mashed at her buttocks.

"Right here, do it right here ... I ask you ..." Sablin muttered. "Here, here ..."

"No..." Sablina freed her lips with some difficulty. "Certainly not—"

"Here, here, I'm begging you, my joy!" Quickly going purple, Sablin got down on his knees.

"No, not for anything in the world ..."

"I'm begging you, Lev Ilyich! For Christ's sake, do it!"

Lev Ilyich embraced Sablina.

"There's a child here, you've lost your mind!"

"On this earth, we are all children, Alexandra Vladimirovna." Mamut smiled.

"I'm begging you, I'm begging you!" Sablin sobbed.

"Not for anything in the world..."

"How enchanting you are, Sashenka! How I envy you!" Rumyantseva raised herself up rapturously.

"I'm begging you, just begging you..." Sablin clambered over to her on his knees.

"Argh, stop it!" Sablina tried to break free, but Lev Ilyich held fast.

"There is no sin in sincere tenderness." Father Andrei plucked at his beard.

Sablin wrapped his arms around his wife's legs and began to pull up her dress. Lev Ilyich squeezed her torso and pressed his lips to her neck. Her shapely legs, without stockings, were exposed, followed by the lace of her undershirt. Sablin grabbed her white underpants and pulled them down.

"No-o-o-o!" Sablina screamed, throwing back her head.

Sablin turned to stone.

Shoving away Lev Ilyich's face, she ran out of the dining room.

Sablin remained seated on the carpet.

"Go after her," he said to Lev Ilyich hoarsely.

Lev Ilyich stood there awkward and red-faced, his hands tensing into claws.

"Go after her!" Sablin shouted so loudly that the chandelier's crystal prisms shuddered.

Lev Ilyich wandered out of the dining room like a sleepwalker.

Sablin pressed his palms to his face and exhaled heavily, with a shudder.

Mamut broke the silence: "Go easy on yourself, Sergei Arkadeyevich."

Sablin took out a handkerchief and slowly wiped the sweat from his face.

"How beautiful she is." Rumyantseva stood up, shaking her head. "How maniacally beautiful she is!"

"Some champagne," Sablin said in a quiet tone, staring at the pattern on the carpet.

Lev Ilyich walked up the stairs and pushed on the Sablins' bedroom door. It turned out to be locked.

"Sasha," he said hollowly.

"Let me be," he heard from inside the room.

"Sasha."

For the love of Christ, go away!"

"Sasha."

"What do you want from me?"

"Sasha."

She opened the door. Lev Ilyich put his arms around her waist, lifted her up, and carried her over to the bed.

"You like to play the fool? You like indulging him, do you?" she muttered. "To submit to this . . . this . . . Can it really be that all of this pleases you? All of this . . . this . . . base ambiguity? This stupid, vulgar theater?"

Dropping her onto the apricot-colored silk of the bedcover, Lev Ilyich ripped off her tight, coffee-colored dress.

"He indulges his peasant nature . . . he . . . he's only three generations removed . . . no . . . two generations . . . he still blows his nose right onto the ground . . . but you! You! You're an intelligent, honest, complex individual . . . you . . . you understand all the ambiguity of my—agh, don't tear it like that—all the absurdity of my . . . my God . . . how has my life become this?!"

Once he was done with her dress, Lev Ilyich tore off her lace undershirt and, on his knees now, began to unbutton his pants with shaking hands.

"If we . . . if we already know everything . . . if we're ready for anything . . . if we know that we love each other . . . and . . . that there's no other way...that...each of our stars shines for the other's," she muttered, looking at the stucco crown molding of the ceiling. "If we met...perhaps it was awful and awkward, perhaps it was even stupid...as is everything that happens so suddenly...then we must cherish this tiny spark...this weak ray...let us take cherish it as something fragile and precious...we must try...ahh!"

Lev Ilyich entered her.

Pavlushka opened the champagne clumsily. Foam gushed from the bottle and onto the tray.

"Give it here, half-wit!" Sablin took the bottle. "And get out!"

The lackey doubled over, as if he'd received an invisible blow to the belly, then left the room.

"Why do Russians so hate to serve?" Mamut asked.

"Pride," Father Andrei replied.

"Boorishness is the greatest of Russian qualities," Rumyantsev sighed.

"We're to blame." Rumyantseva tenderly stroked the tablecloth. "We must do a better job in educating our servants."

"Flog them, you mean? That's no solution." Sablin scowled as he poured wine into everyone's glasses with a scowl. "Sometimes it's necessary, of course, but I don't like doing it."

"I'm also against flogging," said Father Andrei. "The whip doesn't educate—it embitters."

"Flogging must only be done in the proper way," Rumyantseva remarked.

"Of course, of course!" Arina suddenly grew excited. "When she was alive, I once saw something like that at Tanechka Boksheyeva's house! We were stopping by her place after gymnasium because she'd promised to lend me the new Charskaya, but, when we got there, it was a shambles! The governess had broken a vase. And Tanechka's father was punishing her for everyone to see. He says, 'It's good you've come, miladies. You can play the role of spectators.' I didn't understand anything at first: the governess was howling, the cook was laying out an oilcloth on the table, and Tanya's mother was holding a bottle of ammonia. And he says to the governess: 'Well now, you little wretch, take off your clothes!' She lifted up her skirt, lay bosom-first onto the oilcloth, and the cook immediately pinned her. Tanechka's father ripped off her underpants, and I saw her behind was covered in scars! How he attacked her with that belt, how violent it was! She was yelling, so the cook shoved wadding into her mouth! Then he whipped her. Again! Again! And again! Then Tanechnka nudged me and said, 'Look at how she—'"

"Enough," Mamut interrupted.

"To simply flog is barbaric." Rumyantseva raised the hissing glass to her nose and closed her eyes. "Lizkhen has been serving us for four years. It's almost like she's a part of the family. On her very first day, Viktor and I brought her into the bedroom and locked the door. We got undressed, lay down on the bed, and made love. She was watching the whole time. Then I pinned her head between my legs and lifted up her skirt and Viktor whipped her with a riding crop. So hard that the poor darling pissed herself! I smeared goose fat across her derrière, took her by the hand, and said, 'So Lizkhen, did you see everything?' 'Yes, madame.' 'Did you understand everything?' 'Yes, madame.' Then I say, 'You didn't understand anything.' We dressed her in my ball gown, took her into the dining room, sat her down at the table, and fed her lunch. Viktor cut the food and I put it in her mouth with a golden spoon—into her little, little, little mouth. We made her drink a bottle of Madeira. She's sitting there like a drunk doll, giggling, 'I've understood everything, madame.' 'Is that so?' I say. So we lock her in the wardrobe. We kept her in there for three days and three nights. For the first two nights she howled, but, on the third she fell silent. I let her out and looked her in the eye. 'Now, my little dove, you've understood everything.' None of my vases have been broken since."

"Most reasonable." Mamut rubbed thoughtfully at the bridge of his broad nose.

"Ladies and gentlemen, I have a toast." Father Andrei stood up, his cassock rustling decisively. "I propose we drink to my friend Sergei Arkadeyevich Sablin."

"About time," said Rumyantseva with a smirk.

Sablin looked gloomily at the priest.

"Our Russia is as big as a Bolshinskian swamp," Father Andrei began. "We live like we're standing on stilts, guessing where next to step and where to rest our weight. It's not because our Russian people is so beastly, but because the metaphysics of our country has always been like this. It's a savage, uninhabitable place. It's terribly drafty. And the people are no angels. The decaying and the rotten are a dime a dozen. Another's hand pulls you on, speaks of honor, swears to holy friendship, but you squeeze the hand a little harder and maggots come pouring out. Therefore, what I appreciate more than anything else in people is strength of spirit. Sergei Arkadeyevich and I have been childhood friends, classmates, and revelers in arms at university. But we're more than that. We are brothers in spirit. Brothers in strength of spirit. We hold to our inviolable principles—we each have our own stronghold in this regard. If I had sacrificed my principles, I would be wearing a panagia and serving in the Kazan Cathedral by now. If he had gone against his stronghold, he would have donned a rector's cloak a long time ago. But we did not retreat. Because of that, we are neither rotten nor decayed. We are the solid oaken stilts of Russian statehood, upon which a new, healthy Russia shall learn to walk. To you, my only friend!"

Sablin walked over to him. They exchanged kisses.

"Beautifully put!" Rumyantsev reached out to clink glasses.

"I didn't know that you were at university together." Mamut clinked glasses with them.

"How interesting!" Arina took a drink of her champagne. "Did you both study philosophy?"

"We are both materialists of the soul!" Father Andrei answered and all the men laughed.

"For how long?" asked Rumyantseva.

"Since we were at gymnasium," Sablin answered, rolling up his sleeves, and decisively picking up Nastya's tibia.

"So you studied at gymnasium together too?" Arina asked. "Imagine that!"

"Of course!" Father Andrei pulled a menacing, pleading face, then began to speak in a falsetto: "Sablin and Klyopin, how did you end up in Kamchatka again? Come sit in the front row immediately!"

"Ahh! Three-Grave Arshins!" laughed Sablin. "Three-Grave Arshins!"

"Who's that?" Arina's eyes flashed with interest.

"Our mathematics teacher, Kozma Trofimych Ryazhsky," Father Andrei answered, cutting his meat.

"Three-Grave Arshins! Three-Grave Arshins!"—Sablin laughed, bone in hand.

"Why was that his nickname?" Rumyantseva asked.

"He had a constant refrain about the study of mathematics: any idiot should be able to... a-ha-ha-ha! No... a-ha-ha-ha!" Father Andrei suddenly began to laugh hysterically.

"Ha-ha-ha! Ha-ha-ha!" Sablin also began to laugh. "Three... haha! Three... ha-ha! Three Arshins... a-ha-ha-haaaa!"

"He... a-ha-ha!... he... once he measured an angle with a protractor, do you remember?... a ha!... Bondarenko's angle of idiocy... and he... a-ha-ha! Haaaa!"

Sablin laughed and shook so much, it was as if he'd been put into a galvanic bath. The bone fell from his hands, he leaned back in his chair very violently, the chair wobbled and flipped over, then Sablin fell down onto his back. Father Andrei kept laughing, digging his fingers into his crimson face.

Sablina walked into the dining room wearing a fresh long dress of dark-blue silk. Lev Ilyich followed her in.

Sablin was still writhing around on the rug, laughing.

"What happened?" Alexandra Vladimirovna asked, stopping next to him.

"Gymnasium. Memories," Mamut said as he chewed.

"One of their little rhymes?" She walked over and sat down in her chair.

"What rhymes?" Rumyantsev asked.

"Rhymes! Ha-ha-ha! Oh my God, the rhymes!" Sablin sat up on the carpet. "Oy, I'm dying... I wrote a little poem about my friend

Andrei Klyopin, a Kamchadal...ha-ha-ha...oy...I'll try to calm down...and recite it..."

"Why this laughter?" Sablina asked.

"Don't ask, for the love of Christ, and...he-he-he...we'll die... enough! enough! enough! The poem!"

"Please don't recite that filth in front of me." Sablina picked up her glass and Lev Ilyich filled it with champagne.

"But my joy, we're among friends!"

"Don't recite it in front of me."

"The beginning, just the beginning:

> "I have a good friend named Andrei,
> But often we call him Klyopa.
> His kindness, I cannot downplay,
> with such a fine cock, I say opa!"

"Stop!" Sablina pounded the table. "There's a child here!"

"Whom do you mean?" Arina smiled archly.

> "One day he called over to me
> saying, 'Hey there, my friend!
> I've just bathed in poop and pee
> and fear my soul's been unchristened.'

> 'Your soul is most pure!' I retorted
> 'In this I place great stock:
> As pure as a girl's—'"

"—cunt perverted / Or perhaps as the end of my cock," Arina pronounced, looking sullenly at Sablin.

"Where did you learn that?" Sablin stared at her.

"Father Andrei told me."

"When was that?" Sablin turned his gaze onto the priest.

"Why do you insist on knowing everything, Sergei Arkadych?" Mamut muttered angrily, smearing his meat with horseradish.

Everyone laughed and Arina continued: "I like the end of your poem most of all:

"The end of this rhyme is quite sad:
Klyopa's got only one head—
The one on his dick cut off by his dad,
For raping two girls in a shed."

"Such filth…" Sablina took a drink. "Such beastly filth and tiresome vulgarity."

"Yes!" With a good-natured smile upon his incredibly drunk face, Sablin righted his chair and sat down. "Gymnasium humor! How long ago that was… Do you remember how much Schopenhauer we read?"

"With Redhead?" Father Andrei drank his champagne in a state of utter delight.

"We took three months to read that book aloud! That was when I finally understood what philosophy truly is!"

"And what exactly is it?" Rumyantseva asked.

"The love of wisdom," Mamut explained.

Suddenly, Father Andrei stood up, walked over to Mamut, and froze, fingering his cross.

"Dmitri Andreyevich, I…would like to ask you for your daughter's hand."

Everyone fell silent. Mamut froze with an unchewed piece of meat still in his mouth. Arina went pale.

Mamut swallowed spasmodically, then coughed. "And…how is it…that this…"

"I'm asking you very seriously. Very."

Mamut turned his watery gaze onto his daughter. "Well…"

"No." She shook her head.

"Erm…"

"I'm begging you, Dmitri Andreyevich!" Father Andrei got down onto his knees.

"No, no, no!" Arina shook her head.

"But . . . if you . . . then why not?" Mamut frowned.

"I'm begging! I'm begging you!"

"Well . . . speaking openly . . . I'm . . . not against it . . ."

"No-o-o-o-o!" Arina screeched, leaping up and overturning her chair.

But the Rumyantsevs grabbed her, as lightning-fast as two borzois.

"No-o-o-o-o!" She tried to run to the door, her dress tearing in the process.

Lev Ilyich and Father Andrei grabbed her, then pulled her down to the carpet.

"Behave . . . behave yourself . . . erm . . . the fat . . ." Mamut began to fuss.

"Arinushka . . ." Sablina stood up.

"Pavlushka! Pavlushka!" Sablin cried out.

"No-o-o-o!" Arina screamed.

"A towel! A towel!" Rumyantsev hissed.

Pavlushka ran in.

"Fly like a bullet to the sharpener, there on the right shelf, it's the farthest . . ." Sablin muttered to him, clutching Arina's feet. "Actually, forget it, you fool. I'll do it myself . . ."

Sablin ran out and the lackey followed after him.

"Arina, just . . . calm down . . . pull yourself together . . ." Mamut sank down heavily onto the carpet. "At your age—"

"Please, Papa, have mercy! Have mercy, Papa! Have mercy, Papa!" Arina said very, very quickly as she was pressed against the carpet.

"Nobody has ever died from this." Rumyantseva held onto her head.

"Arina, I'm begging you." Father Andrei stroked her cheek.

"Have mercy, Papa! Have mercy, Papa!"

Sablin ran in with a handsaw. Carrying a thick chunk of wood, Pavlushka was unable to keep up with him. Seeing the handsaw out of the corner of her eye, Arina began to thrash and scream so much that everyone had to hold her down.

"Close her mouth with something!" Sablin demanded, kneeling down and rolling up the right sleeve of his tailcoat.

Mamut shoved a handkerchief into his daughter's mouth and

pinched it shut with two plump fingers. Arina's arm was bared to the shoulder, two belts and a wet towel were tightened around her forearm, Lev Ilyich tied her hand to the piece of wood, and Sablin measured the arm with his yellow, tobacco-stained fingernail:

"Praise the Lord..."

Quick jerks of the saw, a girlish scream from the very bowels, the dull crack of doomed bone, splashes of ruby-colored blood on the carpet, Arina's thrashing legs held fast by four hands.

Sablin completed the sawing quickly. His wife placed bowls beneath the stump.

"Pavlushka"—Sablin handed him the saw—"go tell Mityai to prepare the droshky and bring it out front. Fast as a bullet!"

The lackey ran off.

"Mityai will take you to the village doctor. He'll dress the wound."

"Is it far?" Mamut took the handkerchief out of his daughter's mouth. She'd lost consciousness.

"It's thirty minutes from here. Sashenka! The icon!"

Sablina went out and immediately returned with an icon of the Savior.

Father Andrei crossed himself and knelt down. With an asthmatic bow, Mamut gave him his daughter's hand. Father Andrei accepted it, pressed it to his chest, and kissed the icon.

"God be with you." Mamut bowed once more.

Father Andrei stood up and left the room with the hand in his own hands.

"Leave now! Now!" Sablin hurried them along.

Lev Ilyich picked up Arina and carried her out of the room. Mamut followed him out of the room.

"Gulp down one for the road." Sablin grabbed Mamut by the coattails. "It always takes a minute to get the horses ready."

Having lustily opened the bottle of champagne, he filled the glasses.

"It even splashed on my forehead!" Smiling, Rumyantseva showed them a dot of blood on her tiny lace handkerchief.

"You have a strong daughter, Dmitri Alexeyevich." Rumyantsev raised his glass. "Such healthy, such... firm legs..."

"My deceased wife also . . . this . . . was . . ." Mamut muttered, staring at the blood-spattered carpet.

Sablin handed him a glass.

"To the glorious Mamut family!"

They clinked their glasses and drank.

"Even so . . . you seriously overrate Nietzsche!" Mamut proclaimed with unexpected anger.

Sablin yawned nervously, then shrugged.

"And you underrate him."

"Nietzsche is the idol of all equivocators."

"Nonsense. Nietzsche is the great revivifier of mankind."

"A merchant of dubious truths—"

"Dmitri Andreyevich!" Sablin jerked his head impatiently. "I respect and value you as a member of the Russian intelligentsia, but I place no value in your opinions on philosophy. That's enough!"

"Well, God be with you." Mamut walked over to the door heavily and irritatedly.

"Don't forget to invite us to Arina's birthday!" Rumyantseva reminded him.

"Of course . . ." he growled, then disappeared behind the door.

The clock struck midnight.

"Ay, ay, ay, ay . . ." Rumyantsev stretched out. "Mother of God!"

"Where shall we sleep?" Rumyantseva hugged Sablin from behind.

"In the usual place." He kissed her hand.

"We still haven't had dessert." Sablina rubbed at her temples. "My head's pounding from all of that screaming . . ."

Rumyantseva pressed herself against Sablin's back. "We don't need dessert."

"But we have . . . a delightful cake . . ." Sablin muttered, lighting a cigarette with palpable exhaustion.

Rumyantseva's tight posterior, encased in pecan-colored silk, oscillating waves beginning to pass across her pliable body.

"Ah . . . Sashenka . . . you can't imagine how sweet it is to sleep with your husband . . . how enchantingly fine it is—"

Sablina walked over and poured Rumyantseva's half-finished champagne down her bodice.

"Ay!" Rumyantseva squealed, not looking up from Sablin's back and continuing the same rhythmic motion.

"Mamut is such a clumsy bear," Sablin spoke up with conviction.

"But his daughter's cute," Rumyantsev yawned.

"Yes..." Sablin looked off fixedly at a point in space. "Very..."

Sablina put the empty glass down on the edge of the table, then walked off slowly. Having passed by the dimly lit corridor, she heard voices from the front porch; Lev Ilyich and Mamut were putting Arina into the brichka. Sablina stopped, listened, turned around, then set off through the kitchen. Savely had fallen asleep at the table with his head in his hands. Next to him, the cake, ready to be served, was covered in unlit candles. She walked past the cook, opened the door, then walked down the black staircase and out into the yard.

A warm night, none too dim, a thin slice of moon in the sky, stardust, and the crumbly massifs of linden trees.

Sablina walked through the alley of trees, then stopped and sucked in the warm, humid air with great delight.

The sound of the brichka riding off reached her.

Sablina left the alley, began to walk along the fence, then opened the gate and slipped into the Old Orchard. Apple and plum trees surrounded her shapely figure, which looked as if it had been carved from some noble bone. She kept walking, her dress rustling against the grass, touching the wet branches as she went.

She stopped. Exhaled with a moan. Shook her head. Laughed wearily.

Bent over, lifted up her dress, lowered her underpants, and squatted down.

The periodic sound of digestive gasses being expelled from the body resounded.

"What a glutton I am, oh Lord..." she moaned.

The inaudible tumbling of warm feces to the ground, the growth of its delicate scent, its succulent squelch.

Sablina stood and pulled her underpants back up. Straightened her dress. Walked away. Stopped for a moment. Grabbed at a plum branch. Sighed. Stood up on her tiptoes. Turned around and set off home.

The night had come to an end.

A grayish-pink sky, dewy pollen on the still leaves, a silent flash of light behind the forest; as a magpie dozed on the church's gilded cross, a yellow pin of light pierced its eye.

The magpie opened its eyes wider; the sun sparkled on their surface. Having shaken its wings, the magpie then spread them as if to fly, opened its beak, and froze. The feathers on its neck stood on end. Clacking its beak, it glanced over at the cupola, started forward on its black, clawed feet, pushed off from the faceted beam of the cross, and floated downwards:

cemetery,
meadow,
orchard.

Cold greenery flowed through one of the magpie's glowing eyes. Suddenly, a warm spot flashed forth; the magpie dove down and came to rest on the back of the garden bench.

Feces were lying on the grass. The magpie looked at them, fluttered through the air, came to rest once more next to the feces, then hobbled over. A black pearl shone on the buttery surface of the pile of feces—like shagreen leather. The magpie came to a halt; the feces were looking at the magpie with a single black eye. Opening its beak, it squinted, lowered its head, took one hop, dug out the pearl, then, squeezing it in the tip of its beak, flew off.

Having shot over the garden, the magpie flew past a hillock, fluttered past a willow, and, hurriedly flapping its black-and-white wings, began to fly alongside the shore of the lake.

An entire reflected world swam through the pearl: black sky, black clouds, black lake, black boats, black pines, black juniper, black shallows, black footbridges, black willows, black hillock, black church, black path, black meadow, black alley of trees, black manor, and black woman, opening the black window of a black bedroom.

HORSE SOUP

2000

How DID it begin? Simply, like all that which is inevitable.

July 1980, a Simferopol–Moscow train, 2:35 p.m., an overfull restaurant car, tomato sauce stains on the overstarched tablecloths, a forgotten box of Lvov matches, cigarette ash, bottles of Narzan tinkling in their metal collars by the window, a fluttering curtain, hyperboloids of thick sunbeams, Olya's forearm peeling from a sunburn, Volodya's faded polo, and Vitka's jean skirt embroidered with two poppy heads.

"Guys, please, don't dawdle." The fat waiter rustled his greasy pad. "I've got a line of people to last me all the way to Moscow."

"And what do you ha—" Volodya began to ask before he was interrupted by the words spewing from the waiter's froggy lips:

"We're out of salads and *solyanka*, but we've got *kharcho*, pike perch with mashed potatoes, and steak and eggs."

"There's no beer?"

"There is!" The waiter brushed aside his sweat-soaked bangs. "Two? Three?"

"Four." Volodya relaxed. "And we'll all have the steak."

"Do you have any ice cream?" Vitka put on her dark glasses.

"No." The writer scribbled his pencil across the pad and walked his portly, seal-like body over to the barmaid, who was holding back the line of people waiting. "One more over here, Lyuban!"

"Maybe we don't ne-e-d one? Because we're so co-o-mfy!" Olya sang, lighting her last cigarette, but there was already a man walking down the aisle, chocolatey with sunburn and wearing white pants and a blue shirt.

"Hello." He immediately smiled at the three of them and sat down, quickly looking each of them in the eye.

He was without defining characteristics, had no visible age, and was bald.

A veterinarian, Volodya decided, taking the cigarette from Olya.

Dynin in the flesh. Olya remembered the character from the Klimov film *Welcome, or No Trespassing*.

Some dickhead on his way back from a bachelor party at a resort. Vitka's beautiful lips curled.

The waiter was muttering something to himself when he remembered the new arrival and turned around, but the bald man immediately gave him three rubles.

"Nothing for me, please."

The waiter took the money and, not understanding, furrowed his brow: "But, um—"

"Nothing, nothing." The stranger waved his fingers with their bitten nails. "I'll just sit . . . for a little while. It's nice and comfy here."

"But maybe—a drink? A beer? A glass of Psou? Some Ararat cognac?"

"Nothing, nothing. For now—nothing."

The waiter sailed back into the kitchen silently.

A veterinarian, but a fucking weird one. Volodya squinted at the stranger. Probably some yokel from Siberia. *He breaks his back all winter without complaining, but ships off to the south in the summer to make his pockets a lil' lighter.*

He left his wife back in their compartment. Olya grabbed the cigarette from Volodya and took a drag. *He should've given us those three rubles. Volodka's blowing our last five right now. We'll get back, nothing at home but tumbleweeds, our elders at a sanatorium, one week till they're back, sheer horror.*

This guy cut loose in the south and now he can't get it back together. Vitka looked out the window. *Why do such assholes always have so much money?*

The train crawled through the torrid Ukrainian heat.

"Somehow, some way, we've already had such a hot summer this year," the bald man said, trying to look all three of them in the eye again. "Could it also be that in the fair capital of our motherland the temperature has also reached such catastrophic heights?"

"We don't have a clue," said Vitka speaking for all of them, glancing disdainfully at his nails.

"Where were you vacationing?" The baldie smiled with his small, dirty teeth.

In your mom's pussy! Volodya thought to himself angrily, then said, "You know what, we got overheated and want to sleep. And when we want to sleep, we also want to eat, but we do not, not under any circumstances, want to talk."

Olya and Vitka giggled contentedly.

"A siesta, you mean?" The baldie squinted ingratiatingly.

"A siesta." Volodya put out his cigarette butt, remembering the similar title of a Hemingway novel that he'd started but never finished.

"For me, it's just the opposite." The stranger bent down to the table like a doomed man to the chopping block. "Whenever I get sunburnt, an incredible cheerfulness comes over me, such incredible strength rushes through my body—"

Suddenly, he broke off and froze, as if he'd been bitten by a snake. The waiter put three plates on the table, plates that contained overcooked pieces of meat framed by calloused sticks of potato that were supposedly "fries," limp feathers of dill, green peas, and three fried eggs. True, the eggs weren't overcooked or runny and looked rather appetizing. From the two pockets of his unclean white apron, the waiter took out four bottles of cold Simferopol beer, set them down loudly, opened them, then sailed off once again.

Glory be to labor! With palpable relief, Volodya picked up a bottle that had already begun to sweat. *He was really chewing our ears off with all that cheerfulness of his.*

The beer flowed and hissed into the glasses. All three of them began to drink: Volodya—greedily, in a single gulp, until his teeth began to ache; Vitka—without rushing, with pleasure; Olya—in characteristically cold-blooded fashion—only demi-sec champagne could set her insides atremble.

Having forgotten about their neighbor, who'd now shut up, all three of them attacked their food. They hadn't eaten anything since morning, and they'd been drinking in their compartment the day before from the time the train departed and well into the night, finishing three bottles of Mukuzani, "lacquered over" with a quarter bottle of local rotgut (Russia-brand vodka), all of which was severely affecting their well-being today.

They ate as they drank—in different ways.

Volodya heavily salted and peppered his egg, speared it with his fork, put it in his mouth whole, and, having swallowed, washed it down with beer; then, putting three potato sticks on his fork, he stuck it into the tough meat, cut off a decently sized piece, put five peas on it with his knife, maneuvered the whole construction into his mouth, crammed in a piece of white bread, and began to chew while gazing out the window at the cables flashing by and thinking about what might come to pass if Bryan Ferry and Brian Eno happened to get together to form a band.

They would call it something weird. He chewed with so much pleasure that tears came to his eyes. *Maybe BB. Or Rose of Blue. Or, like, Miracle No. 7.*

Vitka put the egg on her meat, nervously mashed it down with her fork, speared a potato stick, dipped it in the yolk, put it in her mouth, cut off a piece of meat, dipped it in the yolk, put it in her mouth, took a drink, then, while chewing, began to quickly collect disobedient peas and pass them through her lips, which were yellow with egg. She was looking at the silver ring on the ring finger of the bald man's left hand. *That ring is all I need to see: I've had it up to here with divorcés. I wonder if he boned anyone down in Crimea. Some kinda Aunt Klava from a sanatorium cafeteria. Or, no, maybe a single mother, a fat-ass Jewish mama. He was holding her place in a line to buy cherries and, on a nude beach, she gave it to him on the sly . . .*

Olya ate calmly, cutting her meat into little pieces and washing down each bite with beer, pinching off bits of white bread and completely ignoring the accompanying food items. Her gaze swam absent-mindedly over her plate. *I wonder if my headache'll go away after this beer?* I swear *I'm never gonna drink that disgusting vodka again, but Vovik seems like he'd have some* even *now. I've* gotta *call Natashka right away, I wonder if she xeroxed the music. If not, I won't return that Bártok to her on principle. Getting her to do anything is a hopeless business. But if she needs something, we'd all better hop to, like that one time with the ensemble . . . God, why is he looking at me like that?*

Olya stopped chewing.

The baldie looked at her crazily with his watery greenish-blue eyes. His face wasn't just deathly pale, it was also terribly ghoulish, as if he'd just borne witness to something horrifying that went against his very nature.

An overthrown face, Olya thought, laying her knife and fork down on the edge of her plate. "Why are you . . . watching me like that?"

Vitka and Volodya also stopped eating and stared at the baldie. A grimace passed over his face, he clutched at his temples, he was blinking furiously, and his whole body was shuddering.

"Forgive me . . . I . . . this . . ."

The train was going over a bridge, steel pillars flashed by thunderously, it smelled of cinder.

The stranger rubbed at his pale cheeks furiously, then reached into the breast pocket of his shirt, pulled out a piece of paper, and silently handed it to Volodya. It was a certificate of release from a correctional labor camp issued to one Boris Ilyich Burmistrov. Olya and Vitka glanced at the paper.

"Seven years, guys, seven years. And all because of some stupid sack of citric acid," the baldie pronounced before taking back the paper. "Forgive me, I don't want to disturb . . . to interfere . . . and so on. I just have one enormous request. A very sizable one."

"D'you need money?" Volodya asked, imagining that the three rubles he'd given to the waiter had only been a trick calibrated for external effect.

"Whaddaya think?" Burmistrov smirked, pulling a thick leather wallet out of his pants and throwing it down on the table. "I'm made of money."

The young people stared silently at the wallet, from which protruded bills of various denominations.

"Money is generally...well..." The stranger waved his hand nervously. "It comes, it goes, and so on. But the request. Well...I dunno. First lemme tell you a story."

He won't let us eat! Volodya looked longingly at what remained of his steak.

Weird dude. Vitka sipped her beer.

A criminal! Gosh! Olya looked at him distrustfully.

Burmistrov put away his wallet and rubbed at his small chin. "Well, as for the circumstances of the case, let's leave them to one side. Not interesting. I'll say just one thing: I'm a construction manager by trade and a businessman by vocation. But in times of socialism, is there such a thing as honest business? Well...underground there is. Yes. That's how they were able to do away with seven years of my life. It's been two months since I was released. Our camp was forgotten by God, all the way in Kazakhstan. Ah, forgive me! Not *ours* any longer!" He laughed delicately. "It's *theirs* now... theirs...This is how I, a man with two degrees, began to work at a brick factory. It wasn't the only thing I did there, but I mostly just shaped bricks. Yep. A little bit later, just before I got released, I used my connections to work in a killer spot: the kitchen. But our camp, God, I was sick of it, had a big problem: it was too small. Only two hundred and sixty-two people. And none of us should've been there in the first place. We were inside for financial crimes of mild severity, so to speak. Long sentences. Calm, serious people. We didn't rebel, didn't drink chifir, didn't try to run away... And the provisions were disgusting. Yes...generally speaking, every day for those seven years I only ate one thing: horse-meat pottage. "Horse soup," we called it. There was a big horse factory right next to us and they sent their culled horses over and into our pots."

He grinned and looked out the window.

"And what else was in the soup?" Vitka asked.

"Millet, rice, or flour," Burmistrov said with a smile. "The ratios changed all the time. But horse, the main "byproduct," so to speak, was always there. Our daily ration. And every day our lil' camp would eat a whole horse. A skinny, old horse."

"Where did they get so many horses?" Volodya asked.

"Are you kidding me? Kazakhstan is full of horses! A lot more than they have in Moscow!" Burmistrov laughed, and Olya and Vitka smiled.

"Isn't that unhealthy—horse every day?" Volodya asked.

"No, horse meat is the healthiest. Much better than beef or pork."

"And you really only ate that for seven years?" Olya looked at his restless forehead, upon which freckles were drowning in sunburn.

"Is that so hard to believe?" He looked into her eyes.

"It is," she responded gravely.

"It's hard for me too. But, look"—he spread out his hands—"seven years have vanished into thin air, two regiments of horses have been devoured, and I'm alive!"

"That's terribly dreary—every day exactly the same!" Vitka shook her head. "If they even made me eat this steak every day, I'd go insane!"

"Well, man can get used to anything . . .". Burmistrov shook his bald head. "In the beginning, I ate everything, then I stopped being able to eat the meat, picked it out of the soup, and drank only the broth. Then I did the opposite and started to eat the meat plain with bread. Then I stopped giving a damn and would mash it all together, but by the end of my sentence . . . it's hard to explain."

He lost himself in thought.

If he isn't lying, this is fuckin' crazy. Volodya poured himself some beer.

Now, he must want to gobble up everything he sees. Vitka looked at Burmistrov as if he were an outlandish reptile. *But he didn't order anything! He probably had too much to eat in Crimea, the poor thing.*

I just can't . . . figure him out, thought Olya. *He acts like he's coming from a funeral . . .*

"Y'know, when they moved me to the kitchen," Burmistrov continued, "I saw the whole process of how the chow got cooked. Every day. It started early in the morning. They'd bring in a horse carcass from the freezer on a cart, and we'd put it on three wooden blocks that were knocked together. Then the cook called for Two-Axe Tolya. He was a convict who'd once worked as a butcher in Alma-Ata but got locked up *big time*. A robust fella with two axes. He'd come and start cutting up the skinny, frozen carcass like a head of cabbage. It was his greatest delight. He cut it up like an artist, each cut coming from the heart. Then he left and we dumped the meat into cauldrons, boiled it, poured in the grains . . . We boiled it for a long time, until the meat came off of the bones. And then . . . then—forgive me, what's your name?"

He stared at Olya fixedly.

"Olga," she replied calmly.

"Olga, can I ask you a favor? Only you."

"Depends what."

Burmistrov clutched at the table with his hands, as if he were preparing to tear it off the ground: "Can you eat for me? Here. Now."

"What do you mean 'for you'?"

"Erm, so that I can watch. I just want to watch."

Olga exchanged a look with Volodya.

I knew he was a nut. Volodya sighed emphatically. "You know, we came here with a concrete—"

"I understand, I understand, I understand." Burmistrov grimaced. "I don't want to bother you, I don't want anything but to watch you—that's seriously all I need! I don't have a family, don't have relatives, and now I don't even have any friends, don't have a home or a hearth, but *this*"—he gestured toward the plate with his lips, somehow like a dog—"*this* is all I have left."

"What—food?" Vitka asked.

"No, no, no!" He shook his head. "Not food! But to watch how a good person eats. How a beautiful person eats. To see how Olga eats. Yes. Now, right away, so that there're no more questions . . ." He took out his wallet once more, extracted a twenty-five-ruble note from it, and put it down on the table.

Here we go! Vitka covered her mouth with her hand so as not to burst out laughing. *Mother of God, if we tell this story to people in Moscow, no one'll believe us...*

He's seriously sick. Olya looked at the money.

What nonsense. Volodya smirked.

"I'm going back to our compartment." Olya stood up.

Burmistrov shuddered, as if he'd been shocked. "Olga, I'm asking you, begging you, please don't go!"

"Thanks, but I'm already full." Olga began to squeeze her way out from between Volodya and the table.

"I'm begging you! I'm begging you!" Burmistrov shouted loudly.

The guests at the neighboring tables turned to them.

"Hold on," Volodya grabbed her by the arm. "This is interesting."

"Yes, very!" she snorted.

"Please believe me, Olga, this minute of you eating will be enough to last me a whole year!" Burmistrov muttered, pressing himself against the table and looking up into her eyes. "You...you eat in such a remarkable way...it's simply divine...it's like, it's like...I've got something here that—" He pressed his hands to his sunken chest. "Here it's...it's just that it...so strongly, so strongly that...that I see nothing else..."

His voice was quivering.

It's hard not to feel for him, but he's crazy. Olya squinted at him.

It was silent but for the knocking of the wheels.

"What's the problem, then?" Volodya blurted out. "What's the big deal if someone wants to watch you eat?"

"I don't like it when people look into my mouth. And I also"—she looked out the window—"I try to avoid crazy people."

"I'm not a psycho, Olga, please believe me!" Burmistrov waved his hands. "I'm a totally normal Soviet person."

"I can tell!" she smirked.

"Maybe I could eat for you instead?" Vitka glanced at the twenty-five-ruble note shivering in the draft passing over the table.

"You...forgive me, what's your name?"

"Vita."

"Vita...Vitochka, y'understand, I only experience this with certain people, please don't be offended! And, more generally...this is the first time I've felt it. Don't be offended."

"I rarely get offended. I'm more likely to offend." Vita straightened her dark glasses. "Ol, eat the meat. Give the dude his pleasure."

"I'm begging you, Olga, just for a few minutes! And such a joy for me! This...this would be...I dunno...more than joy." Burmistrov's voice was shaking once more.

Now he'll start shouting again. She looked at the passengers who were glancing furtively over at them. *Of course, they sat him here with us—Murphy's Law—and not with the two fat ladies over there...*

"All right, I'll finish my food." She sat down in her chair without looking at Burmistrov. "But put your money away."

"Oh Olga, I'm begging you!" He pressed his hands to his chest. "Don't offend me! I really want you to take the money—just you, necessarily you!"

"You can pretend that she took it." Volodya reached for the money, but Burmistrov covered it with his palms warningly, as if he were protecting a candle from the wind.

"No, no, no! I'm asking that Olga take it, only Olga! To take it out of the kindliness in her heart, to take it simply...as an ordinary... well...like a...like nothing at all!"

"Take it, Ol." Vitka nodded. "Don't upset the man."

"Take it, Olga, I'm begging you!"

"Take it, take it..." Volodya frowned.

Hesitating another minute, Olga finally took the money and put it away in the pocket of her jeans.

"Thank you, thank you so so much!" Burmistrov shook his bald head.

Olga gloomily brought her fork and knife over to the meat as if it were a piece of steel lying on her plate.

The train rocked violently.

She gulped, stuck her fork into the meat, then resolutely cut off a piece.

"Just don't rush, I'm begging you, don't rush..." Burmistrov whispered.

Volodya poured her some beer. Olya speared the meat with her fork, brought it to her lips, plucked it off the fork with her teeth, then began to slowly chew while staring at the plate.

It was as if Burmistrov's swarthy, sinewy body had turned to stone. Clutching the edge of the table, he stared directly at Olga's mouth. His turbid eyes rolled around and glazed over as if this unhandsome man had been injected with a large dose of narcotics.

"And this is na ..." His gray lips began to murmur, "And this is na ..."

Vitka and Volodya stared at him, their eyes wide.

The guy's really getting his rocks off, huh?! What in tarnation ...

Fuck this! Just fuck this ...

Olya ate, having given herself the strict order not to look at Burmistrov even once. At first, this worked and she wasn't even in a rush to finish her food, forking up potato sticks and raking up green peas. But Burmistrov's babbling became even more insistent, as if something were tearing itself out of his chest and forcing itself through his clenched teeth, his thin shoulders trembled and his head shivered gently.

"This is na! And this is na-a-o! And this is na-a-o!"

Don't look! Olya ordered herself, spearing another piece of meat, cutting it off and dipping it in the viscous yolk of the cool egg.

Burmistrov moaned and shivered more and more violently as foam appeared at the corners of his bloodless lips.

"And this is na-a-o! This is na-a-o! And this is na-a-o!"

Not able to stop herself, Olga glanced over. She immediately shrank back from his glassy eyes and choked, remembering Repin's painting *Ivan the Terrible and His Son Ivan*. Volodya held out a glass of beer.

Don't look, you idiot! she told herself angrily, taking a drink from the glass.

As seen through the yellow beer, Burmistrov's blue shirt was the color of seaweed.

"And this is na-a-o! This is na-a-o!"

Olya felt like she was about to vomit.

Think about the sea! she ordered herself, fixing her eyes on the "seaweed" and remembering how she and Volodya had swum out to an ichthyologist's platform one evening and lengthily made love on its warm steel floor, which hadn't yet had time to cool from the sun. Vitka stayed on the shore and cooked mussels over a bonfire with two local guys. Volodya forced Olya onto her knees and entered her from behind; Olya pressed her cheek to the smooth iron floor, listening to the weak nocturnal waves beat against the platform . . .

Having speared the last piece of meat, she rubbed it in the egg yolk and put it in her mouth.

"And this is na-a-a-a-o!" Burmistrov trembled and roared with such force that the restaurant car became quiet and the waiter rushed over to their table.

"What the hell is this?" He bent over them with a furrowed brow.

"Everything's . . . fine." Volodya was the first one to shake off his stupor.

Burmistrov went limp, his lip drooped, his face was sweaty, but he was still staring at Olya's mouth.

"You ill or somethin'?" The waiter furrowed his brow.

"No, everything's fine," Volodya answered for him. "Could we . . . pay?"

"Four twenty," the waiter said immediately.

Volodya handed him five rubles and began to stand up. Vitka and Olya stood up immediately afterwards. Burmistrov was hunched over and soundlessly moving his wet lips. He was sweating profusely.

"Let me by," Volodya said.

Burmistrov stood up like a robot and strode into the aisle. The waiter gave Volodya his change, but Volodya refused it and led Olya over to the exit. Vitka hurried after them, grinning and wagging her skinny hips.

Burmistrov stood there hunched over and looking down at the floor.

"You need to lie down." The waiter touched his sweaty back, having finally decided that Burmistrov was simply in a normal phase of a prolonged holiday binge.

"Huh?" Burmistrov raised his eyes to look at him.

"Get some rest is what I'm saying. And, this evening, right before we get into Moscow, come find me for some hair of the dog," the waiter whispered to him.

Burmistrov turned around and walked away.

Back in their compartment, Olya had climbed up into one of the top bunks, while Vitka and Volodya were down below discussing the crazy Burmistrov. The fourth person in their compartment, a portly, talkative accountant from Podolsk, was sleeping loudly on one of the bottom beds, having had several glasses of pepper vodka and chased it with a little bit of sausage.

"I couldn't even finish my beer!" Volodya took out a deck of cards. "Like the Taganka Theater, like a horror movie, like Hitchcock! He's totally off his rocker!"

"I was afraid you'd choke, Ol!" Vitka excitedly rubbed her narrow palms together. "Well, guys, umm, I'm not sure what to say...When my friend Marik was in the army and went AWOL, they made him spend three months in an asylum. He came out with a lotta stories, but nothing like this!"

"Do you definitely have that money Ol?" Volodya laughed. "Maybe we just imagined it? I mean, what the fuck!"

"You promised you wouldn't swear like that anymore." Olya looked at the chrome handle on the compartment's gray ceiling.

"Do you guys want to go back to the restaurant in a little while?" Vitka proposed.

"Just so he can sit with us again?" Volodya cracked the deck.

"You can charge him an evening fare! Half a ruble per peek, right!? I'll even lend you my lipstick, Ol!"

Vitka and Volodya laughed so hard that the accountant stopped snoring and began to talk in his sleep.

Olya was staring at the ceiling, running her hand along the wall's corrugated yellow surface.

So many sickos...she thought, then yawned, remembering how Tanya Batashova once had an epileptic seizure in a harmony exam.

It's good I didn't throw up. He had ears just like ... like a little boy's. What a creep.

She closed her eyes and dozed off.

She dreams that she's in Kratovo, she's riding her cousin Vanya's moun-tain bike down Chekhov Street with a violin case over her shoulder, making her way to the home of the elderly Fatyanovs, who breed tulips, which is where the administration of the Gnessin Institute has organized a Secret Graduation Audition over which Pavel Korgan will be presid-ing; she rides easily and freely, manipulating the obedient pedals, of-fering her face to the warm country breeze, the rural air, the fresh air, accelerating up the hill near the Gornostayevs' dacha, then allowing herself to roll down it, past mossily stirring fences, behind which an endless pack of dogs lies in wait, nursing their torpid anger, then turn-ing onto Marshal Zhukov Street; she sees that the entire street from fence to fence, its every inch, has been converted into the deepest of trenches and that, over this trench, right at the center of the street, hangs a monorail; it is entirely straight and shines bright in the sun; How will I get past? I'm already late! *she thinks in horror, braking sharply; sand, country sand, fine white sand, crunches beneath the bike tires; the roots of a pine tree stand in the bicycle's way; cabbage white butterflies zoom into her eyes, then fly off into the nettles, while, down below, in the gloomy trench, a line of people waiting for kvass fidgets in the dark; the line is short, silent, and unfamiliar; Olya looks at the monorail;* "Hey miss, you've gotta take off your tires," *someone advises from down below;* "How can I take them off? I don't have any tools!" *she begins to grow cold;* "Ask the installer!"; *Olya raises her head and looks up; there, high up in the pine trees, high up in the orange-blue pines, installers live with steel claws on their feet; one comes down to her from his tree;* "We've each got two axes," *he says and takes out two enormous axes; they shine in the sun; grunting, the mechanic deftly hacks the tires off of the wheels of the bike;* "Thank you!" *she's overjoyed;* "Now pay me!" *The installer, who reeks of vodka and sausage, blocks her path toward the monorail;* "How can I pay you?"; "With cooked meat! You're wearin' ridin' breeches*

made of meat! You've been growin' 'em all summer, you lil' dragonfly!"
Olya looks at her legs in their shorts; on her thighs are giant growths
made of cooked meat; she palpates them with horror and fascination;
"Stand normal!" the installer orders and cuts off the riding-breech
growths with two sharp blows; "Now, I'm gonna bake 'em in dough and
make me some capital chow!" he shouts in Olya's face; the meat disap-
pears into the installer's bottomless pockets; "Get outta here! Don't
dawdle! I changed the tracks!" the installer shouts; Olya puts the rim
of her front wheel onto the monorail, pushes off of the ground with one
foot to gain speed, then begins to ride over the dark, bottomless trench
uncertainly; at first—unsteadily—then more and more freely, she ac-
celerates and the wind whistles in her ears.

    Jerk.

          Clang.

               Jerk.

Olya woke up and wiped at her wet mouth.

The train jerked again, then quietly came to a crawl. The sun had grown weaker. Their compartment was stuffy, dusty, and smelled of sausages. Volodya was sleeping on the bunk across from hers.

Olya shook her head, moved her hand through her hair, looked down. Vitka was sleeping. The accountant was gone.

She looked at her watch: 7:37 p.m.

"Excellent." She yawned, getting down from the bed.

Having found her sandals, she examined herself in the mirror on the door, rubbed her face, combed her hair, and turned the door handle. The mirror moved off to the side.

It was chillier in the hallway. Two toddlers, laughing and stamping their feet, were playing tag; in the neighboring compartment, someone was noisily spreading dominoes, someone's low, smoky voice rumbled, and their friend the accountant's high, feminine voice rang out.

Olya went into the bathroom. Slamming the door behind her, she locked it with a twist of the damp bolt, rinsed her face, lowered her pants, and, with some difficulty, squatted down over the toilet. A colorless stream flowed down into the excrement-stained bowl.

I dreamt . . . about Katovo . . . She tried to remember her dream. *God, three more hours of getting jostled around in here . . . Something about Kogan . . . Oh yeah! Meat breeches!*

She laughed and stroked her tan hip. Having finished peeing, she passed her hand across her genitals, rubbed the moisture collected there onto her hand, stood up, rinsed her hand, zipped her pants, and looked at herself in the spattered mirror: a pink Hungarian tank top with spaghetti straps, shoulder-length flaxen hair, a broad-cheeked face with chestnut eyes, and a hickey from Volodya above her collar bone.

"And that was my trip to Crimea," she declared, then opened the door.

Standing directly in front of the door was Burmistrov.

She glanced at him with no surprise.

Now he's gonna ask for his money back, she realized. *The crazy idiot!*

"Forgive me, please, Olga, but I wanted to talk to you . . . I really need to."

"In the bathroom?"

"No, no, if you want, we could go over to my compartment in the seventh car . . . if . . . or . . . here." He stood to the side to let her by.

"And what if I don't want to?" She stepped out of the bathroom and looked point-blank at Burmistrov. *Of course it couldn't end that easily! Now he won't leave me alone . . . the goddamn slug.*

She took the twenty-five-ruble note out of her pocket and quickly put it back into the pocket of his shirt, from which a few papers and a pair of dark glasses protruded. "Take this back and let me be."

"No . . . no please . . ." Attempting to come to his senses, he reached into his pocket. "Why are you—"

Olya turned away from him to leave, but he grabbed her by the arm. "I'm begging you, please don't go!"

"I'm gonna call my husband over," she said, immediately getting angry with herself for this cowardly lie. *Now I'm married too!*

"What do you want from me?!"

"I'm begging you, I'm begging you . . ." He noticed a man in the hallway walking their way. "I'll just say two words, let's go . . . erm . . . over to the vestibule."

Burmistrov elicited no fear in her; internally, Olga sensed that this man wasn't capable of doing anything frightening or *heavy*. This didn't make him any less unbearable.

"Which vestibule do you mean exactly?" She smirked scornfully and squinted at the approaching man; he was vulgarly mustached, had striped pajamas, and purred to himself, carrying a transparent plastic bag of food scraps in both hands. It was as if this bag filled with chicken bones, egg shells, and apple cores had given her a shove and she began to walk over to the vestibule. Burmistrov hurried after her.

In the vestibule, it was dirty, dark, and thunderously loud.

Leaning against the chill, muddy-green wall, Olya folded her arms over her beautiful bosom and looked at Burmistrov. He dug feverishly in his breast pocket.

"Why did you . . . I did this in honest fashion . . . and you—"

In pulling out the bill, he accidentally hooked several other papers, which fell to the floor. He rushed to pick them up. One photograph had fallen at Olya's feet. As she was a decent juggler, she lifted it up into the air with her foot, caught it in her hands, and looked at it: against the background of the Swallow's Nest, a castle in Crimea, Burmistrov was embracing a lean, swarthy-complexioned young man with close-set eyes; the young man was wearing a sailor-striped tank top and had several tattoos on his shoulders and arms. One of a snake crawling up his wrist stood out: it was emblazoned with the name IRA in the same spot where it was pierced through with a sword.

"Your little . . . *friend*?" Olya gave back the picture.

"Well, yes, yes, my friend. We saw each other in Yalta."

"He was in jail too?"

"Yes, but not with me. He had . . . he did . . . something else—"

"What'd he do? Kill Ira? Or just love her too much?"

"Ah—you want to talk about that!" Burmistrov smiled exhaustedly. "Well, no, it has nothing to do with a person named Ira. It's a prison tattoo: I RUIN ACTIVES."

"What's an *active*?"

"They're big *bugry**—bad guys."

"Big *bugry*?"

"Olga," he said sternly and held out the money. "Take it. Please don't offend me."

"Tell me what it is you need from me." She tucked her hands into her armpits.

"I need . . ." he began to speak in a decisive manner, then suddenly got down on his knees. "I saw you in Yalta, Olga."

"What?"

"I . . . back in Yalta . . . in that café on the embankment . . . the Anchor. It was the first time. You were there with your husband. You were eating tomato salad and . . . these . . . meatballs. Kiev-style meatballs. You ate there two more times. And then on the beach, you ate cherries. I gave them to you."

"Hold on." Olya tried to remember. "On the beach . . . cherries—a cornet of cherries! That was you? You gave them to us? In the newspaper cone?"

"Me, me me!" He shook his bald head.

Olya remembered a strange resort-goer with an ingratiating smile who had thrust a cornet of yellow cherries at her and muttered something in a strange tone. Then, suddenly, at that very moment, she for some reason remembered her entire dream about Kratovo: the monorail, the trench, and the installer with the two axes.

"God, what a vision!" she said, laughing.

While this fit of laughter shook her young, shapely body, Burmistrov, still on his knees, stared at her with a pitiful smile.

"That was you?" she repeated after she was done laughing.

"Yes! Yes! Yes!" He was nearly screaming. He rubbed his face with

---

*"Бугер" is prison slang for upper-level inmates—"OG" would be a passable American equivalent.

his fist, the twenty-five-ruble note still clutched in it. "I . . . forgive me . . . Olga . . . I haven't been able to sleep for four nights. Since Yalta."

"You . . . because of me?"

"Yes."

"And you were, what? Following me?"

"No, well . . . I just found out when you were leaving. Just . . . from the, erm, landlady—where you were staying."

"Why?"

"So that I could see how you eat again."

Olya stared at him silently. The door opened and a heavyset man with five bottles of beer pressed to his naked chest stepped out into the vestibule. Burmistrov remained on his knees. Glancing at him and Olya, the man passed by.

"Get up," Olya sighed.

Burmistrov stood up heavily.

"What do you want from me?"

"I . . . Olga . . . please don't misunderstand. . . ."

"What do you want from me?"

He inhaled deeply of the air of the vestibule, which smelled of creosote. "I want us to see each other once a month and for you to eat for me."

"And what will I get out of it?"

"One hundred rubles. Every time."

She reflected.

"This won't be in a public place," Burmistrov muttered. "It will be in a safe, secluded spot and the food won't be anything like—"

"I'll do it," Olya interrupted him. "Once a month. Only once a month."

"Only once a month," he repeated in an ecstatic whisper, then, closing his eyes, leaned against the vibrating wall with total relief. "Oh, I'm so happy!"

"But I'm not going to give you my address or my phone number."

"You don't need to, no need . . . We'll find somewhere to meet . . . We'll establish a day and a time . . . That'll be better, much better. When's a good time for you?"

"Well..." she thought, "I'm done early on Mondays. At one ten. Let's meet at one thirty...in front of the Pushkin monument."

"In front of the Pushkin monument..." he echoed her words.

"Yeah...and do you live in Moscow?"

"I'll be living in Golutvin. They won't let me register in the capital."

"That's all, then. And, please, don't follow me to the bathroom again!" She turned and grabbed hold of the door handle.

"Wait...which Monday?" he asked, not yet opening his eyes.

"Which? Well...at the start of the month. On the first Monday of the month."

"The first Monday of every month."

Nodding, Olya walked out.

In her compartment, Volodya had woken up and was waiting for her with a puffy face and disheveled hair. Vitka was still sleeping.

Climbing onto one of the top beds, they kissed for a little while, then lay in silence.

The train was entering the Moscow suburbs.

I forgot to take back the money, Olya remembered, ruffling Volodya's hair. *Once a month. So what? Let him watch. OK, enough, time to get our stuff together, we're almost there...*

The dusty pillow of a sun-kissed Moscow summer tumbled down onto Olga. She spent August at her family's dacha in Kratovo.

A hammock, pine trees, Sibelius's Violin Concerto—she was learning it for an exam—an old pond, a new edition of Proust, afternoon tea with fresh cherry jam, Volodya coming to visit, which invariably ended with a hurried sex act in the old fir grove, games of badminton with their timid neighbor, a mathematician who was always covered in burs, bike rides with stupid Tamara and nervous Larissa, long evenings spent around the table at the Petrovskys, an afternoon nap in the hammock, and a good night's sleep in the attic on grandpa's squashed sofa.

During the whole of August, she didn't think about her adventure on the train even once and would probably have totally forgotten about it had it not been for one unexpected event. On the first Monday of September, she was performing the first part of the Sibelius concerto for her teacher Mikhail Yakovlevich, a small, rotund man who looked like a restless hamster. In the middle of her playing, he interrupted her by snapping his tiny, plump fingers, as he often did.

"Nao, nao, nao. Naot like that. Too typical—naot like that!" he mumbled, with the intentional Georgian accent that often came out when his students were playing badly. "Olenka, there's something going on with the sound here that's nao, nao, nao. You're not throwing yourself into the music. You're not taking yourself in hand, my golden darling. You must throw yourself into it, throw yourself right in, my child, and don't just sit there on the rests. The sound is good, but there's no meat to it. No meat to it, my golden darling! You're sleeping on the rests. Throw yourself into it, throw yourself into it and don't look back, that's what I'm saying. It's better to overdo it than to not give enough. And here"—he leafed through the music— "your chords went off, rang out, rang out . . . then you got lost on the neck! Got lo-o-o-ost! Totally lost! Push yourself forward! Push yourself! Push yourself to the climax! If you don't, you'll cripple the sound, slow the tempo, and we're left with nao tempo and nao sound, you un-dar-stand? And this is na . . . and this is na . . . !"

This "na" . . . who says that? Olya thought, looking over the violin's tuning pegs at Mikhail Yakovlevich's smooth Jewish forehead *And this is na . . .* steak and eggs!

At that moment, she remembered the steak and eggs, the train, and Burmistrov, then her mouth broke into a broad grin.

"What're you so happy for?" Mikhail Yakovlevich suddenly reached both hands into his pockets to look for his cigarettes. "Summer's over and your piece hasn't budged."

At half-past one, Olya was standing in front of the Pushkin monument with her violin case over her shoulder. In the crowd of people sitting on benches around the statue, she saw Burmistrov immediately get up—still skinny and bald, now wearing a beige slicker—and walk toward her with a rushed and awkward gait.

That tan came off of him real fast. Olya watched Burmistrov with great interest, as if he were an outlandish plant who'd not only managed *not* to wilt in the last month and a half but also to grow, to lead his own mysterious life, to eat, to drink, to sleep, and to wear a slicker, a turtleneck, and a new pair of suede boots.

A construction manager . . . She began to remember his words on the train. *Two degrees. The Tin Man has a brain, then.*

Burmistrov approached her. "Hello, Olga," he said, bowing his head but not offering his hand.

"Hello."

His face was calmer and more balanced than when she last saw him, and his greenish-blue eyes staring at her with benevolent attention.

"I suspected you were out of town back in August and that was why you didn't show up."

"That's true."

"I wasn't very worried."

"Why not?"

"I was sure that you'd show up in September." He smiled tensely and shyly.

"That so?" Olya grinned, shaking her hair. "Such confidence!"

"Are you . . . a musician?" He'd noticed the violin case.

"Almost."

"Are you studying at a conservatory?"

"Almost."

"What do you mean 'almost'?"

"Too many questions."

"Forgive me . . ." He began to fuss about in his usual way.

"Let's . . . over there . . . we'll get a cab."

He walked ahead of Olya toward the boulevard.

I wonder if he's got a woman. Olga watched his long, nervous stride, his gray pants, and his suede boots. *Guys like him either have a lot of 'em or nobody.*

On the boulevard, Burmistrov caught a banana-yellow Zaporozhets, helped Olya get in the back seat, sat next to the gloomy driver, then, thirty minutes later, helped Olya get out when the car stopped across from Avtozavodskaya station.

"Is it far?" asked Olya, getting out of the Zaporozhets.

"Two steps from here, that building there." He gestured with his hand.

They walked into a nine-story apartment building and went up to the sixth floor in the elevator. Burmistrov opened the cheaply upholstered door into apartment number 24 and let Olya lead the way. She entered the one-room apartment, poorly furnished but carefully cleaned. In the middle of the room stood a table covered with a white tablecloth and set for one person. There was no food on the table.

"Right . . . here." Burmistrov gestured toward the table, fidgeting continuously. "Come in, please . . . take your coat off."

He helped her take off her slicker. She put the violin case on top of the refrigerator in the hallway, then walked into the main room. Burmistrov quickly took off his slicker, then ran his palms through the few hairs that were sprouting from his almost completely bald head.

"Olga, please, sit down."

"May I wash my hands?"

"Yes, of course . . ."

He turned on the bathroom light and opened the door for her.

Washing her hands in the rust-streaked sink, Olya looked at herself in the mirror.

Let us re-re-rejoice in our life, in crazy Olka and the happy blade . . . He's getting ready to cut you up with it . . . Right when the staaaaarlight is scattered and the siiiilent world by night and dark is battered . . . No. . . . He won't cut me. He's peaceful. Peaceful like Pa-Papa. Or like Pa-Pa-Pavel. Fear not, Ole Lukøje. She was simultaneously riffing on a Russian folk song and a song from the Russian musical of *The Three Musketeers*.

She wiped her hands off with an old terry-cloth towel, left the bathroom, then sat down at the table. Burmistrov disappeared into the kitchen and came back with a serving dish in his hands. On the dish were pieces of chicken, boiled potatoes, and cucumbers. He walked over to the right of Olya and began to carefully fill her plate.

"Did you cook this yourself?" asked Olya.

"No, of course not … I can't really … cook … this." Once he'd served her. Burmistrov disappeared into the kitchen with the serving dish, scurried back, took a pillow off the bed, then, holding the pillow out in front of him, stood facing Olya.

"What do you need that for?" She looked at the pillow.

"It's … so … that I'm not too loud," he muttered, his voice beginning to quiver. "Please … can … please … I'm asking you …"

"Do you have anything to drink?"

"You don't need it … can't have it …" Burmistrov pronounced harshly. "Eat, please. Please only eat."

That's a new one! Olya chose the tastiest-looking bit of chicken, cut a piece from it, and put it in her mouth.

Burmistrov's face immediately went pale and his eyes rolled in his head.

"And this … and this …" he mumbled pitifully.

Olga began to eat. The chicken was tastily prepared.

"And this is na-a-o … And this is na-a-o!" Burmistrov lowed, clutching the pillow.

It's probably chicken from the farmer's market, steamed chicken, Olya thought, chewing and swallowing the meat slowly. *I wonder if he rents this apartment? Or if it just belongs to his friends … It hasn't been remodeled for at least twenty years … and the furniture …* "Hey Slavs! We stand firm-iture!"

Burmistrov's body had been possessed by shudders. He was drawing in air with a whistle and roaring "This is na!" into the pillow, staring fixedly at the pieces of meat that were disappearing between Olya's lips. His trembling legs gave out and he fell to his knees.

Look around him, not at him, Olya ordered herself.

A plastic donkey stood on top of the old television.

Eeyore! Glancing at him, she almost choked. *Nothing to wash it down with … eat slowly, you idiot …*

Burmistrov's cries gained strength, merging into an unintelligible roar, his bald head trembling.

Olya swallowed the last piece and pushed the plate away.

Burmistrov immediately fell silent, went limp, and let the pillow fall from his hands. Catching his breath, he took a handkerchief from his pocket and wiped at his sweaty face.

"Is that all?" asked Olya.

"Yes, yes..." He blew his nose loudly.

She got up from the table, walked into the hallway, and began to get her slicker on.

"Just a sec..." Burmistrov tossed and turned on the floor to get up.

He walked into the hallway, helped Olya into her slicker, then handed her the money: 125 rubles.

"You forgot to take it the first time."

He remembers... Olya took the money, immediately sensing and realizing how important she was to this shabby, half-crazed man. *Some kinda dream...*

"Forgive me, Olga... I... can't... I won't be able to take you back..." Burmistrov muttered.

He looked pitiful.

"The metro's right here." Olya slung the violin case over her shoulder.

"In a month... I'm begging you..." He looked down at the shabby parquetry beneath his feet.

Olya nodded silently and took her leave.

She took the elevator down, dumbly reading the crass graffiti on the wooden doors, then walked out through the dim entryway, and set off for the metro.

It was a cloudy September day, but it wasn't raining.

I want a drink. Olya noticed a soda machine.

She walked over to it. The machine was working, but there were no cups left. Olya walked into a grocery store. There was a big line in the meat section. One woman was shouting angrily. Someone pushed someone else away from the counter. A flushed, finely dressed woman emerged from the lined-up crowd, holding a string bag. Four pairs of yellow chicken legs were sticking out of it. Walking away, the woman half-turned back to everyone else and made a pronouncement:

"*This* lady wanted chicken! You worthless trash!"

And left the store.

A fit of laughter came over Olya. She keeled over and burst into loud laughter, covering her mouth with both palms and staggering around, coming to a stop in the dry-goods section; there, she *truly* doubled over with laughter, her violin case flew off her shoulder, and she barely managed to catch it, now laughing so much that everyone around her in the almost-empty dry-goods section fell silent. Tears were streaming from her eyes. Leaning against a column decorated with white tiles, Olya laughed, moaned, then shook her head.

"Someone's got the giggles!" the canned-food seller called out to her.

Olya wiped away her tears. "Have you got mineral water?"

"Only Drogobych."

"And...do you serve it in a glass?"

"No." He looked her over with a smile.

Olya walked out of the market. She took the metro to Oktyabrsky station, then got on bus number 33, got off near the Mineral Waters store, and thirstily drank two glasses of Borjomi there.

One hundred and twenty-five rubles! And he didn't give me any bread, she remembered, walking home along Gubkin Street. *He wouldn't let me drink either. Why not? He didn't ask me to eat more than what I did, even though there was still some left. Oh well, if someone's an idiot, then that's forever. One hundred and twenty-five rubles... how horrible! And it all began on that beach in Yalta. He was sitting next to us, just sitting there with his paper cap and a cornet of cherries, and he turned to me and said, "Help yourself." And I did.*

Awaiting her arrival at home were her quiet mother (her loud mathematician father was at the university where he taught), their Irish setter named Ready, Polish perch with rice, and her endless Proust.

Having refused lunch, Olya went into her room, dialed Volodya's number to tell him everything that had happened, but right when he answered, she hung up the phone.

"Why would I?" she asked her reflection in the mirror on the shelf. "Better no one knows."

The next day, she went to a black marketeer and bought two Pirastro strings (an A and an E) for forty rubles each and bought a blue-and-white French scarf for thirty-two rubles at a vintage store on Sretenka Street.

One month later, at 1:30 p.m., she was standing in front of the Push-kin monument.

Burmistrov arrived a little late, then took her to the same apart-ment, where, having given her a plate of roasted pork with vegetables and roared to his heart's content, he paid her the hundred rubles.

Olya decided to begin saving up for a good violin. She put the hundred in a volume of Proust that she'd finished and moved it to the upper level of her bookshelf.

It's too bad I can only do this once a month, she thought as she fell asleep. *Imagine if I could do it once a week! I'd be playing a Schneider by junior year!*

A year passed. Olya began her third year at the Gnessin Institute, broke up with Volodya, pushed to the side by the beautiful and phlegmatic pianist Ilya, learned a concerto by Mozart, played reason-ably well with a quartet in a university contest, read Nabokov's *Lo-lita*, and tried hash and anal sex.

Her meetings with Burmistrov happened regularly on the first Monday of every month.

In December, she arrived at the monument with a fever of 100 degrees and, dripping snot, was barely able to finish the meat ragout with a side of Burmistrov's moans; in April, she felt very nauseous after eating a fatty piece of sturgeon; in May, after eating quail with cranberries, she awoke at night with a cry; she'd dreamt that Burmistrov had an enormously fat python coming out of his mouth; in July, after eating liver in sour cream, she was tormented by vicious stomach cramps. But, in August, she was tanning on the beach in Koktebel, resting on Ilya's plump chest, which was overgrown with red hair.

Olya thought of Burmistrov sometimes, having given him the nickname "Horse Soup." She felt that he played a particular role in her life, but she wasn't sure quite what it was. The phrase "This is na," however, stayed with her; she used it often, muttering it when something surprised or disappointed her.

"Well, this is na!" And she would stamp her foot when she was playing violin and her fingers wouldn't obey.

"This is na!" And she would shake her head seeing long lines in stores.

"This is na-a-a . . ." she would whisper in Ilya's ear as he was bringing her to orgasm.

One day, rushing off to meet Burmistrov, she even declined to go to a closed screening of *From Russia with Love* with Ilya.

"Have you met someone else?" the incisive Ilya asked.

"Horse Soup," she replied cheerfully.

"What's that?"

"You wouldn't understand."

As with Volodya, she didn't tell Ilya anything.

Nineteen-eighty-two came around. Brezhnev died. Ready died after eating rat poison. Olya started her senior year at the institute and bought herself a violin made by the German master Schneider for 1,600 rubles, lying to her poor parents that a girlfriend who'd dropped out of school and married a Georgian had given it to her. She continued to meet Burmistrov at the same apartment. She'd grown so used to Horse Soup's roar that she paid no attention to it anymore, simply focusing on the food she was to devour.

Not enough garnish . . . the cauliflower's boiled and not fried in breadcrumbs . . . but the meat is good . . . and the salad is fresh . . .

Having received her money, she would go to a nearby cafeteria, ask for a glass of *kompot*, and drink it quickly—without sitting down. She wasn't saving money anymore, spending it on herself instead.

Thus passed another six months.

Then, something began to happen to the food that Burmistrov served to her. There was no less of it and it was still of the same high quality, but it was now presented to her in particulate form. The meat, fish, and vegetables were cut into small pieces, and all of these pieces were mixed together as if it were a salad. Olya ate without asking extraneous questions and Horse Soup howled his habitual "This is na-a-o!" Eventually, the food was cut up so finely that it was hard for Olya to figure out what was in the fastidious *okroshka* of meat (or fish) and vegetables on the plate before her.

What's he having me eat now? She would look distrustfully at the full plate but, having tasted it, would realize that it was still normal food and calm down.

One day, Burmistrov put a plate in front of her with his monthly concoction of foods taking up only one half of the plate—the other half was completely empty.

What kind of magic trick is this? Olya bent her brows. *Did he eat the other half himself?*

But she silently picked up her fork and began to eat the mixture of turkey, salad, and boiled potatoes. This time, Burmistrov's howling was especially protracted. His bald head quivered and his hands mashed at the pillow convulsively.

"And this is na-a-a-a-a-o! Na-a-a-a-a-o!" he bleated.

Having finished her food, Olya put down her fork and stood up.

"You haven't finished yet . . ." Horse Soup muttered huskily, gazing out from behind his pillow. "Finish, please . . ."

Olya looked at the empty plate. "I *have* finished."

"You haven't even touched the other half."

"I ate everything. Look. Can't you see?"

"I see better than you do!" he cried shrilly. "You didn't even touch the other half! There's food on that side too! Eat!"

Olya looked at him dumbly. *Has he, like, totally lost his shit now?*

Burmistrov writhed around on the floor. "Don't torment me like this, Olga, please eat!"

"But there's nothing there..." She grinned nervously.

"Stop tormenting me!" he cried.

She sank back into her chair.

"Eat, eat, eat!"

He's seeing things! Olya sighed, picked up the fork, scooped up the invisible food, and maneuvered it in her mouth.

"And this is na-a-o! And this is na-a-a-o!" Burmistrov howled.

I'm a mime now! Olya grinned to herself, lifted her fork to her mouth slowly, took the invisible chow off it with her lips, chewed it, then swallowed it.

She even came to like this game. After a little while, she put down her fork.

"There's still some left... but that's okay... actually—why rush?" muttered Burmistrov, still moaning.

What a pain in the ass! Olya calmly *finished* the invisible food.

He paid her one hundred rubles as usual and, helping her get dressed, said, "We're going to meet in a different apartment from now on, Olga, so, next month, don't go to the Pushkin monument. Go to Tsvetnoy Boulevard."

"And where will we meet there?"

"Outside the market. Same time."

Olya nodded and left.

The apartment on Tsvetnoy Boulevard was much nicer than the previous one: a two-bedroom spot, comfortable, luxuriously furnished, with high ceilings. Burmistrov entertained Olya in the living room. The dinner table was tastefully set: silver utensils on crystal under-plates, porcelain plates, and napkins in silver rings. However, there was still neither bread nor water. And her plate was still only half full. Burmistrov stood in front of the table holding a silvery-pink silk pillow at the ready.

It's like an exam. She squinted over at Burmistrov and began to eat. *OK... meat and mushrooms... and he has a new suit—he get rich or something?*

Horse Soup howled into the pillow.

She ate the visible food. Then the invisible food. She ate calmly, not hurrying at all.

Without saying anything, Burmistrov blew his nose as he usually did, wiped off his sweaty face, then gave Olya her money.

Still, I don't get it—why me? she thought, walking to the metro. *It's been two years... It's a miracle I haven't lost it! And it's only me... So many women in Moscow... He's a real sicko... Schizophrenic, maybe? Or maybe there's another name for his condition... I should do a little shopping at Passage, my tights are a catastrophe... Real nice out today...*

Their meetings continued with businesslike regularity. But there was less and less visible food on her plate each time. The invisible half, however, expanded, and Olya diligently ate the invisible food, bending down to the plate carefully so as not to drop any food, bringing it up to her mouth, wiping her lips, chewing, then, finally, attentively scraping what was left on the plate onto her fork and putting the final bite into her mouth.

On February 7, 1983, a slushy Monday, she sat down at the table as expected. Burmistrov came out of the kitchen with a serving dish in hand. On the dish was only the silver spatula that he typically used to serve Olya. Putting the serving dish down on the edge of the table, Burmistrov began to carefully mete out the invisible food to Olya.

So this is what it's come to, she thought and smiled. *I should get a bonus for my acting ability.*

Burmistrov left with the serving dish, then came back with his pillow.

Olya looked at the empty plate.

"And this... And this..." mumbled Burmistrov.

"In your hoo-use, I spent my yo-o-uth, its go-o-lden dreams," Olya sang part of Tchaikovsky's *Eugene Onegin* to herself, scooping emptiness from her empty plate with an empty fork.

Two more years crawled duskily by. Andropov and Chernenko died. A spaniel named Artaud appeared in Olya's family. Her father left his department at Moscow State University. Vitka got married. In the USSR, it was the beginning of perestroika. Olya completed her degree at the Gnessin Institute and, thanks to an advantageous connection, joined the regional philharmonic orchestra. Ilya moved away to Israel with his family. Olya had two lovers: a tall, skinny, long-haired guitarist named Oleg and a calm, thorough doctor and beautician named Zhenya. Zhenya had a wife and a car. Olya made love with Oleg in his artist friend's studio. She made love with Zhenya wherever they could—mostly in his car.

Nothing changed with Burmistrov: she'd eat yet another plate of invisible food, he roared and gave her money.

After her father's departure from MSU, the family had far less money, so the hundred rubles she got from Horse Soup every month were very useful. She got ninety-six rubles a month from the orchestra.

Perestroika flew off clumsily into the night, leaving the stormy and merciless nineties in its stead. Olya's mother had her right breast removed; Olya's disgraced grandmother died, finally freeing up her one-bedroom apartment near the VDNKh; Olya had her second abortion and left the orchestra in order to become a music teacher at a school for foreign students.

Something began to happen with Burmistrov: he changed their meeting place several times, sometimes feeding her in a stand-alone office at the Hotel Metropole, sometimes in half-empty apartments that exemplified failed attempts at European design. Burmistrov now roared with no pillow, apparently not worried about anyone hearing. He drove Olya around in a Lada Samara, then in a Honda, then in the back seat of an SUV, as he now had a chauffeur with a fat neck. Burmistrov began to dress like a New Russian, if not an especially young one, and to shave his head. The sum he gave Olya accumulated more and more Russian zeros then, like a butterfly under glass, it petrified into an American 100-dollar bill.

Olya would eat her invisible food with great appetite, and Burmistrov would howl "This is na," writhing and spattering his expensive suit with foamy spittle.

On October 19, 1994, she married Alyosha, a beautician and a colleague of her ex-boyfriend Zhenya. They began to remodel her grandma's apartment, run down and fouled by the old woman's six cats, getting set up with new furniture, a huge television, and an Irish setter named Karo. Alyosha, a broad-shouldered redhead, loved Olya, French cinema, sports, and cars, and he made good money. She left her job at the music school with the intention of having kids. That summer, they were preparing to set off for a twenty-four-day trip around Europe organized by Alyosha's father, a functionary in the foreign affairs office. Olya had never been abroad. Alyosha, on the other hand, had spent his childhood in France and longed to disrobe Europe for his wife.

As she packed her bags, Olya remembered that she had a meeting with Burmistrov the next day. *I won't be there. I'm done chewing air —basta, Horse Soup!*

Penetrating Europe's soft body through the quiet expanse of Finland, they passed through Sweden, Denmark, Norway, Iceland, witnessed London's crass beauty, crossed the English Channel, nibbled their way across the deliciousness of France, and ended up in immaculate Switzerland.

Right up until Geneva, Olya was incredibly happy. There, she suddenly became very ill. In the evening, she and Alyosha were sitting at a restaurant with a view of a lake and unhurriedly eating a huge grilled lobster, washing down the juicy snow-white meat with Fendant les Murettes from the south of Switzerland. Slightly tanned from two weeks of traveling, Alyosha was telling Olya about the problems they had with theft at his father's dacha in Barvikha.

"The people around there've lost it—and that's putting it mildly!

If you don't lock the gate for even a minute, they fly in and take everything they can. Maybe there's a hammock—they cut if off the trees; maybe there're some linens—they drag those away; if there's a shovel, they take the shovel; if there's a barrel—hey, you OK?"

Now deathly pale, Olya stared glassily at the piece of lobster at the end of her fork. It was as if a heavy orb had burst inside her head and the endless void had begun to resound. For the first time in her life, Olya *saw* the food that people ate. The sight of this food was horrifying. Worst of all was that it was so heavy, endowed with its own grievous and *final* weight. The lobster, which seemed to have been smelted of white lead, reeked of death. In a cold sweat, Olya raised herself up on her wooden arms and vomited onto the table. It seemed to her that she was throwing up gravestones. After paying twenty francs for *les dégâts*, Alyosha took her back to the hotel. Olya vomited three times on the way. She was turned inside out by her illness that night, but Alyosha was afraid to call a doctor because of the risk that circumstance would force them to stay in Geneva.

"It's just a little bug, bunny." He pressed ice against her temple. "We shared all of our food. If something was off, then I would've thrown up too. Breathe deeper and think about snow, snow, snow, new-fallen Russian snow."

Olya fell asleep toward morning, woke up at 2:00 p.m., shook her heavy head, and peeled apart her dry lips. The nausea had passed. She wanted orange juice and toast with strawberry jam. Alyosha was slumbering next to her.

"Let's go eat, big boy." She stood up.

"You're OK, bunny?" He stretched. "I told you—just a little bug. But it surprises me that there're any bugs in Switzerland! You could eat off the sidewalk here!"

Olya took a shower and did her makeup.

It's good to throw up sometimes. Smooths out wrinkles.

Downstairs in the chill foyer, a glorious Swiss buffet with an abundance of fruits and seafood awaited them. Olya served herself juice, toast, an egg, and a kiwi. As usual, Alyosha filled his plate with salads and covered them over abundantly with dressings.

They sat down at their favorite table on the terrace, which was covered with ferns and calla lilies.

"The heat's gonna break today, so let's go to Chillon Castle," Alyosha decided. "No more locking ourselves away, 'kay bunny?"

"OK." Olya drank her juice thirstily, hit the egg with her spoon, peeled it, poked it, watched the yolk run out of it with pleasure, salted it, put both yolk and trembling white on her spoon, and brought the spoon to her mouth. Then froze: the egg reeked of death. That same resounding void rang out once more in Olya's head. She shifted her crazed eyes away from the egg. The kiwi lying next to it hovered like a heavy, mossy cobblestone, and the grilled toast crawled forth like a tombstone. Olya dropped the spoon and clasped her hands over her face.

"No..."

"Is it happening again, bunny?" Alyosha stopped his cheerful chewing.

"No, no, no..."

Olya stood up and walked over to the elevator. Alyosha came quick on her heels.

"Could I be pregnant?" She stroked her belly as she lay on the hotel bed. "No—it's never felt like this before."

"You should've stayed in bed, bunny. Stay here. I'll order us lunch here."

"Don't talk to me about lunch!" she panted.

"Just have some juice."

There was no minibar in their room, so Alyosha went downstairs and came back with a portly yellow bottle.

Juice flowed into glass. Olya brought it to her mouth and swallowed with great difficulty. It felt like she was drinking melted butter. She put the heavy glass down on her bedside table.

"Later."

But later she couldn't even bring herself to sip it. Any thought of food put her into a stupor and filled her body with a *menacing* heaviness that swiftly turned to nausea.

"It's nothing but a nervous condition," Alyosha thought aloud. "Anorexia brought on by an alarming excess of impressions. I have Relanium. I always take it for hangovers. Take a couple. It'll calm you down."

Olya took the two pills, flipped through a copy of *Vogue*, then dozed off. She woke up at four, took another shower, then got dressed.

"You know what, big boy, I just won't eat today. Let's go to that castle of yours."

They spent the evening in Montreux. Alyosha ate a sausage and potato salad and drank a glass of beer. While he ate, Olya strolled along the embankment. They got back to Geneva at midnight and went to sleep.

In the morning, Olya woke up at seven, quietly got ready, and, not waking her husband, went downstairs; she had a strong desire to eat. Having walked out of the elevator and said "morning" to the waitresses in their white aprons, she took a big warm plate and a fork and knife wrapped in a napkin, then moved toward the food. But when she caught sight of the fatal mounds of salad, cheese, ham, fish, and fruit, her legs buckled and her plate fell from her hands. Olya vomited bile onto the carpet.

Despite the fact that everything was in order with their insurance, Alyosha was still afraid to call a local doctor. *They'll say she has some horrible infectious disease and send her straight to the hospital.*

He instead found the addresses of three Geneva psychiatrists.

"I'm not gonna see a shrink." Olya pushed away the card in Alyosha's hand. "Get me some water."

Alyosha handed her a glass. She could still drink water.

"When are we leaving for Italy?" she asked, sitting on the bed and leaning against the wall.

"The day after tomorrow."

"What's the plan for today?"

"Le Valais. A wine cellar in Vétroz."

"Let's go." She stood up decisively.

The air was cool in Serge Roh's wine cellar. Moldy stacks of bottles under brick arches, just like in Burgundy, called forth a feeling of peace and security in Olya. But still she couldn't bring herself to drink the wine. To Olya, the glass of ruby-red Cornalin weighed a whole ton of death as she swirled it around heavily, a liquid nightmare that engulfed any and all safe, familiar feelings; its thick, ominous glare made Olya's heart stop.

Alyosha, on the other hand, drank so much that Olya had to prop him up as they walked to the train station.

That night in their hotel room, as she was giving herself to Alyosha, who still wasn't entirely sober, Olya gazed up at the ceiling, piebald with spots of light, and tried to understand what was happening to her.

Maybe I'm just overtired? Or traumatized by the West? Marina Vlady wrote that Vysotsky vomited on Kurfürstendamm when he first went to Berlin and saw its affluence. He yelled "Who won the war, motherlover?!" Or maybe we're traveling too much ... Or it's an abnormal pregnancy ... Meaning, I'm gonna have a baby.

Instead, two days later in Rome, Olya got her period. She was very sick. Not having eaten anything for three days, she lay in bed trembling, drinking only water. Alyosha called his father in Moscow, who got in touch with the Russian embassy. Soon, a somber embassy doctor was taking Olya's weak pulse. Having examined her, he went out into the hallway to talk to her husband.

"It could be exhaustion, but it could also be depression." He rubbed uncertainly at the bridge of his thick nose as he talked to Alyosha in the hotel hallway.

"What about ... our trip?" Alyosha said thoughtfully, looking at a reproduction of one of Leonardo's drawings in a lurid frame.

"Tell you what, colleague, I'll give your wife an injection of Seduxen with a touch of barbital. Then you let her sleep. Starting in the morning, you can give her Relanium to continue your trip. But in Moscow you *must* take her to a psychiatrist."

Olya slept for fourteen hours and woke up calm and visibly well rested. Alyosha gave her a pill. She took it, then, having eaten nothing for breakfast, set off with her husband for some sightseeing around the city.

"Let's just pretend I'm on a diet!" she joked.

But by the evening she was terribly tired and had a terrible need to eat.

"Order me some tea and a sandwich from room service," she requested.

Alyosha ordered for her. When the food arrived, Olya looked at the sliced roll, ham protruding from the cut along its side, and the cup of tea from a distance:

"Leave me alone for a minute, big boy?"

Alyosha kissed her and walked out of the room.

What's going on with me? I mean *really*! Olya looked sullenly at the food. *Go over there, pick it up, and eat!*

She walked over to the table decisively. Two steps later, however, her legs seemed to have turned to plasticine and that plasticine, made up of viscous fear, was melting. The fatal sandwich was grinning, sticking out its dead, leaden tongue at her. Olya collapsed onto the bed and began to sob.

"How's it going, bunny?" Alyosha glanced into the room a little while later.

"Take it away...take it away," she sobbed.

Alyosha took the food into the bathroom, sat down on the toilet, ate the sandwich, washed it down with tea, and, still chewing, came back into the room.

"Just let me lie here ..." Olya stared at the cheap white material covering the wall with her moist eyes.

Alyosha sat down next to her on the bed and wiped the tears from her cheek.

"Listen—what if you tried eating with a blindfold?"

"Just let me lie here ..." she repeated.

"I'll go down to the square, OK?"

"Mm-hmm."

Alyosha left.

*Of course it would happen here, in this ugly room ... Murphy's Law ...
What'd I do to deserve this?* She palpated the wall.

The feebleness that comes after tears put her to sleep once more.

*Olya dreams that she's in the hospital where her mother had her breast
removed and she's walking down the hospital hallway to her; she enters
room no. 16 and sees her mother sitting on the bed and looking at herself
in Olya's grandmother's circular hand mirror; her mother is completely
naked and very cheerful; "Look how they cut me, Olenka!" She hands
her the mirror; but, even without the mirror; Olya can see that both of
her mother's breasts are intact: "They tricked you, Mom, they haven't
done anything." Olya palpates her mother's right breast indignantly
and feels the hard tumor still inside it; "You're not looking at it right,"
her mother insists as she take the mirror. "Look over there!" Olya looks
at her mother's body in the mirror and sees that she has a hideous chunk
carved out of her body—her right breast and shoulder have simply
vanished. "Now you need to look from this angle." Her mother smiles.
"That way you can see the most important thing: what needs to be done."
Olya shifts her view and, indeed, begins to see everything very differently,
everything as it truly is; like a magnifying glass, she moves the image of
her mother's body and superimposes it over the view of Moscow through
the window; she sees a neon sign that reads MIXED FEED. "Hurry
up, they close at five," her mother advises. "Run straight through the
dump." Olya runs through the enormous dump, the stinking waste
reaching up to her waist, makes it out to the street, then finds herself in
front of the enormous building with the neon sign—MIXED FEED;
Olya tries the door handle, but it's locked; I'm gonna starve to death,
Olya thinks with horror and knocks on the door; "What are you bangin'
down the door for, miss! They always close at five!" a voice resounds
nearby; Olya sees an old woman; "I'm dying of hunger," Olya sobs; "Go
to the back door and talk to the warehouseman," the old woman suggests;
Olya slides into the darkness through the cracked door and finds herself
in a huge storage room filled with all manner of objects; she walks and
walks, then suddenly sees a small table in the corner; Horse Soup is*

sitting at the table with a can of food in his hand; he's young and hand-
some in a sad, solemn way; paying no attention to Olya, he opens the
can of food in his hand with a can opener; in the can is only void, but
this void is also REAL CHOW; an unbelievably strong and intoxicat-
ingly delicious smell wafts over to her; Horse Soup takes out a spoon and
begins to eat from the can; "Gimme some! Gimme some!" Olya cries
out, crawling toward him on her knees, but he doesn't hear or see her;
she tries to catch the spoon with her mouth, but it's moving as fast as a
propeller; can-to-mouth, can-to-mouth, can-to-mouth; Olya puts her
mouth even closer and is hit very hard by the spoon, which knocks out
several of her teeth.

"Bunny! Bunny! Bunny!" Alyosha was shaking her chin.

"What?" She was up now.

"You screamed. Can I give you another pill?"

Olya sat up and wiped tears from her face. She had understood everything. This understanding did not frighten her but, on the contrary, soothed her.

"We need to go back to Moscow, big boy."

"What about Greece?"

"I'm really ill. I need to go back."

"But . . . we'll waste our tickets and have to buy new ones. Another thousand bucks."

"Then I'll go back alone."

"Don't be silly, bunny!"

"Then pack and let's go."

"C'mon, bunny, let's put our heads together and be reasonable, let's not do anything ra—"

"*I need to go to Moscow!*" Olya screamed.

They caught a flight that evening.

Moscow greeted them with the broad darkness of its dusty streets and its deeply familiar, yet wild smells.

That night, she got to sleep with a Reladorm, but the next morning barely had she woken up when Alyosha made an announcement.

"I'm going to get the doctor, bunny."

"I don't need any doctor." She stretched out her tired body.

"He's a real incisive neuropathologist—he'll look you over. Lie down and wait for me to come back."

Alyosha left.

Olya quickly got up, dressed, combed her hair, had a drink of water, found some money, and left the apartment. Her head was spinning, but still thinking clearly and quickly. Olya was aware of the weakness in her body but at the same time was experiencing the tender satisfaction of feeling a lot younger.

She hailed a taxi on Korolyov Prospect.

"Myasnitskaya Street."

She remembered that Horse Soup had once stopped the car there and run into his office for something.

Getting out of the car on Myasnitskaya, she was quick to find the recently remodeled grayish-pink building with a metal plaque polished until it looked like a mirror. On the plaque was engraved

PRAGMAS
Joint-Stock Company

She went through the door.

In the large, bright entryway, a security guard in a black uniform loomed and a young female porter was seated.

"Hello, who are you here to see?" she asked with a smile.

"I'm here to see your . . . boss," Olya said, then realized that she'd forgotten Horse Soup's last name, remembering only his first—Boris.

"We have two of those." The receptionist smiled. "Do you want to see the director or the chairman?"

"I'm here for Boris—" Olya began.

"Boris Ilyich?" the receptionist interrupted her. "Does he know you're here?"

"No. It's . . . a personal matter."

"You're lucky he's in. Who shall I say is here to see him?"

"Olya Slavina," Olya said, not realizing that she'd never told Horse Soup her last name.

"OK." The girl picked up the phone. "Marina Vasilievna, I have a visitor here for Boris Ilyich on a personal matter. Her name's Olya Slavina . . . Yes, Slavina."

The girl waited for a minute, nodding politely at Olya, then put down the phone.

"You can go up now. Second floor. Last office on your right."

Olya climbed the marble staircase with no trouble, but, in the hallway, her head began to spin and she had to lean against the wall for support.

Please don't kick me out, Horse Soup . . .

Coming back to her senses, she made her way to Burmistrov's waiting room.

"Head on in—Boris Ilyich is waiting for you," said his secretary, opening the door.

Holding her breath, Olya walked into the office. Burmistrov was sitting at his desk and talking on the phone. Taking a quick look at Olya, he raised his index finger and began to stand up from his chair as he finished his conversation.

"I'm telling you for the third time—they don't need gas masks, they only need the metal part and the filters, do you understand? What? Well, tell him to wear those masks on his dick! What? What??? Vitya! Were you born yesterday or somethin'? Just get twenty suckers, put 'em on the barge, and they'll disassemble it in a day! Throw the masks over the side. End of conversation. Goodbye."

He slammed down the phone.

Olya was standing at the center of his office.

Burmistrov circumnavigated his desk with a frown, went over to Olya, and stared at her silently for a long time.

Olya's lips and knees were shaking.

"So, were you trying to cash in your chips?" he asked her good-naturedly, then slapped her across the face.

Completely exhausted, Olya fell to the floor.

"How many days has it been since you last ate?"

"Four...five..." she mumbled.

"Idiot..." He picked up the phone and dialed a number. "Polina Andreyevna? Hello. I need you today. Yes. Please get there as fast as you can, start cooking right now. We'll see you in ... how much time do you need? Let's say an hour. Yes. Thank you."

Still on the floor, Olya sat up.

"Sit over there." Burmistrov nodded at two armchairs around a coffee table.

She stood up, walked over, sat down.

Burmistrov sat on the edge of his desk and folded his arms across his chest. "Where were you?"

"I was traveling with my husband."

"You got married?"

"Yes."

"What was the last thing you ate?"

"I...don't remember...lobster."

"Tasty...You fuckin' idiot. You wanna die?"

"No," Olya whispered, leaning back into the armchair exhaustedly. Sweet tears began to flow down her face.

"A pig, a total pig..." Burmistrov shook his head.

A smug brunette in a white jacket walked in without knocking. "It's coming up roses, Boris!"

"What the hell?" Boris grunted with a scowl.

"They're taking thirty in cash and eighteen bonds. And the Ukrainian piece of shit is still gonna get twenty to twenty-five from those fuckheads."

"What about Larin?"

"What do we need Larin for? He got his piece of the pie—that's how it goes."

"But he's their underwriter now."

"What's he gotta dick around like that for?" the man replied with a big smile, then squinted over at Olya. "There's no reason for it. Get Malakov to knock out a new contract. We'll get the wholesalers to sign today—why wait?"

Burmistrov bit his lip, looking down at the parquetry. "You know what . . . here. I'll go have a chat with the old man myself. In the meantime, you get Zhenka started, got it?"

"Got it." The man left.

Burmistrov dialed a number on the phone and began to speak in a mix of Russian and Ukrainian: "Oles', hello again! We gotta talk terms. They just put a good offer in front of me. Yes. Yes, just now . . . Almost . . . No, those are Vitya's wholesalers. Yes. Yes. Listen, let's meet by the pipe? Yep. Fantastic! Ok, I'm leaving now."

He walked out of the office.

The door had barely shut behind him when another fit of sweet tears came over Olya. She wept silently, resting her head against the soft, chill leather of the armchair. Her successful reunion with Horse Soup filled her body, heretofore so tormented by fear and hunger, with the sweet oil of tenderness. She was no longer afraid to spill this oil.

"This is na . . . This is na . . ." she repeated over and over, like a baby, smiling through her tears.

Burmistrov returned an hour later—cheerful and satisfied.

"Let's go!"

Her face puffy from crying, Olya stood up.

"Were you crying?" He glanced at her eyes.

She nodded.

"How wonderful!" He grinned and opened the door.

Downstairs, a big black SUV was waiting for them with both a chauffeur and a security guard inside. Olya and Burmistrov sat down in the back seat. The SUV turned onto the Garden Ring and sped up.

We're headed toward Kursk Station again, she realized.

The Stalin-era building (with the highest arch in Moscow) where she'd been eating invisible food for the last six months was located on Kursk. She also knew that Sakharov, the famous academician, had lived in that building not long ago.

Burmistrov looked out through his tinted window. His smoothly shaven head, his unhandsome face, his turbid eyes, his fiddly hands— all of this was deeply familiar to her.

Olya suddenly realized that she was truly happy.

Thank God he forgave me. She took a deep breath. *What if he hadn't? What would I do then? May pedestrians stumble awkwardly through horror.* She improvised this last line on the theme of the Russian birthday song.

"Oh yeah . . ." Burmistrov suddenly remembered something, took out his cell phone, and started to dial a number.

The driver made a sharp turn to overtake another car, and Burmistrov's cell phone flew out of his hand and onto the floor.

"Forgive me, Boris Ilyich," the driver mumbled.

"I'll fuckin' fire you, Vasya!" Burmistrov looked down at his feet with a broad grin.

"I'll get it." Olya bent down happily.

This was the first time that Olya had ever seen a cell phone up close, which added ever so slightly to her general feeling of happiness. Looking under the seat, she immediately saw it. The cell phone had an illuminated keypad, like an as-of-yet-undiscovered nocturnal insect from a faraway tropical land, and was lying near Burmistrov's beautiful shoes. Olya moved over to the phone and touched Horse Soup's thin, bony ankle with quiet delight:

Strong and *intelligent*, she thought.

Suddenly, there was a sound like the car had driven into a dead tree whose dead branches then pitter-pattered over the roof.

"'Fuck!" the driver said loudly.

The SUV swerved violently. Olya sprawled forward, right next to Burmistrov's shoes.

And the dry branches pitter-pattered over the car once more. And the glass crumbled delicately.

The car swerved again, then came to a shrieking halt, then started to move again very slowly. Burmistrov's beautiful shoes kicked at Olya violently.

What's he doing? she asked herself and started to get up.

The car was going very slowly.

Olya raised her head and looked around.

Ten narrow rays of sunshine pierced the car's murky light. Dust gathered in the rays. Olya looked around, not immediately realizing that the sun was shining through ten neat little holes.

Burmistrov's monstrously deformed face was swollen with bubbles of blood, his hands were trembling very slightly, and his legs twitched like a doll's. The driver had five tiny holes in his neck and shoulders and had fallen onto the steering wheel, his body still shuddering. The security guard leaned against the window, one cheek gone.

Olya watched.

The car continued crawling forward for a little while, hit a scaffold, then came to a halt.

Burmistrov's legs went still.

Absolute silence reigned inside the car.

But something was moving.

Olya looked over.

Bits of Burmistrov's brain were sliding down the tinted window.

Olya felt for the door handle, squeezed it, jerked the door open, and tumbled out of the SUV.

So flat . . . She pressed her cheek to the calm, dusty asphalt.

And suddenly all around her, cars were braking, doors were slamming, and legs, legs, legs were running.

Flat, but not familiar . . . Olya got up on all fours, began to stand, then, surprising herself, sprinted off, still hunched over and covering her mouth with her hand.

She ran down a lane on half-bent legs and remembered how, during her junior year, she and Lena Kopteyeva had once raced from the barberry bushes to the gate and back and how Lenka had growled when she fell behind.

Tatyana Doronina . . . Olya saw a full-figured woman who was carrying tightly wrapped rolls of wallpaper.

The woman looked Olya over with her gloomy gaze.

"What's the number for the police?" asked Olya and stopped running.

She was clutching the cell phone in her left hand and holding the purse hanging from her shoulder with her right.

"0-2?" she asked, already beginning to dial it on the phone.

But the phone could only buzz or stay silent.

What now? Olya looked at a grayish-white cat sitting in a window. The cat licked at its paw.

"Let's go, let's go, let's go..." Putting the phone in her purse, she began to stride quickly down the lane, making it to Chistoprudny Boulevard in a few minutes.

I need something to drink. She saw a street vendor, walked over, bought a plastic bottle of Coca-Cola, and began to twist off the red cap as she walked. Pink foam rose up from under the cap. Olya stopped to look at the foam and felt the fatal heaviness that had been slumbering inside her for the last few days begin to rise up from her stomach and into her esophagus like mercury. Olya vomited bile. Dropping the bottle, she made her way to a bench and sat down.

"He's dead," she said and the whole world shrank.

Very suddenly, everything in the world was visible to her. Everything was heavy and everything was dead. And no one in this pitch-black, leaden world could help her. To whom could she turn? In a daze, she went through her friends and relatives, doctors and pets, businessmen and street magicians: but none of them—not one of them—had any *food*. Nobody on earth could feed Olya. Not even God? Olya didn't believe in God and had never understood religious people.

She suddenly remembered the apartment where Horse Soup would feed her invisible food.

"There's food there!" Olya whispered in a hoarse voice. "There— of course! There and only there!"

She stood up, walked to the metro, and hailed a taxi, then in a daze, she was driven to the building with the highest arch in Moscow. She went up in the elevator, found the apartment, and rang the doorbell. A short, elderly woman with a calm, sweet face opened the door.

"Hello! Everything's been ready for a long time."

The woman's name was Polina Andreyevna; she helped Burmistrov by cooking the food but always left before the process began. Olya entered the spacious foyer.

"And where's Boris Ilyich?" Polina Andreyevna walked into the kitchen.

"He's...currently..." Olya glanced into the dining room.

There stood the old familiar table set for one.

"I've been waiting! Waiting!" Polina Andreyevna said loudly from the kitchen. "I thought he'd canceled! But then he would've called, right?!"

Olya passed into the kitchen. A dry void was ringing out inside her head. Her heart beat hungrily and heavily. Polina Andreyevna put something away in the refrigerator, shut it, then noticed Olya in the threshold. "Huh?"

Olya walked in silently, moving her eyes hungrily from side to side.

"You lookin' for something?" asked Polina Andreyevna.

"Where's the food?"

"What food?"

"My food."

Polina Andreyevna looked at her with an uncomprehending smile. "Uhhh...we've only got apples and kefir in the fridge. Shall I wash an apple for you?"

Olya looked at her fixedly. Polina Andreyevna went quiet and stopped smiling.

Olya noticed something with a towel over it on the kitchen table. She removed the towel. Under it was the porcelain dish from which Horse Soup served invisible food. But on this dish was only void.

Olya looked in the refrigerator. She saw apples, a lemon, two packets of margarine, and an open bottle of kefir. In the freezer was only ice.

Olya began to open cupboards and rifle through drawers.

But her food was nowhere to be found.

Horror took possession of Olya. Her face turned green and she froze in the middle of the kitchen.

Polina Andreyevna moved cautiously to the corner.

Olya looked at the electric stove. On the stove were stacked three empty pots and, next to them, a frying pan. In the frying pan lay an unopened can with no label.

Olya picked up the can. It was heavy, slightly larger than an average can.

Olya's heart beat heavily and a gruff, inarticulate moan escaped from her lips. Her whole body now shivering, Olya began to search for a can opener. But she couldn't find one anywhere. Then, putting the can on the table, she pulled out the largest knife from the wooden knife block. It was as heavy as a hammer and as sharp as a razor. Olya picked it up with both of her hands wrapped around its comfortable black handle. Trying to suppress her trembling, she drew back and plunged the knife into the can.

The heavy blade sliced through the tin like paper.

"You didn't know!" Olya grinned wickedly, staring back at Polina Andreyevna, who'd been struck dumb, and pressing down on the knife.

She'd never before opened a can this way. Jerking the knife a couple of times and jaggedly cutting the tin, Olya trembled and stamped her foot with impatience. She pushed the knife in the other direction in an attempt to make a bigger hole. She was using her left hand to clutch the edge of the can, but it slipped and collided with the knife. Blood dripped onto the table and the can. Olya paid no attention to the blood, looking instead at the monstrous, slowly expanding slit she'd made—like the Tin Man's mouth.

"Trying to hide it . . . bitch . . ."

The tin lips slowly parted.

The Tin Man's mouth was filled with liquid shit.

Olya's hair stood on end: the can was filled with eggplant spread.

"No!" She laughed and turned to Polina Andreyevna. "No, this . . . no . . ."

Polina Andreyevna watched her with quiet horror.

Olya exhaled, noticed how bloody her hand was, took another dish towel, on which a hedgehog was carrying a mushroom, off its hook, wrapped it around her hand, then left the apartment.

She descended the chill staircase.

The cell phone rang delicately in her purse. Olya took it out, looked at it, pressed the red button with a picture of a telephone on it, and pressed it to her ear.

"Borya?" someone said through the phone.

Parting her dry lips, Olya made an indefinable guttural sound.

"OK, so I got sixteen guys and they estimated, well, they guessed that they'd disassemble it within the day. But here's why I'm callin': we threw the masks into the water and they won't fucking sink! You see the problem, six thousand masks . . . This could be bad, it's the Moscow River, the water cops could come and, well . . . I can't even get the car to the docks 'cause of these huge mountains of trash! Bor, you gotta just get in touch with Samsonov so that he can drive a couple of those shit-suckers out to us, we'll throw the masks to the bank of the river, and the shit-suckers'll, well, suck 'em up with their pipes, right out of the water, and then—" . . ."

Olya dropped the phone down the building's garbage chute.

Outside, the sun had gone behind the clouds and the occasional drop of drizzle was falling.

Olya wandered aimlessly, squeezing her left hand with her right. The dead world flowed around Olya and parted heavily and indifferently before her. She made it to Paveletskaya station, saw the tram tracks spattered with rain beneath her feet, and froze.

It was pleasant to look at the steel bars of the tram tracks. They calmed her. They were calming her. They flowed, flowed, and flowed. They were cold and heavy. They were in no rush. They moved properly and steadily, one always parallel to the next. They were like a ski run laid down by good, kind people, who were honest and reliable, brave and attentive, who knew how to have a good laugh, knew many—oh so many!—proper and heroic tales, they knew many formulas regarding both physics and chemistry, they knew many—oh so many!—wonderful songs to play on the guitar, songs about geologists and mountain climbers, about beautiful and inaccessible alpine peaks, peaks covered in snow, white snow, sparkling snow, snow that never melts, cold snow, kind snow, eternal snow.

Olya walked along the tram tracks toward the center of the city.

Her legs moved of their own accord, taking her deeper and deeper into the rain-washed metropolis.

The rain ceased and the timid sun peeked out from behind the clouds.

Olya slowly made her way to Novy Arbat Avenue, bought ice cream, looked at it, threw it in the trash, turned, walked past the Shchukin Institute, then turned down a lane.

Suddenly, something blankly familiar drew her gaze. On this lane bristled a café, recently built from red brick. And behind the window was sitting the very man in the white blazer Olya had seen in Burmistrov's office.

She stopped.

Two other men were sitting at the table with White Jacket: a tall, broad-shouldered blond and a skinny guy with close-set eyes. Olya recognized the second man right away: Simferopol–Moscow, the vestibule, Burmistrov on his knees, the picture lying at Olya's feet. A tattoo on his wrist.

"IRA . . ." Olya pronounced.

The three of them were eating and conversing.

Olya walked into the café. Pouring a beer, the bartender looked at her indifferently.

The café was filled with cigarette smoke and unbeautiful people. But there were some open spots. The table where White Jacket, the blondie, and IRA were sitting was right in the corner. Olya sat at an uncleared table nearby, her back turned to them.

IRA stood up and left.

White Jacket finished his beer and lit up. The blondie was chewing.

"With the first one, everything's cool, so don't resend anything. Got it? But you should resend the second one, the white one."

"Yeah, I get that, but why the fuck—"

"Stop wasting time, we don't have much of it."

"Right when they get it, then, it'll get done."

"That's right, motherfucker."

They fell silent. Soon, IRA was back, wiping his wet hands with a napkin.

"I always take a dump after I do *business*."

"That's just fuckin' natural law." The blondie chewed. "I took a shit this morning."

"Hey, didn't he have a dacha too?" IRA took a sip of beer.

"Yeah. In Malakhovka," White Jacket replied. "But I don't re-member the address. And anyways it wasn't that . . . I guess it was all right. The shack wasn't great, but it was on a good plot of land."

"Find the address."

"It's ain't anywhere."

"OK, let's do a little boozin', then."

The carafe made a glugging sound as the vodka was poured.

"Here's to Boris the Sucker havin' somethin' to drink and someone to fuck on the other side!"

"Mm-hmm . . ."

"Cheers."

They drank and chased it with food.

Olya looked at the dirty, sauce-covered butter knife next to her hand. Touched its rounded end. Then opened her purse, rummaged through it, pulled out a pair of nail clippers, stood up, walked over to White Jacket, who was still chewing, and, with all her remaining strength, jammed the clippers into his neck.

"Aii?" cried the man, as if he'd been stung by a bee, then grabbed the clippers buried in his neck with both hands.

The blondie leapt up like lightning, knocking down his chair in the process, jumped over to Olya, brought his hands to his chest like a kangaroo, and easily, but with terrifying force, kicked her in her left side. Never in her life had Olya been dealt a blow like this. She flew back, hit the wall, and slid down to the floor. IRA stood up, a pistol suddenly in his hand.

"Ai! Aiii! Aiiiiiii!!!" White Jacket cried out, getting up from the table.

Everyone in the café had fallen silent, staring dumbly at the events unfolding.

Olya didn't lose consciousness from the brutal kick but found herself unable to breathe. Her heart fluttered somehow mortally.

Leaning back against the wall, she palpated the left side of her torso. She felt the depression where her ribs had cracked; this was so terribly out of the ordinary. Trembling and hiccuping, Olya attempted to pull in even a drOp even a drOp even a drOOOOOOOOOOOp of air, but the air wouldn't come in-in-into her mouth and it was like an abortion

        like an abortion

                like anesTHESIA

       like anesTHESIA

       and a drO

            drO

                drO

                    drO

they're pink they're red
they're burning and pEEErfect
MOMMY
anesTHESIA already?
yes

       yes

           yes

               yes

                  yes

"HAS SLAVINA BEEN ANESTHETIZED?"
"gramma, will my boobs grow?"
"HAS SLAVINA BEEN ANESTHETIZED?"
"sweetbootssweetboots."
"HAS SLAVINA BEEN ANESTHETIZED?"
"the little hedgehog carries the mushroom."
"HAS SLAVINA BEEN ANESTHETIZED?"
"don't fuckin' pull it, it'll knock out the glue!"
"HAS SLAVINA BEEN ANESTHETIZED?"
"Olya, what's up with your sonatina?"
"HAS SLAVINA BEEN ANESTHETIZED?"
"the bitch was with him!"
"HAS SLAVINA BEEN ANESTHETIZED?"

"but Rudik showed Anka some stupid things!"
"HAS SLAVINA BEEN ANESTHETIZED?"
"should we bathe Olenka on the terrace, Nadya?"
"HAS SLAVINA BEEN ANESTHETIZED?"
"to the wall, assholes!"
"HAS SLAVINA BEEN ANESTHETIZED?"
"doll-ballerina-dreamer-gossip"
"HAS SLAVINA BEEN ANESTHETIZED?"
"Natashka's cat gave birth to five kittens."
"HAS SLAVINA BEEN ANESTHETIZED?"
"quietquietquietquietquietquiet."
"HAS SLAVINA BEEN ANESTHETIZED?"
"give back the jump rope, Ol!"
"HAS SLAVINA BEEN ANESTHETIZED?"
"i won't do it anymore, Mommy."
"HAS SLAVINA BEEN ANESTHETIZED?"
"i won't anymore, Mommy."
"HAS SLAVINA BEEN ANESTHETIZED?"
"i won't, Mommy."

The blondie held up White Blazer, who was moaning because of the clippers sticking out of his neck. The bartender put a napkin to his busted lip. Two men in athletic clothing were chewing something or another, standing by the wall with their hands in the air. A beer bottle rolled across the floor. IRA shifted the pistol to his left hand and pulled a three-fluted awl out of its leather sheath. Walked over to Olya. Kneeled down precipitously. The awl entered Olya's heart.

But she couldn't feel anything anymore.

THE BLACK HORSE WITH THE WHITE EYE

2004

IT WASN'T just that all of them mowed in different ways, they each also got ready for the mowing and rested between passes after their own fashion.

After three consecutive rows of mowing, Grandpa Yakov would pronounce, "Sabbath!," exhale noisily, fall to one knee, grab a bunch of cut grass with his swarthy, crab-claw hand, wipe his scythe with it, take a touchstone out of the little leather sheath strapped to his belt, and begin to quickly sharpen the blade of the scythe, muttering something into his wispy red beard as he did. His oldest son Filya— or Khvilya,* as everyone called him—was always silent and half asleep, with the same red beard and short, strong arms his father had; he'd lay his scythe down on the grass, walk over to the edge of the field, where Mother and Dasha were sitting beneath an oak tree, take a couple gulps from a linden-wood demijohn, wipe his face off with his sleeve, squat down, and just stay there, looking off to the sides and squinting. His middle son, Grisha, who resembled his mother in terms of his face, angularity, and thinness, would repeat after his father, "If it's time for the Sabbath, then it's time for the Sabbath!" then take his scythe and, breathing heavily, wander over to the half-dried-up linden tree split in twain by lightning that stuck up in the middle of the meadow, where he'd sit down and slowly sharpen his scythe. The youngest, Vanya, who wasn't even fifteen yet, a thin,

*In Ukrainian, *khvilya* means "wave."

sharp-shouldered, big-eared, freckled boy who mowed with a small scythe that had been adjusted to his height and always lagged far behind the other mowers, would take his scythe and follow after his middle brother, then lie down on his stomach beneath the linden tree, prop up his sharp chin with his rough fists, and wait for Grisha to finish with his own scythe at which point he'd sharpen his little brother's little scythe.

Dasha sat beneath the little oak, her back leaning against it, looked at the mowers, at the meadow, the forest, the bugs, the bumblebees, the butterflies, and the lonely buzzard, occasionally sliding through the blue heights above the meadow and the forest. Dasha liked the fact that the motley buzzard would fly in such even circles, then, most unexpectedly, begin to hover in the air in one spot, quickly flapping its wings and squealing plaintively, like a spring chicken, before finally—and with equal unexpectedness—plunging downwards. Her mother would sit next to her, leaning against the other side of the oak tree and knitting a sock from gray goat fleece. She would occasionally get up and rake at the cut grass, which still hadn't become hay. Then Dasha would pick up her walnut cane, at the end of which was a slingshot, and help her mother rake.

The Panins' meadow was real fine: even, smooth, close to the village and to the turnpike. It'd been signed over to them back in '35 thanks to the old chairman, Mother's brother-in-law.

This was the first day the Panins were mowing—the entire village had already been mowing, raking, and ricking on the meadows of the collective farm—on the right side of the Bolva—for half a month. They'd gotten lucky with the weather—it was a hot, dry-winded June; as Grandpa Yakov would say, "So much durn hay, slides onto the porch with no delay."

Yesterday Dasha had turned ten. Grandpa had woven her new bast shoes, her father had given her a clay whistle, and her mother had given her a white handkerchief with red hemming. Dasha was content. She tucked the handkerchief into her grandma's bosom, then walked over to the mowing in the spacious, woven bast shoes she still had room to grow into, bringing the clay whistle with her. Each time her father came over to the oak tree to squat down and take a drink, Dasha would take the whistle from the pocket on the bodice of her chintz dress, sewn in Zheltoukhi by a visiting tailor, and whistle with it. Her father would gaze at her approvingly and scratch his beard, smiling with his eyes. He was a silent man.

Mother wasn't too talkative either. Among the Panins, only Grandpa Yakov had a jaunty tongue.

"What're ye walkin' all quiet for, Dashukha?" he asked her on the way to the mowing. "The shoes ain't let ye walk or somethin'? Do they reach up to yer behind?"

Everyone laughed, then Dasha grabbed Grandpa by his crooked, work-darkened finger with its thick black nail and ran alongside him, shuffling her new bast shoes across the dusty ground of the turnpike.

Once the mowers had mowed a third of the meadow and the sun had risen over their heads, baking them up real nice, Grandpa Yakov waved. "Lunchtime!"

Having thrown down their scythes, the mowers stretched out beneath the oaks. While they were drinking thirstily, passing the demijohn from person to person, Mother and Dasha spread out a piece of ragged canvas and began to take the chow they'd packed out of a wicker basket: half a loaf of rye bread, a heap of green onions, a dozen baked potatoes, a clay pot of baked milk, a little piece of lard wrapped in a rag, and salt in a paper cone.

"Oh Lord, bless this repast." Grandpa Yakov sighed exhaustedly, picked up the bread, pressed it to his chest, and cut it dexterously into slices using a big ole knife with a darkened, worn-out wooden handle.

The brothers each took a slice and immediately began to eat.

Grandpa Yakov crossed himself, dipped a piece of bread into the salt, took a bite, grabbed a long green onion, crumpled it up, put it in his mouth, and began to chew quickly, oh so quickly, which made his wispy beard move in a funny way. Dasha liked to watch Grandpa while he was eating. It seemed to her that Grandpa Yakov suddenly turned into a comical hare when he ate. The brothers ate somehow seriously, as if they were working, becoming dull and gloomy. Furthermore, the youngest immediately seemed to become more mature as he ate, taking on an aspect that was every bit as manly as Grisha's and his father's.

Mother cut the lard into eight bits and gave them out to the men. The lard was old and yellow; the hog had perished last summer from an uncomprehended illness and they'd only acquired a new piglet in the spring. But they had Docha, a cow. And she gave good milk.

Mother put the pot of baked milk in the middle of the canvas, handed out wooden spoons, used her own to pierce the dark-brown skin that had formed in the pot's throat, and stirred. "Eat up, y'all..."

The flesh-colored milk was mixed with the thick white sour cream that had accumulated on top of it. Having quickly swallowed the lard, the men slid their spoons into the pot. Dasha and Mother waited for the men to scoop out their shares of baked milk, then they slid their own spoons into the pot.

The milk was cool and delicious. Dasha scooped it up, slurping at it noisily and chasing it with bread. What she liked more than anything else about the baked milk were the yellow crumbs of butter in it. At home, they would churn butter only around Easter, when Grandma would bake buckwheat blini. The butter smelled so good and melted immediately onto the blini. There was never very much of it.

Mother was eating in her usual way—unhurriedly, carrying the spoon of milk over her palm, swallowing quietly, submissively bowing her lil' head, bound round with a discolored pale-blue kerchief, off to the side.

The men ate the milk, grunting loudly as they did.

"The dew dried up real durn quick today," Grisha muttered, wiping the milk from his chin. "To mow the dry grass...that's what ye want..."

"It's real hot out, course it's dry." Khvilya broke apart a baked potato, dipped it in salt, and took a bite.

"Ain't bad. We'll get it all down by evenin'." Grandpa Yakov slurped hastily at the milk. "We ain't goan break our ribs, but we'll do it real steady 'n' real calm. And it'll get done."

"Long's it all dries." Mother scooped out a big spoonful of sour cream and handed it to Dasha. "Here ye go—ye get the top..."

Dasha licked her spoon and put it down on the canvas. Then took the spoon absolutely filled with sour cream from the top of the baked milk from Mother with both hands. Thick and white, it barely fit on the new wooden spoon, trying its best to climb over its edge. Dasha cautiously brought the spoon to her mouth. The sour cream swayed, then settled. Its surface was ridged. A ray of midday sun beat through the foliage of the oak tree, fell onto the semicircular white surface of the sour cream, and radiated outward. Tiny crumbs of butter flickered within the sour cream. Dasha opened her mouth. Then, suddenly, something dark appeared in this most tender, radiant whiteness. Dasha looked around.

A black horse was standing right nearby.

Dasha shuddered. The sour cream tore itself from the spoon and flopped down onto her dress. Then everyone saw the horse.

"Ach, what the hay!" Grandpa Yakov jerked in surprise and furrowed his brow.

The horse shied away from the people sitting beneath the oaks, walked away, and stood somewhere off in the distance, whipping itself with its tangled black tail. It was of a deep raven shade, squat, broad-chested, big-boned, as peasant horses tend to be, with a big head, small ears, and a thick, shaggy, long-uncropped mane. There were burdocks woven densely into that mane. Horseflies clambered over the horse's glossy back.

"Oh, dear Mama . . ." Mother sighed, crossed herself, then placed her hand upon her smallish bosom. "How ye put the fear into us . . ."

"Whose mare is that?" Grisha started to stand up.

"Sure ain't ours." Grandpa Yakov put down his spoon. "We ain't never had no raven-coloreduns."

Grisha set off for the horse, pulling the belt from his trousers as he walked. Standing perpendicular to him, the horse turned its snout toward the approaching man, cantered down, and flared its nostrils. And everyone immediately noticed that its left eye was entirely white.

"Take a gander, she's totally blind in one eye!" Grisha grinned as he approached. "Hey there, don't be afeard . . . don't be afeard . . ."

The horse reared off to the side. And presented its left flank.

"Approach from the left, Grish, where she got that blind eye," Grandpa Yakov advised. "She musta got loose from Bytosha, the lil' tramp."

"No way, Pop, she got loose from the Gypsies." Khvilya looked gloomily at the horse as he pushed up from the ground. "They got a camp set up in Zheltoukhi again. She got loose from them. And look how shaggy she is . . ."

Grisha carefully approached the horse, made a ring from the belt, and held it behind his back. But the horse reared away from him again.

"Ach, ye viper . . ." Grisha chuckled.

"Hold on, Grishan." Khvilya broke off a bit of bread and walked over to the horse. "Hey there, shaggyun, take this . . ."

Together, they began to cautiously approach the horse from both sides—like hunters. It froze, snorted, and perked up its small ears. Grisha and Khvilya began to move very slowly, as if in a dream. And, for whatever reason, all of this began to make Dasha *most* unquiet. Her heart set to beating very hard. Holding her breath, she watched how insidiously the people approached the horse: her father with a piece of bread in his hand and Uncle Grisha with a looped belt behind his back.

"Don't be afeard . . . don't be afeard . . ." Grisha muttered.

Coming right up to the horse, the muzhiks stopped. Khvilya held out the bread almost to the horse's very snout. Grisha went tense and bit his lip. The paralyzed horse snorted and rushed between them. The muzhiks rushed at it and grabbed its mane. Dasha closed her eyes. The horse whinnied.

Please let them stop doing that! Dasha suddenly prayed without opening her eyes.

She heard the horse's whinnying and the men's swearing.

Then the whinnying stopped.

"Ach, ye motherlover . . ." her father pronounced furiously.

"Wild bitch . . ." Grisha pronounced.

Dasha realized that they hadn't caught the horse. And opened her eyes.

Her father and Grisha were standing in the meadow. There was no horse.

"Ach, ye cretins!" Grandpa Yakov waved his hand at them furiously. "Y'all cain't even catch a mare!"

"She's a wild one, Pop." Grisha began to put the belt back into his trousers, which had begun to fall down.

"The slut's runnin' through the forest." Her father picked up the bread he'd dropped, walked over, and put it down on the canvas.

"If she's blind and wild too, what's the point in catchin' her?" Mother muttered and began to collect the sour cream from the hem of Dasha's skirt with a spoon.

Dasha's knees were trembling.

"What's with ye? Ye get afeard?" Mother smiled.

Dasha shook her head. She was *very* happy that they hadn't caught the mare. Mother once more held the spoon of sour cream out to her. Dasha took it and eagerly swallowed the thick, cold sour cream. The muzhiks who'd leapt up sat down once more, picked up their spoons, and set to gobbling down what remained of the baked milk. The appearance and disappearance of the wild mare had aroused them. They began to speak about horses, about the Gypsies that pilfered them, about the rascal of a new chairman, about the collapsed roof of the collective farm stables, about buckwheat, about the clover on the other side, about the nighttime fellings in the glades near Mokroye, about the Mokroye carpenters, then suddenly began to argue about where it'd be better to split shingles from a stolen fir—in their own barn or in Kostya's bathhouse.

Dasha wasn't listening to them. After the horse had run off, she'd begun to feel light and good.

"What're ye just sittin' there for, Dash?" Mother straightened her out-of-place kerchief. "Hurry on 'n' gather some berries."

Dasha stood up reluctantly, took the empty basket, slung it over her shoulder, then set off for the far edge of the meadow.

"Don't go far." Her father was licking his spoon.

First, Dasha walked through the mown stubble, her new bast shoes rustling loudly, then through the standing grass, frightening off the chirring grasshoppers. The grass had grown hot in the sun and it was hot on her feet. Dasha walked through the entire meadow, looked around. The men had gotten back up to mow. Dasha pulled her whistle out of her pocket and whistled loudly. Mother waved at her. The birds in the forest surrounding the meadow responded to the whistle. Dasha whistled again. She heard the birdcalls. Whistled. Put away the whistle and entered the sparse forest at the narrow end of the meadow. Here stood a young birch forest teaming with with wild strawberries. Dasha began to walk beneath the birch trees, removed the hard birch basket from her shoulder, put it down in the grass, then began to pick berries and lay them in the basket. There were many strawberries and nobody had picked any yet. Dasha picked berries both ripe and not, tossed them into the basket, eating the ones that were a bit bigger than the others. The strawberries were sweet. Having gathered all of the berries in one glade, Dasha carried her basket into another. Suddenly, some kind of bird fluttered up from beneath her feet, fluttered its wings, flew away, then landed on a birch. Dasha pulled out her whistle and blew into it. The bird called back with a thin, discontinuous squeak, precisely like the whistle's. Dasha was surprised. And she whistled again. The bird called back. Dasha walked over to the bird. The bird took wing, flew off, and landed somewhere else. Dasha had time to notice that the bird was motley, just like a buzzard, only much smaller. Dasha whistled. The bird called back. Grandpa Yakov had told Dasha that birds spoke in their own language and that only holy people and fowlers could understand this language.

"The whistle speaks birdish!" Dasha whispered.

She wanted to ask the bird about life in the forest and about the treasures that, according to her grandma, were guarded by hunchbacked forest goblins. She walked toward the bird through the birch forest, blowing the whistle as she did. The bird called back. But, after allowing Dasha to come closer than it had before, it took wing and flew off once more, its wings flapping. Past the birch forest began a thick, old fir forest. The bird had flown there.

"Where'd ye go, ye stinker?" Dasha cried out in the same way that grown-ups yelled at naughty cattle.

She thought that the bird had flown to her nest, as chickens do. And such birds' nests are always set up in secluded places so's no one would bother them. Therefore, here, in the dark fir forest, would be a good place for this bird's nest. There, the bird would land, calm down, and tell Dasha all about hidden treasures, showing the way to secret places. Then she and Pop would set to with a spade, yep, and dig 'em up. And buy a horse. And ride to Lyudinovo on it. And buy up all sorts of good stuff there.

Dasha walked out of the birch forest, made her way between two huge, bushy hazelnut trees with warm, soft leaves, stepped over a rotten tree grown over with moss and shriveled toadstools, then lifted her gaze.

The gloomy wall of a fir grove stood before her. Dasha entered it. Tall firs loomed over her. And the sun hid itself away. The bast shoes suddenly began to step softer. It was cool and very quiet in the grove. Dasha whistled. In the depths of the forest, she heard the faint squeak of the bird calling back.

"Ooh, you rascal!" Dasha muttered and followed the bird's call.

She was walking across the soft soil studded with needles and cones, between the trunks of firs. It grew even duskier and quieter around her. Dasha stopped; the trunks of the firs were crowded together in front of her in the semidarkness. It seemed as if night itself lay before her. And she could enter into it. She grew afraid. Dasha glanced back and could still see the sun-drenched birch grove. There, in the meadow, her father and mother were waiting. But she had to find the bird. Dasha whistled. The forest was silent. She whistled again. The bird called back ahead of her. And Dasha strode forwards, into the night, toward the bird's voice. Stepped across the soft earth, hunched over and palpating the rough tree trunks, circumnavigating stumps, tearing through cobwebs, and stepping over dry branches. Then suddenly came into a perfectly regular alley of trees. Thick fir trees stood before her in two rows, as if someone had planted them a long, long time ago. The fir trees were enormous, old, and close to death. Their trunks—eaten out by beetles—were spotted with gapingly dark hollows and divergent fissures full of hardened resin.

Dasha entered this alley. It was completely dark up ahead. It reeked of decay. Dasha whistled. The bird called back. Dasha set off through the alley. The dusk thickened; powerful fir branches were intertwined above her head, hiding both sky and sun. Something small and white appeared up ahead.

The bird! Dasha first thought, before remembering that the bird was motley.

The little spot of white was hanging in the middle of the alley.

Dasha walked closer to the white. It hung there motionless. Then vanished. Then appeared again. Dasha got right up to it. The white vanished once more. Then appeared. Dasha watched attentively. And suddenly realized that the *little white* was the horse's white eye. It was blinking. Dasha took a closer look. And saw the whole black horse. The very one. The horse was standing in the dark alley. It was barely discernable in the semidarkness. It was as if its black body had merged with the gloomy air, which smelled of resin and needles.

Dasha stood there, frozen.

She wasn't remotely afraid. But she didn't know what to do.

The horse didn't move at all. It didn't chew at its lips or draw air through its nostrils.

Is it sleeping? Dasha asked herself and looked at the mare's *healthy* eye. Moist and dark-lilac like a plum, the eye was looking somewhere off to the side. Not at Dasha at all.

"Don't be afeared," Dasha pronounced.

The horse shuddered as if it had just awoken. Its nostrils filled with air.

"Don't be afeared," Dasha repeated.

The horse still stood there just as motionlessly. Dasha reached out her hand and put it on the horse's lips. They were warm and velvety.

"Don't be afeared ... don't be afeared ..." Dasha stroked the horse's lips, her fingers sticky with wild strawberry.

The horse slowly lowered its head. Sniffed at the coniferous earth. And froze with its head lowered. Continuing to stroke the mare's lips and nostrils, Dasha squatted down. The white eye was terribly close to her. Dasha stared at it. The eye wasn't entirely white. In its center darkened a small black pupil with a subtle bluish rim. Dasha brought her face closer to this uncommon eye. It blinked. The horse still stood just as motionlessly with its head bowed. Dasha examined the eye. It reminded her of the tube that their teacher Varvara Stepanovna had brought from Lyudinovo and showed them in class. The tube had a long, grown-up name that started with the letter *k*. Dasha couldn't remember the word and called the tube a "colander-scope," thinking "colander" started with a *k*. There was a little hole in the tube. You had to look into this hole and turn the other end of the tube toward the light. A beautiful flower was then visible in the tube. If you turned the "kolander-scope," the flower would transform into other flowers, and soon there were so many of them, and all of them were so beautiful and different, that it took your breath away and you could spend your whole life just twirling and twirling this tube.

Dasha gazed into the horse's eye.

She was certain that everything in the horse's eye was totally, totally white—like in winter. But there turned out to be nothing white in the white eye at all. On the contrary. Everything in the eye turned out to be red. And the eye was packed so full of red and it was somehow so big and so *deep*, like the whirlpool by the mill, and it was somehow very, very, very *thick* and *greedy*, and somehow just hovered there and oozed *threateningly*, rising and swelling like dough. Dasha remembered how they would chop the heads off cocks. And how their red throats would slosh.

Then, suddenly, she saw this Red Throat in the horse's eye very *clearly*. And there was *so much* of it.

And Dasha grew so afraid that she froze like an icicle.

The white eye blinked.

The horse exhaled. Snorted. Lifted its head, noisily sucking in gloomy air through its nostrils. Then, paying no attention to Dasha, set off into the depths of the forest.

Dasha squatted down, not even breathing. Then suddenly *realized* that she would never again see this black mare in her life. The mare had left Dasha's life as if it were nothing but a stable. It wandered off, still snorting. And soon disappeared among the trees.

Dasha sat down on the ground. Her hands fell onto the fir needles. And the fear immediately passed. Dasha felt somehow melancholy. She felt *terribly* tired. And very thirsty.

She stood up and set off into the clearing. Leaving the grove, she squinted in the bright sunlight. During this time, it had become even hotter. In the clearing in the birch forest, she found her basket, hung it over her shoulder, and set off into the meadow.

The muzhiks had already reached the middle of the meadow with their scythes. Mother was raking hay. Dasha walked over to her.

"Hey there—ye gather a lotta berries?" Having adjusted the kerchief that had slipped over her eyes, Mother looked into the basket and laughed. "That much?! Not bad!"

"I . . . saw into the horse's eye. There was a Red Throat in it," Dasha pronounced, then suddenly burst into tears.

"Ye wha'?" Mother took her into her arms and touched her forehead. "My girly got overheated . . ."

Mother carried Dasha under the oaks and splashed water on the weeping girl. Having cried her fill, Dasha drank some water and fell into a deep sleep. She woke up in her father's arms as he carried her home—to their village. The sun was setting, the cows coming home mooed, and the dogs barked.

At home, her grandma and her three-year-old brother Vovka were waiting for her. They sat down to their repast when it was already growing dark, lighting their meal with a kerosene lamp. Grandma took a pot of warm pottage out of the oven. They ate it in silence, accompanied by fresh-baked bread. Dasha gulped the pottage greedily, chewing the fresh and tasty bread as she did. Mother touched her forehead.

"It's passed . . ."

"Gramma's lil' girl got overheated!" Grandpa Yakov winked at Dasha.

"The sun got into her blood, clear as clear can be . . ." Her strong-bodied, big-mouthed grandmother nodded.

Having eaten their fill, everyone wandered off exhaustedly to sleep wherever they fell: Grandpa Yakov went to sleep in the garden, Grisha and Vanya—in the hayloft, Mother and little Vova—in the hut, and Grandma—on the stove. Yawning, Father began to extinguish the copper-faced, delicious-smelling kerosene lamp. But Dasha grabbed his trouser leg.

"What about the page, Pop?"

"The page . . ." Father remembered, grinning into his beard.

Every evening, Dasha tore off a page from the calendar, which hung on the wall next to the pendulum clock and the wood-framed photographs. Inside the frame were photographs of Father in a soldier's uniform, Mother and Father holding flowers, kissing doves painted all around them, Grandpa Yakov with a rifle during World War I, and Grandpa Yakov again with an old chairman at a fair in Bryansk, a KV tank, Stalin, Budyonny, and the actress Lyubov Orlova.

Father lifted up Dasha and she tore a page from the calendar.

"Well then, read me what's goan be tomorrow," Father said—as he always did.

"The twenty-second of June . . . Sun—Sunday . . ." Dasha read aloud.

Father put her back down on the ground. "Sunday. We're gonna mow again tomorrow . . . Sleep!" And he jokingly spanked Dasha on the behind.

MONOCLONE

2009

Monoclonius: A large, herbivorous dinosaur from the Jurassic period of the Mesozoic era. Walked on four legs. A large horn rose from its testaceous head, and a peltate collar wrapped round its neck.

VIKTOR Nikaolayevich woke up from a strange and ridiculous dream. He had dreamt of his deceased father, of Vesyegonsk before the war, and of his uncle Semyon and aunt Anna's wedding, at which he had been a guest when he was ten. In the dream, everything was almost exactly as it had been back in faraway 1938, but, for some reason he was already the old man he'd since become and his dad was calling him Grandpa Vitya. They sat him down at the head of the table, his father was sitting next to him and continually pouring him delicious moonshine, as light as birch juice, which caused Grandpa Vitya, still essentially a child, to get very drunk—he lost the ability to sit, fell under the table, and laughingly began to grab at everyone's legs, which made the assembled company so angry that they began to kick at him violently, hitting him with their boots and clamoring that Grandpa Vitya had made a fool of himself. They then grabbed him and dragged him out of the house, and he was so intoxicated he couldn't move his arms or his legs, and he found this so funny, so hilarious, that he laughed and laughed and laughed until he burst into tears.

His tear-filled eyes having shot open, he began to blink frantically. Tears rolled down his cheeks and onto his pillow. He lay still for a long time, looking up at the ceiling with the Czech crystal chandelier, which his late wife had bought in the mid-seventies at Svet—the store on Leninsky Prospect.

This foolish dream had confused his thoughts. Lying there and fiddling with the edge of his comforter, Viktor Nikolayevich tried to put them back in order: at twelve, Valya was coming to do the final injection, then he had to go to the bakery; after lunch, Korzhev had promised to come by to play some chess; and he was expecting Volodya in the evening. Plus, tomorrow he had to go get his pension. And tomorrow, his washing would be ready—Volodya was going to stop by and get it. It was too bad it wouldn't be ready today. If it were, Volodya could stop by and grab it on his way over. Instead, he'd have to make another round trip tomorrow.

"Vesyegonsk..." he pronounced, throwing off the blanket and sitting up in bed.

Feeling around for his slippers with his feet, he squinted at his bedside table: a Yantar watch, an issue of *Izvestiya*, a collection of crossword puzzles, Suvorov's *Icebreaker*, a little book of Veronika Tushnova's poems, a glass of boiled water, reading glasses, a Darth Vader action figure given to him by his seven-year-old great-grandson, a single Valocordin, a package of Cerebrolysin with one last ampoule in it, packages of Nootropil, Sonapax, phenazepam, furosemide, No-Spa, and papasolum.

He picked up the Sonapax, squeezed a pill out of the cartridge, put it in his mouth, and washed it down with water.

Sat for a moment, squinting at the sun through the gaps between the curtains, slapped himself across the knees, and stood up. Walked into the bathroom, shuffling his slippers across the old parquetry.

"Vesyegonsk...Ves-ye-gonsk..."

Turned on the bathroom light, went in, lowered his striped pajama pants, sat down cautiously on the toilet. Sat for a moment, chewing at his dry lips and scratching his knee. Urinated slowly and intermittently. Twisted round, still chewing his lip and grabbing seriously at his knees. Tensed up and lowered his head. The flabby folds of his neck gathered beneath his obstinate chin.

He groaned, pushing out. Froze. Then exhaled displeasedly, shook his head, relaxed, straightened up, and quoted Lermontov: "Mountain peaks slumber in dead of night..."

Stood, pulled up his pants, flushed, walked over to the sink, glanced in the mirror. The eighty-two-year-old Viktor Nikolayevich was staring back at him.

"*Guten Morgen*," Viktor Nikolayevich said to him, picked up his toothbrush, squeezed toothpaste onto it with a slightly trembling hand, then began to brush his *new*, even teeth.

Having finished brushing, he spat, rinsed out his mouth, washed his face, and wiped it with a pink towel for a long time. Then removed his pajamas, hung them on a hook, and carefully, without rushing, stepped over the edge of the bath, grabbed a metal ring, and brought his other leg over. Turned on the tap, adjusted the temperature, picked up the showerhead from the little levers it was sitting on, like a prewar telephone, depressed the switch to make the water come out of the showerhead, then directed the stream toward his thin legs. After making sure that the water was warm, he directed it over his thin, swarthy body with its saggy belly. There were two old scars on this body: one on his left hip, which he'd gotten while hunting in '58, when he was gored by the tusks of a wounded boar, and one on his right elbow, from when he'd broken his arm in '91 by slipping outside the entrance to his building. There were also two tattoos visible on his body: an eagle clawing at a snake in the middle of his chest and a heart penetrated by two daggers with the barely visible inscription NINA on his left shoulder. Both tattoos were old, from the fifties.

Viktor Nikolayevich poured water on his body from the showerhead and bowed his head, as a result of which the wrinkles on his neck gathered menacingly, his lower lip sagging gloomily. "The rails run off to the ends of the earth..." he began, remembering Pugacheva's song. "Along the rails... and the ties, the ties, the ties..."

Turning off the water, he grabbed the ring and brought his body cautiously out of the shower and onto the bath mat. Picked up the towel and dried himself off for a long time. Dressed himself in a robe of red silk, sighed, left the bathroom, then headed for the kitchen, shuffling along in his slippers. But, outside the windows of the apartment's main room something was dinning. Viktor Nikolayevich shuffled into the main room of the apartment, then went over to the window.

His gray brows crawled upwards in surprise: all of Leninsky Prospect, spreading beneath his windows, was overflowing with youths dressed in identical silver spacesuits and white helmets inscribed with USSR.

"Cosmonauts!" Viktor Nikolayevich muttered in surprise.

Then he immediately remembered: "Today's the twelfth of April! Cosmonauts' Day, you darling bastards! Honest Mother!"

Wonderstruck, he shook his head. Hundreds and thousands of cosmonauts filled the street. There were no cars. Rubberneckers darkened the edges of the street outside the apartment buildings.

In the forty years he'd lived on Leninsky Prospect, he'd never seen anything like it. This was where the communists had held demonstrations in Yeltsin's time; and in 1993 there had been a famous massacre on Gagarin Square three hundred meters from his apartment—when patriots from Labor Moscow had clashed with Yeltsin's OMON. But *this* had never happened before.

Viktor Nikolayevich opened the window, leaned out, and looked joyfully from side to side. "Holy cow! Cosmonauts! Lil' cosmonauts!" he laughed rapturously. The spring wind stirred his sparse gray hair.

Some kind of motion spread through the crowd of cosmonauts, some sort of preparation. At its center, in a mishmash of bodies shining in the sun, a rocket with the emblem of Russia on its hull began to rise. It had only just been placed upright when its nose tilted back and a figure in a spacesuit appeared inside it. The crowd piped up joyfully. The figure in the rocket greeted everyone, waving his hands. Then he flipped up his helmet's visor and raised his hand, asking for silence. The crowd fell silent. From the sixth floor, Viktor Nikolayevich looked down at the guy's face appearing through the open visor: black-browed with high cheekbones and a birdlike nose.

"Dear friends!" the guy began in a high, peppy voice and loud-speakers carried his voice down the prospect. "Today is the twelfth of April: Cosmonauts' Day. On this day, Yuri Gagarin made his heroic flight and conquered the cosmos. Our country made itself known to the whole world, declared itself at the top of its lungs. Here, today, on Gagarin Square, thirty thousand young Russians have gathered around the monument to the man who was the first to discover space. Each of you is prepared to repeat Gagarin's feat. Because love for your country abides in each of your souls, along with the desire to make it more powerful and more free! And, to me sitting in this rocket right now, my friends, it seems that each of you is named Yuri!"

The crowd dinned.

"Every Russian patriot is a cosmonaut of the soul! And our president is the number one cosmonaut!

The crowd applauded.

"And our prime minister is the cosmonaut of all cosmonauts!"

The crowd roared with joy.

The speaker waited for the din to die down, held his pause, then began to sing: "Our maps of space have been tucked into their cases—"

"And the navigator confirms the route for one last time!" the crowd immediately picked up.

"Come on, guys, let's have a smoke before we launch, we've only fourteen minutes left to go-o-o-o-o!!!" Viktor Nikolayevich sang down to the crowd from the sixth floor.

Behind him in the room, a phone rang on his desk. Viktor Nikolayevich turned around unhappily, rushed over to the desk, picked up the phone, put it to his ear, then returned to the window. His son Volodya was calling.

"You won't believe what's happening outside my windows, Vov! Thirty thousand cosmonauts!"

Speaking on the phone, he leaned out the window. "Hmm? What? It's not nonsense, my dear, it's beau-ti-ful! Listen to them sing!"

He put his hand with the phone out the window. His thin arm swayed in the open air. Viktor Nikolayevich waited for a moment, then pulled it back into the room and put the receiver to his ear.

"You heard? There! It's those…what're they called…well, the

ones that march? 'All Together'? What're they called? Yeah! Yeah! Thirty thousand of them are gathered here, can you imagine? Today is Cosmonauts' Day, son! There you go! Hmm? What? No! What do you mean? Valya? Then she'll be here at twelve. Yeah? Well, she can come earlier, I don't mind. I'll just go to the bakery later...Yeah. Okay, Vov. It's just fantastic right now! A won-der-ful mood! We're all set to launch! I'm going out into orbit! Yeah. Yeah. And the laundry tomorrow. Okay. I'll be waiting this evening."

He pressed the red button on the phone and put it back in its cradle. A shining crowd was singing outside of his window:

> On the dusty paths
> of distant planets,
> our tracks shall remain.

Smiling and singing along, Viktor Nikolayevich torqued his head and looked around: Which of his neighbors were also watching the proceedings? It turned out that only the young Rubinshteins on the third floor, the Gorbunova girly on the fourth floor, and a couple down below were sticking their heads out their windows. And no one had opened the windows on the fifth or sixth floors.

Viktor Nikolayevich clenched his sinewy fist, thrust it through the window, and cried out "Glory to the heroes of the cosmos!"

The Rubinshteins and the Gorbunova girly heard, looked up from down below, and waved.

The doorbell rang.

"What on earth?" He turned around displeasedly.

He realized that it was Valya, who had shown up early, as Volodya had just warned him she would.

"Motherlover...!" Viktor Nikolayevich spat through the spring air. "Always on time!"

Shaking his head, he shuffled to the entryway.

"It occurred to her just now...where does the evening taxi fly... fly, fly, and take me away..."

Muttering and singing unhappily, he unlocked the door and swung it open recklessly. "Come quick, Valya! I've really got something to show you!"

Three men were standing outside the door. One of them immediately shoved Viktor Nikolayevich's chest. Viktor Nikolayevich stumbled, staggered back, but didn't fall. The three men stepped into the dark entryway and slammed the door behind them.

"A good day," one of them, a little taller than the others, calmly pronounced as he came out of the entryway.

"Who're you?" Viktor Nikolayevich asked, not yet afraid.

The man approached Viktor Nikolayevich, took off his hat, and said "Monoclone."

Viktor Nikolayevich froze.

The man was very elderly, just like Viktor Nikolayevich. Right in the middle of his forehead was a growth reminiscent of a sawed-off horn. A deep, old scar crossed his left brow, which made it look as if his left eye were peering through a crack. His light-gray right eye, however, had an intelligent and decisive cast to it.

"You've recognized me." Monoclone smiled, then hung his hat on the back of a chair, looked around, unhurriedly took off his beige slicker, and gave it to one of the men who'd come in with him. The man hung the slicker on a coatrack.

Viktor Nikaolayevich stumbled back into the main room. Monoclone followed him.

"I promised you."

Still moving backwards, Viktor Nikaolayevich stumbled over to the oval dining table standing in the middle of the room, bumped into it, then stopped. Monoclone walked over, then stopped directly in front of him. The two other men stood next to him. They were young, able-bodied, wearing leather jackets, with virile faces. One of the men was holding a leather bag.

"Three years is too long to wait for what was promised," Monoclone pronounced and held out his hand.

The guy with the bag took something oblong wrapped in black velvet out of it and handed it to Monoclone. Monoclone took it and put it down on the table.

"What's this?" Monoclone asked the owner of the apartment, nodding at the bundle.

But it was as if Viktor Nikaolayevich's face had ossified. Standing in his red silk robe and his slippers, he stared at the bundle.

"Valyok," Monoclone ordered.

One of the guys undid the bundle. The pick of an ordinary pick-axe was lying atop the black velvet. But it was perfectly polished and sparkled in the sunlight like an expensive Japanese sword. Valyok picked up the shining, smoothly curved piece of iron and brought it up to Viktor Nikolayevich's face. On one side of the pick was engraved:

PROCUL DUBIO

On the other:

AD MEMORANDUM

Viktor Nikaolayevich stared at the shining metal. Monoclone glanced into the eyes of his *beholder* and nodded, satisfied.

"He remembers."

The guys exchanged a smirking look. The wind stirred the curtains, which depicted camels walking against a background of palm trees and pyramids. Outside the window, the crowd dinned and laughed. But the visitors paid no attention to this *human* sound.

"Time!" Monoclone ordered.

The guys grabbed Viktor Nikolayevich, tore off his robe, and bound his mouth with green duct tape. Monoclone brushed chess pieces, a vase, and an issue of *Zavtra* off the table. The vase shattered and the pieces rolled across the floor. The guys dropped Viktor Nikaolayevich chest first onto the table, leaning on him heavily and pressing down his thin, swarthy body. Outside the window, the crowd was singing a song about how Earth was awaiting the return of its sons and daughters from the cosmos.

Monoclone pulled a sledgehammer out of his bag. Holding Viktor Nikaolayevich down, the guys used their free hands to grab his flabby buttocks covered with the scars of old injections, then pulled them apart. Monoclone inserted the sharp end of the pick into the old man's hemorrhoidal anus, pressing down on it and driving it deeper. Viktor Nikaolayevich roared, thrashing around in the guys' hands. But they were holding him tight. Cradling his weapon, Monoclone swung back and then hammered down on the pick's wide end. The steel entered his shuddering body. The victim's legs performed a disorderly jig. Monoclone swung back and hit the pick even harder. The steel went deeper. It was as if Viktor Nikaolayevich's body had turned to stone. Only one leg beat evenly against one of the table legs—as if to keep time.

Monoclone swung back and smashed down with all his might. The metal had almost entirely entered the old man's body and the sharp edge came out just above his waist on the left side of his body, tearing through the swarthy yellow skin, pushing ribs apart, and letting forth a trickle of blood. Its appearance put an end to the punishment; the leg ceased beating time and the body went limp. The guys let Viktor Nikaolayevich go. Monoclone gazed at the brilliant metal that had passed through the old man's body and put down the sledgehammer.

"Well, there . . ."

Breathing heavily—asthmatically—he handed off the sledgehammer to one of the guys. Monoclone's sunken cheeks had gone crimson. Gazing at the motionless body, he slapped at his pockets, then remembered: "In the slicker."

Valyok returned to the entryway, took a pack of filterless German cigarettes and a golden lighter from the slicker, and handed them to Monoclone. He lit up, skillfully shielding flame from wind. Both of his hands were maimed: the little finger was missing from his right and the fourth and little fingers on his left didn't bend.

"That all?" one of the guys asked, putting the sledgehammer and the velvet away into the bag.

"That's all." Exhaling smoke, Monoclone turned around so as to leave this apartment for all time, but his gaze lingered on the photographs hanging on the wall over the desk. He walked over, his feet crunching through shards of crystal from the vase. There were six photographs, all in neat frames: Viktor Nikaolayevich's parents, his wife, son, grandson, great-grandson, the young Viktor Nikaolayevich in an MGB senior lieutenant's uniform with a crooked inscription in the corner—NORILSK 1952—and a group photograph of the graduates of the Kazan University law department from 1949.

Monoclone brought his face up to this last photograph. In the second row, Viktor Nikaolayevich was standing third from the left. Monoclone was standing next to him. His face had been fuller and rounder back then, but the growth on his forehead was precisely the same as it was now.

He took a drag from the cigarette, then began to slowly blow smoke on the photograph.

Meanwhile, the guys had cautiously approached the window and were looking outside without sticking their heads out. The iridescent crowd was singing:

> I'm the Earth, I send off my little birds,
> my sons and daughters, sayin'—
> fly all the way to the sun,
> then come back real quick.

After standing in front of the photographs for a moment, Monoclone turned sharply and left the room. The guys rushed after him. Valyok helped him to put on his slicker and hat. Monoclone pulled up the collar of the slicker and nodded to the guy by the door. The guy looked out through the peephole. "It's clear."

He opened the door. They left, quietly shutting the door behind them. The lock clicked.

In the main room, the old man's iron-pierced body was still lying atop the table. The pickaxe's wide end protruded from the anus, oozing blood, and its narrow end peeked out of his left side. The camel-patterned curtains swayed weakly in the wind. The crowd had stopped singing and was now shouting loudly.

"Ooh-ahh! Look at you!" the thick-browed guy's voice resounded from the speakers.

"We're all cosmonauts!" the crowd roared.

"Ooh-ahh! Look at you!"

"We're all cosmonauts!!!"

"Ooh-ahh! Look at you!"

"We're all cos-mo-nauts!!!"

The old man's legs stirred. His arms came to life, his hands crawling across the table toward his head. His body shifted, sliding down from the table and tumbling onto the floor. The old man moaned. He felt at the tape covering his mouth with trembling hands and tore it from his lips. A hiss crept forth from his mouth. He sobbed hoarsely and crawled under the table, shaking his head. Crawled over to the window. Blood oozed avariciously from his anus, his legs smearing it across the parquetry. He crawled and crawled—through the broken crystal of the vase and the scattered chess pieces. Crawled over to the radiator, grabbed it with both hands, hitched up his right leg, and pulled himself up in a single jerk, with moans and hisses, grabbed the windowsill, growling and wheezing, then began to wag and drag his body, peeling his motionless left leg up off the ground. His head was shaking violently. With incredible effort—moving like an old mannequin—he brought his chest to the windowsill, grabbed it, pulled himself up. His face appeared in the opening of the window. He saw precisely the same crowd of iridescent cosmonauts. He opened his mouth to scream. But only the blood that had accumulated in his punctured stomach gushed from his mouth. Blood splashed on the bottom of the window frame, painted by his grandson last fall, flowed back onto the windowsill, then dripped down onto the parquetry. Only a single drop leapt up, bypassing the green slope of the drain, tore down, flashed ruby in the sun, then took wing, carried upwards by moist air. The wind carried the drop away from the building and dripped it on the iridescent crowd.

The drop fell down onto the helmet of a laughing sixteen-year-old guy named Viktor. But he didn't feel it.

TINY TIM

2009

THE SALESWOMEN Moksheva, Golubko, and Abdulloeva went into Sotnikova's office without knocking. Wearing fashionably narrow glasses with a thin gold frame, Ekaterina Stanislavovna was flipping through their third-quarter tax report.

"Yes..." she pronounced without looking at them, flipping through the neatly filed sheets of paper.

The saleswomen stood silently in the middle of the office with bored tension inscribed on their faces.

"Yes?" She looked up, saw the women who'd come in, took off her glasses, rubbed at the bridge of her nose, her swarthy hand ending in enormous, fake milk-white-painted nails and adorned with two golden rings. This circumstance, taken as a whole, created the impression of a Venetian mask.

The saleswomen were silent.

"So..." She blinked, stretching her stiff neck. "Where's Nina Karlovna?"

"She's coming from the packing room," Golubko grunted.

Sotnikova pulled out a thin cigarette from a flat pack of Slims and lit up. "So, we don't understand human speech?"

The saleswomen looked at her silently.

"And don't wish to work in a professional manner?"

"We wanna work." The stumpy Abdulloeva with her overgrown black brows replied for everyone.

The small, round Nina Karlovna burst into the office. "What happened, Katerin Stanislavna?"

"*It* happened—*it* happened again." Sotnikova nodded her head, blowing smoke through her plump lips. "They stand there and chatter, stand there and chatter. Again!"

"Girls." Nina Karlovna turned reproachfully to the saleswomen.

"We were discussing the air-conditioning," Moksheva said.

"What?" Sotnikova's lips curled.

"It's really cold in our section," Moksheva said.

"It's fifteen degrees, just as it should be." Nina Karlovna shook the clips of her earrings. "You're wearing sweatshirts underneath your aprons. What's the problem?"

"The ai-i-ir conditioning!" Sotnikova leaned back into her chair and rocked it. "She lies and doesn't even blush."

"We really were discussing the air-conditioning." Golubko looked at her sullenly.

"Then why were you laughing like donkeys, hmm?" Sotnikova raised her voice. "Because of the cold?"

"Everyone has their own counter: sausages, meats, preprepared foods..." Nina Karlovna elaborated. "Everyone stands at their own counter, everyone is responsible for their place, everyone takes care of the customers, everyone looks them in the eye, smiles, and sells them gro—"

"They stand there and chatter, stand there and chatter." Sotnikova waved her hand. "They're still chattering like they were a week ago. What is this? A political protest? Are you the opposition?"

"We're not the opposition," Golubko answered with a smile. "It won't happen again, Katerina Stanislavovna."

"This ain't the Cherkizovsky Market, girls." Sotnikova knocked the ashes from her cigarette nimbly. "We're already losing customers, these are diff-i-cult times. And you're stabbing me in the back. Like— here you go, Ekaterina Stanislavovna, a knife right in the back!"

"You'll lose your bonus." Nina Karlovna shook her round head. "You'll lose your bonus."

"That's right!" Sotnikova rocked in her chair. "Not even close to everyone gets a New Year's bonus. And that's not just 'cause of the crisis. Certainly not."

"We'll try harder. We won't talk." Golubko smiled.

"We'll work in silence," Abdulloeva nodded.

"Draw your conclusions, girls," Nina Karlovna advised.

"And this'll be the last time!" Sotnikova raised her finger with its milk-colored nail.

"We promise," Golubko nodded.

"And so do I. Leave!" Sotnikova shook her head.

The saleswomen left.

"You go too." Sotnikova returned to the tax report unhappily. "It's simply gotten out of hand—nothing to be done!"

Nina Karlovna left.

Her secretary Zoya peeked into the office. "Katerin Stanislavna, your merchandising meeting."

"Everyone's ready?" Sotnikova didn't raise her head.

"Yes."

"I'll be right there."

Zoya closed the door.

Sotnikova moved the report off to the side, stood up, yawned, and stretched out. Raising her arms, she came out from behind her desk and into the middle of the office. Spread out her long, strong legs shoulder-width apart and placed her hands against the back of her head. Began to make circular motions to the left and to the right, exhaling sharply. She was wearing flared light-gray trousers with thin white stripes, a thick belt, and a white blouse embroidered with silver lilies.

Her cell phone rang. She walked over to the desk, took it, looked at the number calling, lowered her hand holding the cell phone, licked her lips thoughtfully. Exhaled. Put the cell phone to her ear quickly. "Yes."

"Hello," a woman's voice replied.

"Hello, Olga Olegovna."

"I'm coming to you."

"Where?"

"You know where. What is it, you're not at work?"

"I'm here ... but—"

"What is this *but*? I'm already on your prospect."

"But here, well, I've got ... it's not ... really—"

"Oh, it *really* is. I'm driving up now—come out and meet me."

The conversation was cut off.

"Whore ..." Sotnikova dropped her cell phone onto the desk, resting against its antique surface, and shook her head violently.

Her short, thick, smooth hair dyed the color of ripe rye shot round in a wave, fell back down. "Oh, what a fuckin' whore ..." She sighed, grabbed her cell phone, and left the office, her high heels clattering loudly.

"Zoy, nobody can see me for an hour. Nobody!" she exclaimed as she walked past the secretary.

"Got it," Zoya nodded.

Sotnikova set off down the hallway and went into the main hall of the supermarket. Here, all twelve merchandisers were huddled round in their blue aprons, waiting for her with their notepads. "We're pushing it back to five!" she announced loudly as she passed through the group.

Moving through the main hall, winding through shelves and customers, she shook her head indignantly.

"Whore ... I mean ... my God ... what a fuckin' whore ..."

As she walked, she noticed a pack of marshmallows on the floor, picked it up, dropped it into a mesh receptacle filled with toy piglets. Passed through a register with no line.

"Hey there," a young, plump cashier said.

Sotnikova walked through the entryway with its ATMs, lockers, and film development kiosk; the glass doors slid open, she stepped out onto the cobblestones, then stopped. It was still too hot, too sunny, and too dry outside, never mind that it was the beginning of October. Young chestnut and linden trees weren't even thinking of turning yellow yet. Three stray dogs were slumbering on the dusty grass.

Sotnikova walked hastily away from the entrance to the supermarket toward the flower beds outside, then back again, turned, and saw a black Volga approaching. She indicated a free space in the parking lot with her milk-colored nail. The Volga turned and parked. The miniature Malavets got out of the car wearing the uniform of a counselor of justice of the second degree and moved toward the entrance.

"The little shit's here…" Sotnikova muttered, squinting angrily at Malavets.

Malavets was walking with her usual gait: quick, purposefully businesslike, and slightly funny, as if she were a toy.

"Hello, Olga Olegovna," Sotnikova pronounced as Malavets approached.

"Hey, Katya." Without looking at Sotnikova, Malavets surveyed the square around the entrance to the supermarket with her restless grayish-blue, slightly bulging eyes.

Her thin, sharp-nosed face was pale yellow and intensely preoccupied, as it always was. Her restless eyes examined everything. She was about nine years older than Sotnikova.

"Olga Olegovna," Sotnikova sighed, "the thing is that I've got a lot of people today, really a lot of people, which is wh—"

"Which is why you're gonna kick 'em all out," Malavets pronounced, licking at her dry, pearly-pink, made-up lips and looking over at a man with a Labrador on a leash.

"Please understand, it's *unreal* how impossible it is here. I just can't—"

"It's possible. Let's go."

Malavets resolutely directed her thin, little body in uniform toward the entrance to the supermarket. Her legs were shapely enough, but her arms were stubby. A woman's purse hung from her gnarled left arm, a purse that seemed too big for Malavets.

Sotnikova went in after her. "Come on, Olga Olegovna, come over to my place tomorrow."

"I have a trial tomorrow. And the day after that. And the day after that," Malavets pronounced.

"This evening, then."

"I'll be chilling out this evening. Let's go, there's no time."

Malavets went through the turnstile, turned into the fruit section, grabbed a bottle of freshly squeezed pineapple juice lying in ice as she walked, opened it, took a drink, stopped, and looked around.

"Which way...I forget..."

"Follow me," Sotnikova barked unhappily, her heels clattering loudly.

Malavets followed her. Sotnikova crossed through the main hall of the market, entered a hallway, and turned toward her own office. Her cell phone rang, she glanced at it, turned it off, then opened the door.

"Lapshin called, Katerin Stanislavna," Zoya reported, sipping at her coffee.

"Zoy, nobody can see me for an hour. Nobody!"

"Got it," Zoya muttered.

Malavets came into the secretary's office with the juice in hand.

"Hey there." Zoya nodded at her, squinting down at her uniform.

"What shall I say to Lapshin?"

"In an hour."

Sotnikova shoved open the door to the office, letting Malavets in. Malavets entered. Sotnikova shut and locked the door behind them, sat down on the edge of the meeting table, crossed her arms across her chest, and glanced unhappily at the commendation from the Moscow Patriarch on the wall. Malavets sat down at Sotnikova's desk, moved the tax report off to the side, then put her purse and juice on the desk. Opened her purse, took out an old silver powder box, and opened it. Took a bone tube from the purse, stuck one end of it into her nostril, bent down to the powder box, and took a big snort into one nostril, then the other. Froze, inhaled deeply. Grabbed the bottle of juice and took a drink. Then turned off her cell phone.

"C'mon."

Sotnikova sighed. "Well, I arrived shortly after eight, as agreed upon."

"All right, first thing is sit a little closer, over here." Malavets pointed at a chair.

Sotnikova sat down, crossing her legs.

"And sit normally." Malavets pawed her over with her eyes. "You're sitting kinda provocatively."

"There's nothing provocative about it." Sotnikova removed her right leg from over her left leg and ran her fingernails across her knees.

"That's a bit more natural." Malavets sank back into her chair.

"I arrived, rang the bell. He opened the door, I come in and say, 'I'm the new cook—from your ex-wife. My name's Viktoria.' And he says, 'You can't imagine what a perfect moment this is. I'm so hungry and I bought some crucian carp, but I have no idea how to cook them.' So there. I say, 'Don't worry, I'll manage everything.' He says, 'Wonderful! I'm gonna go take a bath then. And you can settle down and get started.' So there. He goes into the bathroom, I go into the kitchen, and there, on the table, a white apron is already laid out. I put it on. And the fish were in the sink. I took out a knife and started to clean the carp. And then he comes into the kitchen all soundlessly, but comes up behind me quickly, grabs me by the ass, and I—"

"Stop!" Malavets claps her scrawny hands together. "Stop."

Sotnikova sighed and scratched her knees with her nails.

"What are you telling me?" Malavets asked.

"Well . . . a story—"

"What story?"

"What, um, happened between us."

"You're telling a passionate tale. Pass-ion-ate. And sec-ret. I came here, having put off two important meetings so that you would tell me a passionate and secret tale. One which no one else knows. And one that nobody shall ever know except for you and me. Therefore, if you deprive me of all of the en-chant-ing details, I'll spit on your case tomorrow and hand it off to *whomever*. Then, you'll know how holy is the Lord and how strict our judgment. Got it?"

"All right, I got it," Sotnikova sighed.

"Tell me calmly and unhurriedly. And without omitting any details. That clear?'

"Yep."

"Please, then." Malavets stuck her hand under her skirt and squeezed her thighs together.

"He came out of the bathroom and I heard him, even though he was walking barefoot."

"How were you dressed?"

"I was wearing a very short skirt with no tights and no panties. As agreed upon."

"As agreed upon." Malavets nodded. "Go on."

"And a singlet. With no bra. And the white apron. He grabbed me by the ass with both of his hands and began to rub it. First through the skirt, then he got underneath the skirt. And he was saying, 'Keep going, keep going.' I didn't turn around and kept on cleaning the carp. Then he got down on his knees, spread my buttocks apart, and started to lick my anus."

"Not anus but booty. Your sweet booty."

"Yes, my sweet booty."

"Did he stick his little tongue inside it?"

"Yes."

"Deep?" Malavets's head jerked.

"Not deep at first, then deep."

"And what were you doing?" Malavets was drawing her thighs apart, then pushing them together.

"It felt really good."

"Was it sweet for you?

"It was sweet."

"He can work his little tongue so sweet—right? Side to side—real sweet, right? Real sweet in Katenka's booty? Side to side. Really sticking in his little tongue, right?"

"He stuck his tongue into my little booty," Sotnikova nodded.

"And what was Katenka doing at that moment?"

"Cleaning the carp."

"She was cleaning the sweet, little carpies and that *deviant* stuck his tongue into her booty...into her sweet little booty?"

"He stuck his tongue in..." Sotnikova nodded, looking at her nails. "And then—"

"Hold on!" Malavets cried out, exhaling heavily. "What was he . . . was he . . . moaning?"

"He was moaning."

"Moaning sweetly, yeah?"

"Sweetly."

"Moaning into your little booty . . . and he was sticking his tongue deeper and deeper into it . . . yeah? yeah? yeah? yea-a-a-a-ah!"

Malavets cried out helplessly, her head trembling minutely and her hand moving under her skirt. Then she grabbed the tax report and hurled it violently at Sotnikova.

"You bitch!"

Startled, Sotnikova stumbled away, jumped up, and ran toward the door.

Shaking her head, Malavets closed her eyes, then cried out—it was both a moan and an expression of relief:

"A-a-a-a-a-a-a-ah"

Then immediately extended her free hand to Sotnikova.

"Sorry, sorry."

Sotnikova stood indecisively by the door.

"Sorry." Malavets inhaled, then exhaled with relief. "It's that . . . it's nothing . . . nerves . . . sit down. Sit down. Sit down!"

Sotnikova picked up the report, then put it down on the meeting table. Sat down in her chair.

Malavets opened the powder box and took a snort into her right nostril. Had a drink of juice. Wrinkled her nose.

They were silent: Sotnikova was looking at the wall—Malavets sighing and stroking at her cheeks, on which two pinks blotches had appeared.

"Understand me, Kat, please," Malavets began to speak. "I want you to get me right."

"I wanna smoke," Sotnikova barked.

"Smoke, of course, smoke."

Sotnikova took the cigarettes and lighter off the desk, lit up, and crossed her legs.

"You understand, every person has their own conception of the sacred. Not in terms of belief, God, or miracles. But simply their own, personal conception of the sacred. Which is always with them. And each person should always respect another person's conception of the sacred if they want to be considered human. I'm ready to accept your conception of the sacred. Always. I'll never trample on it or deride it. Because, first of all, I respect myself as an individual, as a *thinking reed*. And respect my own conception of the sacred. And yours. I'll always understand you. Just as I understood what the deal with your case was. And I had every reason not to understand you or Samoilov or Vasilenko. But I understood you and Samoilov and even that asshole Vasilenko. And now you live a normal human life, nothing's threatening that yet."

"Yet." Sotnikova exhaled smoke.

"Yet," Malavets nodded, leaning back in her chair. "Of course *not yet*! We all live in the *not yet*. Only the dead don't live in the *not yet*. Or angels. Instead of *not yet*, they have eternity. *Ewigkeit*. And we have la dolce vita. That's how we differ from them."

They were silent.

"I have a really tough day today." Sotnikova blew smoke with a sigh.

"Me too."

"Important people are coming to see me."

"And two deputies of the State Duma are sitting in my waiting room. Sitting there and drinking coffee. And waiting for me. Sit normally."

Sotnikova uncrossed her legs displeasedly.

"And don't smoke so much. You're a beautiful young woman. Why are you smoking? People smoke out of a lack of identification with who they are."

"I smoke because I want to."

"You even inhale the smoke! Think about it just this once: you're inhaling smoke. That's completely insane—to breathe in smoke and get pleasure from it."

"And snorting cocaine isn't insane?"

Malavets's face became stern. "Cocaine is the most physically harmless drug. Do you know how many hours vodka stays in the body? Twelve. And cocaine stays in it for only three. With no come-down."

"What about addiction?" Sotnikova put out the cigarette butt.

"Where do you see any addiction in this?" Malavets's narrow, plucked brows arched. "Where?"

Sotnikova smoked in silence, looking away.

Malavets waved her hand. "There's no addiction, my little fish. But I won't offer you any."

"And I won't ask for any."

Malavets closed the powder box. "What did he do with you after that?"

"After that . . . well, he hugged me by the legs from behind. Snug-gled up to me. I realized he was naked. And I felt his cock."

"Not his cock!" Malavets slammed the desk. "But his divine phallus!"

"His divine phallus."

"How did you feel it?"

"Like . . ." Sotnikova's eyes scanned the office.

"Can you speak without saying 'like'?"

"When he was squeezing me from behind, he was on his knees . . ."

"Okay . . ." Malavets stuck her hand under her skirt.

"And his co— His divine phallus was right here . . . between my knees."

"And then?"

"He started to rub it between them and I squeezed it with them."

"Did you squeeze it tight?"

"Tight enough."

"And what was he doing during all of this?"

"The phallus?"

"No—him!"

"He was still violating my little booty with his tongue."

"O-o-o . . . such a good word . . ." Malavets smiled nervously, mov-ing her hand around under her skirt. "Violated . . . precisely violated. A precise word! Vi-o-lat-ed! And did it feel good?"

"Yes, it felt good. His tongue was so . . . persistent."

"And the phallus?"

"The phallus was hot."

"And strong?"

"Strong. Solid."

"Big and solid. He does have a big one, right? Did you feel that right away?"

"Yes." Sotnikova grabbed her hips with her hands, sighed, straightened up, then puffed out her bosom. "It passed between my knees and stuck out."

"Do you know how long it is?"

"No."

"Guess." Malavets smiled nervously, shaking her head.

The blotches on her cheeks became even more pronounced.

"Twenty centimeters?"

"Twenty-four centimeters. That's how divine my ex-husband's phallus is. And the glans of that phallus is like a big apricot. Only it's crimson. Did you see the glans?"

"Yeah, I was looking down even though I was still cleaning the fish."

"You ... out of the corner of your eye, then? With your own little peephole, yeah? Out of the corner of ... saw out of the corner of your eye how he was ... yeah?"

"Mm-hmm."

"How it stuck out ... all springy, right? Back and forth, right? Back and forth ... through your little white legs, yeah?"

"Yeah."

"And he was ... what ... he was what? He was what?"

"He was bleating."

"Bleating into your little booty?"

"Bleating into my little booty."

"With his little tongue inside it, yeah? Yeah? His little tongue in your little booty and his divine phallus ... between your smooth little white legs, yeah? Do you depilate your legs or shave them?"

"I just shave them."

"Yourself?"

"Yeah."

"Well done. Yourself! You made sure to shave them yourself the night before, yeah?"

"Yeah."

"Shaved them, shaved them in secret, stroked your little legs, prepared yourself so that it'd be sweeter for him, more tender for his phallus, yeah?"

"Yeah."

"So that it'd slide . . . slide all tender between your tender . . . between Katenka's little legs . . . just like that . . . slide slide slide sli-i-ide sli-i-ide . . . a-a-a-a-h!!!"

Malavets froze, her mouth open and her eyes rolled in her head. Her cry turned into a wheeze. Sotnikova watched her gloomily, her arms crossed across her chest.

"Oy, I can't . . ." Malavets dropped her head down onto the desk, went silent, and began to sob weakly.

Sotnikova lit a cigarette.

"Oy . . . a nightmare . . . a little nightmare." Malavets breathed, raising and lowering her thin, narrow shoulders.

Having caught her breath, she took a snort from the powder box. Took a drink of juice from the bottle. Leaned back in the chair.

"Don't look at me so *evilly*, Kat. There's no need."

Sotnikova turned away.

"You and I made a deal: three sentences. Two of them have already passed. Stop by his place when he comes back from his holiday for one last time and that'll be the end of it."

"I'd rather pay you." Sotnikova stood up, took a bottle of mineral water out of a refrigerator, and poured herself a glass of it.

"I don't need any money from you. As I've already declared: I don't take bribes."

"A pointless principle."

"Don't be rude to me, Kat. I'm older than you, you know. I've seen things you haven't even dreamed of, Katenka."

"Maybe I could still give you money?" Sotnikova walked over to Malavets and sat down on the edge of the desk with glass in hand.

"Not everything in life can be measured by money." Malavets put her small hand on Sotnikova's knee.

"Maybe it can though?" Sotnikova looked furiously at Malavets.

"We made a deal, Kat."

"Maybe though?"

"Kat..." Malavets sighed decisively and clasped her fingers together.

"Maybe though?" Sotnikova's voice trembled.

"Katya!" Malavets slammed her palm against the table.

"Maybe though?!" Sotnikova cried out, her full red lips trembling and her glass dropping to the floor.

Without shattering, the glass rolled across the floor.

Malavets stood up and hugged her around the shoulders. "Katya. Let's be nice."

Sotnikova turned away. Malavets sighed, leapt up, and sat down next to her atop the desk.

"I'm going to tell you a story now. And you'll understand everything. There's a couple. Him and her. They met. They fell in love. It soon became clear that they didn't merely love each other, they also couldn't live without each other. They match like two halves of one beautiful shell. And inside it is a pearl. The big pearl of love. And it shines in the darkness. They're happy. Happy both physiologically and spiritually. They get colossal pleasure from the act of love. Both of them had had relationships before. Boyfriends and girlfriends. But all of those faded compared with *reality*, so to speak. The entire past faded. I mean to say, their intimacy was something... Sparks flew and the heart stopped. Sometimes she even lost consciousness. And when he was coming, he'd cry like a baby. That's how strong it was. And they were so happy, so happy that... it's simply impossible to express in words. Happy together, as they say. And un-bel-iev-a-bly happy! There. Then she got pregnant. They really wanted a baby. And he was born—a buoyant, healthy baby boy. The fruit of their love. She fed him from her bosom and had lots of milk. And her husband helped her not to get mastitis by milking her. Then he started to just suck her milk, to just drink it. He really liked the taste of her milk, he liked everything about her, he blessed her, just as she blessed him.

She was feeding her two beloved men from her bosom—her son and her husband. And she was happy. And that continued for a whole year. Then she stopped feeding her son. But her husband continued to drink her milk. He had a real preference for a particular position during intercourse: he would sit down in a chair, and she would sit on him and face him. And during the act, he would suck at her bosom. And she gave him milk. And it never ended, it just poured into his mouth, poured forth in a sweet stream, a stream of love and gratitude toward this man, gratitude that he existed, that she'd met him, and that they were together. And this continued. For ten years. Unbelievable, yeah? Nobody would believe such a thing! For ten years, she fed her beloved with her own milk. Fed him at night. There . . . But then, she began to feel a deadly weakness. She had a lot of work, she was making a serious career for herself. She started having dizzy spells and losing weight. She went to a doctor and told him about their sweet secret. The doctor said that it was very harmful to her health. And so she stopped feeding her husband with her own milk. Of course he understood the situation, he himself told her to stop, naturally he wanted only the best for her, he was thinking about their happiness and their future together. They wanted more children. Her career was picking up steam, and he was making a decent amount too. After she stopped feeding him with her own milk, she recovered and the dizzy spells went away. She got pregnant, but the baby girl was born dead. And a year later he left her for another woman. Another woman . . ." Malavets stroked Sotnikova's shoulder and fell silent.

"She took his leaving terribly. Worse than terribly. One might even say she couldn't take it. Not at all. She couldn't make peace with her loss. She tried to forget herself in her work. This had a decent outcome—she became *somebody*. A man appeared in her life. But with him, she didn't feel a tenth of what she'd felt with her ex-husband. To put it simply—she couldn't come. Then another man appeared in her life. The same problem. Her husband had been an unusual sexual partner, a very unusual one. No, he wasn't a pervert, he did all of the normal stuff, but . . . he had a . . . so to speak . . . special and unique flame—a *factory*—that no one else had. He could simply put his hand on the small of her back and she'd immediately lose her mind with desire. And he also truly loved sex. Loved it for real. He didn't just love it—he adored it. Adored it. There was something maniacal about this love. And she adored him. Yeah . . . To put it simply, she broke up with those two guys. Then lived alone with her son. The other thing is she remained friends with her husband. She loved him too much to really break things off. And she raised their son. The fruit of their love. They called each other every week. And once, he complained that he didn't have a cook. And she helped him out and sent her cleaning lady to him—she cooked pretty well too. The cleaning lady came back and told her how the man had unexpectedly taken possession of her when she was cleaning a fish. And when the cook was saying this, I started to feel so good that . . ."

Malavets fell silent. Her bulging grayish-blue eyes filled up with tears.

Sotnikova slid off the desk, took out a cigarette, and lit up.

Malavets was sitting on the desk, her little hands now outside of the skirt of her uniform.

"Why didn't you tell me right away?" Sotnikova asked, standing with her back to Malavets.

"Don't ask stupid questions."

Still seated on the desk, Malavets wiped away her tears, wrinkled her nose, pulled a packet of tissues out of her purse, and blew her nose. Picked up the powder box, looked at herself in its little mirror, put the tube into the powder, and snorted.

Sotnikova walked thoughtfully over to the safe, pecked at it twice with her fingernail, then turned sharply on her heels. "When will the third sentence be?"

"Well . . ." Wrinkling her nose, Malavets made an uncertain gesture with her hand. "Maybe next week."

"I can't any later. We're going to Rhodes."

"Okay. He's still in Moscow."

"No later," Sotnikova repeated.

"I'll arrange it with him for next weekend. A third sentence."

"A third sentence." Sotnikova nodded in a businesslike way.

"Then both your case and Samoilov's will be closed. You have my word as Olga Malavets. And everything will be *frickin' awesome*, as my son would say. So put out your cigarette and come sit over here."

Sotnikova put out her cigarette and sat down on the desk.

"Closer."

She moved over to Sotnikova. Malavets took her by the hand, then stuck her other hand under her skirt.

"Then what did he do?"

Sotnikova licked her lips as she recollected: "Then . . . Then he got up off his knees and stuck his cock—his phallus, I mean—a little ways into my vagina and seemed to freeze. And stopped breathing. First, I thought that something had happened to him. And he was standing totally still with his arms around me. And I stopped too . . . I stopped."

"Stopped what?"

"Cleaning the fish."

"So you froze in place, yeah?" Malavets began to trifle with herself under her skirt.

"Yeah. He was standing there like a statue. And holding me with his hands. And I was also just standing there."

"And what about his divine phallus?"

"It went a little ways inside me."

"Into your little pussy . . . yeah?"

"Yeah."

"Into your pussy, yeah?"

"Yeah."

"He licked your little ass clean . . . licked it clean with his persistent tongue . . . the tongue of a real man . . . and put it into your pussy?"

"Yeah. Then suddenly—"

"Hold on!" Malavets grabbed her by the shoulder. "Hold on, hold on, hold on . . ."

Sotnikova fell silent.

Malavets covered her eyes and began to fiddle around more slowly, nibbling her thin lower lip as she did. "No need to rush . . . all is calm . . . all is good . . ."

Sotnikova stared blankly ahead.

"And what happened next?" Malavets asked quickly.

"Then he shoved himself all the way inside me."

"Inside where?"

"Inside my vagina."

"With what?"

"His phallus."

"Was it hot?"

"Yeah."

"Decisively?"

"Yeah."

"Passionately?"

"Yeah."

"Shoved it in deep?"

"Yeah."

"What did he say to you?"

"He grabbed my whole body and whispered into my ear: 'I'm beatin' it into you, pussycat.'"

"He whispered into your little ear?"

"Yeah, right into my ear."

"He whispered hotly?"

"Yeah."

"Then what happened?" Malavets sobbed.

"Then he started to move inside me."

"To move?"

"To move."

"To move?"

"To move."

"And to move?"

"And to move."

"And then? And then?"

"Then he started to come inside me."

"To come?! He started to come?!"

"To come. And to moan."

"He was moaning?!"

"Moaning and repeating: 'I'm beating it into you, pussycat.'"

"He beat it into you?!" Malavets cried out with a sob.

"He beat it into me!"

"He beat it into you?!"

"He beat it into me."

"He bea-a-a-a-a-at i-i-i-it into-o-o-o-o yo-o-o-o-u!" Malavets roared, her eyes rolling in her head.

Sotnikova froze tensely.

Convulsions swept over Malavets's slender body and a growl burst from her open mouth. She dug her fingers into Sotnikova's shoulder. Sotnikova sat as still as if she'd turned to stone, looking disdainfully at Malavets's trembling legs.

Finally, Malavets stopped jerking around, let go of Sotnikova's shoulder, and put her palms to her hot face. "Enough...enough... enough..."

With a sigh of relief, Sotnikova slid off the desk, took a cigarette, and lit up, pacing around the office as she did.

"Enough." Malavets sat down on the desk, kicked her feet around in their tight black shoes, slowly got down off the desk, took a few steps, then stopped.

There were two crimson blotches on her cheeks. The stately Sotnikova paced around, smoking and paying no attention to Malavets. Malavets picked her powder box up from the desk, held it in her hands for a moment, then closed it sharply.

"No more of that. Gimme a cigarette, I guess."

Sotnikova gave her one and brought the lighter up to her face.

Malavets lit up. Her face immediately became more serious.

"There you go, Katya." She grabbed herself by the elbows.

"It's time for me to work." Sotnikova finished her cigarette quickly and greedily, then stubbed it out in the ashtray.

"Yeah." Malavets searched through the office with her transparent eyes, as if she were seeing it for the first time.

Sotnikova unlocked the door and peered out into her secretary's office. Zoya was sitting at her desk and straightening her eyelashes with shining metal tongs.

"Lapshin called twice. So did Markovich and the customs officers," she reported.

Sotnikova returned to her office.

"Do you have a little coffee for me to drink?" Malavets asked, puffing at a cigarette without inhaling.

"Our coffee machine broke," Sotnikova lied. "And I've got an avalanche of work."

"Okay, I'll go get one at Coffeemania." Malavets dropped her unfinished cigarette into the ashtray and picked up her purse. "See me out."

Sotnikova nodded reluctantly.

They left the office and walked down the hallway.

"Thank you." Malavets suddenly put her arm around Sotnikova's white waist.

Sotnikova walked purposefully, not reacting.

"I tried to get our former cleaning lady Lyubka to do it. But couldn't convince her. I frickin' fired her. And he won't tolerate hookers."

Ahead of them, heartrending female cries sounded out in the main hall of the supermarket.

"What the hell's that?" Malavets muttered.

"I dunno." Sotnikova furrowed her brow, quickening her step. "Someone must've stolen someone's wallet or something."

"There's so much pickpocketing these days." Malavets shook her head, falling behind as she did. "It's a crisis, really."

They entered the main hall.

There was no one behind the long glass display windows of the meat and fish sections.

"Wonderful..." Sotnikova muttered.

A woman's cry, which turned into a whimper, then a mumble, was coming from behind the shelves of soft drinks. Sotnikova walked around behind them. A salesgirl in a blue apron was lying in a pool of blood on the floor. Her glasses and notepad had fallen next to her. A middle-aged woman trembling slightly was sitting on the floor with her back resting against the shelf. Next to them was a shopping cart full of groceries. A very plump police lieutenant colonel was attentively examining the contents of the cart.

"Mhmm . . . you really do need to eat more organic food," he said, then, noticing Sotnikova, turned around.

"Who—" Sotnikova stopped next to the corpse and dug her nails into her lips.

"Killed her?" the lieutenant colonel arched his brows. "I did."

Sotnikova stared at him. His swarthy, sleek face had no particular expression. His slightly bloodshot eyes looked entirely normal. Sotnikova saw the pistol in his hands. Malavets came up from behind her.

"Oh, the prosecutor's office." The lieutenant colonel glanced at Malavets's uniform. "Already?"

"What's . . . happening here . . ." Malavets muttered, her eyes fixed on the body stretched out on the floor.

"A shooting," the lieutenant colonel informed her. "Conducted according to the principle of beauty."

Both women froze. The seated woman whined.

"The most beautiful are to be catapulted into a better world," the lieutenant colonel pronounced, nodding at the seated woman. "This one clearly doesn't fit the bill. Get outta here, you consumer of processed foods!"

He kicked the woman lightly. She crawled obediently away, whining in horror.

"A woman in uniform." The lieutenant colonel squinted at Malavets. "That's beautiful, I can't argue with that. But you yourself aren't beautiful."

Malavets looked at him, paralyzed.

"You, on the other hand, do." He turned his gaze to Sotnikova. "You're beautiful. Really beautiful."

He pointed the pistol at Sotnikova and fired. The bullet entered Sotnikova's bosom, passed right through it, pierced four packages of Dobry apple juice, then came to rest in a bag of semolina. Sotnikova keeled over backwards.

The lieutenant colonel turned away and disappeared behind the shelves of groceries.

"Kat..." Malavets exhaled.

Sotnikova was lying on her back with her arms outstretched, looking up at the ceiling. Her full lips moved weakly, almost indistinguishably, gasping for air. She began to hiccup.

"Katya..." Malavets whispered, clutching at her still-red cheeks.

Sotnikova was looking at the elongated, rectangular ceiling light. The light shined with the light of day. The light shined, shined, shined, then took Sotnikova away with it. She flew behind the light, rushing, rushing, rushing, rushing. And came to rest in a closed space. Behind this space, as if behind a transparent wall, stood a hamster of human height. His fur shimmered with flashes of rainbow light, two zigzags darkened behind his ears, and white whiskers shone forth from his chubby cheeks. Sotnikova immediately recognized him. This was her hamster Tiny Tim, which her grandma had bought for Katya at the Moscow Pet Market when she was eight. The hamster had immediately become her closest friend in the family, in which the arguments between her drinking, hard-partying mother who worked as a waitress at a restaurant called Yakor and her hysterical father, who believed deeply in God and was a junior research fellow at MoscowHydroProject, rose up and tumbled down like avalanches of snow. Katya loved the hamster, squeezed him tight, talked to him, gave him little presents, indulged him with cookies, told him about her time at school, about her girlfriends, about boys, about teachers and assignments, took this warm, furry little ball into her hands and blew her warm breath on it, at which point Tiny Tim would screw his eyes up with pleasure. With her father, Katya always felt guilty, always responsible for everything that went wrong because she got mediocre grades, but her mother loved her and took care of her when she was sober. When she was drunk, however, she became someone else, became incomprehensible, she either wouldn't notice Katya or she would squeeze her tight and kiss her weepingly, as if she were bidding her farewell for all time, which was very frightening. When Katya's mother would weep and lock herself in the bathroom after fights with her father, Katya was also beside herself. There was her grandma too, she was good and big, always kind, but she lived in Bronnitsy with her goats, chickens, and a dog named Valyok and would only ever come to Katya's parents' one-bedroom apartment in Kuntsevo for a day at a time. Katya and Tiny Tim would visit Grandma in the summer. She also loved the goats and chickens and spoke with them just as she spoke with Tiny Tim. But the goats and chickens didn't understand Katya like Tiny Tim did. And it was difficult to talk to Valyok; he was chained up and angry all the time. Tiny Tim lived in the kitchen in an aquarium filled with straw and cotton wool. He drank his water from one half of a plastic soap dish, ate from the lid of a can, and slept bundled up in cotton wool. Coming home from school when her parents were still at work, Katya would feed Tiny Tim, talk to him, warm him with her breath, then let him out to run around the apartment. Tiny Tim would run around, his little legs scrambling as he sniffed at everything. Tiny Tim lived with Katenka's family for a year. Then, one winter day, Katya let him out to run around and turned on the TV to watch the Olympics—figure skating. Then she went to the bathroom, but heard them announcing that her favorite skaters, Linichuk and Karponosova, were on, rushed out of the bathroom, and threw open the door so hard that it smashed into her father's skis, which were standing up in the hallway, the skis fell down onto the floor, and Katya heard Tiny Tim's squeak. The skis had fallen down onto Tiny Tim. He died in Katya's hands a few minutes later: his little black eyes were filled up with tears, he helplessly kicked his back feet, and his mouth was open. Then he was still. Katya laid him down on the table, then wept until the evening. Her father was the first to come home from work. As always, he was exhausted and unhappy.

"Your skis killed Tiny Tim!" Katya screamed at him, crying angrily.

Seeing the dead hamster on the table, her father immediately grew serious, the fatigue of the day and his habitual irritability left him. He sat down at the table, straightened his glasses, took Katya by the hand, and began to speak calmly and seriously. "Don't cry. There's no such thing as death. Tiny Tim didn't die. He's gone to be with God."

"He . . . he's here . . . he's still warm . . ." Katya disagreed, sobbing.

"That isn't Tiny Tim anymore," her father continued. "It's just his body. His soul is in the next world. Someday, we're all going to go there and we're all going to see each other. Your Tiny Tim will meet you when you go there. And your deceased grandpa. And Uncle Semyon. And my grandma and grandpa. And all of your friends and all of your relatives. The Lord shall bring them all back. Now, let's go bury Tiny Tim."

They got dressed, her father took out a trowel, Katya took Tiny Tim, and they went down into the courtyard in the elevator, dug through the snow around a linden tree, and buried Tiny Tim in the not-too-frozen earth. A lot of snow fell the next day; the janitor shoveled it away, and a drift grew up around the tree. As she walked to school, Katya spoke to the snow drift: "I'm going to school, Tiny Tim."

Coming back from school, she spoke to him again: "I'm back from school, Tiny Tim."

For some reason, they didn't buy her a new hamster. Then she forgot about Tiny Tim. And now he was standing before her, as big as a bear, beautiful and noble, looking at her attentively with shining eyes. This was her Tiny Tim, but entirely new and transformed. Unbelievable grace flowed forth from him. But an even greater grace trembled and wavered with unearthly light behind his back. A graceful sea of light trembled behind Tiny Tim's back. An all-consuming state of joyful peace emanated from this sea. And this sea was waiting for Sotnikova. And she wanted to go into this sea terribly. The sea drew her toward it, it was filled with the Other, the Joyful, and the Great. In comparison with this sea of light, all of Sotnikova's former life suddenly seemed to her to be something small, insignificant, shriveled, and shrunken, like her grandma's glove in her old chest of drawers. But the sea wouldn't let her in; Tiny Tim was standing in the way. She understood that she had to give Tiny Tim something so that he'd let her pass into the Kingdom of Eternal Joy. Tiny Tim's shining eyes told her exactly *what* he awaited from her. And she immediately understood and remembered: the prosphora! The holy bread! Katya remembered that she'd once put Tiny Tim onto the table so that he could gnaw at the prosphora her father had brought back from church. Honestly, Katya hadn't done this purposefully to annoy her bothersome father, but just because it made her feel happy

208 · VLADIMIR SOROKIN

and good that Tiny Tim was eating the prosphora that her father had brought back from church with such a significant air and would let only Katya and her younger brother Lyosha eat it on an empty stomach. Tiny Tim picked up the prosphora with his paws, pressed it to his white paunch, and began to gnaw at it.

"Eat, Tiny Tim, and become holy!" Katya said and laughed. "If you eat all of it, you shall become Saint Tiny Tim!"

Tiny Tim ate quickly, filling up his cheek pouches. He ate almost two thirds of the prosphora, leaving only a crescent-moon-shaped slice. Then, suddenly, a key ground in the front-door lock: her father was coming back from the store. Katya quickly grabbed the partially devoured prosphora from Tiny Tim and looked around—where could she put it?—she had no pockets in her dress, if she threw it under the sofa, they'd sweep it out with a broom, then punish her, and it was too late to flush it down the toilet—her father was already taking off his coat in the entryway. Katya ran over to a chest of drawers and looked behind it, but the space behind it was so wide that everything in it was visible and the prosphora would be visible too. Next to the chest of drawers was a Rigonda turntable with a receiver attached. Katya looked and saw that behind the beautiful Rigonda was a cardboard lid with two little holes in it and two big holes in it. Katya had barely managed to shove the crescent moon of prosphora into the holes when her father came in with a string bag full of groceries.

"Where's Mom, Kat?"

"At Aunt Sonya's," Katya replied, laying her hands on the Rigonda.

Her father looked at her gloomily through his glasses and took the string bag into the kitchen. "The hamster on the table again?" his displeased voice rang out.

"I'll come get him, Daddy," Katya replied.

Katya double-checked: the crescent moon of holy bread had disappeared into the Rigonda without a trace. She took Tiny Tim, who was still exploring, off the table, brought him into the kitchen, and lowered him into his little glass home.

"The table's for people and the floor is for hamsters," her father muttered, sorting through the bags of food. "We eat on the table.

The refection I bless every day goes on the table. This is the last time, got it?"

"Got it," Katya replied.

Her father didn't ask about the prosphora that day or the next. And now Tiny Tim wanted the remaining piece of holy bread that had been stuck into the Rigonda.

Sotnikova opened her eyes. She was lying in an intensive care unit. And she realized that she hadn't made it into the Shining Sea of Joy. The wretched earthly world once again surrounded her. Next to her, in blue-and-white scrubs, stood two bearded men. She looked at them displeasedly. She recognized that one of them was her husband Vasily. The other bearded man was a doctor.

"Katenka," said Vasily, taking her by the hand.

She looked at him as if she were seeing him for the first time, even though she remembered who he was in her earthly life.

"Do you hear me, Katenka?"

She moved her lips. They were dry and her rough tongue rubbed against them. She swallowed. Swallowing was very painful, almost impossible. But there was neither pain nor heaviness where she'd been shot in the chest.

"Yeah," she whispered and felt a tube in her right nostril.

"You're alive, darling," Vasily smiled.

"Yeah," she agreed mournfully.

"It's a miracle. The bullet didn't hit your heart, spine, esophagus, or any internal organs!" Vasily's voice trembled with joy. "A miracle, Katyusha! A miracle, my joy!"

She looked at his sunken-cheeked, bearded face. This dull, emaciated face so absorbed by earthly life promised the return of precisely the same gray, limited, wretched, familiar-to-the-point-of-nausea earthly life.

"Come closer," Sotnikova whispered.

"You shouldn't talk much," the doctor warned, then went over to the next patient, who was lying with eyes closed beneath a drop counter—with precisely the same oxygen tube stuck into her nose.

Vasily brought his face closer, which made it even more unbearable for Katya. Every wrinkle on the face and every hair in the beard seemed to say to her: "This is our life and there shall be no other."

Sotnikova ran her tongue across her lips and spoke up softly: "Do you remember the Rigonda at my dad's place?"

"The Rigonda?" Vasily furrowed his brow.

"The Rigonda turntable. At his place. In front of the piano."

"Yes, yes, of course I remember," he nodded, stroking her hand. "Your dad's also terribly worried, he even wanted—"

"Open the back panel of the Rigonda and you'll find a piece of prosphora in it."

Vasily nodded seriously.

"And bring it here to me. Immediately."

Vasily glanced at the doctor. Having called a nurse over, he was occupied with the neighboring patient.

"You need rest, Katenka . . ." Vasily's face whispered.

"Immediately," she pronounced, looking away. "Immediately. Immediately."

"Okay, okay, I'll do it." He shook his balding head in a way that was both disgusting and familiar.

"Today. Immediately," she whispered hoarsely.

"Okay." He nodded. "They wouldn't let Sasha in. He's here too, in the hallway. He cried so much when he found out."

She remembered that she had a son. This realization didn't call forth any emotion in her. Then she remembered her father in his wheelchair. Her father seemed *so distant* to her, as if seen through inverted binoculars. She remembered that her mother had died a long time ago. And that her kind grandmother had also died.

"Bring it to me today," she repeated.

"I'll do it, darling, don't worry. I'll bring you the prosphora. I'll bring you a little icon too. Polina got them to say a remembrance prayer—when she found out, she immediately went to church and ordered one. But a miracle came to pass, thank God. And they shot that bastard, that cop, the werewolf, the shit, the filthy drug addict . . . He's gone, Katenka, forget about him. He shot four women dead and wounded three. They shot that little slime like a rabid dog. They're talking about you on every channel. You're a hero, Katyusha. Vasilenko called me, Segdeyeva called me, Anya's calling every hour, Nikolai's calling... And that woman from the prosecutor's office, you know, what's her name, Malavets, got through to me, offered to help, to use any of her connections. Such a spiritual woman, she said that everything to do with your case was closed, and we had such a bad opinion of her, huh?"

"Today." Sotnikova closed her eyes in the hopes of once again seeing the radiant Tiny Tim.

But only darkness lay before her.

"It's time for you to go," the doctor's voice rang out. "We generally don't let anyone in here at all, you know."

"I'll be back, Katyush." She felt her husband's beard against her cheek.

But she didn't open her eyes.

She licked her lips.

"Do you want a drink?" a woman's voice rang out.

Sotnikova opened her eyes. A nurse was standing next to her holding a sippy cup.

"Yeah."

The nurse helped her to drink.

"How long have I been here?" Sotnikova asked.

"Since yesterday."

"Is it morning?"

"It's noon. We're gonna have lunch soon."

Sotnikova realized she had to urinate. "Can I stand up?"

"No."

"I want to go to the bathroom."

"You're wearing a diaper."

"Ah..." Sotnikova touched herself through the thin sheet and felt the diaper.

"I...am I badly wounded?"

"Everything turned out miraculously for you," the nurse smiled. "The bullet went straight through and didn't hit anything. Soon, you'll be transferred out of the ICU."

Sotnikova began to urinate, looking at her hands as she did. It was only now that she noticed they'd removed her luxurious fake nails.

Her husband came back in the evening. He brought fresh prosphora and icons of the Virgin Mary and Pantaleon the Healer. Sotnikova wanted to scream at him with all of her remaining strength, but she changed her mind when she realized that this man with his dull face wouldn't be able to help her with anything. She demanded that they let her son come see her. When the thirteen-year-old Sasha came over to her bed and kissed her, she took him by the hand.

"Do me one favor, Sashenka. It's very important."

"You can count on me, Mommy."

"Go to Grandpa's place in Kuntsevo, open the back panel of his old record player, and you'll find a piece of prosphora—it fell in there a long time ago. I really need it. Without it, nothing's gonna work out for me."

"You can count on me, Mommy."

"Don't tell anyone about this. And bring it to me here. Yourself."

"You can count on me, Mommy, don't worry."

The next day, Sasha came to see her. And handed her a thin, dried-out crescent moon of prosphora.

"Thank you, Sashenka." She took the crescent moon and squeezed it in her fist. "Now go. I need to sleep."

Her son kissed her and left.

Forty-two minutes later, her heart stopped.

WHITE SQUARE

2017

HOST: Hello, and welcome to *White Square*! Today, we're going to talk about Russia. Our grand, fantastical, and, in many ways, unpredictable country "shall be unknowable to foreign sages for centuries and centuries," as we sing in an old song. The truth is that Russia continues to prompt questions not only among *foreign sages*—and that's putting it mildly—but also among our own countrymen. An old pal of mine confessed that, after living in Russia for forty-odd years—can you imagine?—he still didn't understand exactly what our country was. And this is an Orthodox man, a patriot, an intellectual deeply familiar with our history and culture. Now, we're not here to discuss our political system. Every schoolkid knows that Russia is a federal, democratic state, with a president and a parliament. But what image does our country call forth in us? What does it look like? What associations does it carry? Everyone has their own image of Russia. I'm sure that many of these images are compatible. Some may not be. And, no, I'm not just talking about what the fifth column thinks. In fact, this diversity simply shows yet again, in all of its ebbs and flows, the deep mysteriousness of Russia. Shows—ebbs and flows! I'm speaking in rhyme, that's how important our topic is today! Let's really talk about this. Today, as always, four guests are sitting around our square white table. You probably recognize some of them. But, you know our rule on *White Square*: first names and professions only. No titles, positions, or regalia. And so: Irina is a municipal employee, Yuri is a military man, Anton is a theater director, and Pavel is a businessman. Respected guests of the program, I have one question for all of you: What do you think Russia looks like? Please!

(Applause)

IRINA: Why is everyone looking at me? *(She laughs.)*

HOST: Ladies first.

IRINA: Of course. Well, in that case, I'll begin. Hm . . . you know what Russia is for me? A song. That sounds a little naive, I bet, doesn't it?

HOST: Not at all.

IRINA: There you go then. A song. A song. A long, slightly sad Russian song. Which I heard when I was still a child, when I knew no words, but someone was singing it nearby, it was winter, I can remember the cold, all the windows in our town were frozen. And that song. Whenever anyone says "Russia," like Russsh-iiaa, I remember that melody, the frost on the windows, my grandma in the kitchen, her dried-sturgeon-spinal-cord pies, my little brother, our furry cats, the street, snowdrifts, our kindly neighbors, games, school, lots of dreams, then, suddenly, um, I remember this childish feeling that, basically, we live in a very large country, a mighty and powerful country, that somewhere out there, really, really far away, is Moscow, with the Kremlin and the Spasskaya Tower, and that, when I grow up, I'll go there and see all of it. And the song goes on and on. Just like it was before. And for as long as it resounds, for as long as we keep singing it, know its words, and remember its melody, Russia shall survive.

(Applause)

HOST: What a fantastic start, Irina! I think a great many people in our country are familiar with this image—that it's very dear to them. You can't imagine Russia without a song. Anton, are you ready for your turn?

ANTON: Yes, of course. Irina put it very well. A song. A song from her childhood. A song's unforgettable. It etches itself into your memory for your whole life. For me, that song is "Blue Wagon." It somehow eclipsed all the other Russian folk songs, even though we sang a lot of 'em in my family and at school. "Blue Wagon" is the one that'll stay with me forever. But I don't want to talk about songs; I want to talk about my image of Russia. I admit that it's a bit different from Irina's. I imagine our country as a huge, enormous—a monstrously large louse. It's also in the deepest hibernation, completely frozen. Geographically speaking, it's as big as Russia: its head and mouth, er, its—whaddya call 'em—its pedipalps are located near our border with Belarus, right around Chop, and its butt hangs out over the Pacific Ocean by Sakhalin Island. And this gigantic louse is sleeping, it's motionless. It doesn't wake up often, but its awakening is a gift for us all. We live atop of this icy monster, slide around on its back, get frightened by it, marvel at its unusual shape, and wait for its awakening. We wait with impatience and horror. For decades sometimes—like we are now, for example.

(*Applause*)

HOST: Hmmm . . . No wonder your plays always cause such scandals, Anton! What's happening with the latest trial you caused with your production of *Dead Souls*?

ANTON: We're definitely gonna win.

HOST: That so?

(*Laughter*)

ANTON: The lawyers' *living souls* will fix everything!

(*Laughter*)

HOST: Send my best to their living souls! In any case, though we shall discuss each image in detail, first everyone must also have the chance to speak. Yuri!

YURI: You know, when I was invited onto *White Square*, they also, I guess I'll reveal the secret, hipped me to the topic of today's discussion. I had a few days to think, to get my thoughts in order. For me, Russia has always resembled a cave. A cave of real mysteries. A huge, dark, endless cave filled with stalactites, stalagmites, and holes, which is to say crags of varying size, pitch black, no end to 'em, you can't see a thing, no bottom at all. An immense cave. And in this cave are treasures. They shine in the darkness. You're walking through the cave, the ground's uneven, danger at every step. You could slip or fall, but just up ahead, you can see a flickering. Those are her riches. The riches of Russia. They shine in the darkness, they're beckoning to you and you move towards them. There're so many of them—you can't even count all the—

HOST: Diamonds in dusky caves?

YURI: Yes! But more than diamonds. We're not just talking about gold, oil, uh, gas. Russia is rich on the inside, in terms of what she has inside . . . in her soul. Rich in spirit! That's our main source of wealth.

(Applause)

HOST: Fantastic! And yet, real variation has immediately become apparent in these images, no? *(Addresses the audience.)* Our guests today truly demonstrate the unpredictability of our country.

(Applause)

PAVEL: It probably won't be terribly original if I say that, for me, Russia has always been connected to the notion of struggle. Struggle for survival, for the right idea, for comfort, for true friends, for love, for family, and, finally, for business. Everyone sitting at this table was born under the Soviet Union and everyone remembers it in one way or another. For example, when my wife gave birth to our daughter, the first thing the Soviet state did was take the baby and carry it off to another ward in the hospital where the mothers weren't really allowed. This was a Soviet tradition that, in my opinion, all of those who gave birth under the Soviet Union will remember. And, of course, the possibility of the father being present at the birth, as now happens the whole world over, wasn't ever discussed. I couldn't even get inside the maternity hospital. All of the fathers were walking in circles around the building, glancing through the windows, trying to catch sight of something. What I did was I gave a nurse three rubles so she'd let my wife into the ward where they kept the babies at night—to see our Olya. Can you even imagine? For money, a mother sneaks around like a thief to go see her baby! The struggle! From its first days, every newborn child was drawn into the struggle. Everyone has had to and shall have to struggle—struggle for everything! Each step is an act of overcoming! That's what Russia is!

(Applause)

HOST: Yes, it's hard for me to even imagine. I was at my wife's side when she gave birth. We got through it together and when my son was born—

PAVEL: They put him on his mother's chest, right?

HOST: Yep, they didn't even wash him, just laid him on my wife's chest. It was...unforgettable. But Pavel, in czarist Russia, they may not have taken children away from their mothers, true, but did all of them survive back then? In small villages, for example? They didn't even have maternity hospitals out there! They had to carry their children out into the barn with the cows! And how many of them died? Even Leo Tolstoy, a count, lost four of his children, if I'm remembering correctly.

PAVEL: But it isn't just humans who put newborn babies on their mother's chests—it's also animals the world over!

ANTON: And it doesn't cost three rubles.

PAVEL: And it doesn't cost three rubles!

HOST: You're complaining about giving a nurse three rubles? What a penny pincher!

(Laughter)

PAVEL: That was a lot of money for us back then.

IRINA: They laid my daughter on my chest, too. Our country was the Russian Federation by then.

HOST: I can only imagine how beautiful that must have been! A painting by Raphael!

(Applause)

PAVEL: Thank God that's how it is in our time...

ANTON: But will it be like that forever? That's the question!

(Applause)

HOST: Let's hope so! In any case, Russia continues to stride forwards. With difficulty and confusion, yes, but forwards nevertheless. And the fact that we can calmly discuss all of this here in the studio is proof of that!

(*Applause*)

HOST: Now, I'm going to start up our voting machine. Those of you who are seated in the studio can vote for any image of Russia outlined by our guests: "Song," "Icy Louse," "Cave," or "Struggle." Let's vote! And, in the meantime, my first question is for Irina. In your steadily improving district, do songs help people build their lives?

IRINA: We sang and danced our hearts out on City Day!

HOST: The senior citizens, too?

IRINA: Of course!

HOST: Were they waving around bills with increased utility rates?

(*Guffaws from the audience.*)

IRINA: The rates in our district haven't gone up for five months. And they're not going to go up in the near future. I promise!

HOST: Well, that sounds like a good song! We'll all join in.

(*Applause*)

HOST: Anton, take a look, here's your icy louse. What does it do? Suck the people's blood?

ANTON: It had its fill of sucking in the twentieth century.

HOST: And now it's digesting?

ANTON: Yes—digesting, meditating, and resting.

HOST: What about us?

ANTON: We admire it, worship it, write songs for it, make films about it.

IRINA: Why do you have such a disgusting image of our country?

ANTON: Look back at the twentieth century. Tens of millions of victims. Innocent victims killed by a monster called the USSR.

IRINA: But we live in the RF.

ANTON: Yeah, new letters, but the monster's genetics have stayed the same. Not everything, no, of course not! Much has changed for the better. But, basically…the genetics of the *state* haven't changed.

YURI: But why a louse and not, for example, a bear?

HOST: Yes! Why not a bear? That's an animal that looks a bit more like Russia: it sleeps for a long time, but when it wakes up, it begins to run around, to howl and scratch itself in such a way that no one will be unimpressed!

(Laughter)

ANTON: A bear is an image from a fairy tale. *The Gulag Archipelago* is not a fairy tale.

HOST: So—a louse?

ANTON: A louse.

HOST: Forgive me Anton, but is this just a louse or is it a pubic crab?

(Guffaws)

ANTON: I don't find it funny. It's sad.

HOST: Well, you have, um, you have every right to be sad ... Pavel, a question: Your "struggle"—does it come from Marx or, forgive me, from *Mein Kampf*?

PAVEL: From neither. It comes from the Stone Age. It's a struggle for survival.

HOST: In that case, has Russia not changed since the Stone Age? Do you have a stone axe instead of an iPhone? Which model? An 8, I hope?

(Laughter)

PAVEL: They make iPhones in America. Russia's problem is that we live our lives apart from the state. There's an abyss between us. And it's growing. That's why our struggle for survival is becoming more difficult every year.

HOST: Irina, do you agree?

IRINA: No. We have problems. But there's no *abyss*.

(Applause)

PAVEL: Well, obviously there's no abyss between you and the state. You're part of the state.

IRINA: And one of the people too. Think about it—are you one of the people?

PAVEL: *(Laughing)* I *am* the people.

HOST: That so?

(Laughter, applause)

220 · VLADIMIR SOROKIN

HOST: Moving on! Yuri, in your hall of the Mountain King, are the diamonds and emeralds of Russian spirituality as inexhaustible as they once were? Or is it at least possible that some of our deposits have been exhausted?

YURI: A lot of it's been wasted, but a lot's been purposefully fouled—

HOST: By the fifth column?

YURI: By bribe takers. And the fifth column. But there are new deposits, new mines, that have only just been discovered—in our time.

(Applause)

ANTON: *(Ironically)* Yes, they just . . . shine in the darkness! Geysers of spirituality bursting with diamonds.

YURI: You're just jealous—so jealous.

ANTON: I wish that were so.

HOST: Does the spirituality of the people bother you?

ANTON: More like their lack of spirituality.

HOST: So, you think that modern Russia is soulless?

ANTON: Basically—yes.

HOST: Have you already been paid for a new play?

(Laughter)

ANTON: Oh yes—I've been paid . . . We're going to elevate the people's spirituality—

YURI: With naked Valkyries?

ANTON: It can't hurt.

HOST: Naked Valkyries are ve-ry ve-ry spiritual!

(Laughter)

IRINA: My daughter's a big fan of yours, Anton. And, after your last play, she said, "There were just too many naked butts, Mom!"

(Laughter)

ANTON: Our government has always had money for naked butts and always will. But it's reluctant to spend much on veterans.

PAVEL: Isn't it a little less reluctant with students and doctors?

YURI: Well, they're at least getting something.

ANTON: Protractors for spiritual measurements?

YURI: Again with the irony. Don't you ever get bored?

("The voting is complete" alert goes off.)

HOST: Friends! The voting on "Images of Russia" is now complete. So: 37 percent of you voted for Song, 31 percent for Cave, 28 percent for Struggle, and 4 percent for Icy Louse. It seems you're in the minority, Anton. Therefore, we have the right *not* to believe your thesis about the soullessness of Russia. Our winner is "Russia as a Song"!

("The Hype is here" alert goes off.)

HOST: It's time for the White Hype!

(The song "The White Hype Is Here, There Are So Many Squares" begins to play.)

HOST: It's time to get moving, my friends! The product is in the studio!

(As the song plays, four enchanting nurses in short white skirts enter the studio; each of them is carrying a tray with a syringe, a tourniquet, a cotton swab, and a vial of rubbing alcohol.)

HOST: Today, our program *White Square* is asking its guests to *get hyped* on a new product that was approved for use a week ago. It's called WH-4! Let's hear it!

(Applause)

HOST: Out enchanting girls—Sonya, Vera, Fatima, and Natasha—will help you out.

(The guests sitting at the white table roll up their sleeves, the nurses give them each an intravenous injection.)

HOST: WH-4 is a remarkable drug. The most remarkable thing about it is its subtlety. It causes cheerfulness and clarity of mind, but it also intensifies the senses, and all of this happens unobtrusively, nonaggressively, most delicately. It's a gentle high, not dragging you along but offering itself up. It has all the well-known features of the WH formula. Compared to WH-3, however, which so many Russians have fallen in love with in the last six months, which our mighty rock bands sing about, which our minister has spoken of so effusively, well, compared to WH-3, it's a little different. But not for the worse! Not at all for the worse, ladies and gentlemen! Now as our guests begin to feel it, we too shall immediately begin to feel *this*! As always, after the White Hype, the discussion will begin to operate on another level, attain a new valence, fill with new energy and new meaning, all of which will be passed on to us! Friends, a lot of interesting stuff lies in store. Let's hear it!

(Applause)

(Having finished the injections, the four nurses take their leave of the studio. The four guests stay seated, pressing cotton swabs into the crooks of their arms.)

HOST: I mean really, what an amazing country we live in! We're ready to discuss its image with such enthusiasm for practically the umpteenth time! It's stunning! Can you imagine such a talk show on French or German television? I won't even say anything about the Americans . . . (*Laughter*) Can you imagine that all of them would seriously reflect on the image of their country? Everything's been clear to them for a long time. For them, it's not even worth asking the question. Every kindergartner knows that Europe has ossified. The Europeans know it too, oh they know! But they stay silent! And as for us? The greatness of Russia is that it changes, evolves, and reveals itself to be shining with new facets, surprising and shocking us literally every day!

(Applause)

PAVEL: Generally, I'm not sure . . . if you want to . . . to even know . . . I mean, to put it simply . . . when you want to do something new and strong, something totally different. Then? Something necessary? Then?

ANTON: Something mighty, right?

PAVEL: Yeah! Powerful! Bright! Something totally different! So that it shines precisely like something "different"! Like a neon sign— and then?

HOST: Here we go—the White Hype has begun!

(Applause)

ANTON: Because you're sick of it.

YURI: So fuckin' sick of it!

ANTON: So sick you'll throw up, you'll puke...

YURI: Had e-fuckin'-nuff! It's dim and pathetic—had e-fuckin'-nuff!

HOST: My dear guests! Though we're able to bleep such words, un-questionably, I would perhaps ask you—

IRINA: *(Standing up and interrupting.)* What would you ask? Huh?

HOST: I would ask you to perhaps...

IRINA: What, what can you ask us, you stump? *(She throws her cotton swab in his face.)*

HOST: Irina...I don't understand your aggression.

IRINA: What are you asking? What do you want? *(She kicks the host.)*

HOST: Hmm...It seems that something's gone wrong. *(Backing away, he bumps into Anton.)*

ANTON: Where do you think you're going, you nit? *(He grabs the host's jacket and pulls violently, splitting a seam at the shoulder.)*

HOST: I would ask you...c'mon, gentlemen...

YURI: *(Stands up.)* Here's *gentlemen* for you! *(He punches the host in the face with great force.)* Little shit stain—

PAVEL: *(Grabs the host and hurls him to the ground.)* You're a... hindrance...a sucker—

HOST: Call security!

YURI: *(Hits the host.)* Here's your security. Here's your...Here's—

IRINA: *(Kicks the host.)* He's still gonna point at me...bastard—

HOST: Security!!!

YURI: *(Sits down on the host.)* Lie the fuck down...

(Two security guards enter, run over.)

GUARD: Um, what's going on here?

YURI: *(Sitting on the host.)* Nothing's going on. He's just been shitting on all of us. Both of you, too. He's a criminal. A federal offender! *(The guards stand next to Yuri.)*

YURI: What regiment did you fellas serve in?

(The guards exchange a silent look. The host starts to shout, but Irina puts her hand over his mouth.)

IRINA: Just lie there—don't push us out!

YURI: *(To the guards.)* I asked you a question: What regiment did you scrve in?

GUARD: The missile forces. What's going on?

ANTON: What's happening is what's supposed to happen, fellas. The radiance of the new!

PAVEL: Exactly! The radiance!

YURI: *(To the second guard.)* And where did you serve?

GUARD: In the Baltics.

YURI: Grab that crab, sailor! *(He extends his arm to the guard.)* As soldiers, do you know what honor and redress are? How is this any different? Hmm? From honor and red dress?
(The guards are silent.)

YURI: And? You're not saying anything—are you jacking your dicks? It's time for you to learn, soldiers: Honor and red dress are better than honor and redress. Than honor and chess. Than honor and stress. Than honor and abscess. And never, under any circumstances, ignore me and try to fucking transgress. As in the case of a federal offender. Am I clear? Everything's under control, guys! You can go!
(The guards leave.)

HOST: *(Desperately.)* Where're you going?! Come back!!! Seryozha, you idiot, they overdosed!

IRINA: *(Covering his mouth.)* You're the one who overdosed, you stump!

ANTON: No, there are no limits for the new in the process of tearing down old walls! It's like a battering ram! I feel like a battering ram! I can crush old junk, crush it, shatter it into a new, prospective something that shall shine out a way for the new icy louse! This louse shall shine away all of our old doubts, all the old meanness and abomination, all of it will bounce off the louse, fly off it, all the dummies, the mummies, the Mickey Mouses, the Richard Strausses, Mr. Santa Claus, the useless laws, the Pikachus and the Gucci shoes. Only the honest will remain. Only the new.

PAVEL: Shining! Like the sun!

ANTON: Shining for all eternity! Forever!!! And why don't I hear any applause?! Huh?
(Applause.)

YURI: So. We'll need four belts.

PAVEL: What kind of belts?

YURI: Strong! Faithful! Durable!

ANTON: *(Takes off his belt.)* Here! For the new!

PAVEL: Take mine too! *(Takes off his belt.)* For the shiny!

IRINA: *(Still holding the moaning host's mouth shut.)* I ... don't have a belt. But I should also ... should also give something up for the new. *(She takes off her blouse.)*

HOST: Call the police, you idiots! You're gonna be fired and put in jail!

YURI: Take the belt off the past! *(He jabs his fist at the host's face.)* *(Irina takes the host's belt off; Yuri takes off his own belt.)*

YURI: Brothers and sisters, let us lift up the past!

(They lift up the host, who is screaming, groaning, and swearing.)

YURI: Put him on that table.

ANTON: New! Everything is new, cheerful, and good!

PAVEL: And shining!

YURI: Bind his hands and feet to the corners of the table.

(The host is lying on the table, his hands and feet are bound to its four corners with belts and a twisted-up blouse).

HOST: Seryozha!! Call the police!!! What are you waiting for?!! You idiot!!!

YURI: *(Gagging the host with his handkerchief.)* The evil of the past.

IRINA: How much evil! Yet it seems kind. Curly haired. Have we been tricked?

YURI: He tricked us. Tricked us. And Russia too.

PAVEL: Our eternal Russia! Its eternal ices shining in the sun! Such spectacular ices!

ANTON: Deception? How can it be so?! This ... shocks me. It rends my soul. *(He sobs.)*

IRINA: Calm down! I love you!

ANTON: And I love you! *(He kisses Irina.)*

PAVEL: I love all of you! *(He kisses Irina and Anton.)* I love you so unbelievably much!

ANTON: We must clear the old from the new path, smash, destroy, and sprinkle the dust and ashes of the past into the wind! Ahead lies only the new, the strong, and the bright!

YURI: We have to do everything properly. Otherwise, it's already too late. It'll be impossible to fix!

IRINA: We must do everything properly! My darlings! Let's do this right!

PAVEL: There's no other way! The new and the proper! The shining and the good! In the name of Shining Russia!

ANTON: She's shining! Ahead! For all of us!

(Applause)

YURI: *(Takes an AK-47 knife out of his pocket and opens it.)* Here. Hello my old and faithful friend. You've seen so much! I've always carried, carry, and shall carry you with me. *(He kisses its blade.)* You've never betrayed me. Please help us now! *(He cuts the clothes off the host, who is crucified to the table; the others help him.)*

ANTON: *(Drops the cut-up clothing on the floor.)* This is the past. The bad.

PAVEL: Very bad! Evil!

IRINA: Naked evil. Beastly evil! *(She spits in the host's face.)*

ANTON: The evil of the past must be overcome. So that it cannot obstruct the shining of Eternal Russia!

(Applause.)

PAVEL: Together, we shall overcome all of this!

YURI: Brothers and sisters! Take up your work properly! And amicably!

(Yuri makes a deep cut on the Host's hands and feet; the other four peel back his skin, flaying him; at first he twitches, roars, struggles, but, soon, he falls silent.)

YURI: A grand act! *(He unties the Host's corpse from the table, pushes it onto the floor, and moves it under the table with his foot.)* Now, we must do that which is important. Let us begin, brothers and sisters! *(They stretch the host's skin over the table.)*

YURI: Carefully! It might tear! There's no rush!

ANTON: Carefully! Consistently! Exactly! *(He covers Irina's shoulders with warning kisses.)*

(The skin is completely taut.)

YURI: We have done a grand and important thing!

(Applause)

PAVEL: Victory!

IRINA: Happiness!

ANTON: *(To Irina.)* The time of joy has come! Of new joy!

PAVEL: *(To Irina.)* Of shining joy!

YURI: *(Cuts Irina's underclothes off with his knife.)* Bring us joy! You must!

(They help Irina, now naked, clamber up onto the table.)

IRINA: *(Throws her hands into the air and begins to quickly spin around on the table.)*

Ababara!

Akhakhara!

Atatara!

(Puts her hands to her groin and squeezes her thighs together.)

Ababonia!

Amamonia!

Akhakhonia!

(Shakes from the force of her orgasm.)

Mamo rokhma-a-a-a-a!

(Howls and shakes, spreads her legs, urinates onto the tables.)

Mamo I can't bocomo like a hordo-o-o-o-o!!!

No need to becomo together and then like a hordo-o-o-o-o!!!

Now that they have bocomo like all of us a hordo-o-o-o-o!!!

Nothing to bocomo if Mamo's not already a hordo-o-o-o-o!!!

Everyone becomo everyone and everyone's a hordo Mamo's a hordo and everyonnnneeeeee!!!

(Irina falls weakly from the table. Yuri, Pavel, and Anton catch her. She moans with exhaustion.)

ANTON: *(Shakes his head rhythmically, trembles, and stomps his feet.)* Let's go, brothers! Brothers, let's go! Let's go, brothers! Brothers, let's go!

YURI: *(Makes painful motions with his buttocks.)* To do-do-do-do-do-do-do that which is good.

PAVEL: *(Squirms)* And shining! Shining in the darkness! In the dark darkness, the dork dungeon, they built something good, necessary, shining dmomiate dmomiate dmomiate! For centuries! Centuries!!!

(The three moaning and sobbing men carry Irina out of the studio, greedily licking and sucking on her limbs.)

A VOICE: The show is now over! We ask that everyone leave the studio!

(The audience leaves. A little while later, a group of people comes in: the managing director of the channel, the assistant director of the channel, a chemist, the director of the show, and the guards.)

MANAGING DIRECTOR: *(Approaches the table.) Finita.* First-rate.

ASSISTANT DIRECTOR: The product proved itself. Really frickin' proved itself, huh? Maybe a little too much though.

CHEMIST: RH-1 well and truly edged out WH-4.

DIRECTOR OF SHOW: *(Shakes his head.)* I can't believe it. *Awesome*!

MANAGING DIRECTOR: *(Slaps him on the back.)* You'd better believe it! RH's time has come.

CHEMIST: We need to make some adjustments.

MANAGING DIRECTOR: That goes without saying... *(He looks under the table.)* Otherwise, we'll run out of hosts.... Mhm... The product solved two problems in one go. Right? "Bumbarash!" as my deceased dad used to say in this sort of situation.

DIRECTOR OF SHOW: Bumbarash! Yeah! I mean... totally!

ASSISTANT DIRECTOR: Nobody was expecting this, right? Were you expecting it? None of us were! That's what we mean by extra milligrams, right?

CHEMIST: Half a square. We'll need some adjustments, some new R-tests. It'll take two or three weeks. We'll need a new crop of donors—quite a small one.

MANAGING DIRECTOR: *(Not listening to the chemist.)* Mhmm... and the third thing: a mythical tale played out. Arbitrarily! And inevitably.

ASSISTANT DIRECTOR: What do you mean?

MANAGING DIRECTOR: The Flaying of Marsyas. You don't know it? Look it up.

ASSISTANT DIRECTOR: *(Looks at his tablet, finds it, and reads.)* Ah! Dope! But Marsyas was punished by Apollo for winning a contest. Right?

MANAGING DIRECTOR: *(Pokes the corpse under the table with the toe of his shoe.)* Apollo won a competition too. More precisely—he didn't lose. *(To the guards.)* Take the body away. *(To the assistant director.)* Mark this down as an occupational injury, fatal.

ASSISTANT DIRECTOR: *(Tapping on his tablet.)* Doing that now. *(The guards drag the corpse away.)*

MANAGING DIRECTOR: Take the skin off the table. And fold it up neatly.

GUARD: But ... it's covered in urine. And blood ...

MANAGING DIRECTOR: So?

GUARD: Maybe we could wash it first?

MANAGING DIRECTOR: Urine is environmentally friendly. Blood too. Do what I say! Fold it tighter.

(The guards take the skin off the table and fold it up neatly.)

DIRECTOR OF SHOW: *(Touches the blood-soaked table.)* Listen, if we've got more of a Red Hype goin' down, maybe we should change the name? Like, *Red Square*?

MANAGING DIRECTOR: That'll just get lumped together with the Red project: Bolsheviks, Lenin, the Revolution ... Fuck that! We'll stick with *White Square*. It's a brand everyone knows.

ASSISTANT DIRECTOR: We can just redo the song: "The Red Hype is here ..."

DIRECTOR OF SHOW: "... There are so many squares"?

MANAGING DIRECTOR: Yeah. And we'll keep the table white.

DIRECTOR OF SHOW: That'll cost money.

MANAGING DIRECTOR: We'll help out. I won't refuse you anything.

DIRECTOR OF SHOW: And the host?

(The managing director spreads his hands with an affirmative sigh.)

DIRECTOR OF SHOW: What ... again?

ASSISTANT DIRECTOR: *(With a reproachful laugh.)* Who else could we get? Are there other options?

DIRECTOR OF SHOW: *(Grimaces.)* No, but maybe—

MANAGING DIRECTOR: It's not worth it. Time, time.

DIRECTOR OF SHOW: But, at least—

MANAGING DIRECTOR: We have no choice. You know the year we have coming. It's crawling in like a glacier.

ASSISTANT DIRECTOR: *(To the director of the show.)* What? Are you afraid you won't work well together? Get that thought out of your head. We've got him by the balls. He'll do what he has to.

DIRECTOR OF SHOW: No, no, listen, it's not really about—

MANAGING DIRECTOR: *(Interrupts.)* You *will* work together. You have no choice!

DIRECTOR OF SHOW: *(Disagrees.)* No one asked me if I wanted to get partnered up. It's just like last time, dammit! Why?

ASSISTANT DIRECTOR: Because you have to, old man! We're all in the same boat. You're a genius. Everyone knows that. We'll help you. This'll be the hit of the year.

MANAGING DIRECTOR: *(To the guards.)* Did you finish folding it? *(The guards show him the skin, which has been rolled into a tube.)*

MANAGING DIRECTOR: *(Takes the skin and sniffs it. Puts the two ends of the tube together and hands it to the guard.)* Hold it like that . . .

(The guard holds it. The managing director takes a gold pin out of his tie and sticks it through the two ends of the tube. It becomes a ring.)

MANAGING DIRECTOR: *(Puts the tube around the Director's neck.)* Check it out! Wear that for a little while. For inspiration.

DIRECTOR OF SHOW: *(Gives a tired, ironic laugh.)* Well-l-l-l tha-a-ank you!

MANAGING DIRECTOR: I'm off! *(Slaps the director on the shoulder and palpates the ring of skin.)* So beautiful. It suits you. Bring it back to me in a little while. We'll knock back a few glasses.

(All, except for the Director, leave the studio. He walks over to the window and opens it. Lights up. Observes the city, Moscow, at night. A light snow is falling.)

DIRECTOR OF SHOW: The Flaying of Marsyas . . . *(Laughs.)* The same cocksuckin' boat . . . *(Begins to sing an old Russian song.)*

Doubts away, into the night, another . . . *(Pauses, smirks.)* Another bit of madness.

(Takes the ring off his neck, sniffs it, and frowns.)

(Addresses the ring.) I never raised my voice at you, buddy. And you yelled at me so often. A star! *(Grins.)*

(Puts the ring around his arm and begins to spin it.)

But, I mean . . . how can I put this . . . generally speaking . . . well . . . as the genius says: nothing but gratitude will come out of my mouth. Forever. I'm being . . . honest. No, really. No fuckin' joke. Thank you for everything. We did good work. Awesome! We did some quality work. And you were a pro. Always. So . . . White Hype or Red . . . it's what-the-fuck-ever. What-the-fuck-ever, what-the-fuck-ever, what the fuck. The main thing is being a pro. We're pros. Pro, pro, pro. Whatever, what the fuck, what-the-fuck-ever. Pro, pro, pro. That's decisive. That, that, that. That, that, that. *(The ring begins to spin faster and faster.)* Pro, pro, pro . . . What-the-fuck-ever, what-the-fuck-ever, what the fuck . . . Pro, pro, pro . . . What-the-fuck-ever, what-the-fuck-ever, what the fu—

(The ring flies off his arm and out the window.)

Motherfucker! *(Looks out the window, pulls out his iPhone, and makes a call.)* Yes, Seryozha, run and ask the guards to go downstairs right now, just outside, to the right of the entrance, on the lawn, they'll find a sort of . . . ring—how can I put this—well . . . it's made of papier-mâché . . . no, it's basically folded parchment. They've gotta find it! They must! They've gotta look! Tell 'em it's the managing director's ring! His property! We need it to shoot the show! *(Leaves the studio carrying his iPhone.)*

A crow perched on a telephone pole saw the ring of skin fall from the seventh floor onto the snow-powdered lawn. Took off from the pole, glided down, and landed next to the ring. Squinted at the ring and pecked at it several times. Picked up the ring in its beak and flew off with it with some difficulty. Flew over a steel fence and past a parking lot, almost hitting several cars with the ring. Two other crows noticed the first crow, took off, and flew after it. Sensing that it was being followed, the crow flapped its wings faster, rising higher. The other crows caught up to it as it flew over an overpass. A brief tussle in the air and the crow dropped the ring. It fell onto the roof of a large semi going over the overpass. The semi got onto the Yaroslavl' highway and stayed on it for six hours and eighteen minutes. During this time, the ring moved to the front of the body of the semi, moving slightly forward each time the driver braked hard. The semi turned off the highway and onto a road, then turned left, right, then left again. During the last turn, the ring of skin flew off the roof and landed in a ditch. Forty-two minutes later, a stray dog found it, picked it up, and ran off. When the dog was running across the square and past a shop, Andruykha Smirnov, a cripple everyone called "Earwax," caught sight of it. He walked through the open door of the shop to buy some bread, then stopped, smoked, and leaned on his cane. Watching the dog run with the ring of skin between its teeth, he noticed that something on the ring was shining. Hungover as he was, he seemed to see an expensive women's watch. Earwax spat out his cigarette butt, drew back his arm, then threw his cane, carved from young ash, at the dog. The cane hit the dog in the legs. The dog yelped, dropped the ring, and rushed off. Earwax hobbled over. He picked up the ring with a grunt. Removed the golden tie pin, brought it to his face.

"Aha..."

Footsteps resounded behind him. Earwax quickly put the pin in the pocket of his *vatnik* jacket, picked up his cane, and turned around. A big, portly fella, Sasha Losev, walked up to him, having come to buy bread as well.

"What the hell are you doing?" Sasha growled.

"Hey there, Sashok!" Earwax turned his *ushanka*-clad head to him ingratiatingly. "Look what I got from that mutt!"

He showed Sasha the ring of skin, which was now beginning to straighten out.

"What the hell?" Sasha scowled dismally.

"It's kind of a... sausage, y'see. It must have come way the fuck over from the factory 'cause I got hold of it over here!"

"What kinda sausage is that?" Sasha looked at it dismally.

"Huh!" Earwax turned the ring over and sniffed at it with his squashed nose. "No, you know what this is? Sheep gut. Damn straight! They fill it with liver. See? Stuffed right into the tube!"

Squinting at the ring with swollen eyes, Sasha pulled a pack of Parliaments and a lighter from the pocket of his vatnik. "When y'goan pay me back?"

Earwax pressed the ring to his dark-gray vatnik. "Holy crow, Sash! Lemme fuckin' swear to you that, when Ma's pension comes, I'm gonna be good for it—a hundred percent—or you can rip out my teeth!"

Sasha lit up in silence. Spat. "It's been two months."

"Sashok, I don't have shit right now, I swear. This is what we could scrape together for bread, Ma's been beggin' me to go to the store since morning. Our chow's nothin' but potatoes and cabbage, *empty* tea with no sugar. Home's no fun right now."

Sasha kept silent and blew a cloud of smoke. "Here's how it's gonna be—if you don't get it before the holidays, I'm goan come over on the thirty-first and break your windows. Your New Year might be a little breezy."

"Sash, I swear, I ain't goan fuck you—"

"I'm goan fuck *you* if you don't get it to me. Fuck you with the freezing cold."

"I got it, Sash. At least take this . . . tripe. It's real fine. Back when we kept sheep, Grandma would make tripe soup all the time—delicious! Take it. Take it!"

Earwax stuffed the ring into Sasha's bag. Sasha mutely walked over to the store. Bought a stale loaf of rye bread and two warm loaves of white bread after waiting in line. Set off home through the village.

At home, his wife had almost finished stoking the stove. Sasha put a warm loaf of white bread onto the table, took the ring of skin out of his bag, and handed it to his wife:

"Here."

"What the hell is this?" His wife looked at it suspiciously.

"Mutton tripe from the factory. I found it . . . or, um, Earwax *racketeered* it. Someone brought it to him."

His wife took the ring, looked at it, and sniffed.

"The fucker still doesn't have the thousand. He swears he'll have it before the holidays." Sasha took his *shapka* off his head and removed his woolen gloves.

His wife tossed the ring onto a little table by the stove along with two pots, a peeled potato, a chunk of lard, and an onion.

"Even stinky-ass Earwax's got friends at the factory. We got no one!"

"It sucks shit . . ." Sasha took his vatnik and hung it on a nail in the door. "Seryoga got fired, Sanyok ran off. But we'll find someone, don't you worry."

"We goan find somebody, we goan fi-i-ind somebo-o-ody!" his wife began to sing mockingly, narrowing her already thin lips. "The whole village is stuffed with sausages and all we can do is sniff at 'em."

Sasha shook his heavy head, sat down at the table, tore off the heel of the warm loaf, and began to chew. His wife put the potato, the lard, and the onion into a small pot, added some water, salted it, put the lid back on, then pushed it into the stove with an oven fork. Straightening back up, she put her hands to her narrow hips.

"And what'm I s'posed to do with this tripe?"

"I dunno."

"It needs to be washed!"

"It's been washed—it's all twisted up."

"There's some dried blood on it."

"Len, if it hadn't been washed, it wouldn't have been twisted. No doubt! The blood's from a surface cut. The inside's washed."

His wife took the ring. Sniffed at it again. "It reeks . . ."

"It's tripe! It's s'posed t'reek. It's nutritious. They don't fill it with liver for nothin'."

His wife quickly washed the ring in the sink, put it down on the cutting board, then cut it into pieces. She then put them into a big pot of already boiled cabbage soup, put the cast-iron lid back on, picked up the oven fork, and, with a hiccupping sound, pushed it into the stove. She grabbed a long poker and raked the glowing coals over to the pot.

"Gimme somethin' to drink and I'll go," Sasha said, chewing the last of the heel.

His wife poured him tea into a big mug emblazoned with intertwined Soviet and American flags and the phrase SUMMIT 1987. He picked up a jar of currant jam, cut a slice of bread, spread some jam on it, then began to eat while sipping the tea. His wife poured herself some tea, put some jam in it, sipped, sat down, but immediately leapt back up.

"I'll pack you somethin' to munch on."

She cut a slice of rye bread, put a piece of lard on it, cut off a piece of a pirozhok filled with the same currant jam, then wrapped all of it in newspaper. Put it into Sasha's bag. Also put a couple of apples, a crooked cucumber, and half of a head of garlic in the bag. Sasha glanced at his watch.

"Okay, I'm off."

He started to get up, bumped the table with his heavy body, then got out from behind it. Put on his vatnik and shapka, took out a cigarette, stuck it in his mouth, and lit up.

His wife sipped at her tea, picked up a tin flap that was leaning against the stove, shut the mouth of the stove, stood up on her tiptoes, then closed the damper in the chimney pipe. "Will you be back earlier today?"

"I dunno how it'll play out. Today's a holiday. Two services."

"Ahhh..."

With his bag over his shoulder, he went out into the breezeway and opened a closet. Took out an old-looking suitcase, a square panel that had been painted white, four bars that were bound together, and a folding chair. Went out onto the porch, walked down the stairs, then strode across the snow-dusted ground, puffing at his cigarette. The village had already woken up and stoked their stoves. Sasha got to the bus stop, glanced at his watch. Four others were standing at the bus stop. He knew two of the fellas there, but he didn't talk to them, just stood there, turned away, and finished his cigarette. The bus came. Sasha got on last with all his things, put his suitcase in the aisle, then leaned the white panel, the bars, and the chair against it.

He pulled out his travel card and showed it to the driver. The bus wasn't full. Sasha got off at the fourth stop. There were already cars crowded around the Church of Saint Pantaleon the Healer, which towered up right by the road. People were walking into a liturgy that had begun thirty minutes earlier. Sasha walked over to the fence and put his heavy suitcase down on the asphalt. As always, two beggars sat by the entrance: the young, one-legged Kolya and the puffy, elderly Oksana. Not far from Oksana, an old woman named Nastya was selling dried herbs, jam, and wooden spoons from a tray. It made Sasha happy that there were no other hawkers of wares. Oksana and Kolya greeted him. "Hey there," he growled, then unbound the bars, placed them upright, and connected them with steel rods, creating an underframe. Placed the white, square panel onto the underframe. Opened his suitcase. Inside of it were twenty-six jars of honey: sixteen small and ten big. Sasha placed them on the panel, shut the suitcase, unfolded his chair, but didn't sit down yet. Instead, he lit a cigarette and looked around. People were walking. Not one *people*, but separate individuals. A large number of them had already been in the church, from which the singing of a small choir and the voice of the priest could be heard.

The old man from Ukhtoma's not here today, Sasha thought content-edly. *That's good. Maybe he got sick. Hopefully for a long-ass time . . .*

The old man from Ukhtoma was the main source of dangerous competition for Sasha in the honey trade. Basically, Sasha had begun to occupy himself with honey only at the end of August. In August, Vovka Maltsev and a guy who was on the run from Dagestan robbed the apiary in Kukoboi. They got away with sixty frames full of honey using the Dagestanian guy's Ford. The Dagestanian made an offer to Vovka. The kind of offer that doesn't come along every day. They got to work immediately after the nighttime raid: they cooked a hundred liters of fake honey using molasses, old honey, and starch, poured it into jars, and put a piece of real honeycomb that they'd cut out of the stolen frames into each jar. The jars turned out real pretty. There were a lot of them: 368. The Dagestanian guy took half of them and Vovka got the rest. He hid them in his attic. His wife and mother-in-law first started selling it by Vladychny Convent, but they already had quite a few honey hawkers there—they sold real honey too. So, they began to dip their toes at various markets, but it wasn't much use. They'd never had a car and to carry the jars on their own backs was a piss-poor notion. Then, yet again, Vovka got put "in the slammer" for two years. There was no good reason for it: he lost his shit at a bunch of Azeris at a tea house, wouldn't stop, a fight broke out, and someone pulled a knife. They cut Vovka, but he managed to smash an Azeri's skull with a bottle. Then—in short—the Azeris had an "in" with the cops and Vovka got put in jail. That was when his wife reached out to Sasha and Lena: *Help us move the jars and we'll split the profits.* Lenka immediately refused to sell the jars herself. She wouldn't have been able to, as she didn't know how to smile or talk to customers. Sasha, then, had to immerse himself in a new trade. He had no choice, since they had no money—as usual. Starting out at the markets, he soon realized that they were a dead end. So he moved on to the Church of Saint Pantaleon the Healer, a roadside establishment. He set up his stand on Sundays and on holidays. It started out pretty good: he sold forty jars in September. The half-liter jar cost four hundred rubles and the small one cost two hundred. Then, one dark day, on the Feast of the Cross, that old man from Ukhtoma appeared. He rolled up in a green Zhiguli carrying a battery of jars filled with real honey, as well as appetizing frames of honeycomb with beebread, beeswax, and propolis. He set up two tables and spread out his goods. At first, he wanted to set up next to Sasha, but Sasha caught on immediately.

"Find another spot, old man. More money that way."

"Whatever you say, my dear, whatever you say."

The old man was little, quick, kind, and a chatterbox. He shined bright against the background of Sasha's gloominess and heavy motionlessness. He called girls "my darling" and fellas "my dear." His first questions made Sasha tense up and freeze. They had to do with bees, and Sasha didn't know a damn thing about beekeeping.

"My dear, how was the swarming? Your bees didn't fly away?"

"Do you make the queen cell yourself or do you buy it at the store?"

"How many times did you feed them?"

"How was their hibernation?"

His questions stung...like bees. And Sasha had to wave them away like a bear. Fortunately, they weren't the first questions he'd gotten about these mysterious insects, so incomprehensible to him.

"How's the varroosis going for you?" one dude had asked.

"Nothin' to complain about yet." Sasha grinned, thinking that the man was asking about varicose veins, which Sasha's deceased mother had had a lot of.

"We're in big trouble in Sheksna: almost all of our hives are infected."

It turned out he wasn't talking about varicosis, but varroosis, a bee sickness. Another time, someone asked whether he used an electric honey extractor or if he did it by hand. Almost everyone asked what kind of honey he was selling.

"Mixed grass, mixed grass honey," Sasha blurted out.

After he'd grown comfortable in his new spot, Sasha thought of a straightforward fib: his brother tended to the apiary and he just sold the honey. With this shield, he could defend himself against all questions.

After an hour and a half, the service came to an end and people poured out of the church. Now, it was time to work. Energized by the lard, garlic, bread, and cucumber, Sasha began to feign liveliness: he clapped his big, chubby hands together, swayed back and forth, stamped his feet, and muttered, "Honey, Russian Orthodox honey, you gotta buy it, don't pass this offer by!"

But the people, as always, passed right by.

"Russian Orthodox honey. Mixed-grass honey. Smells like meadows, smells so sweet."

Even while muttering all of this, Sasha could not shake his innate gloominess. The old man from Ukhtoma flogged his wares so loudly the whole district heard. Sasha could bark loudly and sincerely like that only when he was getting the Krapivinys' goat to leave his vegetable garden. The people who were now leaving the church called forth no enthusiasm in him, but, logically, he knew that they were the only people who might buy his jars of false honey. He still couldn't overcome his gloomy nature.

"Have some honey, some Russian Orthodox honey."

A woman and her lil' daughter walked over. Tried it. Walked away. Two women walked over. One tried it. "I'll get one for them," she said, buying a small jar. Having made two hundred, he spread all the money out between the jars like Lena told him to: for luck. A stout, gray-haired man with a wide red nose and an unhappy face walked over, tried it. Walked away, unsatisfied. A family walked over, tried everything twice, then walked away. An old woman walked over and immediately bought a small jar. Then Seryozha, the police officer, came over.

"How's it goin'?"

"It's goin'," Sasha replied.

Sasha paid Seryozha a thousand a month. Seryozha glanced at the jars with his indifferent gaze, then walked away.

Because of the holiday, the church was open all day. People came to light candles, then drove off. Sasha would also sometimes go into the church and light a candle "for his health," but he didn't believe in God. Lenka didn't believe in God either, but she thought that "fate exists, so you better sniff out your path in life." Before the evening service, Sasha ate the pirog and the apples and began to feel slightly chilled despite the two sweaters he was wearing underneath his vatnik. He went to the church three times to warm up and went to the bushes twice to relieve himself. He followed the people with his swollen gaze, trying to guess how much money they had, what their family circumstances were, and where they lived. These people were so different, but they still somehow resembled one another. How exactly, Sasha couldn't explain. There was always something incomprehensibly unpleasant about people . . . His thoughts jumped around like fleas from one passerby to the next: he estimated, judged, reasoned, ridiculed, approved, and compared. The people passing by forced him to remember other people: his relatives, neighbors, and friends from the army or from his childhood in Rybinsk. Back then, life was good, cheerful, and satisfying, his father worked at an electromechanics factory called Magma, earning decent wages. Sasha went to Sambo class and was also learning to play the *bayan*. But then Magma closed and his father got fired. Sasha ended up in the army. Came back, got married. His mother died, his father died. And another life began . . . At moments like these, he would almost invariably begin to think about the old man from Ukhtoma. Why did he have to come precisely here?

"What the fuck, huh?" Sasha muttered, looking at all the people.

What was stopping him from selling his honey in Ukhtoma? What with his car, he could go anywhere he wanted. Even to Yaroslavl'. Even to Moscow. Sasha turned green with envy when he saw someone buy from the old man. He clenched his jaw with rage. If Vovka weren't in prison, he'd give him a thousand to pop the old man's tires. Or just to scare him a little. Doing it himself would be too much. The police were nearby too. Weighing in at 110 kilos, Sasha could smash the fidgety old man like a fly, but, unfortunately, it just wasn't possible.

Right before the evening service, it had begun to grow dark. Big flakes of snow floated down now and again. Waiting for the people to come pouring out of the church, Sasha was freezing his ass off, so he stomped his boots and walked back and forth in front of the fence. The beggars and Nastya, the old lady, had all left.

At last, they started to come out. Walking, walking; almost no one walked over to Sasha. Eventually, however, a lady in a fur coat bought a big jar. Sasha did the math in his head: 200 + 200 + 400 = 800. Not bad.

Once everyone had left, Sasha started to pack up. Put the jars in his suitcase, took down the white panel, dismantled the underframe, bound the bars together, folded up his chair. Picked up everything and strode over to the bus stop.

At home, it was warm and the air was filled with the cabbagey scent of *shchi*.

"Pour me a drink—I froze like a dog!" Sasha said as he walked in.

His wife silently took out a liter bottle of home-brewed potato moonshine and poured a glass. Without taking off his shapka or his vatnik, Sasha drank it in one gulp, took a piece of rye bread from the table, brought it up to his nose, sniffed at it noisily, salted it, then ate it.

"So, how'd it go?" Lena looked at him fixedly with her black, perpetually serious eyes.

"Two little ones, one big one."

"Well, thanks be to God. Sit down, everything's been ready for a while. I've been waiting for you."

Sasha took off his shapka, vatnik, and one of his sweaters, pulled off his felt boots, put on short felt boots, and sat down at the table. Lena set out one bowl with pickled cucumbers, another with sauerkraut, and a third with sliced lard. They each drank half a glass and started to eat. Lena served the *shchi*. Amongst the dark cabbage, they could see pale, swollen pieces of curled-up skin.

"There's no sour cream," his wife announced.

"To hell with it."

Sasha picked up his favorite wooden spoon and started to eat the *shchi*. Lena also started to eat. Sasha ate greedily. He was hungry. Lena chewed the skin.

"Dang…the tripe's real soft…"

"Well, well …" Sasha muttered reproachfully. "And you were asking what to do with it …"

"It softened up in the soup…"

"Nutritious …"

Sasha chewed.

His face became even gloomier as he ate, as if he were eating in order to spite someone else. His front teeth were still all right, if also discolored by smoking. One had been chipped when Sasha was young. He had been riding Alyoshkin's moped and flew off it into the corner of a fence. There were also problems with his molars. Sasha had lost his first tooth when he was in tenth grade—when his whole cheek had swelled up from an abscess. The tooth was ruined; the dentist didn't bother trying to save it and just pulled it out. He had lost three more teeth in the army: his periosteum got inflamed because of bad sleep, bad food, and the cold in the barracks. Because of this, he got to spend some time in a warm hospital. After that, Sasha had problems with two more teeth. They had to pull out one of them. After selling the apartment in Rybinsky, he got a little money and had two bridges put in. Six years later, the tooth under the left bridge got inflamed. They removed the bridge and wanted to do some work on the tooth, but Sasha didn't have enough money. They pulled out the tooth. He still had the right bridge. Sasha now chewed everything on the right.

Lena chewed.

When she ate, her face lost its dismal seriousness, relaxed, and grew attractive. While chewing, she often moaned as if she were preparing to sing. But she didn't know how to sing at all. Lena's teeth were reasonably good even though she rarely brushed them. She'd only had three teeth removed in her life: a baby tooth in third grade and two upper teeth that were growing in the wrong places when she was twenty.

They finished the *shchi*. Sasha asked for seconds and Lena gave him some, along with potatoes braised in lard and onions. Sasha drank another half glass. He started to eat the *shchi* and potatoes. Picked up the remote for their small television, which was sitting on their small refrigerator. Pressed the red button.

The white square of the screen blurred. Sasha flipped through the channels. Stopped on a scene from the 1947 movie *Secret Agent*. A bald traitor was standing in front of an SS-Gruppenführer. They were listening to a radio that was playing a Russian song.

"The music's not bad, isn't that so?" the Gruppenführer asks.

"I don't like Russian music, Mr. General," the baldie replies.

"What kind of music do you like?"

"I'm a Ukrainian, Mr. General. Moscow has its songs, we have ours."

The frame froze and the round-faced, feline host of the show walked into the frame, gesticulating energetically.

"That's where it all began! Here lie the roots of contemporary Ukrofascism!"

"Sash, I'm sick of the war." Lena furrowed her brow.

Sasha changed the channel. In a large, bright studio, the tanned, beautifully dressed host made an inviting gesture with his hands and began to speak:

Hello, and welcome to *White Square*! Today, we're going to talk about Russia. Our grand, fantastical, and, in many ways, unpredictable country "shall be unknowable to foreign sages for centuries and centuries," as we sing in an old song. The truth is that Russia continues to prompt questions not only among *foreign sages*—and that's putting it mildly—but also among our own countrymen. An old pal of mine confessed that, after living in Russia for forty-odd years—can you imagine?—he still didn't understand exactly what our country was. And this is an Orthodox man, a patriot, an intellectual deeply familiar with our history and culture. Now, we're not here to discuss our political system. Every schoolkid knows that Russia is a federal, democratic state, with a president and a parliament. But what image does our country call forth in us? What does it look like? What associations does it carry? Everyone has their own image of Russia. I'm sure that many of these images are compatible. Some may not be. And, no, I'm not just talking about what the fifth column thinks. In fact, this diversity simply shows yet again, in all of its ebbs and flows, the deep mysteriousness of Russia. Shows—ebbs and flows! I'm speaking in rhyme, that's how important our topic is today! Let's really talk about this. Today, as always, four guests are sitting around our square white table. You probably recognize some of them. But, you know our rule on *White Square*: first names and professions only. No titles, positions, or regalia. And so: Irina is a municipal employee, Yuri is a military man, Anton is a theater director, and Pavel is a businessman. Respected guests of the program, I have one question for all of you: What do you think Russia looks like? Please!

All movement stops. Everyone in the studio freezes as if the frame were frozen. Alex, the protagonist of Kubrick's *A Clockwork Orange*, walks into the studio. He's wearing a tight white jumpsuit and black boots, with a cane in his hand. Two of his droogs follow him in, dressed the same way.

ALEX: Dooby doo?

DROOG 1: Dooby doo!

DROOG 2: Dooby doo!

ALEX: Dooby dooby doo?

DROOG 1, DROOG 2: Dooby dooby doo!

ALEX: Dooby dooby dooby doo?

DROOG 1, DROOG 2: Dooby dooby dooby doo!

ALEX: *(Tapping at the white table with his cane.)* What's this?

DROOG 1: It's moloko vellocet.

DROOG 2: Yeah, Alex, it's moloko vellocet.

ALEX: Moloko vellocet?

DROOG 1, DROOG 2: Moloko vellocet!

ALEX: *(After a beat.)* My dear, old, darling droogs. Do you take me for a gloopy devotchka?

DROOG 1: No, Alex.

DROOG 2: What do you mean, Alex? You're not a gloopy devotchka!

DROOG 1: You're our droog and our leader.

DROOG 2: Yeah, Alex! Our droog and our leader.

ALEX: Does that mean you did everything horrorshow?

DROOG 1: We did everything horrorshow, Alex.

DROOG 2: We did everything, absolutely everything, absolutely horrorshow, brother!

ALEX: Horrorshow?

DROOG 1, DROOG 2: Horrorshow!

(Alex smiles, then sharply whacks both of his droogs on their codpieces with his cane. The droogs fall writhing to the floor.)

ALEX: No, you didn't do everything horrorshow, droogs. But you must. You're obligated. To do everything in the horrorshow way.

Alex begins to move IN REVERSE through the *White Square* pavilion. Having left the studio, he enters Sasha and Lena's house, then finds himself outside the Church of Saint Pantaleon the Healer, on the bus, in Sasha and Lena's house once more, then, finally, in the square by the store. The dog running across the square lets the ring of skin fall from his mouth after being hit by Earwax's cane. Alex picks up the ring, puts it around his cane, and, beginning to twirl the ring, leaves the *White Square* pavilion. A giant blue expanse spreads out before him, on which the names of various pavilions are lit in red. Whistling the melody to "Singing in the Rain" and twirling the ring around his cane, Alex moves hastily through the blue space. A pavilion catches his eye: VICTORY DAY. He begins walking toward it. He enters the space of the pavilion. He finds himself on Red Square. Month of May, blue sky, sunshine. Everything's ready for a parade and the frame freezes. Two pigeons are even frozen in flight over the square. Near the Historical Museum stand rows of convicts, wrapped in their vatniks and pushing wooden wheelbarrows. Wooden watchtowers with machine gunners tower up at the edges of the column. Alex walks through the empty square toward the gray column. His boots knock against the cobblestones and the sound rings out over the frozen square. Zoomorphs are standing atop Lenin's Mausoleum in bright summer suits with the heads of hyenas, crocodiles, and rhinoceroses. Alex takes the ring of skin off his cane, winds up, and tosses it toward the mausoleum. The ring flies through the vernal air, its golden tiepin shining in the sun, then falls onto a rhinoceros's horn and dangles from it. Continuing on, Alex whistles and applauds himself, tucking his cane under his armpit. He walks up to the first row of the column. Convicts stand before him. They're of various ages, dressed in vatniks new and old, pushing wheelbarrows new and old. In the wheelbarrows are books, clothing, liturgical objects, radio equipment, toys, dishes, glasses, hats, shoes, bed linens, sculptures, paintings, locksmith and carpentry tools, musical instruments... Whistling, Alex paces around inspecting the unmoving convicts, knocking his cane against their wheelbarrows, examining their contents. Then, he strides forwards, turns his back to the convicts, and makes a sharp motion with his cane. The convicts come to life. They draw air into their lungs and sing out "It's Victory Da-a-a-ay!"

The column begins to move. The convicts sing in their gloomy voices, pushing their wheelbarrows. Alex walks just ahead of the column, throwing his cane from hand to hand and dancing in time with the convicts' song. The zoomorphs standing atop the mausoleum cheer for the parade.

RED PYRAMID

2017

TO PUT it plainly, Yura confused Fryazino with Fryazevo and went the wrong way. Natasha had explained everything to him: Go to Yaroslavsky station and take the train toward Fryazevo or toward Shchyolkovo. Her station was Zagoryanskaya and not all trains stopped there. The train toward Fryazevo did, but the train toward Fryazino didn't. Yura ended up on the train toward Fryazino.

"There's a train at six fifteen. It runs regularly on the weekdays," Natasha had said, standing in front of Dinamo station and licking at the ice cream sandwiched between two round waffles that Yura had treated her to. "That train always stops at our station."

"And how many hours . . . mmm . . . does it take to get there?" Yura quipped, chomping at his ice cream and waffles.

"Forty-five minutes." Natasha smiled. "You'll be at my stop by seven."

This was the third time they'd met, but, for some reason, they were still using the formal word for "you."

"Will it be a big group?"

"I don't like small ones!" Natasha laughed, shaking her head.

She always shook her head when she said something funny. When she did this, she came off as too sincere, perhaps even foolishly naive, but she wasn't stupid, Yura quickly figured that out. He liked her more and more all the time: short, slender, swarthy, nimble, and always smiling. There was clearly some southern blood running through her veins. Moldavian or Armenian. Maybe even Jewish. Yura hadn't asked about her *roots* yet. There was always a wave of joy emanating from Natasha. Her hair was black, tied up into two tight braids that encircled her head.

"So, can I expect to meet a whole cohort of your admirers?" he asked, finishing his drippy ice cream.

"No doubt!" Natasha shook her head again.

"D'you have any dueling pistols?"

"My dad's got a shotgun."

"I'll provide the ammunition."

"Deal!"

Looking at her lips, smiling and wet with ice cream, Yura imagined their first kiss. Perhaps . . . in front of a lilac bush.

"Are there any lilac bushes at your house?" he asked.

"We had one. It was ex-quis-ite! But it started to wither. Dad cut it down. There's just the ti-i-iniest bit left."

Natasha finished her dessert, took a handkerchief from her jacket pocket, wiped off her lips, picked up her briefcase, which had been leaning against her swarthy, slender legs this whole time, wrapped both of her arms around it, and pressed it to her stomach. "Well, I'm off."

Then, bowing her head forward and looking almost sullenly at Yura, added, "See you Saturday, Yuri."

"See you Saturday, Natasha!" Yura raised and clenched his fist.

Natasha turned away quickly and hurried down into the subway. She turned away from him just as quickly as she'd walked across the balance beam in the gym the first time he'd seen her. Then, she'd done an easy cartwheel along the beam, pushed off of it, jumped up into the air, spread her hands wide, and threw back her radiant face.

She was a first-rank student athlete studying at a pedagogical institute and participating in a student Spartakiade, about which Yura, a second-year student in the journalism department of Moscow State University, was doing a report for the university periodical. That was where they'd met. Then they'd gone to a French film, *Under the Roofs of Paris*, which they'd both already seen: Yura had seen it once and Natasha—three times.

Then they'd taken a stroll through Gorky Park.

Then Natasha had invited him to her birthday party.

And now…Yura had missed his chance

He was bearing a bottle of champagne and a book of poems by Walt Whitman translated by Korney Chukovsky as gifts. The book, beautifully printed by Akademia Publishers, had been nestled among the many other books collected by his grandfather in Yura's home. Yura had only glanced at it once, flipping through it quickly and putting it back onto the shelf. Then recalled its existence only when he started to think about what to get for Natasha. He'd already spent his student stipend on three American jazz records, which he'd bought from profiteers on Kuznetsky. The remaining money was only enough for the champagne. Yura had basically not asked his parents for money in two months.

A good poet and a beautiful book … he thought and put Whitman, along with the champagne, into his yellow leather bag, slinging its strap over his shoulder.

On the train, he got caught up in Whitman. And realized too late that he was heading the wrong way.

"Could you tell me when we'll be at Zagoryanka?" he asked a thin, gloomy old man with a cane and a pail in a string bag.

"Never," the old man replied laconically. "You got on the wrong train."

"What?"

"Well…The train to Fryazino has never, ever stopped in Zagory-anka."

Yura leapt up and looked out the window. Bushes and telegraph poles were crawling by.

"And what the heck—"

"The next stop is Green Pine. Get off there, take this train back to Mytishchi, then get on the train toward Fryazevo."

"Damn!" Yura punched his palm impotently.

"There's no reason to swear," the old man said and looked gloomily out the window.

Cursing his own idiocy, Yura picked up his bag and walked out into the vestibule. The door here was missing, so the June air blustered in.

"Hey, buddy, gimme a smoke!" a voice rang out behind him.

Yura turned around. A guy who looked kinda like a crook was leaning against the wall in one corner of the vestibule. Yura hadn't noticed him at all when he'd walked in. Looking unhappily at the guy, Yura took a half-empty pack of Astra cigarettes and a box of matches from his pants pocket. He then took out one cigarette for himself and proffered the pack to his companion. The guy pushed himself off the wall, strode over to Yura in his loose black pants, silently pulled out a cigarette, and stuck it between his prominent lips. Yura lit his cigarette and threw the spent match over his shoulder.

"Gimme a light too!" the guy demanded.

Yura hesitated, thinking of telling him it was "time to start carrying your own," but ended up lighting a match and putting it to the tip of his cigarette. The guy sucked in smoke. He had a thin, pale face with wide cheekbones and a sloped chin.

"Is Green Pine soon?" Yura asked unhappily.

"Who the hell knows?" the guy answered. "I'm goin' to see some dudes in Ivanteyevka. I'm not from here. Same with you, huh?"

Yura nodded.

The guy examined Yura dully, then leaned back against the wall and, with the cigarette between his moist lips, half closed his eyes.

Yura turned away and blew smoke out through the door frame.

The electric train rolled along unhurriedly.

We're crawling like a tortoise, Yura thought, furious. *Cretinoid. Idiotium. Stuposaurus...*

He quickly finished off his cigarette and threw the butt into the dusty greenery passing by. Went back into the carriage. The exact same passengers were sitting in their exact same seats. Some of them were looking at Yura and, he thought, smirking at him.

I'm capable only of inciting mirth. And rightly so.

Yura opened Whitman and again began to read. Eight pages later, a hoarse voice on the intercom announced "Green Pine." Yura picked up his bag, walked out into the vestibule, the lippy man now gone, and took his place next to three women of various ages: an old woman, a full-figured lady, and a young girl.

The train braked with an unpleasant screech. Yura got off with the women and looked around. A small number of other passengers were also getting down onto the wooden platform, then setting off in the direction of the village houses visible through the greenery in the distance. The train crawled off. Realizing that he had to get over to the opposite platform, Yura jumped onto the railroad ties and crossed the tracks, stepping over the rails that'd grown hot in the sun. As he approached the other side, he surveyed the platform, found a set of wooden steps, then climbed them. There was nobody on the platform. Some cigarette butts lay on the ground. On the long, latticed sign, only the word PINE remained. Where the word GREEN had been, Yura could distinguish just the outlines of the letters that'd once been there.

"The green's being refurbished, then..." Yura joked gloomily, walked over to a bench with peeling white paint, and sat down.

He glanced at his Luch watch, which his father had given him when he'd gotten into Moscow State: 6:42.

"They'll start without me..."

He pulled out his cigarettes, then thought better of it. Put them away.

"Idiotium!" he pronounced, looking at the rays of light caught in the branches of the pine trees and spat on the dusty, foot-destroyed boards.

Twelve minutes passed.

Then thirteen more.

Then twenty more.

The train wasn't coming.

"Frick me. Happy birthday, Natasha!"

Yura stood up and walked along the platform. There was still not a soul to be seen. The sun was sinking lower, making its way between the trunks of the pine trees.

With his bag over his shoulder, Yura began to walk across the dusty boards, slapping his sandals against them angrily:

"Shitomometer!"

"Tearassium!"

"Shitassium!"

The boards groaned stupidly under the blows of Yura's feet. Their groans made him absolutely furious. Having walked down the entire platform, he turned around, started to run, and tried to do a long jump like a track-and-field athlete, compressing all of his fury into his impact with the shabby boards:

"Fooloplesius!"

"Shitokneadius!"

The boards rattled.

Yura reached the latticed sign with the word PINE on it.

"A pine day!!"

"I pine for the train!!"

"OH, SUCK A PINUS!!! WHEN! WILL! IT! COME!?"

"In eight minutes," someone shouted.

Yura turned around. A man was sitting on the bench past which he'd just jumped. This was so unexpected that Yura stopped in his tracks. A fat, puffy-faced man in light summer clothes sat looking at Yura.

"What..." muttered Yura, not believing his own eyes.

"The train will be here in eight minutes," the man pronounced.

There was no expression on the man's large, mealy white, pear-shaped face. No expression at all. *Absolutely* no expression at all. It was the first time in his life that Yura had seen a face like that.

"What train?" he asked, unable to look away from the man's face.

"Your electric locomotive."

His small, *expressionless* eyes were fixed on Yura. It seemed to Yura as if his face were frozen. And that the man himself was... from the morgue. A corpse. A dead man. Yura suddenly began to feel ill, just as he'd felt when he'd had sunstroke in Baku the previous summer. His legs started to tremble.

"Sit down," the man's frozen lips pronounced. "It's obvious you have sunstroke. It's very hot for the beginning of June."

Yura plopped down on the bench. He inhaled, coming back to his senses now, and ran his hand across his sweaty forehead.

"It's better not to practice your *long jump* in this kind of heat," the man pronounced.

Yura noticed just how fat the man was. He hadn't moved at all and was still staring straight ahead, frozen. His summer clothing was old-fashioned: a white panama hat, a beige summer suit, and a white *kosovorotka* with an embroidered collar. White calico shoes peeked out from underneath his loose beige trousers. A fun friend of Yura's deceased grandfather had worn clothes like this in the summer: a numismatist, a joker, and a drunkard. Also deceased. The fat man's comical shoes—really, they were ankle boots—brought Yura back to his senses. He exhaled. Inhaled. Exhaled again. He was calmer already. The gloom had suddenly passed. He felt light and cheerful.

Where did he come from? Yura thought. *Totally out of the blue ... Why didn't I notice him? Did I really, like, overheat?*

The fat man stared straight ahead with calm indifference and without changing his position.

"Eight minutes, huh. You know the schedule?" Yura asked.

"And not only that."

Yura glanced at his watch. "In eight minutes?"

"Seven now."

"Do you have a mental stopwatch or something?"

"And not only that."

Yura began to feel even lighter and more cheerful. He laughed with relief and scratched at the nape of his neck. "So, you know everything there is to know?"

"Almost."

"Okay. What's *Mittelspiel*?"

"It's the middle of a game of chess."

"Right. What about ... Betelgeuse?"

"A star in Orion's Belt. A red supergiant with roughly the same diameter as Jupiter's orbit around the sun."

"Exactly right! Now tell me who Dave Brubeck is."

His frozen lips puckered and began to whistle a pretty decent "Take Five."

"Jeepers..." Yura gasped in shock, slapped his knees, then laughed. "You're a musician. That's it, right? And musicians are usually good at chess too, right? You play jazz?"

"No," the fat man replied calmly.

"C'mon, that's gotta be it! What do you play? Sax? Trumpet?"

The fat man was silent.

"Okay. A guessing game... Then tell me this: Where is... hmm... Rotten Marsh?"

"In the Selizharovsky District of Tverskaya Oblast."

Yura was shocked. Rotten Marsh was a place known only in the small village where he used to go hunting with his father and grandfather. The village was called Khutor and it was indeed in the Selizharovsky District. Rotten Marsh was a swamp surrounded by a forest. Waterfowl loved nesting there.

How does he know that?

The fat man was still sitting there without changing position.

A telepath? A hypnotist? Definitely a hypnotist! Probably used to work with Wolf Messing... Right. Gotta trip him up somehow...

Yura examined his surroundings. Then, suddenly, in the middle distance, in front of a one-story building made of white silicate brick, he saw a faded poster on a panel: OUR GOAL IS COMMUNISM!

Lenin's profile was visible beneath the slogan.

"Please tell me who Vladimir Ilyich Lenin was, then," Yura demanded loudly, folding his arms victoriously across his chest.

"The man who called forth the pyramid of the red roar," the fat man replied calmly.

Yura's mouth fell open.

"What? The pyramid? Of the red—what?"

"The red roar."

"What kind of pyramid is that?"

"The source of the endless red roar."

"And where is that?"

"In the center of our capital."

"Where exactly?"

"Where the center is."

"In the Kremlin?"

"No. On Red Square."

"On the square itself? A pyramid?"

"Yes."

"But where is it on the square? In concrete terms."

"Its base takes up the entire square."

"The entire square?"

Yura laughed. The fat man was still sitting with the same imperturbable calm.

"Y'know," Yura spoke up, "I live pretty close to Red Square, on Pyatnitskaya. But I've never noticed a red pyramid around there."

"You can't see it."

"But *you* can?"

"Yes."

Okay, then. This guy has hallucinations . . .

"And what does this pyramid do?"

"Emits the red roar."

"Like . . . a loudspeaker?"

"More or less. But it emits a different kind of sound wave. Different vibrations."

"And why does it . . . emit them?"

"To infect people with the red roar."

"Why?"

"To destroy mankind's intrinsic structure."

"Destroy it? Why?"

"So that humans stop being humans."

This sounds seditious, Yura thought and looked around.

But there was still no one on the platform.

"So, Lenin built this pyramid?"

"No. He simply called it into being."

"So he, like . . . flipped a switch?"

"Something like that."

"Who built it then?"

"You wouldn't know them."

"The Germans, then? Or Marx maybe? Engels?" Yura grinned.

"No, not the Germans."

"The Yanks, then?"

"No."

"Well then—who? Where're they from?"

"From there," the fat man replied, then added: "Your train's coming from there."

Yura looked out into the hot air, gazing to the left at the tracks shrinking off into the distance, didn't see anything, but still stood up and put the strap of his bag over his shoulder. Turned his gaze back to the poster of Lenin.

"What about . . . communism?"

"What about communism?" The fat man trained his frozen eyes on Yura.

"Well . . . isn't it our . . . radiant future?"

"It isn't our radiant future, but the red roar of the present day."

At that precise moment, a horn sounded off in the distance. And Yura saw his train. It was still far away and impossible to hear its movement. Yura wanted to say goodbye to the fat man, wanted to say something humorous and offensive, but suddenly thought the better of it. He stood there, swaying in place as he loved to do, and stared at the strange man. And the man was still sitting there, looking straight ahead. Yura could hear the train now. It crawled up to the platform. Yura suddenly had the keen impression that he would never see this unusual man again. He was absolutely certain that the man would just keep sitting there on this empty, dusty platform. He wouldn't get on the train to Moscow. Maybe he wouldn't get on any train at all. It was unclear where this man could possibly want to go. He seemed to have grown up out of the bench itself. Yura suddenly became bitterly sad. So much so that eyes filled with tears.

The train crawled up to him with its familiar screech.

Yura strode inside mechanically. Entered the car and sat down. Wiped at his eyes with the back of his hand. Looked out the window at the platform. The fat man was still sitting in the exact same way on the bench. And looking straight ahead. There was something painfully *familiar* about him. Something *native*.

The train shoved off.

Yura was frozen in place. He felt an intense yearning. A quiet yearning. He didn't want to go anywhere. And he had no thoughts to think. Instead of thinking, he simply remembered the fat man's last sentence:

The red roar of the present day.

In a state of total paralysis, Yura stared out the window at the greenery, the telegraph poles, the little houses, the cars, the dumps, the warehouses, the cranes, the piles of coal, the heating plants, the people, the birds, the goats, the dogs . . .

And completely forgot about Natasha's birthday party.

And missed the stop for Mytishchi.

He only came to his senses when the train was pulling into Yaroslavsky station. The moment it stopped, his paralysis passed. Yura stood up. He left the train, got down onto the platform with the other passengers, and immediately moved away from the crowd. He stopped and took out his cigarettes.

And what about the birthday party? Zagoryanka? Natasha? He remembered everything. *I'm such a dumbass . . .*

He walked along the platform. "You idiot!" he spat furiously.

He lit up. Wandered through the evening streets of Moscow. Crossed the Garden Ring. Walked to his apartment on Pyatnitskaya.

The cigarette brought him back down to earth.

"He must've been a hypnotist," Yura decided, then started laughing. "And I got taken in like a little idiot. Red roar! Red ro-o-o-oar! A pyramid!"

Wandering through the evening streets, he pulled the bottle of champagne from his bag and opened it without stopping. The cork flew out with a loud pop, scaring an old lady, and knocked into a building's facade. The warm, demi-sec champagne erupted from the bottle and Yura lapped at it, drenching himself in the process.

He drank the whole sticky bottle on his way home, then put it down on someone's windowsill.

At home, he read a fresh issue of *Youth*, then went to bed earlier than usual.

Sunday passed by.

On Monday, Yura had two tests. And, on Tuesday, he set off to Dinamo, where the Spartakiade was coming to an end. Walking into the gymnasium, he nearly bumped into Natasha. In dark-blue tights, with palms white with talcum powder, she was walking toward the locker room.

"Hi!" he said, stopping.

"Hi," she replied with her eternal smile, then continued walking.

They never saw each other again.

Yura graduated from journalism school and married Albina, the daughter of his parents' old friends. With the help of his father, a prominent functionary in the Ministry of Transport, he got a job with *Komsomolskaya Pravda*. He and Albina had a son named Vyacheslav. At the end of the sixties, Yura joined the party and got a job with *Izvestiya*. They had a daughter named Yulia. In the middle of the seventies, he was offered a position as department head for *Ogoniok*. He stopped working at *Izvestiya* and started working at *Ogoniok*.

One July morning, he had a quick breakfast as he always did, got into his father's old white Volga, then set off for the editorial office. The moment he drove onto Moskvoretsky Bridge, his heart clenched and fluttered in such a way that he couldn't catch his breath. Yuri stopped his car next to the curb. He took evenly spaced breaths and massaged the Hegu points on his hands as his doctor had taught him to. Yuri had already had heart problems. They'd started after the scandal around the publication of his controversial article in *Izvestiya*, which had been "rashly" approved by the assistant editor-in-chief while the editor in chief was on vacation. Yuri was called to testify before the City Party Committee. "You've crossed the line of that which is permissible," a man with the face of an old wolf had said to him. The assistant editor-in-chief was removed from his position with lightning speed. Yuri's career hung by a thread. He managed to hang on to it by a miracle; his father's Party connections came in handy like never before. But his heart went out of whack. The doctors said that Yuri had suffered a small heart attack. He spent two months with Albina at a sanatorium. The second time his heart acted up, his son had been implicated in a disgusting story: a gang rape in a student dorm. Yuri's son had come under suspicion. Yuri's father had recently died and there was no one to appeal to for help *up there*. Yuri had to go to a lot of people's offices, asking for favors and humiliating himself. His son was saved: he was only put on probation. But, after those six months, Yuri had to start taking pills for his heart. Then the problem had gone away.

But now, now, now.

His heart was fluttering.

It had never felt like this before. Yuri just couldn't catch his breath. He got out of his car and walked over to the railing of the bridge, laid his hands on the chill granite, and tried to breathe normally, looking out at the morning light over the Moscow River. The water exuded freshness and Yuri could feel it there, on the bridge. He tried to calm himself down. But his heart was still fluttering. Like a small animal beating around in a . . . trap-trap . . .

Doing the can-can.

Dressed in a caf-tan.

Its paws going bam-bam.

Yuri breathed, breathed, breathed.

His head spun and two steel cicadas buzzed in his ears.

"Stop, stop, stop . . ." Yuri tried to calm himself down.

The cicadas continued to buzz. His legs trembled. He grabbed hold of the railing and leaned over it. The water was shining below him. The water was shining. The shining water shined with shiny shininess.

"Stop, stop, stop . . ." he whispered to himself.

The he-art. The h-ea-rt. His h-e-a-r-t. Stopped fluttering.

Stopped. Sto

pped.

Stopped for good.

Inside Yuri reigned

SILENCE.

With the last of his strength, he straightened up.

Clutched the railing.

And suddenly saw the red pyramid.

It towered up over Red Square, its base taking up its entire area. The pyramid vibrated as it emitted the red roar. The roar came forth in waves, flooding everything around it like a tsunami, flowing off beyond the horizon and toward all four corners of the earth. The human race was drowning in this red roar. Drowning as it tried to paddle through. Walking, driving, standing, sitting, sleeping—men, women, old people, children. The red roar overwhelmed all of it. Its waves beat beat furiously against every person person inside every person person light light and the red roar roar beats beats out of the pyramid pyramid in order to extinguish extinguish the light light of man man and extinguish extinguish cannot cannot and why why beats beats this frighteningly frighteningly and dumbly dumbly red waves waves beat beat and cannot cannot beat beat and cannot cannot why why beat beat this stupidly stupidly furiously furiously stupidly stupidly six-wingèd six-wingèd you here here next to next to six-wingèd six-wingèd you bright bright you most most you eternal eternal you hello hello six-wingèd six-wingèd back then back then you were were different different fat fat funny funny white white shoes ankle boots shoes your name name will will you not not tell tell me your your name name name.

"A pine day..." Yuri muttered, trying to smile as his lips went white.

And keeled over.

VIOLET SWANS

2018

CROOKED November moon. The sky's belly.

Torn open.

The snow, spilling out and coming down. The first snow. Onto the midnight streets of Moscow.

"Ashhhhhhhhhhh..."

Wind.

Flakes.

Three snakes:

      blizzard

                whiteout

                        drifting snow.

"Y-y-you c-c-can't g-g-g-grasp at what's g-g-g-gone."

Stuttering.

Shed snakeskins of snow. Down the streets.

The streets emptied of humans.

Trash sleeping on squares. Frozen corpses.

In the frightened mouths of gateways.

"The-e-e-e-ey fo-o-o-o-ound i-i-i-it..."

In the courtyards:

      people,

                campfires,

                        whispers.

"Forty-eight black cranes. Rose up. They made three circles around the Kremlin."

"And it got *fecked up*?"

"It all turned into a crane."

"Black mages . . ."

"They smeared themselves with African pus."

"The entire inner circle."

"Did they fly the FUCK away?!"

"The patriarch was with 'em too."

"And waved a weng at us . . ."

"Oh-a-fuck-a-duck-a!"

"Pus?!"

"They roasted a bishop on a spit on Yakimanka Street; they extracted his lard and made candles from it. They use 'em for black masses . . ."

"Wooooaauuugggghhh . . ."

"Chechens and Chinese. A new contract! Signed. In Russian blood."

"A hundred poods, in any case, I'll fuckin' do the fuck out of it . . ."

"And the Dzerzhinsky Division swore an oath . . ."

"They saw a two-headed dog on Ostozhenka today."

"They stole for twenty years!"

"Stale 'em!"

"Sucked 'em!"

"Sooked 'em dry."

"And chewed over!"

"And chawed over?"

"To the bones!"

"No wonder he was flying with the cranes, then . . ."

"Knowwhathefuckimsayin???"

"Go??"

"Lo!"

"Warlock . . ."

"Amanullah!"

"What else?!"

"They

       fecked

             it

                  up!"

"It leaked."

"The info laked?"

"Of course it leaked leaked leaked into a jar of white gold, black african pus a fresh batch of medium thickness to be kept in a refrigerator at a temperature not lower than five degrees paracelsus as they called it and knew it at the plenary session of the lower-basement ward through the gray masses the last time the president sang the moscow windows and the orchestra of the bolshoi theater but the parliamentary rubbing of african pus onto the backs of popular deputies and the law about the subliminal and the criminal demolition of all heating plants and the intensive growth of cranes' feathers when the black wings don't dare to fly out over the fatherland but to provide soft-bodied family packaging for superbulletproof containers and, first of all, the president's administration flies and the new elite of power structures when it is urgently indispensable to drill all of the antiaircraft complexes and to launch intelligent, grand, and grateful worms into them by default and antiaircraft guns from the second world war fill the throats with lead or bread or dread but flight makes a man freer like sergey brin."

Evgeny opened his eyes. The helicopter had begun its descent.

"Au-a-a-a-a…" he yawned, then took off his headphones with their attached microphone. "Black cranes, huh? *Cool*."

"What, Evgeny Borisovich?" his assistant was shouting over the sound of the blades as he also took off his headphones.

"Dreams, dreams, dreams…"

Evgeny fastened his seat belt and rolled his sharp shoulders.

"Shall I continue?" his assistant shouted, holding up the tablet. "He turned water into lamp oil eighteen times, and they've gotten so used to it at the monastery that they've started to sell the oil. Everyone

264 · VLADIMIR SOROKIN

knows about the three people he brought back to life, and I've already told you about the woman with the brain tumor and about the hot tea for the brotherhood. All of this has already become old hat for them at the monastery. Yep! Here's what's really important for us: Seven and a half months ago, a monk—he was an artist out in the world—began to paint a wall in the refectory. One day, he started chatting and fooling around and forgot to eat his prosphora after communion. And, by the time he remembered to eat it, it had turned to stone."

"It'd dried up?"

"No, it'd *really* turned to stone. Transformed. Its shape and color were the same, but it was a stone. That's how his elder punished him for his 'worldly engagements.'"

"What sort of stone was it? Granite? Marble?"

"I don't know. The abbot has it."

"Can we find out? The molecular structure of the stone?" Evgeny yawned violently.

"We'll need to take it from him to find that out."

"That'll be hard to do, huh?" Evgeny stretched out, his thin lips curling up in ironically maudlin fashion.

"I only received this information yesterday, Evgeny Borisovich. The mind reels! Fedot Chelyabinsk, Anfisa the Wet, now this—"

"Shooting at a game bird that's already flown away..."

"Excuse me—what?" His assistant hadn't heard him.

"I won't excuse you," Evgeny yawned again.

"I didn't hear you! Can I continue?"

"You can't! That's enough yelling!"

The helicopter landed. Evgeny pulled out a thin cigarette from a narrow golden cigarette case and looked out the window: cliff, sea, monastery. A white helicopter with an image of a six-winged seraphim on its fuselage began to take off nearby.

"What the hell?" Evgeny arched his black brows.

His assistant glanced at the tablet. "The patriarch is leaving, Evgeny Borisovich. *He* didn't accept the patriarch!"

"How wonderful..." Evgeny took a drag from his cigarette and laughed, exhaling smoke.

"It's ... unbelievable!" His assistant shook his head.

A flight attendant emerged from behind a screen, opened the door, and put down a ramp. Two guards came out right behind him and walked down the ramp. Hot southern air tore through the open door. Evgeny stepped down onto the stony earth, which was covered with grass that'd been burnt by the sun, and, squinting in the sunlight, gazed up at the patriarch's rising helicopter.

"My carriage, bring my carriage round ... Mhmm ..." He thought of the lines from Chatsky's final monologue in *Woe from Wit*.

He looked around with the cigarette in his mouth. It was hot and bright. It smelled of the sea and of dry sagebrush. The sun beat down. He got out his dark glasses and put them on. There were two buses waiting nearby: one was blue and belonged to the monastery, and the other was greenish-gray and belonged to the National Guard. There were two sparse groups of people standing in front of them. They were cordoned off by the National Guard. A little farther away, he could see a massive military apparatus, reminiscent of a powerful crane with a telescoping jib. Four sentries with machine guns were patrolling its perimeter.

Surrounded by his guards and his assistant, Evgeny moved toward the buses. Two people moved away from the buses to greet Evgeny: the general and the abbot of the monastery, Abbot Kharlampy. The abbot was wearing black, and the general was wearing a summer field uniform.

Evgeny threw his cigarette forward like a dart, then stepped on it with his pointed boot as he walked. The general was the first to reach him with his sweeping gait and extended his long arm, as thick as a log.

"He didn't accept the patriarch, Zhenya!"

"So I've heard." Evgeny held out his narrow palm and bowed to the abbot as he approached.

The abbot bowed his head with its black capuche back to Evgeny.

"Yesterday—the president, and today—the patriarch. How's that possible?" The general's sloped shoulders jerked. "Any idea, Holy Father?"

"I'm not a holy father, I'm a priest," the abbot corrected him, calmly fingering his rosary. "And I've been telling you that the elder hasn't accepted government officials or hierarchs for four years."

"Then he won't accept us either!"

"That's possible. It's up to him."

"Did you tell him about us?" Evgeny asked.

"I don't have to tell him. He already knows. And he observes his own rules, which we have no right to interfere with."

"So, he doesn't listen to you?" the general grunted.

"He doesn't listen to anyone down here," the abbot said, turning his calm gaze toward the cliff.

Evgeny and the general turned toward the cliff. It was low, like all of the foothills, but still almost sheer. A narrow wooden staircase moved in a zigzag across its grayish-pinkish-yellow face in three flights, resting on pieces of rebar cut into the stone. The staircase looked flimsy. Instead of a railing, along the edge of the zigzag was a rope that the climber was supposed to hold on to. The zigzag ended at the pharynx of a cave, reminiscent of a human face with one eye. From down on the ground, one could see how the entrance of the cave was covered up by stones, with only a small space left open.

"The ascetic has been walling himself in from the inside for a year now," Evgeny's assistant whispered into his ear. "He cuts the stones, then hews them. He only has one stone left to put in."

"And they bring him cement from down here?" Evgeny asked, almost laughing.

"Instead of cement, the elder uses his own excrement."

"That's very...wise. Who are those people by the bus, Boris?" Evgeny asked the general.

"Ah, the people!" An evil smile lit up the general's sweaty face. "Those people, Zhenya, are our beloved public. The info leaked! Looks like they already know everything, huh? Government secrets don't exist anymore? Why the hell'd they come to us, huh?! What a leaky country! Right, Zhenya? And why is that?"

"You're asking me?"

"Who the fuck else would I be asking?!"

Evgeny took out his cigarette case and opened it.

"Better not to smoke here," the abbot pronounced. "And much better not to swear."

The general waved his hand. "We get it . . ."

"And what does this public want? When did they arrive, Father?" Evgeny put away the cigarette case.

"This morning."

"And, uh, what do they want?"

The general giggled. "What do you mean 'what'? The public wants an audience! They've already been fed twice."

"Okay, then let's go over to them." Evgeny made out some familiar figures in the assembled company.

"Let's go!" the general grunted angrily and strode forward.

"But, Zhenya, all of this is already, like—whoa!" He chopped his broad neck with the edge of his palm as he walked. "Like, way too much for me!"

"Calm down, Borya."

"Yes, calm! I am calm!" the general snapped.

Tall, healthy, and narrow-shouldered, the general looked like an insomniac bear driven out of his warm den by a small spot of bother cropping up outside it. What expressed discontent more than anything were his arms: long and strong, they dangled menacingly as he walked, as if they were inertial balances accumulating the energy to eventually deliver the blows of a professional boxer, blows that the general would award to this entire Moscow public with great delight, never mind whatever bullshit reason they'd flocked here for.

The ring of National Guard soldiers parted, letting them through, and a solid man in bright summer clothing with a handsome white mustache and a sleek, tanned face broke off from the gathered company to walk over to them.

"Zhenya! Zhenechka! My dear! Finally! We've waited so long!" he cried out in a high voice.

He embraced Evgeny, softly wrapping his arms around him, pressing him into his broad chest, then kissed his thin cheeks three times, tickling him with his mustache. He'd already managed to hug and kiss the general. Evgeny was entirely passive in his embrace.

"My darlings, my precious dears, what on earth is this?" Without letting go of Evgeny, the white-mustached man peeled off to the side. "Zhenya! Borya! What's going on? Why have these good fellows with machine guns come here? To make arres-s-s-s-s-s-sts? To detain? To *not let go*? To di-vide? Us-s-s?! To divide?! At this precise moment? My dear ones, have you lost your minds? If all of this is truly happening, if it isn't mere gossip, and I can already feel, can sense right here, right he-e-ere"—he poked at his broad chest with his finger—"that it's true, true, true, that it reeks of truth, then how can this be?! Wherefore this division? What in the hell is this *cordoning off*?"

A potbellied man with a face reminiscent of a potato tuber and an icon on his stomach depicting Yuri Gagarin surrounded by a golden nimbus walked over to them and began to mutter loudly, gesturing with his short-fingered hand, which was bent into the shape of a trowel, as he spoke:

"Russia has pupated! Its shell has cracked! The dazzling butterfly of Russian statehood breaks free to reveal itself to humanity in all of its spiritual splendor! It soars above the world as a shining missile carrier, marking a new era of humanity! The physiognomies of Sergius of Radonezh and Joseph Stalin upon its wings! It emits unfabricated rays of Russian spirituality! They penetrate the earth! The voice of a trumpet rings out over the world: peoples and states, 'tis time to repent, to gather beneath the banners of the Fifth Empire and behold the Earth's grand transfiguration!"

He was handily pushed off to the side by a man with a stern face in a dark-blue silk two-piece suit, a black bow tie, and jockey boots. He was clutching a cane, the knob of which was shaped like a snake's head.

"My dear people!" he began to speak, manipulating his facial muscles with affected courageousness. "You know that I'm a pirate, a cynic, and a villain. Up until yesterday, I'd spew a daily Niagara of bile onto our church and its ministers, but today I get down onto my knees before it"—he gently fell to his knees—"and am prepared to be the first to crawl up this staircase to the great elder. I'd even do so naked, sprinkling my head with the dirt from the side of this very road."

"We are dealing with an incredible lack of mutual trust and elementary common un-der-stand-ing!" pronounced a thin man with watery eyes in an almost singsong tone; he had a prickly beard, a disorderly mass of white hair, and was wearing a carmine-colored sari with a slanted collar embroidered with Russian Orthodox crosses and displaying a medal awarded "For the Defense of Donbass," as well as white pants and yellow sneakers.

"Who are you?" the general grunted.

"URA."

"What the hell is that?"

"A representative of the Union of Russian Arts," Evgeny's assistant clarified.

The man crossed his thin, sinewy arms across his chest. "We can and should talk about everything, not just whisper off in the corner like liberal fungi—we should talk every day, every night, every hour, and every second in order to understand just what a great country we live in and how much we can accomplish together, how much lies before us, what a wonderful president we have, what wonderful warriors, generals, elders, and saints, fathers, mothers, brothers, wives, and children we have—we'll overcome and solve everything, but only if we talk, talk, and talk!"

"I agree entirely! We must talk!" A man with glasses, a gray mop of hair, the bearded face of a wise goat, and wearing a checkered shirt and a nankeen vest raised his index finger significantly.

"And what're you doing here?" the general grunted unhappily. "Filming and news reports aren't allowed."

"We're here, Mr. General, as ordinary citizens of our country," the shaggy man answered with a cocky half smile, two of his front teeth protruding through his lips. "We have an equally keen concern in all that concerns you!"

"Evgeny, please just tell us honestly," a woman of athletic build with an enormous red head of hair and a lizard's face asked in a voice that sounded like the Russian Pinocchio's in the old children's film, "is it all . . . true?"

Everyone froze. Evgeny took a beat, then began to speak.

"It's true."

Everyone standing around them was entirely still for a moment. Then began to stir—all in their own ways. The paunchy man fell to his knees, crossed himself, and muttered, "I live to serve the Most High." The man with the cane, on the other hand, leapt ably to his feet and exclaimed, "Wonderful! Fantastic! I was certain! Let's go up the stairs!"

"We've lived to see it, you bastards!" the shaggy man pronounced loudly, shaking his gray head of hair.

The man from the URA grabbed his sari with knotty fingers and his eyes rolled back into his head:

"Everything! Everything! We can overcome absolutely everything so that everyone can be happy and healthy—fathers, mothers, wives, children, even sheep..."

The curly-red-haired woman chuckled nervously. And the white-mustached man began to cry out, his lament almost feminine. "Hold on, hold on, Zhenechka, if that's so, if that—if that's tru-u-ue, then, ladies and gentlemen, my dear, darling compatriots, citizens, and fellow subjects, they'll simply grab us by the throats as a wolf grabs a lamb, by our itsy-bitsy throats"—he grabbed himself by the throat with his tanned hand and its two intricate golden rings—"and they'll cho-o-o-oke us, cho-o-o-oke us all the way to *goddamn hell*!"

His mustache trembled and tears glittered in his dark eyes.

"Let's go up there, my friends! It's only by a miracle that Russia has survived thus far—let it also be saved by a miracle." The stern-faced man gesticulated with his cane. "And this miracle is to be scientifically sound! It shall contradict neither chemistry nor quantum mechanics! Let's all of us, everyone, go up there together, Evgeny first, then everyone else. Forwards! Upwards!"

"Shut up!!!" the red-haired woman screamed so loudly that everyone turned to look at her.

She wrapped her arms around her torso trying to calm herself down but couldn't manage to.

"That's enough... Enough playing the fool... That's enough... enough of this squabbling, these disagreements, these shitty ambitions, all of this BS—vatnik, liberal faggot, European agent, patriot..."

We need to get rid of all this and rally round our president! Rally round the Kremlin!"

"It's too late, my dove, too late..." the man with the cane retorted spitefully, brushing the dust from the knees of his silk pants.

"No! It's not too late! It's not too late!"

"We have to rally round the general now. And just for a little while..."

The general was silent. His bearish little eyes watched what was happening just as calmly and warily as they always did, even when he was drunk or lost his temper, but, in his soul, with each passing minute, a black tower of fear was piling itself up, building itself forth from swirling black cubes. And it was growing because the general, having lived through three actual wars and a single long career, having grown steel fangs of character and been reinforced by a shell of strength and spikes of glory, having raised himself up onto one of the peaks of Russian authority, didn't understand what was going on for only the second time in his life. The last time this had happened had been in his early childhood, when he was five years old, and had seen a cow giving birth in a village stable. Everything that he'd heard in the last twenty-four hours—from soldiers, officials, scientists, the president, and now from these clowns—called forth in him a single desire: to destroy *all of it* with bazookas and machine guns, to riddle it with bullets, to break it up into little bits so that those bits would fly far, far away, to douse it with napalm, then to get into this helicopter himself and fly beyond the three seas where, on the sandy shore, he'd be met by his beloved wife, his children, and a swarm of coconut crabs.

He opened his sweaty lips so as to say something rude, but a stone suddenly fell to the ground nearby.

Everyone looked at it. The abbot walked over and picked up the stone. And shifted his gaze up to the opening in the cave's masonry. The stone was no bigger than a tennis ball. And it wasn't simply a stone, but a chunk of white bread that had been suddenly turned to stone by a human's force of will. The abbot picked up the stone. A dial and an arrow glittered inside it. An old, cracked compass had been kneaded into the stone.

"A compass?" Evgeny asked as he walked over.

"It's *his* compass," the abbot corrected him. "Please, let's all stand in a circle."

Without any quarreling, everyone obediently formed a circle. With the stone in his hands, the abbot got into the center of the circle. The compass's arrow began to spin, then stopped. The abbot raised his eyes and saw Evgeny's assistant. "The elder is ready to receive you."

Everyone standing in the circle stared at Evgeny's assistant. His young, lively, intelligent face didn't express anything in particular.

"Well, well!" Evgeny grinned and sighed. "Looks like you've got a bigger role to play than I do, Sasha."

He pulled out his cigarette case. "I'm gonna go have a smoke..." And he set off toward the buses.

"Might I puff along with you, Evgeny?" the man with the cane exclaimed languidly and menacingly, as he pulled out a pipe.

"Come right ahead..."

"I'll come too!" the goat-bearded man nodded, his hair bobbing.

"What the hell is this..." The general glanced spitefully at Sasha, turned away angrily, then began to follow Evgeny with his sweeping gait.

The red-haired woman rested her hands on her muscular hips, then nervously slipped them into the pockets of her tight white trousers.

"Sasha...Alexander...you know what..." she sighed and shook her head, her curls swishing sharply. "You...you...I don't know... hold on...strategically...I don't know how to even—"

"Yes! You don't know!" the white-mustached man said, half-embracing Sasha. "So be quiet! I don't know either! And they don't know! And Father Kharlampy doesn't know! And no one knows! So be qui-i-i-iet!" he half sang in his reedy voice. "Sasha! The elder chose you. This is the finger of God. What a blessing! Don't you understand, my dear? Hmm?"

Sasha was silent.

The white-mustached man's chin trembled. "There—up there—in that cave, lives our sa-vi-or. The sa-vi-or of Rushhh-ia! It's a mystery!

Which should enter you, enter me, enter them, enter all of us"— he knocked his finger against his tanned Adam's apple—"right here! And we should accept it! This mystery! Sip by sip! Si-i-ip by si-i-ip! And if it doesn't enter us, if . . . if this sip of . . . this draft of truth, this draft of God's grace . . . if we can't swallow it, if it gets stuck here, then"—he began to sob—"then we've no reason to live anymore! No re-e-e-eason! We shall choke. We shall suffocate! This shall be the end of the entire country! The e-e-end of everyone and everything! Do you understand? The Russian sun shall set o-o-once and for a-a-all!"

Tears spilled from his eyes.

"Dmitry Donskoy, Peter the Great, and Georgy Zhukov are walking with you, Alexander!" the paunchy man shouted, spraying saliva and stretching out his hand, curved like a trowel, until it was almost touching Sasha's face. "Have no fear! Here and now, next to this cliff, the fate of the Fifth Empire shall be decided! The rays of Eternal Russia have made the sign of the cross on you! You will help to bring our History into being, and our History shall sing and make every atom in your body sparkle with rainbows. It'll sparkle when you climb up there, and it'll sparkle when the great visionary accomplishes that which he's destined to! Long live our great Celestial Russia!"

"The main thing is that we must discuss everything with the great elder . . . We can talk about everything—" the man from the URA started to say, but the white-mustached man interrupted him.

"Shut-uuup! Everyone shut up!" He raised his fist. "That's enough blabbering! We must be silent! And listen! Li-i-isten! Don't you understand?"

Everyone fell silent.

"Run along, Sashenka," the white-mustached man whispered very quietly, still managing to convey his suffering.

Before suddenly howling, "Run alo-o-o-onggg!!!"

And a fat drop of sweat dripped from his mustache, sparkling in the sun like a diamond.

"Go with God." The abbot made the sign of the cross over Sasha and handed him a small plastic bottle. "Give him some water."

Sasha took the bottle and walked over to the military apparatus. The sentries didn't even glance at him. The captain slid out of a big green hut and nodded to another soldier sitting in another hut next to the telescoping jib. There was a metal cube of imposing dimensions at the end of the jib; its doors were locked. The apparatus started up and loudly released a burst of glaucous exhaust. And it was only then that Sasha noticed how the entire apparatus was resting slightly above the ground on six powerful struts. The thick telescoping jib began to move, unhinging itself, and the cube moved down toward the rocky earth. The captain walked over to it, unlocked the doors, and opened them. Inside the cube was a round table made of white plastic. On the table was a black cone surrounded by fragments of something.

"There's a button here on the right wall," the captain showed him. "When you're done, push the button and we'll lower you down."

The captain walked away.

With the bottle and the tablet in hand, Sasha entered the cube. The ceiling of the cube was a little higher than normal human height, and it was very hot and humid inside. But the air conditioner inside immediately began to hum.

The cube moved upwards toward the cave. Sasha put the tablet down on the table and glanced at the earth as it receded. The people standing on the ground silently watched his ascent, shielding their eyes from the sun with their hands. It seemed to Sasha that these were Pioneers saluting him.

Transcendental—for some reason he thought of this word from *Moscow to the End of the Line*, the novel his recently deceased father had so loved quoting and rereading.

The cube approached the cave and delicately docked against the cliff, like a spaceship, leaving only a small gap between the iron and the stone. The masonry of the cave became like a sixth face of the cube. And it grew dim inside the cube. But the lamps on the ceiling flashed into brightness right away. Sasha stood on the iron floor staring at the masonry of the cave with its single dark opening. The masonry was neat; all of its stones had been hewn and fit together evenly, even though they were of various sizes. And there was only a single stone missing in this masonry. Through that opening, it was dark and quiet.

Sasha took a breath, then spoke up loudly. "Hello, Father Pancras!"

"Amen," a muffled voice resounded within the cave.

Sasha stuck his hand through the opening. "Father Kharlampy sent this water for you."

"Christ save you," the voice rang out in response and a cool, invisible hand took the bottle from him.

Through the opening, he could hear rustling and movement. Then everything fell silent. Then the elder's eyes appeared along with the upper part of his face. The face didn't look old. The eyes were distracted and couldn't focus on the visitor.

"What has brought you to me, Sasha?" the elder asked.

"A great woe, Father," Sasha began to speak, then faltered.

"Has your father died?"

"Yes, Father. He has."

The elder was silent. Sasha wasn't at all surprised that the elder knew his name and that his father had recently died.

He licked at his lips. "I—I haven't come to you on a personal matter. But with a very important—how to put it—matter of state. A matter of life or death for our state, for our great—our one and only country—our motherland."

I'm such an idiot... what am I saying? he thought.

"You're not an idiot," the voice said from the opening.

How... shameful.

"It's shameful if you're caught with your pants down. And your pants aren't down."

This statement brought Sasha to his senses. Reaching his hand out toward the black cone on the table, he began to speak:

"Father, before you is a nuclear warhead from an RS-20, a Russian intercontinental ballistic missile. There are ten of these things in every RS-20 missile. In Russia, there are forty-three such missiles kept in a state of operational combat readiness. This is our country's nuclear shield, a guarantee of state security. As I've just said, each of them contains ten nuclear warheads. And yesterday something happened that science isn't capable of explaining. Each of these warheads has two charges: a trigger, or a nuclear fuse, and the main, thermonuclear charge. First the nuclear trigger goes off, which leads to the detonation of the main charge, which is—"

"An uncontrolled thermonuclear reaction," the elder's voice came from inside the cave.

"Yes, a thermonuclear reaction. And there's an explosion . . . the explosion of a hydrogen bomb . . . 500 kilotons in each warhead. So, yesterday our personnel realized that all twelve of the missiles in the Far East had stopped emitting X-rays. Which is to say they were no longer radioactive. Upon dismantling one of the warheads, it became clear that all of the warheads made of uranium-238, plutonium-239, and lithium deuteride had turned into refined sugar. Robust, transparent refined sugar. All 120 warheads had become—"

"Sugarheads."

"Yes." Sasha licked his lips and stopped talking.

The sound of the elder's chewing came forth from the cave. He'd begun to eat something loudly and to sip water from the bottle with audible pleasure. Sasha stood there silently, listening to how patiently the elder ate and drank.

"Father Pancras," Sasha began again, "nobody understands what happened. No one could've switched out all of those warheads. It's . . . simply inexplicable. And there's something else: in the areas where the RS-20 missiles are kept, many people saw flocks of strange birds . . . strangely colored birds. The people said that they were cranes or seagulls, strangely colored seagulls or cranes, orange and blue . . . Both civilians and military personnel saw them. The locals've never seen birds like these in the area."

The elder chewed.

"This incident is a threat to the security of our country and could expose all of us to a terrible catastrophe. Russia could lose its nuclear shield and, with it, its guarantee of state security."

The elder stopped chewing, took a drink, then cleared his throat.

"Can you explain this?" Sasha asked.

The elder was silent.

"Can you help? Everyone knows that, with divine aid, you're able to create ... to do ... to accomplish incredible things."

The elder was silent.

Sasha sighed. "We have no one else to turn to, Father Pancras."

The ascetic's face popped into the opening in the masonry. "What do you have there on the table?"

Sasha looked at the table. "These are fragments of the former warheads. Now, it's just sugar. We've brought them here to show you—"

A gurgling sound came from the cave, then a hand appeared holding an enameled mug.

"I haven't had my tea with sugar for a long time. Break me off a bit, Sasha."

Sasha took the dirty blue enamel mug, the rim of which was chipped. It was filled with water from the bottle he'd given the elder. Dry tea leaves floated on its surface, having apparently just been dropped into the mug by the elder. But, as Sasha turned to the table, the water in the mug began to boil.

Sasha froze and stared at the boiling water. The water was boiling. The mug began to heat up. Sasha carefully put the mug down onto the table. The water came to a full boil, then calmed down.

Sasha stared into the blue mug, utterly enchanted.

"Break off a piece and drop it in the tea."

Having come to his senses, Sasha picked up a piece of the translucent sphere and tried to break off a small fragment but wasn't able to. The sugar was robust. Sasha knocked the sugar against the table. Two fragments broke off it. He dropped them into the mug. Picked it up. It was hot. Sasha proffered the mug through the opening. The ascetic's hand took the mug. The ascetic looked down. Sasha heard him blowing on the tea. Then the elder took a sip. "How glorious ..."

As the elder drank, blowing on the water and snorting, Sasha stood staring at his face through the opening in the masonry. The ascetic kept raising his gaze, then lowering it. But even when his eyes were looking straight through the opening, they still weren't focused on Sasha—it was as if he were looking straight through him.

Time passed. The air conditioner in the cube went on running, blowing cold air. The cold air blew directly onto Sasha's back, but this didn't make him any more comfortable; it actually bothered him. The stream of air, the plastic table with the black warhead and the bits of sugar, the hastily welded iron walls with four bright lamps atop them, and, yes, even Sasha himself in the blue suit he wore to work, his ash-colored French tie, and his English shoes, all of this was somehow stupid and ridiculous in the presence of the rough masonry, the missing stone, and the elder's face.

The ascetic kept sipping at his tea, smacking his lips, mumbling something, sipping again, smacking again, mumbling again ... And, with each sound he made, a feeling of helpless irritation grew in Sasha. He hadn't slept last night—a crazy night full of stressed people, unbelievable commotion, texts, and conversations that turned into shouting matches. What was now happening in this foolish cube felt like a dream falling directly from that crazed night.

Sasha really wanted to wake up.

But suddenly fell to his knees.

And spoke up loudly:

"Listen, Father Pancras! You know where we live, in what country, under what state. Everything here is *as it were*. Calm, as it were, will, as it were, law, as it were, order, as it were, the czar, as it were, boyars, as it were, servants, as it were, nobles, as it were, the church, as it were, kindergarten, as it were, school, as it were, parliament, as it were, court, as it were, hospitals, as it were, meat, as it were, planes, as it were, vodka, as it were, business, as it were, cars, as it were, factories, as it were, roads, as it were, cemeteries, as it were, pensions, as it were, cheese, as it were, peace, as it were, war, as it were, motherland, as it were."

The recluse ceased sipping his tea.

Sasha continued, bitterness and trembling in his voice:

"The only actual thing we have is this warhead here. Only this uranium, only this lithium deuteride. It does what it's meant to do. But if it also becomes *as it were*, then we won't have anything at all. There'll be an enormous empty space. You ... you can transmogrify matter. You have unbelievable abilities. You're a great ascetic. I'm begging you: Turn this sugar back into uranium, back into lithium deuteride. So that we can be as we were before. All of Russia asks you to do this."

He fell silent, but continued to tremble.

It grew quiet in the cave. Then the hand holding the mug popped back into the opening.

"C'mon, Sashok, have a drink!" the elder pronounced loudly.

Sasha got up from his knees with some difficulty. His legs were trembling. He took the hot mug with both hands, afraid of dropping it. His hands were shaking violently. He brought the mug to his lips and took a sip, knocking his teeth against the peeling enamel of its rim. The tea was terribly sweet. And very delicious. As it was in his childhood. The tea calmed him.

Sasha took a deep breath. And another sip.

"Finish it!" the elder ordered.

Sasha finished it both dutifully and eagerly. Proffered the mug through the opening in the masonry.

"Keep it for yourself." The recluse pushed the mug away.

Sasha pulled his hand out of the cave, still holding the mug. It grew quiet in the cave once more.

"What are we to do?" Sasha asked.

The elder was silent for a moment, then asked Sasha a question: "What is your missile's name?"

"The RS-20."

"I'm asking you what its name is."

"It's name is...Satan. Yes. Satan. That's what its engineers... named it."

The elder was silent. Several long minutes passed.

"Father Pancras," Sasha stuck his face through the opening. "What're we to do?"

There was a heavy smell in the cave.

"Sleep!" the elder replied out from the darkness.

"What do you mean...sleep?"

"Sleep deeply!"

"Why?"

"So that you have more dreams."

Sasha took a deep breath and came to his senses. Opened his mouth to ask what that meant, but the elder spoke first: "Run along. Go to sleep!"

In the cave, he heard fussing, grunting, and muttering. Then everything went quiet. Sasha simply stood there with the mug in hand, staring through the warm opening. Some time passed. A stone suddenly appeared in the opening. And closed it up entirely. A light-brown substance squeezed out very slightly along the edges of the stone. But Sasha smelled nothing.

He stood with his gaze fixed on the cave's dull masonry. The foolish air conditioner kept buzzing and blowing, blowing right at his back. Sasha banged the mug against the stones.

"Father Pancras."

No sound came from behind the masonry.

"What am I to do?" Sasha sighed helplessly, his hands falling to his sides.

The wall stood dully before him with all of its declivities, chipped stones, veins between them, and pockmarks. He wanted to spit on it.

"Tell me!!!" Sasha cried furiously, knocking the mug against the stones.

He heard a faint, dull murmur behind the wall. It was barely audible. But it was there. Sasha put his ear to the stones. But couldn't precisely make out the murmuring. The elder was saying something in a singsong tone. Having realized this, Sasha put the mug to the masonry and put his ear to the mug, remembering the last time he'd done this as a teenager, listening in as his older sister gave herself to her classmate, a bearded, thin, cross-eyed guy who taught Sasha how to drink vodka and was always playing the Sergei Nikitin song "Take Me Across the Maidan" on his guitar.

The mug helped: the elder was singing something in his dull cave. It was a very simple motif, familiar to Sasha since his childhood. He plugged his free ear, so as not to hear the humming of the damned air conditioner, and stood entirely still with his ears cocked. He finally made out the words:

Crying bitter tears, I sat there stooped,
I'd eaten so much and more now pooped.

There were no other words. The elder kept repeating that single couplet. Then went completely quiet.

This stupid children's song had the effect on Sasha of an invisible bug bite from a good and powerful insect, a shaggy moth perhaps. He froze completely but, somehow, in a *positive* way. He felt calm and comfortable in his own skin. He had nowhere to go. Suddenly and with great pleasure, he remembered his kindergarten, a school for children with speech impediments, and his friend Marik, who had curly hair and big eyes and had thought up a poem while sitting on the potty.

Toot, toot, toot,
Poop, poop, poop.

Marik was kind, cheerful, and chattered incessantly, even though he stuttered like most of the other children at the school. For his birthday, Marik's father gave his son a book of American stamps, sixteen of which he gave to Sasha. And, very surprisingly and unexpectedly, Marik's little poem spread through the whole kindergarten. It was repeated with great pleasure not just by stuttering, lisping, and burring children, their nannies, and the drunk who was the school's watchman but by their teachers too. Their cheerful music teacher even wrote a "Toot Toot Foxtrot," and Sasha's mom, a cultured, strict, and untalkative woman, developed the habit of saying something that Sasha, with his own impediment, couldn't repeat:

Here's your toot, toot, toot,
Here's your poop, poop, poop.

Sasha knocked the mug against the wall again. And realized there was nothing more to wait for. He looked around and pressed the button on the wall.

The cube shuddered and began to move downwards. Floated down to the ground. The light went off in the cube.

Sasha was in total darkness. With the mug in hand, he stepped out of the cube and onto the ground. And saw that, as it turned out, night had already fallen. The apparatus ceased humming. There was a light shining in the hut. One soldier was visible. But the light soon went out there as well.

Sasha tried to see his surroundings through the pitch-black southern darkness. The air was simultaneously warm and cool. Cicadas were singing in the bushes. The surf rustled in the distance. The moon came out from behind a single cloud and illuminated everything around him: The cliff and the apparatus. And the people sleeping on the ground.

Sasha walked over to them.

The general was lying supine, his legs and arms outstretched, snoring loudly and evenly. The paunchy man, his head resting on the general's left leg, was snoring noisily, mumbling, and squelching his lips together as the moon illuminated the icon on his stomach The white-mustached man, his head resting on the general's right leg, was moaning subtly and plaintively in his sleep, his body periodically shuddering. Evgeny was sleeping next to him; whistling through his nose, the goat-bearded man had his arms tightly wrapped around Evgeny's legs. The man from the URA was lying there too, huddled up and pressing his cheek against Evgeny's hip. Next to him, the man with the stern face was spread out, his palm positioned beneath the general's head and his feet in their jockey boots positioned over the white-mustached man's buttocks, which shuddered as the man slept. The red-haired lady was sleeping on the goat-bearded man's buttocks as if they were a pillow. The National Guard soldiers, the captain, and the general's adjutant were sleeping off in the distance.

The abbot was sleeping in a seated position with his back up against the cliff. His face in the moonlight was a corpsy shade of white.

Why was he so passive? Sasha wondered. *He didn't say anything, just stood there like a tree trunk. Just stood there, just stood there ... like a pillar saint ... like a tree-trunk saint ...*

It suddenly seemed to Sasha that the abbot was dead. Dropping the mug to the ground, he walked over to the abbot. Bent down. The abbot's face shone pale gray. Cold radiated from him. The folds of his facial skin came to life, began to move like scales, shifting one over the other; his eyelids sank down into his eye sockets, sank down to the bottoms to the backs to the blacks of two pitchy dark bark wells bells dells the monster the mouth on the other hand opened with a hiss tore open fell apart like a loose grave held together only by soily strength.

"IN THE THROES OF DOZE!"

Sasha opened his eyes, closed his eyes, opened them again, sighing noisily and powerlessly.

The ceiling is white plastic, the walls are lightly colored wood. The windows are rhomboids. Early sky. Matte sea.

Predawn.

Alya felt him wake up, moved closer, and snuggled up to him with her warm body. "You're already up? Or could you not sleep?"

"Aaaaaah," Sasha sighed once more and threw his hands up toward the ceiling.

"Up for an early-morning swim?"

"Oh no."

"Bad dreams?"

"Oh yeah."

"As usual after eating monkfish?"

"Oh yeah."

"Is it a tradition?"

"Oh no."

"Fatum, then?"

"Oh yeeeeeah," he yawned.

"But it was so taaaaasty," she yawned into Sasha's ear in response, wrapping her arms around him under the sheets.

"I had . . . quite the dream." Sasha reached out, his hands sliding under the displaced pillow.

"Again, the monkfish and the cook are to blame! We'll have them walk the plank! We'll feed them to the eels!"

He grinned sleepily. "All of our stuff's made of sugar now...all the uranium..."

"The whole world's made of sugar?" Alya took the lobe of his ear between her wet lips.

"No, just the uranium. All of the government's uranium turned to refined sugar. Oh yeah! And I dreamt of Zhenya too. Zhenya!"

A weak laugh came to life in Sasha's chest.

"You can't even leave him behind when you're on vacation."

"Zhenya! I went up instead of him...and got down on my knees..."

"On the carpet? In front of Vladimir Vladimirovich?"

"In front of a cave."

"What cave?"

"A mountain cave—"

"I hope I was in the cave? Naked? Fleeing the Minotaur?"

"Of caaaaarse!" he said in a funny Georgian accent.

Sasha burst into a weak fit of laughter. Alya's hand found its way to his warm, sleepy member beneath the silk blanket and squeezed it gently. "Why don't you ever take me at dawn, mister?"

"I'm a sleepy...little mouse...my little fish..."

He stretched out on the light-green sheet, arching his spine and throwing his head back.

The hand gripped his member more tightly. Then relaxed. Then squeezed. Then relaxed.

"Whyyy? Whyyy?"

"Well, like..."

"Whyyy?" She took the lobe of his ear between her teeth.

His member came to life.

"I mean...*why not, honey*?" she said in English.

Her tanned hands pulled back the sheet. She brought her bronzed knee over him, throwing an avalanche of black hair behind her back.

"The nymph wanted to sneeze but stepped on a scorpion. Oh, Ithaca!"

Sasha spread his arms out helplessly atop the green sheet and shut his eyes.

"Give the nymph the gift of your white poison, Scorpio!"

She sat down on his member with cautious confidence. Shook her head and lowered the avalanche of hair down onto the fallen man.

"Aaaaah—how nice it is to do it in the morning!"

Salty hair.

Hips always warm.

Nipples always pointy.

Lips always able.

Her body rolled like a wave.

Sasha put his arms around her and pressed her to him. She breathed into his neck with a wet moan. "I looooove you . . ."

He opened his eyes.

she ably begins to lightly and is ably able ably able ably herself still as a sphinx as a sphinx and everything itself happens to her to her itself to her itself to her is ably able ably able ably has me ably has me and her black hair black hair hair vines vines hair jungles hair black jungles and two hemispheres two hemispheres buttocks hummock hummocks buttock on the edge of the sea on the ledge of the sea hummocks buttock two hummocks no two buttock-fruits two pears no two buttock-melons no two buttock-mangos buttock-mangos two buttock-mangas japanese buttock-mangas buttock-buttock-mangas on the horizon tender strong buttock-mangas on the edge of the sea make me feel good manga makes me feel good lines on the water lines on the wasser lines on the bother lines on the daughter lines on the mutter lines on the brudder lines and dawn and dawn and dawn and dawn already all already all already all already all the more visible two mangas two mangas two mangas two buttock-mangas you were created for pleasure you picturesque burlesque mangas two buttock-mangas and between them a triangle triangle of sea this buttock triangle buttock it's like a shot glass no like a cocktail glass a cocktail glass for dry martinis no wet seaside martinis with their incomprehensible melancholy a buttock triangle of the wet sea of the very wet sea without ice without ice and what's in it and what's in it and what's there what are these violet spots bubbles in a martini in a wet martini of sea in a wet martini of sea some kind of violet bubbles what is this why are there violet spots in the sea what is this why why why and for what reason why and for what reason why and for what reason these spots in a cocktail glass of sea spots in in cocktail glass spots in a cocktail glass where are rushing off to spots where are you swimming where are you rising no hold on where are you where are you where bubbles where bubbles where you bubbles you where you whe-e-e-e-e-e-e-ere?!

He moaned, clutching at her with his hands.

A whisper into neck. "Ahh, Scorpio ... you're already spilling your venom ..."

"What are these ... vi ... ol ... et ... spots ... in the sea, and now ... and now in the sky?"

Her body began to shudder ably.

"Ah, Scorpio, ah, Scorpio, a-a-a-ah, Scorpio, a-a-ah, Scorpio, my venomous little boy, a-a-a-a-a!!"

A ray of sun rising over the Ionian Sea touched the feather-tips of the slumbering leader of a flock of swans. It brought its head out from under its wing. Opened its lilac eye with its black pupil. The sun began to play over the swan's plumage, which flashed with every shade of violet: from bluish violet to yellowish violet. The swan slowly raised its head: a pinkish-violet beak with a crimson-violet edge and a bluish-violet neck, each feather shimmering in the sun.

The leader of the flock lifted its head and shook it. The sun flashed into its pupils. It let forth a cry. All twenty-two swans sleeping on the water began to wake up and shake their plumage.

The leader of the flock let forth a second cry. The other swans began to cry out in response.

It shook its head and opened its wings to greet the sun. The sun shone on its reddish-violet and light-lilac feathers.

The leader of the flock shot off into the air. Its wings flapped against the water and its emerald-violet webbed feet beat into it. The leader began to accelerate. The other swans jerked into action behind it, noisily striking the sea, which had served as their abode for the night, and stretching out their bluish-violet necks.

The leader was the first bird to tear itself from the smooth surface of the sea's morning mirror. The flock followed him up. Having taken off, the swans made a wide circle around the place where they'd slept. Beneath their violet wings, which were dancing in the sunlight, the sea stretched out emptily, except for a lone yacht, white and double-masted, and Ithaca, greenish-blue in the distance.

The leader of the flock let forth a third cry. The swans replied amicably and began to get into formation behind their leader. A smooth violet wedge rose up in the matinal sky. Having completed another smallish circle, the wedge turned around and headed north.

HIROSHIMA

2000

LUKASHEVICH, the vice-president of a small, but impressive bank, and Zeldin, the owner of four supermarkets, were sitting at a table served for three. A Gypsy choir was singing on stage. A birch tree was growing in a tub by the table. On the table itself, a decanter of vodka sparkled and a plate of salmon crimsoned.

The two pals were drunk. They'd begun at Café Pushkin: 850 mL of Russian Standard, cranberry *mors*, beer, pickled porcini mushrooms, stuffed pike, veal pâté, Caesar salad, "Hussar-style" lamb, sturgeon in champagne, crème brûlée, bliny with hot fudge, coffee, cognac, calvados.

Then, they continued at Biscuit: 380 ml of tequila, green tea, fruit salad.

"Nah, Bor"—Lukashevich lit a cigarette sloppily—"those Gypsies ain't doin' it for me . . ."

"You don't like it?" Zeldin filled the glasses, spilling vodka onto the tablecloth. "Well, I love it when they howl."

"I mean, like . . . that's some real-ass longin' . . ." Lukashevich took a glass. Splashed it onto the birch. "Dogshit."

"The vodka?" Zeldin didn't understand.

"Everything."

"Whaddaya mean—everything?"

"I don't like places like this. Let's go to Bridge. Dance with some chicks."

"Right now? Let's drink first! What's with you, Sashok?!" Zeldin hugged Lukashevich. "Everything's still good. Oh yeah!" he remembered, "I didn't finish telling it!"

"What?" Lukashevich looked at him gloomily.

"Like, about the bell!"

"What bell?" Lukashevich was bored.

"Like, on the Cathedral of Christ the Savior! The bass bell! A G-note! Thirty-two tons. On the southwest wing, I think. Yeah. And this broad from Gazprom, well, she's got lung cancer, she heard somewhere that low frequencies destroy cancer cells. She stuffs their pockets full and, every evening, they take her up with the bell ringer, plus she's totally naked ... Sasha, you bitch!!! I still can't believe you came! Motherfuck!!! You came!!! You came, you sweaty asshole!!!"

Overturning the decanter of vodka, Zeldin rushed for Lukashevich and embraced him with all his might. The table rocked. Zeldin's striped jacket tore. Lukashevich growled, his big, mealy fingers squeezing at Zeldin's swarthy neck. Zeldin squeezed at Lukashevich's white neck.

"You Moscow bitch!" Lukashevich growled, then they began to strangle each other.

23:48

A FIVE-STORY BUILDING ON NOVATORY STREET
PREPARED FOR DEMOLITION

Two bums, Valera and Petyukh,* were sitting atop a pile of damp rags in the corner of a ruined apartment. The thin moon shone through a broken window. The bums were drunk. And finishing a bottle of "Russian" vodka. They'd begun drinking in the early morning right

---

*"Petyukh" is a diminutive for Petya, but literally means "rooster" and is also prison slang for the "bitch" of the yard, who is implied to be gay.

outside Yaroslavsky Station: a quarter liter of Istok, a half-loaf of white bread, chicken scraps from a grill bar. Then made it to Sokolniki where they collected empty bottles in the park, turned them in for money, and kept going: three bottles of Ochakovskoye beer and two poppy-seed buns. Then, after they'd slept on a bench for a little while, they made it to Novodevichy Convent, where they begged for alms until evening. Enough for a bottle of "Russian."

"That's it." Valera finished drinking the bottle in the darkness.

"We killed it?" Petyukh croaked. "Motherfuckin' fuck..."

"What?"

"I'm shiverin' like a bitch. 'S'if we hadn't drunk shit. I could use another swallow."

"We'll shift over to Izmailovo tomorrow. We'll really rake it in there! Tomorrow! Tomorrow!" Valera chuckled, then began to sing something incomprehensible.

"Whaddaya mean—tomorrow?" Petyukh hit him.

"What the fuck! I pissed myself, bro! Again! Motherfuckin' bitches!" Valera giggled.

"Asshole...dickmouth..." Petyukh punched him sluggishly.

"Fuck is this...go eat a dick!" Valera hit him back.

They fell silent, a fire truck drove by loudly outside the window.

"Meat wagon?" Petyukh yawned.

"Concrete smasher," Valera retorted authoritatively.

They fell silent.

"Tomorrow! Tomorrrrooooowww, motherfuck! Tomoooooorrr-roooowww!!!" Valera sang once again, then laughed, opening his rotten-toothed mouth wide in the darkness.

"Shut up, you fuck!" Petyukh growled and grabbed him by the throat.

Valera grunted and grabbed him back.

They began to strangle each other.

23:48

AN APARTMENT ON SIVTSEV VRAZHEK LANE

Alex, a dancer, and Nicola, a web designer, lay naked in bed. Mozart's Symphony No. 40 was playing quietly. Nicola was smoking and Alex was cutting lines of cocaine out on *Ambient 1: Music for Airports*, a Brian Eno CD. They'd started a whole twenty-four hours ago at a makeup-artist buddy's birthday party (0.5g + orange juice), then continued at Tabula Rasa (0.3g + still mineral water) and at Niagara (0.8g + still mineral water + 2 cigars). After which, having drunk some green tea at Wineglass, they'd gone to a morning showing of *Attack of the Clones*. Then, they'd gone out to the dacha of some designer chick whom they didn't really know (1.3g + carbonated mineral water + fruit tea +150 mL of whiskey + apple juice + strawberry cake + grapes + candies + 50 mL of apricot liqueur + strawberries + green tea + strawberries with whipped cream). Then, in the evening, they'd gone back to Nicola's place (0.4g).

"Really not a lot, Col. We're gonna finish it," Alex was cutting two puny lines with a discount card for all "Party" stores.

"You mean that's it?" Nicola squinted his beautiful, glassy eyes.

"I mean, like, it's gonna have been it."

They silently snorted the coke through a plastic tube. Alex wiped up the cocaine dust with his little finger and delicately touched it to the head of Nicola's cock. Nicola looked down at his cock:

"Want to?"

"I always want to."

"Listen, do we not have any more whiskey?"

"We never did."

"Really?" Nicola was tensely surprised. "What is there, then?"

"Only vodka," Alex took Nicola's balls into his palm tenderly.

"I feel kinda comatose for some reason . . ." Nicola stretched out.

"I'll bring it."

Alex stood up springily and walked smoothly into the kitchen. Nicola stubbed out the butt of his cigarette in a steel ashtray. Alex returned silently with vodka and glass. Poured it. Nicola drank. Alex got down onto his knees in front of him and ran his tongue slowly over the lilac head of his cock.

"First, let's do it velvet-style, my little hedgehog." Nicola licked at his dry lips.

"Yes, meesa," Alex imitated Jar Jar Binks as he took two velvet women's belts from the chair—one black and one violet.

They lay down onto the bed, pressed in close to one another, and intertwined their legs. Alex wrapped the violet belt around Nicola's neck and Nicola wrapped the black belt around Alex's. Their lips drew closer, parted, and their tongues touched. They began to strangle each other.

23.48

A HUT IN THE VILLAGE OF KOLCHINO

Two old women, Nyura and Matryona, were on their knees and praying to a dark icon case. The lamp's blue flame poorly illuminated the visages of St. Nicholas the Wonderworker, the Savior, and the Virgin Mary. It was damp and dark in the hut.

"Oh Lord Jesus Christ, Son of God, we pray to Your Most Pure Mother, to our reverend and God-bearing fathers and to all the saints—that they might have mercy on us. Amen!" The two women finished their discordant prayer, crossed themselves, bowed, touched the uneven ground with their foreheads, then began the process of standing with a groan.

Matryona was the first to get up. Then grabbed Nyura by her bony elbow.

"Oh mama, oh God..." Nyura straightened up with great difficulty, strode over to a bench, and sat down.

"'Haps y'might still write to Vasily?" Matryona asked, walking over to the table.

"Nah. Haven't the might." Nyura was breathing hard.

"Well, I wrote to my people. That they might come."

"Mine ain't been here for eight months already...oy, feels like somethin's breakin'..." Nyura moaned. "C'mon...no point waitin'..."

Matryona lifted up the tablecloth. On the table, in addition to bread and a salt shaker, there was a plate with a *blin* on it. Matryona picked up the *blin*, sat down next to Nyura, and tore it in half:

"Well then—chow down. Made it in the mornin'."

"Just one?" Nyura took half of the *blin* with her thin, violently shaking fingers.

"What's the issue...? Yeah. One. With butter. Eat."

"So I shall..."

They began to eat in silence. Chewed with toothless mouths. Once she was done, Matryona wiped at her mouth with her brown hand, stood up, and took Nyura by the elbow:

"Time to go with God."

"Time to go...oh Lord..." She had a hard time standing up as she chewed.

They went out into the dark breezeway with its collapsed floor. Light filtered in through holes in the roof. A hemp rope with a noose at either end of it was thrown over the ceiling beam. Matryona led Nyura over to the nooses. Helped her to put one around her neck. Then put the other around her own. Nyura was wearing a new white kerchief with blue polka dots. Matryona had put on her old black one with white polka dots.

Matryona grabbed Nyura by her bony shoulders and pulled her downward. Nyura let forth a sob and a hiccup. The rope became taut and the old women's legs buckled.

23:48

KINDERGARTEN NO. 7

Rita and Masha, both five years old, lay side by side in their beds with open eyes and looked up at the ceiling. The remaining sixteen children were asleep. Their teacher and the watchman were making love behind the wall.

A car passed by outside the windows. Stripes of light crawled across the ceiling.

"A dragon," Masha said.

"Nope. A giraffe." Rita wrinkled her nose.

Their teacher let forth a muffled gasp behind the wall.

"What the heck is Nina Petrovna up to in there?" Masha asked.

"She and Uncle Misha are stranglin' each other."

"Whaddaya mean?"

"They're lyin' in bed naked and stranglin' each other. With their hands."

"Why?"

"It's where kids come from. Feels nice too. My mom and dad do it all the time. They strip naked and—there y'go. Do yours do it?"

"Well, I don't have a dad."

They fell silent. Another car passed by. Then another.

"Oy... ahhh... oy... umm... Mish... like... I don't want it... like that..." their teacher muttered behind the wall.

Masha raised her head:

"Rit... think we should strangle each other?"

"Then we'll have kids."

They fell silent. Rita thought for a moment:

"No. We won't."

"Why?"

"We're not a man and a lady."

"Aha! Then let's do it, huh?"

"Let's. But, first, we better strip naked."

"C'mon! It's cold! Let's do it like this!"

"If we don't do it naked, it won't work."

"Really?"

"Mhm."

It took them a long time to take off their pajamas. They got into Masha's bed. Grabbed on to each other's necks. And began to strangle each other.

The aforementioned Lukashevich, Valera, Alex, Matryona, and Rita saw *nothing special* during the strangling process.

Zeldin, Petyukh, Nicola, Nyura, and Masha, on the other hand, first observed a series of orange and scarlet flashes, which flowed smoothly into a menacing crimson radiance. Then the crimson light became turbid, went navy, then sky-blue—before suddenly opening up into an enormously endless space. It was an unbelievably spacious ash-gray landscape illuminated by an enormous full moon in the dark-violet sky. Despite the fact that it was nighttime, it was as bright as day. The moon illuminated the low ruins of the incinerated city in great detail. A scattering of stars sparkled in the sky. A naked woman walked amongst the ruins. A bewitching sense of peace emanated from her white, moonlit body. She didn't belong to the world, upon the ashes of which she walked. People destroyed by the blast lay in the ash and ruins. Some were moaning and others were already dead. But the people's moans had no effect on the woman's calm. She moved smoothly, stepping over those who were dead and those in their death throes. She was searching for something *other*. Finally, she stopped. A mortally wounded bitch attempting to whelp lay amongst the melted bricks. The majority of its body had been burnt and its ribs stuck out through tufts of fur and skin. Breathing heavily and squealing weakly, it was attempting to give birth. But it had no might left for delivery. The dog was dying, shuddering with the whole of its mutilated body and straining impotently. Bloody saliva flowed from its scarlet maw and its pink tongue lolled.

The woman lowered herself down into the ashes next to the dog. Put her white hands onto the bitch's singed belly. Pressed. The dog's dirty, bloody legs parted slightly. It whined weakly. Puppies began to issue forth from its loins: a first, a second, a third, a fourth, and a fifth. A spasm passed across the bitch's body. It squinted at the woman with a single crazed, moist eye, then yawned and died. The wet black pups stirred languidly, poking their muzzles into the gray ashes. The woman took them into her arms and pressed them to her bosom. And the blind pups began to drink her milk.

TRANSLATOR'S NOTE

I AM INDEBTED to Yelena Veisman, my eternal *дичь* consultant, as well as Ben Hooyman, Andrei from *The Untranslated*, and Mark Krotov for helpful comments along the way. And to Professor Monika Greenleaf for suggesting I change the name "Timka" to "Tiny Tim." Perhaps the best note I've ever gotten.

The stories proceed chronologically: the first three are from *My First Working Saturday*, then comes "A Month in Dachau," never included in a collection, then two from *Feast*, a food-themed collection, then three from *Monoclone*, then, finally, three from *White Square*.

It's worth adding that the very last story, "Hiroshima," was written by Vladimir somewhere *outside of time* (but was still somehow published in *Playboy*). At a big mahogany desk up in the ether. In 1850, perhaps. Or in 2085. His pipe sits just to the right of his wrist, it's gone out. He's typing furiously. An old Dell computer. The turbulent air whips around him in the form of gale-force winds. The sun sets crimson. The interstellar void threatens to tear his computer away—to dispose of it in a black hole. The interstellar void, then, is on the Kremlin's payroll. But the void does not succeed and Vladimir is able to finish his story—here, somewhere outside of time. He weeps as he writes the story's final paragraphs. And, once it's done, awaiting him on his left side is no glass of milk dotted with condensation—no, that would be far too convenient!—but a ceremonial tea set pilfered from *A Dream of Red Mansions*. We *are* outside of time, after all. Such things are possible here.

The tea is scalding, but not too strong. Just how Vladimir likes it.
He takes a sip. Wipes away his final tear.
And begins to knock out his pipe.
This is not the end.

M.D.L.
Los Angeles, February 5, 2023

OTHER NEW YORK REVIEW CLASSICS

For a complete list of titles, visit www.nyrb.com.

RENATA ADLER Speedboat
DANTE ALIGHIERI Purgatorio; translated by D. M. Black
CLAUDE ANET Ariane, A Russian Girl
HANNAH ARENDT Rahel Varnhagen: The Life of a Jewish Woman
ROBERTO ARLT The Seven Madmen
DIANA ATHILL Don't Look at Me Like That
POLINA BARSKOVA Living Pictures
MAX BEERBOHM Seven Men
ROSALIND BELBEN The Limit
ADOLFO BIOY CASARES The Invention of Morel
ROBERT MONTGOMERY BIRD Sheppard Lee, Written by Himself
HENRI BOSCO The Child and the River
DINO BUZZATI A Love Affair
DINO BUZZATI The Stronghold
LEONORA CARRINGTON The Hearing Trumpet
CAMILO JOSÉ CELA The Hive
EILEEN CHANG Written on Water
FRANÇOIS-RENÉ DE CHATEAUBRIAND Memoirs from Beyond the Grave, 1800–1815
LUCILLE CLIFTON Generations: A Memoir
COLETTE Chéri *and* The End of Chéri
E. E. CUMMINGS The Enormous Room
JÓZEF CZAPSKI Memories of Starobielsk: Essays Between Art and History
ANTONIO DI BENEDETTO The Silentiary
PIERRE DRIEU LA ROCHELLE The Fire Within
FERIT EDGÜ The Wounded Age *and* Eastern Tales
MICHAEL EDWARDS The Bible and Poetry
ROSS FELD Guston in Time: Remembering Philip Guston
BEPPE FENOGLIO A Private Affair
GUSTAVE FLAUBERT The Letters of Gustave Flaubert
WILLIAM GADDIS The Letters of William Gaddis
THÉOPHILE GAUTIER My Fantoms
GE FEI The Invisibility Cloak
NATALIA GINZBURG Family *and* Borghesia
JEAN GIONO The Open Road
ROBERT GLÜCK Margery Kempe
NIKOLAI GOGOL Dead Souls
JEREMIAS GOTTHELF The Black Spider
WILLIAM LINDSAY GRESHAM Nightmare Alley
VASILY GROSSMAN The People Immortal
MARTIN A. HANSEN The Liar
ELIZABETH HARDWICK The Uncollected Essays of Elizabeth Hardwick
GERT HOFMANN Our Philosopher
DOROTHY B. HUGHES In a Lonely Place
MAUDE HUTCHINS Victorine
ERNST JÜNGER On the Marble Cliffs
ANNA KAVAN Machines in the Head: Selected Stories
WALTER KEMPOWSKI An Ordinary Youth
SIGIZMUND KRZHIZHANOVSKY Autobiography of a Corpse
PAUL LAFARGUE The Right to Be Lazy
CURZIO MALAPARTE The Kremlin Ball
JEAN-PATRICK MANCHETTE The N'Gustro Affair